LIVING YOUR BEST LIFE

MAXINE MORREY

B

First published in Great Britain in 2022 by Boldwood Books Ltd.

Copyright © Maxine Morrey, 2022

Cover Design by Debbie Clement Design

Cover Photography: Shutterstock

A CIP catalogue record for this book is available from the British Library.

Paperback ISBN 978-1-80162-632-3

Large Print ISBN 978-1-80162-631-6

Hardback ISBN 978-1-80162-630-9

Ebook ISBN 978-1-80162-633-0

Kindle ISBN 978-1-80162-634-7

Audio CD ISBN 978-1-80162-625-5

MP3 CD ISBN 978-1-80162-626-2

Digital audio download ISBN 978-1-80162-629-3

Boldwood Books Ltd
23 Bowerdean Street
London SW6 3TN
www.boldwoodbooks.com

For the incredible team at Boldwood Books

1

Something was up. We were sitting in our usual huddle at the pub we'd been gathering in since school. Over time the group had swelled as partners and wives and husbands had joined and blended, but most of us had stayed pretty local to the area we'd grown up in. Of course, what was once a ratty pub full of students, with sticky, dark patterned carpets that hid a multitude of sins, and loos that always made you consider just how much you actually needed a wee, had long since been transformed. Now it was a light, airy affair with oak-effect flooring and pale walls that sold gastro-style meals at the appropriately inflated price. We'd been meeting up here for years. As many of us as possible would make the regular meets, and in between there was a mix and match, depending on who was available. Once children popped onto the scene, it made it a little more difficult to schedule, so in the summer we often swapped the location to one of the parks so that the kids could come too. I loved that we'd all done our best to stay close, despite all the changes in our lives. As the ones without children, Tia, Jono, Luca and I had inadvertently formed our own mini group within the larger one and tended to stay closer in touch.

I often met up with just Luca for a quick drink or a meal after work as we both worked in the same area of town, which generally took the edge off a long, tiring day. We'd been friends forever. Well, since we were five anyway. I'd been standing at the back of my first class at primary school, taking it all in and wondering whether anyone would notice if I snuck back out of the door. As I pondered my escape, one of my neatly plaited pigtails was yanked and followed by a giggle. A boy with hair as black as pitch stood next to me, still grinning. His smile faded as I stepped back towards the wall, my bottom lip beginning to wobble. Big, expressive eyes the colour of chocolate widened as a tear plopped onto my cheek. Suddenly I was enveloped in a huge hug.

'I didn't mean to make you cry,' he said as he pulled away. 'I'm sorry.'

I nodded and let him take my hand as he confidently crossed the classroom and found us both a seat. From that day on, we were almost inseparable. Even on the days we yelled at each other, it hadn't taken long before we were hugging and playing again. This group were my people and they got me. But I knew Luca got me just that little bit more.

But tonight, something was different. Tia was sitting next to me, chatting inanely as we waited for everyone to arrive. I squinted at her.

'You all right?'

'Of course! Why?'

'You're acting weird.'

'What do you mean? I am not acting weird. Jono?' She turned to her boyfriend next to her. 'Am I acting weird? Bee says I'm acting weird.'

'You're always weird.' He shrugged then kissed her nose. 'It's one of the things I love about you.'

Tia grinned, showing the beautiful smile I'd always been a little bit jealous of. I had a wide smile too but, while hers worked for her like Julia Roberts's, I'd always felt mine made me look more like the Joker. Luca told me not to be so ridiculous when I'd mentioned it and that was the end of the discussion. But I still had a tendency to keep my teeth to myself when I smiled.

'That is true,' I agreed with Jono. 'But you're extra weird tonight. Like you filled up on Smarties before you got here.'

'Oh, psh.' Tia waved her hand, dismissing my suspicion. 'So, anything new on the love-life front I should know about?'

I took a sip of the drink in front of me. 'Nope.'

She let out a sigh. 'What are we going to do with you?'

I gave her a look over the rim of my glass. 'I don't believe anything needs doing with me.'

Tia gave me the look straight back. 'I'm pretty sure we both know there is plenty that needs doing.' She gave a lascivious wink and I rolled my eyes at her. 'Surely there's got to be someone you're interested in? No one at work?'

'Nope.' I stabbed the olive in my drink with the ironically retro cocktail stick. It was in the shape of a sword and I remembered my parents having plastic ones like it in their drinks cabinet years ago. Entertaining had been their thing – being parents rather less so.

'Nobody at all?' Tia sighed.

'Not one.' I popped the olive in my mouth.

'That's disappointing.'

'Apparently more so to you than me.'

Tia gave me a look.

'Luca agrees, don't you?' She launched at him as Luca joined us and folded his long legs into the bench seat opposite me.

'Hard to say, bearing in mind I don't know the question.' He still had the same fabulous smile he'd had when he was five but now it was surrounded by a face that was all hard planes, a day's growth of dark stubble and long-lashed chocolate-brown eyes a person could lose themselves in if they weren't careful, and many had. All this was accompanied by a body that had a double whammy of excellent genes and fitness training. He gave me a wink as he sat down and I smiled back.

'Bee needs a man.'

Bella and Jesse turned from their own conversation discussing the pros and cons of a particularly trendy buggy and whether to upgrade their daughter's current one in order to listen in on our discussion.

'Oh.' Luca took a sip of his beer, appearing less interested than any of the others.

'See?' Tia turned back to me. 'Luca agrees too.'

'He didn't say anything but "oh". That's not an agreement.'

'It's not a disagreement.' she countered.

'Can we order food yet?' I asked with a sigh, desperate for both sustenance and a change of subject.

'In a minute,' Tia replied, glancing over my head. 'Jack and Lucy aren't here yet. She said they'd be here any minute.'

'Can't they just order when they get here?' I grumped.

'Miss lunch?' Luca asked, the dark eyes fixing on me.

I shrugged. 'There was a meeting.'

He gave a little head shake.

'I saw that.'

'You were supposed to. We've talked about you missing lunch before. It's not good for you and it's not good for us because you get all grouchy.'

'I am not grouchy. I'm just hungry.'

'I'd argue you were both.'

'You'd argue anything if it meant not agreeing with me.'

He tilted his head a little in a 'that's possible' way, before smiling.

I gave a brief eye roll and looked away, mostly because I knew he was right. I'd been about to head out of the door at lunchtime to grab a sandwich when I'd been pulled into a 'five-minute meeting' by my boss.

'You don't mind, do you?' he'd asked, indicating for me to follow him into the boardroom. As usual, the question was rhetorical so I didn't answer and instead just took a seat. An hour and half later, when the meeting finished, my stomach had given up growling, turned its back on my other organs and begun sulking, taking the hunger pangs with it. They were, however, back with a vengeance now.

'Here they are!' Tia practically shot out of her seat, making Luca jump and tip his drink. He gave me a querying look as he mopped up the small spillage with a napkin. I shrugged back at him. Something was most definitely up.

* * *

I waited at the bar, trying to catch the eye of the barman amongst the throng of the evening crowd. Having served five other people, three of whom arrived after me, I finally managed to get his attention and prepared to lean in a bit to make myself heard.

'What can I get you?'

'Three—'

'Two cosmos, one dirty martini and one vodka and lime.' The woman squashed against me, edging me down the bar a little more as she claimed her place.

The barman's glance barely grazed me as he turned to begin making the cocktails. I squished myself in the tiny space I had left, clinging to it grimly, and placed a foot on the rest that ran around the bottom of the bar, gaining a couple of inches' height, and continued the battle of trying to get served. I hated it when it was my round.

'Bloody hell. You were ages! We were beginning to think you'd left,' Bella said as Tia distributed the drinks and I retook my seat.

'I couldn't get anyone's attention. And then when I did get it, I was gazumped.'

'Oh.' They offered sympathetic faces before we all chinked our glasses together. Let's face it, it wasn't the first time I'd taken an age to get served and it wouldn't be the last. Next time I was sending Tia. She'd be back with the drinks inside five minutes. I could guarantee it. People noticed Tia. It wasn't just that she was gorgeous. She just had something about her, a charisma that drew people in. I was a little short on that. I wondered if Amazon stocked it.

We all shuffled together more so that our little clan could fit around the two tables commandeered for the night.

'OK, can we order now? Please?' I looked at Tia.

Luca chuckled. 'She's broken out the puppy-dog eyes. Things must really be serious.'

'One minute.' She held up a finger distractedly before turning back to Jono.

I glanced at Luca. 'I do not do puppy-dog eyes.'

One side of his mouth tilted into a half-grin. 'You so do. The cute thing is you don't even know it. You did them on the first day of school when I pulled your hair and you just did them now.'

'That's not puppy-dog eyes!' I huffed out. 'You're making it sound manipulative. That's just my face.'

'Never said it was intentional, or that there was anything wrong with it. It was just an observation.' Luca shrugged in that relaxed way of his. I wasn't sure if it was his Italian genes that gave him that Mediterranean laid-back air when it came to life, or if that was just his natural setting. Unlike mine, which tended to be rather the opposite. I was always worrying about the 'what if?'s. Luca was more 'what if not?'.

'Well, your observations are wildly inaccurate.'

'Is that so?' he asked, putting his now empty beer glass back on the table.

'Yes.'

He opened his mouth to begin his argument but before any words could leave it, Jono tapped a fork against his beer glass. Half full, it made a duller sound than he anticipated so he swiped my now empty wine glass and tried again. A clear note rang out and the whole pub dropped into silence. Everyone stared.

'As you were!' Tia made a motion to the rest of the crowd with her right hand and, after a moment or two, everyone but our group turned back to their conversations. No one had much of an attention span these days anyway.

Jono looked at her and then at the rest of us. Was he blushing? Tia was definitely the more talkative of the two. Jono was lovely, with a dry, fast wit and happy to chat, but he didn't waste words and had always seemed more content to listen if options were given.

'Thanks to everyone for making it tonight. I know it was all a bit last minute so cheers for that.' He cleared his throat. 'We just wanted you all to be the first to know that last night I proposed to Tia and to my very great relief, and possibly surprise, she said yes.'

At this, Tia flung her left hand out towards us with a small, barely controlled scream. On the third finger sat a large teardrop diamond, set in a white-gold band.

Within moments, we were all one big mass, hugging and

congratulating and mopping up the bride-to-be's happy, excited tears. I couldn't have been more thrilled for my childhood friend. She'd not always had it easy with an intermittently absent father, but she had an immense resource of spirit that I'd admired even back then. It had enabled her to push past those who wanted to hold her back, either due to her gender or her colour. Tia powered through until she got what she wanted. And I knew one of the things she wanted was a good, kind, reliable man with whom she could eventually start a family. Now, she'd finally found him and I felt my smile, teeth and all, grow wide at their obvious joy.

2

'Feeling less grouchy now you've got some food inside you?' We'd shuffled places a few times as we'd each chatted to different people and now Luca was sitting next to me, opposite Tia and Jono.

'I wasn't grouchy.'

Luca said nothing.

'I wasn't.'

'I didn't say anything.'

'You didn't have to. Your face said enough all by itself.'

'So!' Tia rested her elbow on the table and surveyed us both, interrupting what some people called an argument but what Luca and I always referred to as a discussion.

I raised an eyebrow. 'So?'

'You two are the only ones out of us lot free and single now.'

I shrugged. Luca said nothing. Clearly neither of these reactions suited our friend. 'So what are we going to do about it?'

'*We* are not going to do anything about it,' I said, looking pointedly at her. The last time she set me up with someone I'd spent the evening being regaled with the minutiae of Marvel

comics, their characters, and their film creations. I had no particular objection to people enjoying those things, even though they
weren't my cup of tea. But after almost three solid hours of being
talked at on this sole topic, I needed my own Avenger to rescue
me. A brief sojourn to the bathroom typically proved it to be one
without a window, which rather ruled out that exit strategy. I'd
returned instead to the table, ready for another oral onslaught.
However, my date then broke it to me that he never ate dessert
and asked if we should just split the bill there and then. I wasn't
bothered about paying my share. I *was* bothered about missing
out on pudding though – the one thing that had led me to stay
that long in the first place! And then, the proverbial cherry on
top of the non-existent dessert? He'd called Tia on his way home
to say that I 'seemed nice enough but didn't really have much
conversation'!

'You're never going to let me forget about that, are you? I
knew he was into that stuff but, admittedly, perhaps not the
depth to which he enjoyed it. I did apologise.'

'I know. But still no.'

'Fine. So if there's no one at work and you won't let anyone
set you up, there's only one option.'

'A nunnery?'

Luca snorted and I flashed him a look. 'I don't know what
you're laughing at. It's not like you're attached either. Perhaps we
can find a space in a monastery for you.'

He opened his mouth.

'Preferably a silent order,' I added quickly, narrowing my
eyes.

Luca laughed his rich, throaty laugh that usually caused
various women within a generous radius to melt. I could actually
see why they reacted that way. I wasn't blind. But although he

looked and sounded good, I had the life experience to know that all just masked his ability to be incredibly annoying.

'I was, in fact, going to suggest online dating.' Tia grinned. 'I don't think we're quite at *The Sound of Music* stage with you just yet.' Her gaze flicked to Luca. 'And somehow I don't think anywhere would take him. He's far too handsome and if you look up "made for sin" on the web, he'll be staring moodily out of the photo next to it.'

'Don't say things like that!' I said, sliding my arms out on the table and resting my head on them. 'It's hard enough getting his ego out of the door as it is.' This wasn't entirely true. For someone so annoyingly good-looking and personable, Luca was remarkably modest. Most of the time.

'Right here, by the way. Also, I don't stare moodily,' Luca stated, glancing between Tia and me as I looked up at both of them. She waved the protest away, her newly adorned finger sending sparkles of light across my face. He did actually, but I knew it was entirely unintentional and only happened when he was concentrating on something. In those moments, David Gandy's trademark look had serious competition.

I dragged myself back up and rested my head in my hands. Suddenly it felt like a long day. I probably ought to think about heading out into the last vestiges of summer, towards the Tube and home.

'What do you think, then?' Tia was looking from me to Luca and back again.

'About what?' we said together.

'Online dating?'

Luca and I exchanged a look. My expression, I was pretty sure, fitted somewhere in the 'horrified' category. Luca's was, oddly for him, unreadable.

'Surely you can't think it's a good idea?' I asked him.

'Of course, it is!' Tia interjected before Luca got a chance to reply. 'Jono and I met online and look how disgustingly happy we are!'

'Yes, but you two are the exception to the rule. All I've ever heard about online dating is horror stories. You have to admit that a system where 80 per cent of people aren't putting genuine, accurate photos on their profile has a serious flaw. And that's just one of the problems.'

Luca had still said nothing. I nudged him. 'Please say something so that we can move this conversation on to something more comfortable, not to mention sensible.'

He sat back in his seat, folding his arms across his broad chest. The sleeves of his shirt were rolled up part way displaying tanned, muscled forearms and the fabric from his white tailored-fit shirt pulled taut across his chest. In my peripheral vision, I watched a woman who'd had her eye on him all evening turn more towards him and cross her long, perfectly tanned legs as she sat on the bar stool. Luca's eyes flicked up to her briefly, then back to Tia and me.

'It's not the worst idea.'

I felt my mouth drop open.

'What?' Luca asked.

I gathered myself and found the ability to speak again. 'Yes, it is! It is absolutely the worst idea! There isn't any idea that could be worse than this one!'

'Why?'

'For exactly the reasons I already said.'

'But, as Tia pointed out, there can be good results as well. Just because you meet someone in a face-to-face situation and go on a date with them doesn't mean it's going to be a better date than if you had met them online. In fact, you're likely to know even less about them.'

'Yes, but at least you know what the person you're meeting actually looks like and you don't get a fifteen-year-older version of the one you arranged the date with.' I huffed out a sigh. 'You only think it's a good idea because I don't.'

'Not true. That's just a bonus.'

I gave him a side eye and he smiled.

'Why are you even bothered? It's not like you're ever short of offers.' I slid my eyes to the woman on the barstool, who was still undressing Luca with her eyes. By the look on her face, I guessed she was close to his boxers by now.

'Perhaps I'm looking for something more.'

Jono sat up a little and began to look interested as Tia leant forward, eyes wide. 'Are you?' she asked.

Luca looked back at me momentarily then shrugged. I didn't know what to say. Judging by the silence, neither did Tia, which was, in itself, quite the miracle. I stared at Luca for a moment. He'd always been a bit of a good-time guy. There was never anyone particularly serious, and he made that clear from the beginning in the hope of avoiding any awkwardness. The tactic didn't work all the time but that wasn't for any lack of honesty on his part. He worked, he had his friends and he had his passion for adventure, which he pursued doing hobbies that completely terrified me like ice climbing and paragliding. That was another thing we didn't agree on, so he tried not to mention it too much and I tried not to think about it when I knew he was off on one of his escapades. I knew this wasn't a great strategy in life but it worked for the most part, so I was sticking to it. He always video-called when he was done being a Power Ranger just so that I knew he was OK and able to see he was still in one piece. He knew I needed that confirmation. We'd been friends for so long that there was very little we didn't know about each other. Except this bombshell, apparently.

'Are you?' I asked, before I could stop the words falling out of my mouth.

He gave another shrug.

'You never told me that.'

'You never asked.'

He was right. I'd never thought to. None of us had. We'd just assumed he was happy with what he had. But we were all getting older and Luca came from a big, close family. Suddenly it seemed blindingly obvious that he too, at some point, would want that for himself. And for some reason, despite Tia and Jono's announcement, that knowledge felt like the biggest news of the evening.

Luca held my gaze for a long moment then looked away. I squirmed a little in my chair, unable to shake the distinct feeling that he was disappointed.

'So?' Tia prompted.

'So what?' Luca and I said together. She shifted her gaze between us, one brow slightly raised before carrying on.

'Clearly we know Bee's view on the whole online dating thing, despite the image of perfection currently in front of her eyes.' Tia batted her lashes and did a little duck-face pose with the ring, then resumed. 'Do you feel the same?' She looked at Luca.

'Not at all,' he answered, barely pausing.

'You would say that,' I huffed at him.

Luca turned a little to face me more. 'Oh, I would? And why is that?'

'Because you can never agree with me.'

'I do agree with you.'

'Rarely.'

'Enough over the past thirty odd years for us to still be as close as we are, despite how annoying you can be.'

'At least on that front, we're even.'

He gave me a look that suggested he didn't necessarily agree with that statement then looked back at Tia.

'Why do you ask?'

'Well, as you both have such opposing views on the subject, and you're the last two of our group to still be single, what do you say to a little challenge?'

'I say no, thank you,' I replied, politely.

'Absolutely,' answered Luca at exactly the same time.

'How can you agree to a challenge when you don't even know what it is yet?' I asked Luca, incredulous.

'How can you completely reject the idea when you don't know what it is?' He threw his hands up, the Italian blood rising and bringing with it all the classic gestures of his lineage.

'Because I know that if it is remotely connected to online dating, I don't want anything to do with it.'

He pulled a face. 'I should have known.'

'What's that supposed to mean?' I said, pulling myself up. We were still sitting down, which was just as well as Luca had about a foot in height and several stone in weight on me. Sitting at least gave me a little more equality when it came to height.

'It just means that you're doing what you always do. I don't know why I'm surprised.'

'And just what is it that I always do?'

'Take the safe option.'

'You make that sound like a bad thing. Frankly, taking the safe option is a far better life choice than throwing myself off mountains and all the other ridiculous things you choose to spend your time doing.'

'Actually, I try to stay firmly attached to the mountain. It's kind of rule number one in climbing. Throwing yourself off is not recommended.'

'Climbing slippery, icy edifices isn't recommended either and yet you choose to do that.'

'That's because it's fun.'

'No. It's insane. And cold.'

'I enjoy it.'

'That's because you were most likely dropped on your head at some point in your childhood but your mum doesn't want to tell you.'

He gave me a look he'd given me a million times, the dark eyes locking onto mine, shaded by lashes I would never, ever not be jealous of, and a hint of smile on the just full enough lips.

'You up for it, then?' Tia broke into our banter joust.

Luca slung his arm around my shoulder. 'We are.'

'Not,' I added quickly. 'We are *not* up for it.'

He tilted his head against mine, resting it there for a moment. 'Live a little, Bee.'

'I live plenty, thank you!' I said, pulling away as both his and Tia's expressions showed they disagreed on this.

'What? I do. I just do it in a quieter, less flashy way than this one.'

'So quiet, in fact, as to be almost silent.'

'You're such an arse,' I said, going to swig the last of my drink only to find I'd already finished it. 'Fine.' I faced Tia. 'I accept the challenge. Whatever it is.'

She clapped her hands excitedly. 'This is going to be so much fun!'

The knots my stomach was currently tying itself in not only showed I felt that was highly doubtful, but would also likely win me a Cub Scout badge. This was most certainly not going to be fun, but I wasn't about to back down now. I knew Luca always thought I was reserved but in comparison to him, most people were. It was called being normal. But now it appeared that he wasn't the only one of my friends who thought I wasn't exactly 'living my best life', if I was kind to myself. If I wasn't being kind to myself, I could say that they actually thought I was pretty dull. Somewhere deep inside I wasn't entirely convinced they were wrong, but I liked quiet, and security and gentle pastimes. I liked sensible. And safe. Keeping your head down. You had less chance of getting hurt that way, not to mention less chance of hurting others.

'You OK?' Luca touched my arm gently, his voice soft, the teasing note of earlier gone.

'Yep.' I squashed all the unwanted thoughts away, back into the attic of my mind and concentrated on what Tia was saying.

'Right, so. Luca thinks happiness is possible via online, yes?'

'I certainly wouldn't rule it out as a means to finding someone special. You and Jono are the perfect example. There's a few people at work who've also met their partners online.'

'Bee, however, has no faith in it. Is that right?'

It felt a little incongruous to say just how little belief I had in it when Jono and Tia were sitting right in front of me, glowing with happiness.

'I just think you two are the exception to the rule, that's all,' I replied, hoping I'd hit the right balance of honesty and tact.

'Fair enough. So, maybe we should put your theories to the test.'

'How?'

'You both join the same dating site, and commit to actually using it.' Tia gave me a hard, Paddington-worthy stare as she said this. 'After a set amount of time, we'll see whose theory comes closest to being accurate.'

Oh God.

3

I felt the food I had been so desperate for earlier swirl and swoosh around my stomach.

'That's ridiculous. There are so many variables! I mean, look at him. Obviously, he's going to get hundreds of dates.' I gave Luca a glance. 'Well, first ones anyway.'

'You're hardly the back end of a bus, Bee,' Luca said, ignoring my dig.

'Oh, come on! You've got all the patter. You deal with people all the time. You go on dates all the time! It's not a fair trial. I go on... less dates.' Tia and Luca were both looking at me. 'OK, fine! A *lot* less dates. Exactly! I don't have the practice. Or the skills. I mean, just take the woman over there who's been undressing Luca from the moment he got here.'

We all gave a surreptitious look towards the bar. She had her legs crossed sexily, her body language was languid and natural and frankly, I'd been surprised Luca hadn't gone straight over. Right now she was talking to a middle-aged guy in a bespoke suit who radiated wealth, and was flirting expertly with him – but it hadn't stopped her throwing glances Luca's way.

'What about her?' Luca asked.

'I can't do that.'

'Do what?'

'Look all glamorous and artless like that.'

'You could if you wanted.'

'I'm not sure I want to. But either way, the point is moot. I definitely can't. You, unfortunately, were in the same bar the last time I tried that technique. And don't think I can't see that smirk, which exactly proves my point.'

'At least you had clean underwear on.'

'Not helpful.'

'At least you had underwear on, full stop,' Tia added.

'Really not helpful.'

'We're just saying it could have been worse. Bar stools can be tricky things to negotiate at times.'

I gave another glance under my lashes at the siren across the room. 'She seems to be managing just fine.'

'You don't need all that fakery, Bee. You have other qualities. We're all different. It's just about confidence anyway. This could be the perfect opportunity to build on that for you.'

'I'm plenty confident,' I said, with absolutely no confidence at all.

'You know we've known you for like thirty years, right?' Tia said with her classic head tilt that signalled to everyone when she was calling them out.

'Fine,' I said, too tired to argue any more. 'But even if this sort of thing can work, it could take months to find The One. If there is such a thing.'

Luca kicked me under the table.

'Present company excluded obviously,' I added, hurriedly.

Tia accepted the codicil to my statement and continued. 'Agreed. But for the purposes of this experiment, we have to set a deadline. How about Christmas Day? That should give you both enough time to get a definite feeling as to whether online dating has promise, even if it hasn't produced Mr or Ms Right by then. Is it a deal?'

By this point, the rest of the group had turned their attention to our conversation and the gauntlet that had been thrown down. I felt their eyes boring into me. Everyone knew Luca would go for it. That was how he was built. But I wasn't built that way. I wasn't sure they'd even used the same materials to build me. The whole process filled me with dread. But on the other hand, despite the evidence of the friends sitting before me, I knew I was right about this whole online dating lark. I would prove Luca wrong, and that aspect definitely appealed to me. We'd been trying to get one over on each other since reception class and this time things were practically guaranteed to go in my favour.

'Deal?' Luca repeated Tia's question, holding out his hand.

'Deal,' I replied, shaking it.

* * *

The following morning I was rudely woken by the loud, continual revving of an engine. I let out a sigh. I lived in a tiny flat at the end of the DLR, which was fine. Thankfully, I didn't own a cat as there wasn't room to swing one, but I'd made it nice, and I didn't have to share with anyone. Out of all of us, I was the one who lived the furthest out of town, but I was also the one who hadn't finished her degree and who earned the least. The two weren't unconnected. The only way I could have afforded to live closer to the city and the rest of my friends was to share and that wasn't really up my street, excuse the pun. I liked being able to sit and eat crisps in my pants if I so chose. I also liked quiet. On the whole, the area wasn't too bad, but a neighbour to the right of the small block I lived in had a thing about cars. I didn't object to that. Cars were nice. I didn't own one as I couldn't afford to run one and most of the time didn't need one. What I did object to was his propensity to 'fix' them at eight o'clock on a Saturday morning.

The car revved again and suddenly there was a huge bang, followed by a moment's silence, which, in turn, was followed by a trail of expletives a mile long. I smiled to myself and turned back over to get some more sleep. When I woke an hour later, I rolled over and fumbled about for my phone on the bedside. Switching it off flight mode, I checked my messages.

Have you done it yet?

This question was followed by an emoji of a chicken. I noted the message had been sent at half past six this morning when all normal humans, assuming they weren't working or parents of small children, should be in bed, asleep. Luca was neither working, nor a parent. Nor was he normal. But I'd got used to that, which was also why I turned my phone onto flight mode overnight. That, and because banks seemed to think three in the morning was exactly the time people wanted to know how their bank balance was looking.

I wrestled my arms into my dressing gown, shoved my feet into the oversized slippers shaped like teddy-bear feet Luca had got me last Christmas and shuffled into the kitchen, which took all of two seconds. Finding orange juice in the fridge, I poured a glass and then flicked the kettle on before poking around to see what might be lurking that could pass for breakfast. Grocery shopping did not thrill me and I tended to put it off until the absolutely last moment. I was pretty much there now. Luca, weirdly, enjoyed it, but then he also knew what to do with all the stuff once he got it home. He'd inherited his family's joy and talent for cooking while I'd never really mastered either. That being said, I didn't mind because he often invited me round for dinner and I was lucky enough to be regularly included in his family's Sunday lunch invitations too. It'd been that way since we were small and I loved it. Unfortunately, while their appreciation of good food had rubbed off on me, their skills in creating it had failed to. I poked a packet of own-brand super noodles and debated their suitability for breakfast.

Grabbing the extra-large mug of tea and glass of juice, I took them to the small table and set them down. I typed back.

Done what?

Moments later my phone dinged with a one emoji answer – rolly eyes. Luca used that one a lot but I wasn't sure if it was just on me. To be fair, I sent a good number of that particular one his way too, so things probably balanced out. Another message came in.

Your profile. For the dating website. Or did you

– he'd inserted chicken emoji here –

out already?

God, he was annoying.

No. I haven't. Because it's the weekend and early and I'm normal. Unlike you.

So, basically you're in your pjs, drinking tea and trying desperately to find something for breakfast that hasn't grown legs and walked out of the fridge on its own?

Ugh. I hated it that he knew me so well.

Whereas I suppose you've done a marathon and whipped up a gourmet dinner for sixteen already?

Nah, only a half marathon and some fresh pasta.

I hate you.

I hate you too.

He followed this with a winky face and then one sticking its tongue out.

OK, so this meant he'd likely prepped his profile on the agreed dating site and uploaded it. It was also likely he already had forty-two dates lined up. Luca wasn't exactly hard on the eyes, ran his own successful business and actually enjoyed exercise, which helped when you were as good a cook as him.

Ugh. I could not lose this bet. I'd never hear the last of it. I knew I was right. Tia and Jono were most definitely exceptions to the rule when it came to Internet dating and I'd prove that. I didn't know why Luca couldn't just accept that he was wrong. I had no inclination to launch myself onto the crazy merry-go-round of online dating only to be flung off again feeling horribly queasy in a few months' time. If I was supposed to meet someone, I would. Luca, of course, approached things differently. To him, you had to make things happen. And he did, which admittedly had worked out pretty well and I was hugely proud of what he'd achieved with his business. I knew he'd give this challenge his all too. Luca Donato was not someone who tended, or liked, to fail. But then neither was I. OK, I had less of a success rate than him but that didn't mean I enjoyed failing. Circumstances just hadn't always been as conducive to triumph as I would have preferred. But the challenge was on, whether I liked it or not. I pulled my laptop towards me and opened it. Pressing the icon for the Internet, I typed in the dating site's address, took a deep breath and clicked on the 'how to join' tab.

* * *

'This is your profile?' Tia asked when they called round later, on their way out of town for the weekend. She was perched on the arm of my compact sofa as Jono watched my neighbour surreptitiously through the window.

'Nice car,' he observed.

'It needs a new engine if the loud bang this morning was anything to go by. Right now, the longer it stays silent, the nicer I think the car is.'

Jono grinned and slouched down onto the sofa, taking the coffee I'd just made him as Tia looked up at me, a frown creasing her brow.

'What?'

'You're cheating.'

'I most certainly am not!' I fired back.

'Is this live?'

I sat on the sofa, tucked my leg up and stroked the fuzzy fur of my slipper. 'Not quite.'

'There's no grey area here, Bee. Is it uploaded or not?'

'Not.'

'Good. That means we can salvage it.'

'Excuse me?'

'I'm the moderator of this challenge, and I need to know it's being run fairly.'

'When did you get appointed moderator?'

'Last night.'

'By whom?'

'Me.'

'You appointed yourself?'

'Yep. Problem?'

I shrugged. 'Not especially. Oh, apart from the bit where you accused me of cheating.'

'This—' she pointed at the screen '—is cheating.'

'How? I've got a profile ready. I've even chosen the most decent-ish picture I could find.' I wasn't a fan of having my photo taken and selfies seemed to come out even worse. I envied those who always looked amazing in them but was also aware that many of these weren't true-to-life representations. However, faffing about with apps to trim that and smooth this seemed like way too much effort. 'Believe me, there were a lot worse ones I could find.'

'It's not that. The picture is good. It's the rest of the profile. It's boring!'

'Wow. Thanks.'

Tia had now moved to one of the chairs at the bistro set that served as my dining table. She spun to face me. 'But you're not,' she added, hurriedly. 'That's why it looks like you're cheating. As though you're trying to make yourself out to be the dullest duck in the world and get the least number of dates.'

'I'm not!' I looked out of the window towards my neighbour, who was now staring intently at his car as if that might fix it. Tia's accusation had stung but I knew she hadn't meant it unkindly.

She studied me for a moment. 'No. I realise that now. Sorry. I should never have said that.' She leant over and gave me a hug. 'I know you wouldn't cheat, even if it meant getting one over on Luca. It's just this...' She indicated the screen. 'This isn't you.'

'It is.'

'No, hon. It's not. Is this really how you see yourself?'

I shifted in my seat. 'I'm just being honest. My profile is never going to look like Luca's. I don't have all those things going for me like he does.'

'You have plenty going for you,' Tia replied in a tone that brooked no argument. 'And don't you ever think that you don't.'

I slid my eyes to Jono. 'She can actually be quite scary, can't she?'

He grinned, nodding at me. 'Yep.'

'Right. Now. Let's fix this.'

There was no point arguing. I'd known my friend too long to realise when it would be fruitless to try and stop her once she was on a mission. I just hoped her attempt at 'fixing' something didn't end in me trailing as long a string of expletives as next door's.

4

'That doesn't sound anything like me!' I protested when I peered over Tia's shoulder twenty minutes later. 'You can't put that up.'

'Of course it does, and I can. Actually, I already have. You, my sweet girl, are live!'

A groan that was supposed to stay in my head broke out.

'It'll be fine!' Tia said in response. 'Who knows? Maybe you'll even meet The One!'

'But then I lose the bet against Luca.'

She studied me for a moment. 'You really think winning a bet is more important than finding someone to share your life with.'

'No, of course not,' I said, honestly.

Tia raised a perfect brow at me.

'I don't. It's just...' I shrugged '... an automatic reaction. It's what Luca and I do. What we've always done.'

She nodded. 'Yeah, I know. Just don't throw something good away over this, OK?'

'Honestly, I still doubt the likelihood of anything good coming from this anyway, but no, I promise that, should I meet someone great, I will accept my loss of the bet graciously. All the while avoiding the low-flying pigs soaring around me.'

Tia rolled her eyes and Jono gave a chuckle, his eyes fixed on some rugby he'd found channel hopping.

'Hey, let's look at Luca's profile.'

'Oh, I'm not sure I want to see...' But Tia was already searching and scrolling and, a moment later, his profile was up on the screen.

'Ooh, he looks good!' She scanned the screen. 'Sounds good too. He's going to be popular.'

'He could have said he was a pig farmer who lived in the sty and he'd still get dates. Look at him! I can't compete with that.'

Tia gave me a sharp look.

'Not that it's all about the competition, obviously.' The look remained and I knew I hadn't convinced her.

I sat on the chair next to her and brought my knees up, tucking myself into a small, compact ball. 'Did you know he was wanting more from his relationships? I mean, from what he said last night...' I shrugged '... sounds like he's really serious.'

'We've never discussed it as such, but he could see the writing on the wall for me and Jono and he was thrilled. He made a couple of comments that did make me begin to wonder whether he was over the flings and perhaps looking for something more serious.' She tilted her head at me. 'You really had no idea?'

I shook my head.

'Surprising. You two have been practically glued to each other since the first day at school. I thought you told each other everything.'

'So did I.'

'It's not exactly a surprise though. You, of all people, know how much family means to Luca. You've spent enough time with his.'

'True.'

It was true. I was an only child with very sociable parents, but, as those social events rarely included me, I spent a lot of time with a babysitter, who, in turn, spent a lot of time with the boyfriend she wasn't supposed to bring over. This, in effect, meant that I spent a lot of time in my room, on my own. I didn't mind so much. My mother repeatedly said that I'd always been good at entertaining myself. I was never sure if she truly thought this or whether it was something she told herself to lessen any wisps of guilt that might have swirled up from time to time. And then Luca, who could keep a secret until the grave but, conversely, could also have a big mouth, must have mentioned something to his mum. Much of the time when my parents went out, I would do myself a Pot Noodle because the babysitter 'wasn't hungry'. She always took the food she was supposed to cook home, though, so my parents wouldn't know she hadn't prepared it as she was paid to do, and, for some reason, I never said anything. I suppose, deep down, I wasn't sure it would make any difference and instead only cause discord and increase the uncomfortable feeling I had that they viewed me as a stumbling block to their nights out. Mum always looked so glamorous, and so happy when she was getting ready to go out, I didn't want to upset her.

Once Mrs Donato got wind of this situation, she stepped in. I begged Luca to stop her, worried I was going to get into trouble about the babysitting thing, but he hugged me and told me not to worry. He was right. Although she clearly knew what had been happening, Mrs Donato handled the situation with complete tact and diplomacy and even framed it in a way that worked better for my parents than the current arrangements. Getting my mother chatting, she steered the conversation around to evenings out and before I knew it Luca's mum had arranged for me to go and stay over at their house whenever my parents had plans. That way, she pointed out, they didn't have to rush back for the babysitter, and as they already had a houseful, one more would be no bother. My mother protested politely, but not too much, and the deal was done. Suddenly, I no longer felt a sense of heaviness and isolation inside me when I knew they were going out. I couldn't wait! Luca's house was a noisy, busy place full of good food and good humour. I'd always loved going there and now I got to go even more often. They lived in a big rambling house that his grandfather had bought cheap in the days when you could still get inexpensive property in London, and gradually done it up and filled it with family. Even now, Luca and his siblings spent a lot of time there. It was suddenly obvious that he'd want to recreate that for himself in time. And it seemed that time was now.

I leant over and skipped back to my page. 'Did you have to put all that computer stuff in? I sound nerdy.'

'Yes, of course. It's your job. You're a computer genius. That's why you're on all our speed dials.'

'Good to know that's the reason.'

'That came out wrong.'

'I hope so.'

Tia grinned and I knew it wasn't true. But she was right. I was good with computers. We'd done bits at school but I'd taught myself a lot sitting alone in my room all those nights and found it came quite easily to me. I wasn't one of the cool girls and I wasn't sporty. But this, I was good at. That, of course, had its down side as my talents immediately labelled me as a nerd – until someone wanted something fixed and then they were a bit nicer to me, but I didn't care so much. I had Luca and a solid group of friends and that was enough.

But now we were all dispersing. It was inevitable, of course.

We did do our best to meet up as much as possible and had a chat group so there was contact fairly regularly. I'd have felt lost without that, even though occasionally I wondered if I still fitted in so well. Sometimes it felt as if everyone was moving on and I was stuck where I was with no sign of moving anywhere. But Luca had always been there since I was five years old and now it looked like that might change too. I wanted him to be happy. He was my best friend. How could I not? I still didn't hold much faith in a procedure that effectively felt like shopping online for love, but the thought of being the only one at our group meet-ups turning up alone made my stomach churn. I'd felt pitied once before and I never wanted that again. My eyes drifted to the screen and the one picture of me that didn't make me screw my nose up. Maybe this was for the best. Maybe there were more important things in life than winning a bet.

* * *

'I wonder how many dates he's been asked for so far?' Tia asked, nosing over Luca's profile.

'Plenty, I imagine, if his track record is anything to go by,' I answered without looking up.

'Yeah, but don't forget what he said. He's not just looking for a fling.'

'You can't tell anything from a picture and few words. People just put up what they think others want to hear. You've just done the same for mine! These things are hardly representative. Even if he is looking for something more, I'm pretty sure Luca's still going to do some thorough research.'

Tia shrugged. 'Maybe. And yours is representative.'

'It's not. You've made me sound far more interesting and successful than I am. Even if I do get any dates, they're soon going to find out the truth. You may as well have put a ten-year-old photo up as well and gone the whole hog.'

Tia rolled her eyes at me and looked back at the screen. 'You know what's funny?'

I shook my head as I picked a notepad off the table and scanned down my to-do list. 'Nope.'

'Reading this.' She pointed an exquisitely painted, highly decorative nail at my computer where Luca's profile was still smiling out, relaxed, confident and entirely too handsome for his own good. (Even his mother said that, so I knew it was true.) 'Well, it's kind of a shame that you two know each other.'

I looked up from the pad, having reluctantly ticked off 'create and upload profile for ridiculous bet'.

'What do you mean?'

'It's just that, according to this, Luca's looking for someone exactly like you.'

I gave a snort, half laughter, half disbelief and altogether unladylike. Even Jono glanced away from the sports for a moment to raise his eyebrows at his fiancée.

'He is,' Tia persisted. 'It says he's looking for someone kind, caring and genuine with a good sense of humour.'

'Everyone puts that!'

She ignored me and continued on. 'With an appreciation of good food, travel and who understands the importance of family and friends. You're all those things.' I could see the cogs whirring and the steam beginning to build in the engine of my friend's brain.

'Lots of people are all those things. It's pretty generic.' I peered over. 'It also lists his hobbies as "ridiculous macho crap".' OK, it didn't say that exactly. What it actually said was 'enjoys extreme sports' but those two were interchangeable in my eyes. 'And somewhere there must be a requirement list of "legs up to armpits, body of a lingerie model, preferably with the same job to match, and long, glossy hair that wouldn't be out of place in a shampoo commercial".'

'He's not that shallow,' Tia defended him. 'And your hair is long and glossy.'

'I didn't say he was shallow. But when was the last time he turned up with a woman who would have looked out of place in a fashion magazine, or weird perfume advert? I always end up having to surreptitiously move to the other side of the table just so I don't look a complete Ork. I'm just saying, even if it wouldn't be weird, which it totally would be, I'm definitely not Luca's type. We'd drive each other bananas inside a week, not to mention how awkward things would then be. It'd change the whole group dynamic... thing.'

'Specific.'

'You know what I mean.'

'Jesse and Bella got together. It hasn't changed anything.'

'Yes, but we could all see they were made for each other. That was just inevitable.'

Tia gave me a long look.

I let out an exasperated sigh. 'It's not the same thing at all. Not even remotely. And don't even think of mentioning it to Luca! He'd be mortified – if he ever stopped laughing.'

Tia rolled her eyes before fixing me with a no-nonsense look. 'But just fyi, that move you do to get away from Luca and his latest flame? It isn't surreptitious. Everyone notices that you do it every time.'

'They do?' I said, my voice pitching a little higher than usual.

She nodded. I glanced at Jono. He shrugged and gave a head tilt to show he agreed.

'Has Luca noticed?'

'Yep.'

'How do you know he's noticed? I'm sure he would have said something if he had.' Tia was definitely wrong on this. Luca called me out on pretty much everything. The knot that had been building in my stomach began to unravel again. 'He always says something if he doesn't agree with it when it comes to me. Which tends to be most things.'

Tia and Jono exchanged glances.

'What? What was that look about?'

Tia let out a sigh, reaching out and taking my hand briefly to give it a quick, reassuring squeeze. 'He was getting antsy about it one time and was going to tackle you about it...'

'And?'

'And we asked him not to.'

'We? Who's we? And why?'

'All of us.'

I frowned. 'But why? I don't understand.'

'OK. Tell us why you move as soon as you can every time you end up next to one of Luca's girlfriends.'

Jono had lowered the TV's sound and, like Tia, was now focused on me. My face felt hot and pink and my stomach was back doing a demonstration of knots that would put a sailor to shame with an added backflip to finish. 'I just told you...'

They waited.

I cleared my throat. 'OK, fine. I feel dowdy. Every single woman he goes out with is this perfect specimen. Great hair, great clothes, utterly stunning with a body to die for. And then there's me sat next to her. And yes, maybe it is vanity but it's not hard to feel like I'm suffering by comparison and, frankly, I don't need the fact that I'm not like that rubbed in my face, or high-lighted to anyone else. So, I move. I'm sure Luca doesn't even notice most of the time.'

Tia shook her head. 'I can tell you he absolutely does notice. And you should never feel like that. It's not true, is it, Jono?'

Jono shook his head and gave another shrug. 'Honestly, it's not. You're... nice.'

Both of us looked at him. 'Nice?' Tia repeated.

'What?'

'She's much more than nice!'

'I know that!'

'So why did you say it?' his fiancée asked, raising her hands, palms up.

'Because I thought if I said she's kind of hot, which she is, I might get pushed out of a window and we're three storeys up!'

Tia studied him for a moment. 'You're so sweet. Wanna get married?' She winked and he grinned. He gave me a shrug, then turned back to the TV with an audible sigh of relief.

'See?' Tia said. 'You're cute. You don't suffer by comparison and you're gorgeous in your own way. Fine. You're not model height.'

I peered at the pyjama legs that were halfway down my feet now I'd kicked my slippers off.

'I'm model village height.'

Tia laughed, releasing the slight ripple of tension in the room that had built since I'd discovered that Luca – that everyone – had busted my manoeuvre. And that they knew the reason for it. I rubbed my face, unable to shift the feeling of awkwardness entirely.

'You're lovely, hon. Really. You should never feel anything less than that.'

'How come I'm the only one who's single, then?'

'Luca's still single too, remember.'

'Luca is only single when it suits him and, if what he said the other day is true, won't be for long.'

'Because he's putting himself out there. Something you, my friend, have an aversion to doing.'

'I don't have an aversion to it.'

'When we go out, you do your best to wedge yourself between the group like we're your defence shield. You make it pretty hard for any guy to approach you.'

'If they were that bothered, they'd make the effort. Clearly they're not.'

Tia gave me an exasperated look.

'What?'

'You.'

'What about me?'

She shook her head. 'I want to wave a magic wand and give you the confidence you should have. You're intelligent, independent, and, as my fiancé says, kind of hot.' She gave me a grin. 'I just wish you'd believe it yourself.'

'I'm fine.' I waved her away, uncomfortable with how long the spotlight seemed to have been on me. 'Anyway, have you had any thoughts on dresses or anything yet for the wedding?' Tia was a total fashionista so I knew that I was on pretty safe ground on how to transition the conversation away from me. She paused a moment, her look telling me she knew exactly what I was doing, but then turned back to the laptop, pulling it between us. Quickly she typed in an address and Luca's profile disappeared, replaced by a swish-looking website featuring an ethereal-looking wedding dress. Checking Jono couldn't see the screen, she tilted it a little more towards me.

'What do you think?'

5

My pocket squeaked with the arrival of a message as I sat in the coffee shop later that afternoon, staring out at the shoppers as they hurried past the plate-glass window. The pavement was shiny with rain and people pulled their coats around them, heads down as they battled along the busy London street, an array of colourful umbrellas bobbing along above their heads. Pulling the phone out, I clicked on the chat app. It was from Luca.

What you up to?

I put the phone down for a moment, letting it rest in my lap. Ever since Tia had told me that everyone knew about my evasion tactics when it came to Luca's girlfriends I'd been feeling a bit out of sorts. With Luca's surprise disclosure about looking to settle down and the fact he'd never tackled me about my propensity to put distance between me and his latest flame even before the others asked him not to, I was beginning to wonder what else I didn't know about him. A feeling that perhaps we weren't as close as I'd thought we were had begun to swirl inside me and I didn't like it. People often said that friendships come and go in life but I didn't want this one to go. I couldn't remember a time that it wasn't a hugely important part of my life, and I'd thought that Luca felt the same. But if he didn't feel that he could share something as important as wanting a serious relationship, a family or tackle me bluntly about my behaviour as he'd always done, then perhaps he didn't feel the same. Maybe he'd already taken a step or two away. I wasn't sure how I felt about that. Actually, that was a lie. I knew exactly how I felt about that. I hated it. But I also knew I couldn't stop it. I couldn't hold onto something that wasn't to be, or to someone who didn't want me in their life. I'd learned that lesson the hard way and I wasn't about to fight it this time. But I still felt crap that Luca thought I was being rude to him and his dates. It was just a form of self-protection and I'd not meant to hurt his, or anyone else's, feelings. However much of an idiot it might make me look, I had to tell him that. I picked the phone back up.

Not much. Hot chocolate and people watching.

Where?

Neros at More London.

Want some company?

I sent a thumbs up. No time like the present to clear the air.

OK. Be there asap.

Just under a quarter of an hour later, Luca pushed through

the heavy glass door and a group of female American tourists all swivelled their heads towards him. It was hard not to notice Luca Donato. Not only had he won the genes lottery, he was six four, and had the broad-shouldered, solid build of a rugby player. The slight bend in his nose and one-inch scar that left a thin silver line through his left brow was testament to his enjoyment of the sport in previous years. These only added to his charm though. Apparently.

His dark eyes glanced around, the gaze swinging over the women still checking him out before landing on me. A smile broke and he raised one hand in a wave. I smiled back, aware that I was now being scrutinised by his admirers. He placed his order and then strode across the café, confident and relaxed, leaning down to give me a hug before taking the seat next to me on the battered leather sofa I'd nabbed.

'What you doing in town? Got a date already?' He grinned his even white smile, achieved courtesy of two years of braces.

I made a dismissive sound, half laughing. 'Hardly. It's only been a few hours. Why, have you?'

'Yep.'

'Oh.' The laughter died in my throat. 'Right. Wow. That was quick.'

He shrugged.

I didn't know why I was surprised. When Luca decided to do something, he put his heart and soul into it. That determination and commitment had earned him a first-class degree, a happy, stable relationship with his family and a successful business. There was no reason, now he had committed to this, that it would get any less attention or dedication.

'What time is your date?'

'Not for a couple of hours yet.'

'Oh. Going somewhere nice?'

'Some restaurant in the West End she wants to try.'

'Not taking her to Ginelli's?'

He gave me a half-smile. 'Nah. That's only reserved for very special people.'

Ginelli's was Luca's favourite restaurant in London. He knew the staff like family and they treated him the same way. Family celebrations were always held there and I'd been lucky enough to be included in many of those, even on the odd occasions when my parents were home. Whenever I mentioned I'd been invited over for dinner, or a party or a celebration – Italian families always seemed to find things to celebrate, something I loved – my parents never objected, always encouraging me to go. I was more than happy to, of course. But deep down, I occasionally wished that they would suggest that we did something together, just us, for once, have our own celebration. But they never did. The wine and champagne bottles I would see in the recycling told me that celebrations certainly took place, it was just that I was never a part of them. But I always felt a part of the Donatos'. Those cherished times spent with them were bright spots of vivid colour amongst the grey of my childhood memories. I felt as if I owed Luca. Which was why I needed to apologise.

'Luca?' I said, shifting round a little more to face him.

He studied me for a moment. 'Uh oh. This looks serious. What's up?'

'I need to say—'

'Order for Luca.' The barista bellowed across the chatter of the coffee shop.

'Hang on.' He touched my hand briefly before stepping past me, his long legs managing it easily and gracefully. A moment later he was back with a large coffee, a hot chocolate topped with cream and tiny marshmallows and two slices of cake. 'Thought you might want one and I saw there was a distinct lack of cake.'

'I was trying to be good so I didn't order any.'

He shrugged. 'Being good's overrated.' He then waggled his eyebrows for emphasis. I shook my head and took a plate of cake, placing it in front of me before linking my fingers together again on my lap.

'Thanks.'

'Carry on with what you were saying.'

I should have waited until he already had his order. The moment felt lost now.

'No, really, it doesn't matter.'

Luca put his coffee down next to his own cake.

'By the look on your face, I'm pretty sure it does. So just say it. I can sit here until you do.' He gave the briefest hint of a smile. 'You know I can do it.'

'You have been known to be stubborn at times.'

His smile grew. We both knew this was a huge understatement. Mules had nothing on Luca Donato if he put his mind to it.

'But I have an advantage.'

'And what's that?'

'I can sit it out until your deadline if I feel like it today.'

'Deadline?' He frowned.

'Your date?' I reminded him.

'Oh!' He considered this for a moment. 'There will be other dates. Some things are more important. So, tell me now or tell me later. Either way, I'm not moving until you do.'

See? Stubborn. God, he was annoying.

'OK, fine. But only because I don't want you blaming me for you missing your date with Miss Possibly Right.'

He gave me an even look.

I picked up the cake plate and fiddled with the fork for a moment, sectioning off a bite-size piece. Then I put it aside and gave an unnecessary clear of my throat.

'I need to apologise for something.'

Luca shoved some cake in and squinted one eye a little in question. 'Oh?' he asked, having swallowed his mouthful.

'Yes.' I took a deep breath and then let it out slowly. I felt like an idiot but I knew if I didn't do this it would just eat away at me. 'For always moving away from you and your dates when we go out as a group.'

He watched me for a moment. 'Right.'

'I thought I was being subtle.'

'No. You weren't. But I could see how you might think that.'

I couldn't tell what he was thinking. He wasn't smiling.

'I'm sorry. I never meant to offend you, or anyone else. I honestly didn't think anyone noticed.'

'Oh. We all noticed.'

'Yes. So I've been made aware, which is a little bit awkward.'

'Some of them were nice women, you know.'

I looked up quickly from where I'd been studying the patterns in the marble cake. 'It's not that! I'm sure they were. I wasn't... I didn't mean to be rude. I'm...' I did another throat clear. 'I'm really sorry if I embarrassed you or if they thought I was being a snooty moo. I just...'

'Just what?' he asked. 'I have to say, it's bugged me for ages but the others made me promise not to say anything.'

'I wish you had. I'm pretty sure it couldn't have been any more excruciating than it is now!'

'I made a promise. They told me you had your reasons.'

'I did,' I said, dropping my gaze.

'Do I get to hear them?'

I lifted my eyes to his own. They were dark and serious, watching me.

'You wouldn't understand.'

'Try me.'

Shoving my hands over my face, I pushed them back up and through my hair before letting out a big sigh. 'Fine. Because every woman you date makes me feel frumpy, plain and insignificant. They're always tall, glamorous and immaculately put together and I'm... not. I reasoned that if I wasn't slap bang next to them, the difference wouldn't seem quite so obvious.'

Luca stared at me but remained silent.

'Well, I'm so glad I told you because this ensuing silence isn't awkward at all.'

He shook his head as though coming to from a daydream. 'Sorry. I just... I guess I wasn't expecting you to say that.'

'What were you expecting, then? As apparently you and everyone else had noticed I not so stealthily put distance between myself and your latest supermodel. I assume I was just thought of as horribly rude. I'm not sure which is worse now. Being thought rude or actually being pathetic.'

'You're neither of those things.'

I flicked a look at him that suggested I thought otherwise and, having eaten most of the toppings already, disappeared momentarily behind my second huge mug of hot chocolate, making a mental note to add an extra mile to my next walk.

'You're not. I'm just kind of shocked that's how you feel. And also that you never told me.' He shrugged. 'I thought we shared pretty much everything.'

There was a look of hurt in the dark eyes that sent a stab to my own heart. I'd thought that too but it seemed that perhaps both of us had been keeping secrets.

'It's not always as easy as that.'

'Of course it is. It's me.'

I put the mug back down on the table a little heavier than I'd planned and met Luca's gaze.

'And what exactly was I supposed to say?' I began, my voice

low but determined. 'Oh Luca, would you mind not sitting your unfailingly beautiful, long-legged, doe-eyed model-type girl-friends so close to me every time we go out because I already feel inferior to you lot most of the time and them sat there looking like someone just shook them out of a *Vogue* magazine really isn't helping matters.'

He was giving me that look again.

'What?'

'That's really how you feel?' he asked, his voice soft, concern rippling through the words.

I fiddled with a paper napkin, rolling and unrolling it round my finger until it became permanently curled, all the while avoiding answering.

'Bee?' Luca prompted.

'What?' I said, stalling.

He gave me a look I'd seen a million times.

'Yes. It is. There? Happy now? You know all my darkest secrets.'

'Of course I'm not happy this is how you feel about things. Why would I be?'

I didn't answer.

'You think I'd be pleased that I, or anyone, was contributing to making you feel bad about yourself?' He sat back into the corner of the sofa. 'I guess maybe we don't know each other as well as we thought, after all.'

'Well, you've been keeping secrets too, so it's not all on me!' I snapped, feeling unhappy and uncomfortable.

'Me?'

'Yes!'

'Like what?'

'Like the fact that you suddenly want to settle down.'

His eyes narrowed a little but I ploughed on.

'One minute it's all these glamour types and one-night stands, two if they're lucky, and then the next minute you're sat there declaring that you want to find Ms Right and live happily ever after. And you never mentioned it to anyone, let alone me and we're supposed to be best friends! That seems like something pretty important and something I'd certainly have told you if I'd been looking for it.'

'But you're not.'

'It's not that... I... I just don't see it happening for me and anyway we're talking about you, not me.'

'Why don't you see it happening for you?'

'I'm not the type.'

'Rubbish.'

'It's not rubbish. Besides, I imagine that's what my parents thought too. But that didn't exactly work out in the long term either, did it?'

'They seemed happy together until the accident.'

'Oh, yeah, they were happy together. Their big mistake was having a child, which rather put a dent in that happiness.'

Luca shifted his position closer to me, reached out and took my hand. 'Don't ever think that, Bee.'

I let out a sigh, the prickliness of earlier replaced now by that familiar sense of emptiness.

'Oh, come on, Luca.' I bumped my shoulder against his. 'We both know I was obviously unplanned, even if they never admitted it.'

'We don't know that.'

'It doesn't matter. When it comes down to it, there just wasn't enough love there for three people.'

'Have you heard from your mum lately?'

'There was a postcard a couple of months ago, from somewhere in the Med. I don't remember where.'

'She say when she's back?'

'Nope.'

'No messages? Email?'

'Apparently "communication can be patchy" when you're cruising the world on one of the highest spec, most expensive liners in the world.' I gave an eye roll so big I was surprised they didn't roll right out of my head and out of the café door. Luca didn't say anything. We both knew Mum's excuse was bullshit and no kind words would ever be able to hide the truth of that.

6

Eighteen months after my father was killed taking part in the Isle of Man TT motorbike race, my mother met someone else. Within six months they were married and I'd barely seen her since. To be honest, it had been a bit of a relief to begin with, which I knew sounded awful but I'd been exhausted. Mum had completely fallen to pieces the moment she'd heard the news about Dad. I'd been at uni and came home to take care of the arrangements for the funeral as well as Mum herself. Those months had basically consisted of either heart-rending sobbing, hollow-eyed silence or wailing cries of how she 'had nothing and no one'. To begin with I'd tried to tell her that she had me, that she'd always have me and I wouldn't leave to go back to university until she was feeling better. But somehow, at the one time I thought she might actually want – or need – to form a bond with her only child, there was still nothing. Her husband had gone. He had been her world. She didn't want anyone else – not even her own flesh and blood. I still wasn't enough.

But I'd stayed and taken care of things as it soon became apparent Mum was in no fit state to. My friends were all still off at uni, enjoying their new-found freedom, and experiencing life, making new friends and forging new paths – just as I'd begun to. But that had all come to as abrupt a halt as Dad's bike had when it hit the tree. His life had been over from that second, and so was mine. At least the one I'd been working towards, enjoying, planning for. All gone. All for the sake of some stupid adrenalin rush.

'I'm sorry, Bee.'

'What for?' I asked. Luca's deep, smooth voice pulled me from my memories.

'For how your parents acted towards you. For how your mother still does.'

'Doesn't matter. Besides, it's not your fault.'

'I know. But you're right. I probably should have told you I'd begun to think maybe it was time to pull back a bit on the playboy side of life.'

'So, why didn't you?'

'Because I didn't think you'd understand. And because I was worried how you'd react.'

'What does that mean?' The spikiness made a reappearance and I dropped his hand.

'You just said you're not interested in any of that stuff yourself.'

'So? That doesn't mean I can't empathise or be happy for others when they find the person that makes them happy! You make me sound like a… a bloody robot or something! I do have feelings, you know!'

'I know you do! I just…' He ran a hand across a jaw that was dark with stubble and likely hadn't seen a razor since yesterday morning. 'This is exactly why I didn't tell you.'

'Oh, that's crap! I'm upset because you think I wouldn't understand, not because you've told me you want to fall in love!'

At this, all four of the American women at the table next to us swivelled their heads towards Luca.

'Maybe we should pick this conversation up again another time when you're a bit calmer.'

'I'm perfectly calm!' I said, admittedly not exactly backing myself up with my tone. 'It's just nice to know my friends keep things from me because they think I'm not emotionally equipped to deal with it!' I grabbed my coat and stood, shoving my arms in the sleeves.

'It's not that and you know it.'

'Isn't it?'

'Of course it isn't,' Luca stood, taking hold of one sleeve that was resolutely refusing to obey and let my arm inside. 'Here.'

'Thank you,' I said, forcing an inkling of gratitude into my voice. 'It doesn't really matter now, does it? What's done is done. Maybe we're both learning more about each other thanks to this stupid bet than we ever thought we would.'

'Maybe we are,' Luca replied.

'Talking of which, you'd better head off. Wouldn't want you to be late for your date.'

'Are you sure you don't have a potential one?'

'What?'

'A date? It's Saturday night, I know your profile went up. Tia sent me a link.'

'Oh, for God's sake. Why?' I mumbled, now even more irritated. 'Yes, it is live. And no, I don't have a date. Potential or otherwise.'

'When did you check it?'

'What?'

'The profile inbox.'

'What does it matter?'

'You could have a bunch of messages!'

'We both know that's not very likely. Besides, I don't want a date tonight. I'm tired and I just want to go home.'

'You're cheating on the bet. Tia said we both had to make an effort.'

'I am!'

'You're not even checking the messages! How is that making an effort?'

'Oh my God! You're impossible! Here!' I shoved my phone at him. He took it and tapped in my security code, then found the app icon as I belted my coat, ready to head out into air that had cooled substantially now the sun had set.

'You've got five messages.'

'What?'

'There are five messages in there.'

'Oh!'

He tilted his head a little. 'You seem surprised.'

I glanced out of the window, faffed with my belt and avoided answering.

'Why?'

'Why what?'

'Why are you surprised?' Luca sank back down onto the sofa, much to the consternation of a couple who had been heading our way, their eyes focused on the prize of a comfy seat.

'I don't know,' I answered eloquently.

Luca let out a sigh that was part frustration and part something else I couldn't quite place. 'Why do you have such a low opinion of yourself?'

'I don't,' I shot back, but even to my own ears there didn't seem quite enough conviction in the words. 'Anyway, you'd better get going.' I took my phone back and shoved it in my pocket.

'Aren't you going to read the messages?'

'Later.'

'What if one, or more of them, wants to make plans for tonight?'

'Then one, or more of them, can make plans with any number of other women they've probably messaged.'

Luca let his head fall back on his shoulders, his eyes focused on the ceiling. 'And you say I'm impossible.'

'What? I'm not about to jump because some strange bloke says to!'

'That's not what I meant. But you don't even seem interested...' There was no fight in his words.

'Maybe that's because I'm not. I've only signed up to this stupid website because Tia made us.'

'She didn't make us. You just couldn't resist the opportunity to try and prove me wrong on something. As usual.'

'Well... neither could you!' It wasn't a great comeback but it was all I had.

'It's not about that for me. It's about the opportunity to meet someone. Not to beat someone.'

'You'd better go and meet them then. Have a nice dinner.'

Luca stood again, shrugging into his jacket as he did so, looking effortlessly stylish, as always.

'Thanks,' he replied.

I gave him a quick hug, because I couldn't not. Even when I was mad with him I couldn't bear not to say goodbye properly. And I wasn't really mad with him. I was just... feeling a bit odd. Luca's comment about not having confidence in myself had rankled. I'd denied it – obviously. Owning up to it wasn't an option, even though it was true. I hated that I felt that way. But I hated even more the fact that Luca knew. He was my best friend but I still couldn't admit this. Not even to him. How could I? He came from a big, loving family who were interested in him and his life and everything he did. I knew he'd try to understand because that was Luca. But there was no way he could. Not really. And, as I saw him check his watch, I was beginning to realise now that I couldn't rely on Luca as I'd done in the past. Things were changing. What was the point of trying to explain something like this? If this bet worked out for him, he'd be moving into a new phase and the insecurities of a childhood friend would definitely not be top of his priorities.

'You can always talk to me, you know,' he said, catching my hand as I turned to go.

'Yep, I know.' I forced a smile, gave a quick wave and headed out of the coffee shop without looking back.

* * *

I sat on the Tube, listening to the rattle of the carriage against the tracks, staring at an advert for some miracle-working vitamin drink that was guaranteed to give you vitality and pizzazz. I'd tried it. It hadn't made one iota of difference. There was a lot of tiny print at the bottom of the advert and I guessed somewhere in there it noted that all the above was a load of hooey. Or something to that effect anyway.

My gaze drifted around the carriage. A couple of people were asleep and a group of what sounded like Spanish tourists were talking fast and laughing together. The rest of the passengers were all either watching, scrolling or listening to something on their phones bar one man on an end seat who was absorbed in a book. A real book. That made me smile. Although he had the cover bent around the rest of it and as he turned each page, another one added to the curve. That didn't make me smile. I had a thing about not bending books, or their pages, and it was all I could do not to snatch it from his hands and educate him on proper book etiquette. But I didn't. Obviously. I glanced up as the train made the whooshy, whistling sound they let out as they slowed for a station. An announcement came over the tannoy that, due to emergency engineering works, the train would be terminating at the next stop, and that tickets would be accepted on all overground trains, and buses. Groans and sighs filled the carriage. At the next stop, we all filtered out and I made my way up to the surface to find an alternative route home.

Some time later, I was on my second bus and staring blankly out of the window. To distract myself, I pulled my phone from my pocket and went to the dating app. Opening it, I saw the little envelope symbol in the top right-hand corner with a number five next to it. I stared at it for a moment then pressed it. The inbox opened with the five message headings lined up below. My stop wasn't for a while yet. No time like the present then, I told myself, and pressed on the first message.

Hey, foxy lady...

Umm, hello? The seventies called. They want their chat-up line back. I read the next two lines of the message and let's just say things didn't improve. If possible, they actually got worse. My finger found the little rubbish bin and, one satisfying press later, Mr Foxy was gone. With trepidation, I moved on to the next. My eyes bulged a little as it loaded. Had I ever got to finish my degree, I'm not sure even my dissertation would have been this long! However, having dismissed messenger number one, and with both Tia and Luca accusing me of not participating properly, I made an effort to prove them wrong and give option number two a chance.

By the time I got to my stop sometime later, I still hadn't quite finished. I found it hard to believe there was anything I didn't know about this guy! Should I agree to a date with him, I wasn't sure I could think of any questions I'd ask him – there couldn't possibly be anything left to tell me. Certainly not about his previous marriage and the ensuing divorce. He'd been so detailed about that I almost felt I'd been there! But I gave him the benefit of the doubt and decided that perhaps he just wanted to be honest. Get it all out there. And, boy, he'd done a good job of that. Maybe the first ever message might not have been the ideal time to do that but perhaps he was as new to this stuff as I was. His profile pic showed quite a nice-looking guy, with a shy smile and light brown hair worn short and neat. I decided to put him in the possible pile, thanked the bus driver as I got off and slipped my phone back in my pocket. The rest could wait until I got home. I wasn't so desperate to find out who else might have messaged that I was willing to risk life, limb or even just irritation by walking along with my phone in front of my face. I'd get comfy in my pjs and make a nice big cup of tea and settle in to look at the rest.

* * *

So?????

Tia's message pinged as I sat down with my cuppa. I guessed she was talking about the dating thing. This was Tia's modus operandi. You had to keep up because, unlike Responder Number Two on my profile, Tia did not fill in any gaps for you unless specifically asked.

Give me a few minutes…

Luca said you hadn't even checked your inbox earlier! You know he's out on a date already, right?

I let out a sigh.

Luca is such a tattle tale and yes, I did know.

I put the shrug emoji after this, just to emphasise that it made no difference to me. It might be a competition but it wasn't a race.

Do you have a date then?

Tia and I apparently had different concepts of what constituted 'a few minutes'.

Not yet. I'm reading the messages and making a considered decision.

Well, hurry up!

I went back to the other messages and read them. Thankfully, the remaining three were all shorter. I took a deep breath and replied to the fourth one. He looked nice, sounded as if he had a sense of humour and was posing with a dog in his picture, which admittedly swayed me probably more than it should. But he mentioned being an animal lover and, although I wasn't able to have pets in my flat, I'd always loved animals and longed for my own pet. I'd even begged my parents years ago, perhaps sensing that the company might have helped dim the loneliness. They'd always dismissed the idea, saying they didn't have the time or the inclination to look after a pet. After one such exchange I'd unexpectedly fired back with the accusation that they didn't have the time or inclination to look after a child either, but that hadn't stopped them having one. The look on their faces was still etched in my memory now. They never replied and it was never mentioned again. It didn't make any difference in the end but there had been a strange sense of relief on my side that I'd finally said it.

I've messaged one.

One? What about the rest?

What about them?

You have to try a few, Bee! Send some other messages. Unless they're total creeps in which case don't!

Why?

It gives you options!

This was going to be harder work than I thought.

OK. Fine…

I messaged Mr Dissertation and another one that had come in after I got home. I didn't say much, just a simple hi and thank you for the message and one short comment about something in each of their messages.

7

Ten minutes after I'd messaged Mr Animal Lover, I got a reply, which was shortly followed by a reply from the last guy that had contacted me. I clicked on that one and then threw the phone across the sofa! I heard my message app beep but I was too busy wondering where I could buy mental floss. Why would someone do that? Seriously? The phone beeped again. I picked it up. Screwing my eyes up as much as possible while still being able to see just enough, I deleted the last bloke's messages and hit 'block' and 'report' on the contact before switching to the chat app.

Waiting!

Tia prompted.

Sent some more. One most definite NO! Will keep you posted on the rest.

Tia sent a thumbs up and some kisses.
Just as I put my phone down, another notification came in.

So did you read the messages yet?

It was from Luca. I glanced at the clock. I guessed his date was in the loo or something.

Yes. Date going OK?

I saw him typing.

Am home. Not my type after all.

Want to talk about it?

Moments later, my phone sprang to life with an incoming video call. I answered and Luca's annoyingly handsome face filled the screen. And when I say filled, I mean filled. His nose must have been pressed against the glass. I jumped back and he laughed.

'Will you stop doing that?'

'Nah. It makes you jump every time. Why would I stop?'

'Because it's annoying.'

'You've just given me yet another reason not to stop.'

'You know we're not in primary school now, right?'

'Shame. You always looked so cute in those pigtails. You should wear those again. It'd be kind of hot.'

'Oh, ha ha. So why are you home already?'

Sitting back against the soft cream sofa in his apartment, he gave a shrug. 'Like I said. Not my type, and not really compatible. At least not from my perspective.'

'In what way?'

'Well, because the only conversation topic she seemed interested in was monetarily based.'

I frowned, not quite understanding.

'I should have twigged from the moment she asked for the cocktail menu, and then chose the most expensive one. Which she then left half of before requesting a glass of the second most expensive one.'

'Oh. And I'm guessing you weren't splitting the bill.'

Luca gave me a look. He had an old-fashioned streak to him. If a woman insisted on paying half, then he wouldn't make a big thing of it, but generally he reasoned that he'd been the one to ask her out, and so it seemed fair to foot the bill. It was just who he was. I got the feeling tonight's date hadn't offered to split the bill.

'Then she said she was peckish and what she really fancied was oysters.'

'A packet of salt and vinegar Chipsticks usually hits the spot for me but each to their own.'

'Yeah, you're a much cheaper date.'

I pulled a face. 'I'm going to try and form that into a compliment. At some point.'

He grinned. 'It was meant as one.'

'Maybe not one to use on your next date, should it apply. Another woman may not be quite so understanding as me.'

'That's true. You're definitely one of a kind.' He laughed. 'In a good way!' he added quickly.

'Nice save.'

'Thanks.'

'So, what happened after the oysters? I'm assuming you ordered them.'

'Yep. I did. She tried one, turned green and then declared herself not to be hungry after all.'

'Aah.' A picture was beginning to form. 'She did an internet search on you and thinks you're rich.'

'I was trying to be generous but I began to get that impression too. Still, her declaring she wasn't hungry gave me a polite way of ending the date early.'

To be fair, Luca was doing pretty well for himself and a few cocktails, even top-priced ones, and a plate of oysters weren't going to make a dent in his wallet, but I hated that someone had focused on that aspect of him. That his money and success were the only things she'd seen. OK, they wouldn't have been the only things she'd seen. But still, the looks, body and money aside, Luca had so much more to offer than that. He was laughing off the disastrous money-grabbing date but there was something in his eyes, a shadow, a hesitation. Had this been why he'd never stayed with women all that long? Because he was afraid that was all they were after? That he might let himself start feeling something more only to find out they were only in love with his bank account and swanky apartment, not the real Luca Donato.

'Are you OK?' I asked, concern rippling through me. I hated the thought of someone using him.

'Yeah. I'm fine. So how's it going with you? Did you look at those messages yet?'

'Yep. I even replied to a couple.'

'Oh? And have they replied back?'

'The first reply I opened was a dick pic. So I'm just taking time out to recover from that before I open the next one.'

Luca's brow darkened, which made him look even more Italian, and a little bit threatening. Obviously, I know he's a teddy bear so it didn't bother me, but for others not in the know he could definitely look intimidating, even if it was unintentional.

'He did what?'

'It's fine. Thankfully, I was at home so when I threw the phone it landed on something soft. And it's gone now.'

'That's not the only thing that should be gone,' he growled.

I let out a giggle.

'I didn't get much of a look, thank goodness, but, from what I saw, I'm surprised he's that open to showing it around so freely, to be honest.'

This time it was Luca's turn to laugh and I was glad to see his face clear, and the relaxed expression I knew so well take its place.

'You'll be careful with all this, Bee, won't you? I mean, don't take any risks. Make sure one of us knows where you're going if you meet anyone and stuff.'

'I will. Tia's already given me strict instructions saying the same thing.'

'OK. Good. Did you report him to the site?'

'Yep. All done.'

'Good. What a—'

'Dick?'

'Precisely.'

* * *

After I had spoken to Luca and then snuffled about in my cupboards and fridge for food, I turned back to the dating app. I pushed the apprehension I felt to the back of my mind and then opened Mr Animal Lover's reply. Thankfully, no pictures appeared, just a few lines of easy chat. I found myself replying and as the evening moved on we chatted on and off for a couple of hours, the result of which culminated, a little to my surprise, in me having a date for Sunday lunch tomorrow. Dutifully I messaged Tia, gave her the details and then answered the barrage of questions she fired at me between watching whatever reality talent TV show was showing this evening – her ultimate Saturday night entertainment. It had surprised me to learn that

Jono was a fan of them too but decades of Tia's influence had yet to turn either me or Luca into fans.

* * *

Was I supposed to feel sick before a date? Wasn't I supposed to be excited or something? My stomach felt as if it were competing in the floor exercises of an Olympic gymnastics competition with the amount of flips and flops it was doing. The last thing I felt like doing was eating, despite the admittedly delicious smells of Sunday roasts wafting from the pub I was standing outside. I'd wondered about meeting inside but had reasoned with myself that if he didn't turn up it would be less embarrassing to walk away from the outside of a pub than from a table set up for two on a busy Sunday.

'Beatrice?'

I turned to see a man who looked surprisingly like his photograph approaching me. He was dressed smartly although his style was more Country Estate than London Town, but he had a nice smile and, gesturing for me to go through the door first, some pleasant manners, it seemed. So far, so not as bad as I'd expected.

'Hi. Everyone calls me Bee.' I thought about extending my hand but it seemed a bit formal and a kiss seemed too much so I rammed my hands into my pockets and tried not to look as awkward as I felt. Oliver smiled, gestured politely again to enter the pub and followed me in.

As our lunch arrived I'd begun to relax a bit and was, much to my surprise, actually enjoying myself. The pub had a warm, buzzy vibe and Oliver was good company. Maybe Tia and Jono really were on to something. Perhaps Internet dates weren't all horror stories.

'So, is the dog in your profile picture yours?' I asked as I forked another perfectly crisp roast spud into my mouth.

Oliver took a large sip of the red wine he'd ordered, and that I'd passed on, before answering. 'Oh, no, that's just one of the hounds. I know they're working dogs and one shouldn't have favourites but, well, sometimes it just can't be helped. Know what I mean?'

I made an effort to swallow the hot roast potato without giving the roof of my mouth second-degree burns. 'Umm... hounds?'

'Yes,' he replied, loading up his fork.

I was looking at him blankly as he glanced up. A flicker of something crossed his face. If I had to name it, I'd have said it looked remarkably like annoyance.

'I'm sorry... I don't understand,' I began. 'Do you mean hounds as in hunting?'

This time I was absolutely sure it was annoyance. 'Of course. What other sort are there?' He said it with a laugh but his previous expression had already given away his thoughts on my slow understanding of the subject.

'You hunt?'

'When I'm at the country house, obviously. Don't you?'

'I don't have a country house and, even if I did, then no! Of course not.'

He looked genuinely shocked at my reply.

'Really?'

'Yes, really. You mean proper hunting?'

His look gave me the answer.

'But it's illegal!'

He gave me a wink. 'There are lots of loopholes to get around that ridiculous ban.'

'It's not ridiculous! Fox hunting is cruel and barbaric!'

Oliver let his cutlery fall to his plate with a clatter. 'Oh, for God's sake, you're not one of those tree-hugger types, are you? You looked quite normal on your profile.'

'I am normal, thank you! And, yes, I like trees. I also love animals, which, may I remind you, was something you'd put on your profile and was part of the attraction!'

'I do. Absolutely adore my horse, and I already told you about the favourite hound.' He let out a sigh.

'A dog you train to chase, terrify and then kill a defenceless animal! And by the way, I'm not blaming the dog. That's solely reserved for you.'

'Honestly, Beatrice. You're making a far bigger thing of this than you need to. People who don't understand hunting make such a fuss exactly because they don't understand. It's pure ignorance.' He reached over and patted my hand. 'It's fine. I'll explain things and then you'll understand and see why you're wrong.'

I snatched my hand back, knocking my water glass over as I did so, which clattered against my plate, the contents soaking into the tablecloth and beginning a steady drip drip drip onto the floor. Oliver gave me a tight look before clicking his fingers loudly, signalling the nearby waiter over, then gesturing at the table. I felt my cheeks flame at his rudeness. Apparently, those initial manners didn't extend to staff, or to me now that he had clearly decided I was beneath him.

'I'm sorry,' I said to the waiter, smiling apologetically.

He smiled back, pointedly avoiding Oliver as he cleared up the mess. 'It's no problem. Happens all the time.'

Oliver gave a small snort. The waiter flicked his eyes to me momentarily.

'Would you mind bringing the bill?' I asked him.

'I'm not finished,' Oliver blustered.

'Would you mind bringing the bill for my food, please?' I adjusted my request.

'Certainly, madam.' He gave a nod, a private smile and headed off to the till.

'You're just going to leave in the middle of lunch?' Oliver's voice was low and the attractive smile of earlier was now curled into something more like a sneer.

'Yes.'

'Some people have no manners.' He tossed his napkin aside.

'You're right,' I said, looking pointedly at him. 'They don't. And just to save any other women a wasted afternoon, you might want to adjust that whole "animal lover" thing on your profile. It's misleading.'

'Only to uneducated types like you.'

My mouth dropped open a little, which admittedly didn't exactly go with the sophisticated, calm look I was going for.

'Enjoy the rest of your meal. Do try not to choke on it.' With that, I pushed my chair back and met the waiter halfway across the pub, returning with him to the till and paying there. I gave him a generous tip to try and make up for Oliver being such a rude git and headed out of the pub and back towards the nearest Tube station. I'd hardly eaten any of my lunch in the end so I grabbed a king-size Twix from Smith's and headed down to the station platform to catch a train home. Stuffing chocolate with one hand, I tapped out a message with the other to Tia.

On way home.

Moments later a reply pinged in.

Already? Not Mr Right then?

Definitely not. Mr Completely Wrong.

Aww, sorry sweetie.

No worries. I'm fine. Just wanted to let you know I was on my way back.

Thanks. Give me a call when you're in for all the details.

I sent a thumbs up, although I wasn't really in the mood to rehash the disaster that had been my first date in ages. If this was the shape of things to come, Christmas couldn't come fast enough so that I could delete my account and forget about the whole thing. Not to mention win the challenge from Luca. Assuming he hadn't found Miss Perfect by then. That thought lodged in my brain for a moment until the train rushed into the station, pushing a wall of warm air before it, blowing the thought from my mind as it did so.

8

By half past five I was in my pyjamas, heating up a ready meal I'd found in the freezer. The make-up was off and my hair was shoved up messily in a clip in my standard 'at home' look. As the microwave whirred, I idly flicked through Netflix, looking for something to catch my eye. I settled on a documentary about Mount Everest and set it to play as the microwave pinged and I juggled the hot dish onto a lap tray. Just call me Ms Sophistication. I was about to take the first mouthful when my phone rang with a video call. It was Luca. My gaze drifted momentarily to my ready meal then back at the ringing phone. I paused the TV, let out a sigh and answered the phone.

'Before you say anything, I'm hungry and this is all I can be bothered to cook right now.'

Luca and I did not see eye to eye on my propensity towards ready meals.

'You should have come to my place after your date. I could have made you something edible.'

'It is edible,' I said, taking a bite. All right, not remotely tasty, but mostly edible. 'I went out for lunch.'

'True. But as you didn't get to finish your meal, you should have come to me.'

'How do you know I didn't finish it?'

'We all know you didn't finish it.' He grinned at me. 'You know how the gossip grapevine works in the group by now.'

I sighed and shoved another mouthful in.

'What is that?' Luca asked, screwing his nose up.

'Cannelloni.'

'You could have fooled me.'

'You haven't tasted it.'

'I don't need to. I know what your face looks like when you're enjoying food and it doesn't look like that now.'

'Did you call for a reason or just to give me a hard time on my culinary choices?'

'Just wanted to see if you were OK.'

'Why wouldn't I be?'

'Tia said he was a... well, I won't repeat what she said he was, but I get the impression he wasn't the best company.'

'He started off OK. Finding out he was a fan of hunting and of flouting the ban against it rather soured the moment. Things went downhill from there.'

'Didn't deserve your company anyway.'

'No. That's what I thought. Uneducated as I might be.'

'Excuse me?'

'He told me the reason I didn't agree with his choices was because I was uneducated.'

Luca's face took on the *Goodfellas* look again.

'Don't worry about it. I'm fine.'

Luca didn't look convinced. It was no secret I had a hang-up about not having finished my degree and being the only one in the group who didn't have one. Dad's accident had changed a lot of things.

'Honestly, I am, Luca. I promise. Comments like that say more about him than me.'

'They do. So long as you truly believe that.'

'I do,' I said, pushing the mostly empty plastic container away.

'How was the so-called cannelloni?'

'Don't be a food snob.'

He grinned.

'So, what are you doing home? I thought you'd be out on another date by now? Not like you to hang around.'

He gave me a small quirk of one dark brow and shifted into a more comfortable position on his sofa. 'Wasn't really in the mood today.'

'More lined up?'

I received a non-committal noise as my reply. 'What about you?'

'I've got another possible,' I said vaguely, opening my laptop with one hand and going to the desktop version of the website. 'And apparently I have another couple of messages. Obviously a few bored people around on a Sunday.'

'Don't do that.'

'What?'

'Put yourself down.'

'I was joking.'

'You should be, but I've known you for far too long. And you weren't.'

I scratched my leg for something to do and to avoid getting hooked up on Luca's intense I-know-you stare – which he did, and which at times was incredibly inconvenient.

'Anyway...'

'So what are the others like?'

'Haven't looked yet.'

'Look now.'

'No, I'll look later. To be honest, my enthusiasm isn't really at its height after today and I wasn't exactly ebullient about it all in the first place.'

'Fair enough.' He shifted again. 'If you wanted a second opinion on any of them, I wouldn't mind. I mean, if you wanted to ask me, of course.'

I looked back at the screen of my phone. 'Are you offering to vet my options?'

'When you put it like that, it sounds obnoxious.'

'It wasn't meant to. And thanks. If I'm not sure about someone, I might well take you up on that.'

'Although I'm pretty sure I'll find plenty to criticise.'

'You certainly have done in the past.'

He shrugged, unapologetically. 'They were never good enough for you.'

'Says you.'

'Yep. And I was right. Every time.'

'Must be such a burden having to be right all the time.'

'I manage.'

'I want pudding,' I said, changing the subject.

'Meet me after work tomorrow. I'll cook and will ensure there's pudding. I can help you vet your dates then too.'

'I didn't say I was definitely going to show you! Anyway, don't you have a date tomorrow night?'

'Yep. With you.'

'Oh, ha ha. I mean with the possible Ms Right?'

'I'd rather spend the time with you.'

'You're never going to meet her if you waste your spare time hanging out with me.'

'Time spent with you is never wasted.'

'I think my date from earlier might disagree with you there.'

'I think he and I would likely disagree about a lot of things.'

'True. Well, if you're sure you don't mind.'

'Of course not. And Ma was asking today when you're coming round for dinner again. They miss you.'

I smiled at the screen. 'I miss them too.' I did. The Donatos had made me feel like a part of their family and their attention and love had never wavered. Unlike my own relatives'. 'I'll come whenever is good for them. Let them know I'm sorry I haven't been for a while. Work's just been crazy.'

'No improvement on that front, then?'

A sigh escaped.

'I'll take that as a no. Still not recruited anyone to help you?'

'Nope. Melissa doesn't think it's necessary.'

'Melissa doesn't know her arse from her elbow.'

'This is true.'

Melissa was my direct boss. I had more experience, knowledge and expertise than her. She in turn had a degree and great boobs. Both those attributes had impressed my ultimate boss, although when the position had become available – a position I was more than able to do and had effectively been doing unpaid for the previous eight months – it had been only her degree he'd cited as having been the clincher for her getting the position, despite it being obvious to the whole office other factors had most certainly had an impact.

'You know the answer.'

I rolled my head towards my shoulder.

'I'm not coming to work for you.'

'Why not? You're the best IT person I know, and it frustrates the hell out of me I can't get you to come and work with us.'

Luca had been trying to recruit me for his company since he started it. On paper, this seemed like a no-brainer. Whenever I visited their offices, there was this great, relaxed vibe. He had a very low turnover of staff and, when an opportunity did arise, they were inundated with applications, not just because of the good pay and excellent package, but because the company had a reputation as being a great place to work. He'd built the business from nothing and hired people not just on qualifications, but actually took into account their experience, both work and life. I knew he wanted me to run his IT department. The current guy had been talking about retiring for a while now and I could do it with my eyes shut. It was a lot more money than I made now, had a benefits package unlike my current position and I wouldn't have to answer to Melissa or get stuck with the blame when something she hadn't done came back to bite us.

'Because...'

He waited. 'Is there any more to that sentence?' he asked eventually.

'You know why.'

'No. All I know is that you're the best person for the job, which is all I ever want for my company, and you won't accept the position.'

'You'd be my boss!'

'And?'

'And it'd be weird.'

'Why?'

'Because!'

He gave me an eye roll and did a rolling motion with his hand.

'Because! I'd be reporting to you. What if something went wrong? Or you weren't happy with something I did? What if we argued?'

'We've been arguing since we were five. You annoy me. I annoy you. It's how it is. It works just fine.'

He had a point.

'But it's not the same in a work situation.'

'So... I put someone else in between as a line manager. That way you don't have to deal with me directly, if that's the problem.'

'You'd still be my boss, Luca. You own the bloody company!'

Luca said something in Italian and let out a sigh. 'You hate your job. You're taken advantage of at your job. Tell them where to put it and come and work with me. Please.'

'No.'

'Arrgh. Impossible woman! Why would you stay at a job you don't like when a better opportunity is right there on a plate for you? Especially in a company where there's usually plenty of other goodies on plates in the kitchen for employees.'

'Ordinarily I'd take it. Of course I would!'

'So?'

'It's you, Luca. If I messed up, I wouldn't be able to forgive myself.'

'Bee, you're the most conscientious person I know. But we all mess up from time to time. In work. In life. In love.'

'Yes, but it's you,' I repeated. 'It's different. It would mean more.'

He opened his mouth to say something but I stopped him. 'I really do appreciate it, Luca. You know I do. And it practically kills me to know I could be working somewhere so great and not have to listen or look at pneumatic Melissa ever again. But I can't. I can't risk our friendship. That means more.'

'What if I promised you nothing would ever affect that?'

My glance drifted to the dating site still open on my screen. 'You can't promise that. However much you think you can. Things happen. Things change. But thank you.'

The dark eyes studied me for a long moment. 'I'm not going to change your mind on this, am I?'

I shook my head, sadness mixed in with other emotions I

couldn't quite put a name to. 'I think I'm going to head off to bed actually, if you don't mind. I'm not feeling so great.'

'Probably that dodgy ready meal.'

I gave him a watery smile. 'Maybe.'

'Meet me after work tomorrow, then?'

I nodded. 'OK. Thanks.'

'Get some rest, Bee.'

I gave a little wave, blew a kiss as I usually did and hung up.

Why was nothing ever simple?

* * *

On my eighth date in three weeks, my mind began to wander as the guy opposite me continued droning on about himself. We'd been at the bar for over an hour and a half and he'd yet to ask a single question about me. In hindsight I should have left a long time ago. My first clue was when he turned up looking ten years older than his profile picture and dressing fifteen years younger. The second clue was when I'd suggested ordering some food and he'd told me he'd already eaten so it wasn't necessary. I wasn't entirely sure why I was still sitting there, to be honest. The fact that it was pouring outside and dry in here was, realistically, the strongest argument I could make.

None of the previous dates had been any better. One chap who'd looked quite the beefcake in his pic did actually turn out to be one, which was a good start. Unfortunately, that was all he turned out to be. No matter how many times I tried to steer the conversation around to other topics, it soon pinged right back to what amounted to a gym addiction. Questions such as how much could I bench press resulted in blank looks from me. Not because I didn't understand the question, but because I didn't understand why he'd asked me the question. Nowhere on my profile had I (or rather Tia) mentioned that I went to the gym. Like, ever. I did try and keep sort of fit. London had great parks to lose yourself in, and my flat was a twenty-minute walk from the station, which helped get me a decent amount of steps in each day, so I did my best to keep vaguely active.

'Did you hear what I said?' The voice broke into my thoughts and yanked me back to the present – and to my growling stomach. Who ate before a dinner-time date anyway?

'Umm... no. Sorry. I missed that.'

My date sat back in his chair. Not a great look for his burgeoning paunch. If he was thirty-five, I'd eat my hat. Frankly, I was so ravenous by now, I'd eat anyone's hat.

'You don't exactly seem very into this date, if I'm honest.'

'Don't I?' I replied, for lack of anything else to say.

'No. And to be honest, it feels a bit rude.' One thing I had noticed was his propensity to use the word 'honest' in as many sentence variations as possible, which was ironic for someone who had advertised himself with a picture at least a decade old.

I sat up straighter. 'Excuse me?'

'I said it's a bit rude.' He spoke slower, as though I was struggling to comprehend the words. In truth I was, but not for the reason he aimed at. 'Perhaps it's best to just call it a night and I stop wasting my time trying to impress you.'

Impress me?

He gestured sharply to the barman. 'Can you total up my tab?' The barman nodded and turned away.

Silence sat heavy between us. The first of the night but only because he'd finally stopped talking about himself. His accusation of rudeness was whizzing round and round my brain in circles until it eventually fell out of my mouth.

'I'm sorry, but I think you're being rather unfair and if anyone was rude this evening, it was you.'

Astonishment tightened the muscles on his face.

'What?'

'You accused me of being rude,' I said, trying to remain calm and dignified. 'And I think that's unfair.'

He gave a derisive sniff. 'Oh, you do, do you?' he said, snatching the tab from the barman and running his gaze down it. 'Well, I think it's unfair that I've had to sit here with someone who's meek and dull and has no conversation and then had to pay for the privilege.' He threw some notes on the bar. Fire burst inside me. I shoved the notes along the bar towards my date before the guy could pick them up and handed my debit card to the barman instead.

'Please could you put the bill on that? Thanks.' I smiled, as naturally as I could. The look on his face told me I hadn't quite won that game but that I'd at least made a valiant effort.

I turned back to my date. 'For your information, I am not dull and have plenty of conversation should the person I'm with have the manners to actually bother trying to engage me in some. As it is, you have done nothing this evening but sit there and drone on and on about yourself and a whole bunch of people I have never met and will never meet. And frankly, from your "hilarious"—' I put my fingers up and made the shapes for emphasis 'stories, I hope I never do meet them. *To be honest*, they're not actually hilarious at all. In fact, they are at best boring, and, at worst, offensive.

'Also, if you invite someone to meet at dinner time, it's generally accepted that you're either going to call it a day after one drink or you're going to move on to dinner. As is it, you made a point of eating before you arrived. I, however, am absolutely starving. Something you were clearly aware of and have made no attempt to suggest we order food, even if you didn't want any. I've been working all day, barely got lunch and have ended up with a bowl of peanuts for dinner! So before you go around accusing people of having poor manners you might want to take a look in the mirror. Oh, and while you're looking in that mirror, try taking a more up-to-date photograph for the site rather than using one from what you obviously consider your glory years.'

He stared at me open-mouthed like a guppy. Cautiously, the barman pushed the card machine towards me. I paid and met his eyes briefly. Was that a smile?

9

I turned, headed out of the bar and straight into a torrent of rain. Within moments, my hair was plastered to my head, and my dress was plastered to my body. Neither was a good look. Hastily I put the light coat on over the now soaked dress. Had I not been on such a roll I might have thought it through and put it on before I exited onto the street. Although the coat itself was now also sodden, so it seemed as if it was pretty much a case of swings and roundabouts.

I made my way through the downpour towards the Tube station. A Transit van drove by, its direction adjusting noticeably so that it hit the large puddle that had formed at the kerbside, resulting in a perfect arc of filthy water sailing through the air and hitting its target – i.e., me. Great. Now I was not only wet, but dirty and wet. And hungry. And apparently dull, according to my date. I really was having quite the day. At least it couldn't get any worse.

Against my body, I felt my phone vibrate in my bag. Heading to the shelter of a shop doorway not already occupied for the evening, I pulled the phone out. It was Luca.

'Hi.'

'Hi. Sorry, am I interrupting anything?'

'Nope.'

'OK... so are you home?'

'No. Just on the way to the Tube.'

'Your line is closed. That's why I was ringing. Some sort of incident on it.'

I groaned. It had got worse.

'Are they running buses instead, does it say?' I shoved myself closer to the door as a delivery lorry sent up another plume of water nearby.

'It's a bit vague at the moment, but they should do.'

I let out a sigh. 'OK, thanks. Well, I'll head to the station and see what I can find out. Thanks for the heads up.'

'What's that noise?'

'What noise?'

There was a pause on the line. 'Is that your teeth chattering?'

'Umm... maybe. It's only because I've stopped moving. It's fine when I'm walking.'

'It's not that cold, Bee. Are you unwell?'

'I'm fine. Just got a bit damp.'

'Where are you?'

I told him.

'Stay there. I'll pick you up.'

'No, Luca. Really, it's fine. I'm already wet now anyway. I don't think it's physically possible to get any wetter. Don't come out in this.'

'I'm already out. I had a meeting down in Devon today. I'm on my way back and I'm about ten minutes away from you. God knows how long you might be waiting if they haven't sorted out bus replacements yet. You'll freeze to death. Your mother would never forgive me.'

'My mother would neither know nor care,' I answered, honestly.

'Then my mother would never forgive me.'

He was probably on to something with that one.

'I'll be there in a few minutes. All right?'

'I don't mind going to the station. I'm sure it'll be fine.' I wasn't sure it would be fine at all. I'd been there, done that and had the three-hour wait for a phantom bus or train to prove it, but still.

'Bee. I can hear your brain whirring from here. I'm already out. It's no problem and I'd prefer it if you didn't die of hypothermia.'

'OK, thanks, then. That would be great.'

'At least not until I win this challenge and prove you wrong. Again.'

'Oh, ha ha. Just get you and your bloody car here, then, or I'll expire just to spite you.'

The deep, melodic laugh drifted through the phone and wrapped itself around me in a warm hug of friendship.

'You might need some plastic or something on the seat. I'm literally dripping.'

'It's leather. It'll wipe off.'

'If you say so. But don't come to me with a bill!'

'I promise. Now, do try not to expire as per the deal. See you in a few.'

'Bye.'

He disconnected and I tucked the phone back in my bag, before wrapping my arms around me in a vague attempt to get warm. It wasn't working. I squinted at the cars approaching but they were all just lights. I couldn't pick out colours until they were nearer and that was pretty much my limit when it came to cars anyway. Luca's car was black. Helpful.

Ten minutes and one awkward proposition later, a sleek black car flashed its lights and pulled to the kerb. I couldn't see inside but it looked vaguely the same shape as Luca's and I really hoped it was, otherwise there was a chance this could be another embarrassing moment to really finish the evening off. The window buzzed down, Luca's face appeared and I hurried to the car. He leant over and pushed the door open.

'Bloody hell, Bee! That's a little more than damp!'

'Quite damp, then.'

'You sound like those wind-up teeth toys that chatter along.'

'Thanks. My evening is full of compliments tonight.'

Luca pulled out into the traffic and then gave me a sideways look. 'Not great, huh?'

I did a small head shake and inadvertently gave Luca a shower. 'Oops. Sorry. But no, not the best.'

'Want to talk about it?'

'Not right now, if you don't mind.'

He frowned. 'What was that?'

'My stomach.'

'Didn't you eat?'

'No. My date had already eaten.'

'Why did that stop you?'

'I don't know. I just would have felt weird.'

'OK. Here's the plan. One, we need to get you a hot shower and some dry clothes, swiftly followed by some good food.'

'I think I've gone past being hungry, to be honest.'

'I hate to disagree with you—'

'No, you don't. You love it.'

'That's true. But still. Your own stomach clearly disagrees with your previous statement.'

He had me there.

* * *

Luca pulled up at his apartment block, found a space in the underground car park hidden below it and I squelched alongside him to the lift.

'Sorry the date didn't work out. Seems like a waste of a nice dress.'

I looked down. 'It looked better when it wasn't sodden.'

Luca did a maybe-yes maybe-no thing with his head and grinned. 'Doesn't look as bad as you think it does now.'

'Yeah, maybe I should rock the drowned-rat look from the start on my next date. Perhaps I'll have more luck.'

'You didn't miss out. I didn't like to say before, when you said where you were meeting tonight, but that place has terrible reviews for its food anyway.'

'Does it?' I asked, accepting his invitation to enter the lift before him as it opened its doors to greet us. Hesitating, I looked up at him. 'I'm going to leave a puddle.'

'It's not a long ride and who cares?'

I still hesitated. With a sigh, Luca shuffled me in alongside him, leaning across to press the button for his floor. I gave him a look.

'What?'

'I was thinking!'

'About something that didn't require thinking about. And I'm hungry, as are you. I don't have time for you to stand there wondering about leaving a few drips on the floor. Plus, you'll catch your death if you don't get out of those soon.'

'Ah, I didn't know you cared,' I said, with all the maturity of a twelve-year-old.

He gave me a quick side eye before looking back at the

numbers changing on the lift display. 'I do wonder why I bother sometimes.'

'Thanks.' I gave him a smile but a tiny little voice inside my head poked at me. *Did he really think that?*

The lift slowed politely at the correct floor and the doors swooshed back almost silently. Luca nodded me out and I began wandering slowly up the hallway towards his apartment.

'What's the matter?' he asked as he walked beside me, having slowed his normal stride in order for me to keep pace with my ridiculously high shoes. Totally gorgeous but completely wasted this evening. I don't think my date had even noticed them.

'Nothing, why?'

'Because I know you and I can hear your cogs whirring.'

'It's nothing.'

'It's enough to keep you silent, so it's something.'

'I don't talk that much!'

'You do to me.'

He had a point. I wasn't always great at making conversation but it'd never been a problem with Luca, or his family. A very amateur stab at psychology made me guess that it was something to do with how relaxed I was with them all.

'Nothing. Probably just overthinking things because I'm cold and hungry.'

'You have been known to,' he replied, unlocking the door and gesturing me in. I lifted one foot up, using the arm he held the door open with as a support while I pulled off my sodden footwear.

'Nice shoes.' Luca smiled approvingly.

'Again, they looked better when they weren't soaked.'

'You worry too much. You could have walked in that bar looking like you do right now and definitely not been short of attention with that dress and those shoes.'

'Thanks. I'm not sure my date noticed either, if I'm honest.'

'Then he was an idiot that didn't deserve your company anyway. Come on, get inside in the warm.'

I bent and placed the shoes on the mat once Luca had closed the door. He took the coat that had proved to be little protection against the weather and hung it next to his own on a hanger in the warmth of a sleek cupboard whose door blended into the wall. The first time I'd visited, he asked me to grab his jacket when I retrieved mine as we headed out to dinner and it took me several minutes to even locate it. Obviously, Luca had been no help and, once he realised I wasn't back, came to lean on the wall and amuse himself by watching me trying to find the damn door.

'I think I'm just feeling a bit... invisible this evening.'

Luca shook his head, gently placed his hands either side of my cheeks and kissed my forehead.

'You, Bee, are never invisible. No matter what you think. Some people just don't know a good thing when they see it.'

I gave a half-smile and felt some of the insecurities the last few dates had helped reignite begin to crumble away like failing chalk cliffs.

'Do you want a shower to warm up?'

Luca's bathroom was like you got in five-star hotels – all subtle and sleek with a big rainfall shower head, soft fluffy towels and gallons of hot water.

'You sure you don't mind? You've obviously had a long day and it's getting late.'

'So? Just stay over. Unless you have plans tomorrow morning?'

I shook my head and sent out another little spray of droplets. 'Whoops. Sorry.'

He waved it away. 'Go warm up. There's a few of your clothes in the guest bedroom. You know where everything is.'

As there had been plenty of impromptu sleepovers over the past however many years, I'd gradually left a few things here. I had offered to take them back, but Luca said it made sense to leave a change of clothes or two.

'Don't women find it strange that you have these in your wardrobe?'

He shrugged as he shucked off his suit jacket and slung it over the back of a chair. His shirt was bright white, still crisp despite a day's wearing, and did amazing things for his skin and dark eyes.

He gave me an even look. 'Most women, unless they're my sisters or you, don't stay in the guest room...'

'Oh... right. No. Of course.'

He grinned, giving a perfect demonstration as to why women didn't stay in the guest room.

'Are you sure you don't mind?'

'Nope. Go on, I'll start some food. Any requests?' he asked, rolling the expensive cotton of his sleeves back to just below the elbow, exposing strong, tanned forearms that could make a girl's imagination drift off to dangerous places.

'You're going to cook in that white shirt?' I asked, slightly horrified. Thanks to growing up in a household where food was revered and enjoyed, Luca had been instructed well and was a skilled cook, but still.

He looked down then back up, a wicked grin on his handsome face. 'Would you rather I took it off?'

I rolled my eyes at him then turned and headed for the bathroom.

* * *

I sat cross-legged on Luca's sofa, just finishing my second large glass of wine, and let out a sigh.

'That was a good one. Any particular reason for it?'

'Why can't dates be like this?'

He shifted position a little more to face me, the thick-lashed eyes serious. 'What do you mean?'

'You know, relaxed. Interesting. Fun. Feeling like the person you're with actually gives a monkey's banana that you're there in the first place.'

'Have they all been that bad?'

I looked at him. 'I'm assuming yours haven't.' I let out another big sigh. 'Of course, they haven't.'

'If they'd been that great, I wouldn't be here with you, would I?' Before I could speak, Luca had already moved towards me. 'That came out wrong.'

I shrugged, trying to ignore the feelings banging on the door of my brain demanding to be let in. *People only notice you when it's convenient to them...* 'It's fine. It's true.'

'Not in the way it sounded.'

I wasn't sure there was any other way to take it, but Luca seemed determined that I find one and I couldn't stand the look of concern on his face so I made a concerted effort to show that I understood and waved it away.

'Have they not gone well, then?'

'Some have been OK. But that's it. Just OK. Some have been a bit weird. One woman spent the entire evening talking about nothing but her cat. Literally it was the only subject. If I tried to veer off towards something else it ended right back there again.'

'I guess she really loves her cat.'

He raised his hands and shrugged in a very Italian way as he replied. 'I love animals but still...'

'Bit much?'

'Bit much.'

'Any other bad ones?'

'One woman was so nervous she was pretty much silent the whole evening.'

'She didn't relax once you got chatting?'

'Conversation was, to put it mildly, a little stilted.'

I raised one brow. 'You can talk the hind legs off a donkey!'

'Thanks.'

'Welcome.'

'It's still a little tricky when you get pretty much nothing back.'

'Yep, I could see how that could make it a little more challenging.'

'I felt bad for her. She seemed really sweet so I hope she finds a way to be less anxious, or someone she really does feel relaxed with.'

'Yeah. Me too. It's nerve-wracking at the best of times.'

'It can be.'

I made a scoffing noise. 'Luca Donato, you have never, ever found dating nerve-wracking.'

He drew himself up a little. 'Says who?'

'Oh, I don't know. Everyone? You don't find anything nerve-wracking. You just do it. Go for it. Grab the bull by the horns. All those metaphors.'

'What other choice is there? It doesn't mean I'm not still nervous about things.'

'You never say you are. And you certainly don't look it.'

He shrugged. 'I guess looks can be deceiving at times.'

Silence floated around us for a moment. The noise from the street below was silenced by expensive and efficient double glazing. The album he'd set to play via his smart speaker earlier had now finished. All was quiet.

'Why have you never told me?' I asked.

'Because you'd want to fix it for me.'

'And?'

'And you can't. Like I couldn't fix it for my date. Some things you just have to fix yourself.'

'That doesn't mean I wouldn't want to know.'

He met my gaze. 'I didn't want you feeling bad for me or pitying me.'

'Believe me, I wouldn't pity you! You're far too good-looking and successful to qualify for that, I'm afraid.'

'Is that so?'

'Yep.'

'When did I stop qualifying for that, then, according to the rules of Bee?'

'Oh, when you were about five and a half.'

He laughed and leant over to give me a squeeze.

'I still wish you'd tell me though,' I said as he pulled back, his eyes on mine as I looked up to meet them. The long, thick lashes I'd envied for decades cast shadows on his cheeks in the low light.

'I'm sorry.'

I shrugged. 'It's OK. I guess I sort of forget sometimes that you have your family to talk to. I'm assuming they know?'

He paused, holding my gaze a moment longer before looking away. 'Yeah, they know everything.'

10
———

Luca was already up and about when I made my way out from the bedroom the next morning. He'd always been an early bird. It had driven me bonkers on holidays we'd taken together when I'd wanted to lie in but, to be fair, I'd probably seen a lot more of the places we'd visited than I would have done otherwise. I was better these days but between the drinks I had at the restaurant on an empty stomach and the two large glasses of full-bodied red I enjoyed with Luca's delicious supper, I slept rather heavier than I usually did. Also, Luca's guest bedroom had the same five-star vibe as his bathroom. I always slept well here. I wasn't exactly sure what the magic ingredient was, but I wish I knew so that I could bottle it, take it home and use it on the nights I'd lie awake in the dark, willing sleep to come and claim me.

'Morning. Juice?'

'Morning. Yes, please.'

'Any preference?'

'Nope.'

He nodded and two minutes later I was sitting at his marbled black-ceramic-topped kitchen island with a large glass of cool, fresh blood-orange juice while thick rashers of back bacon sizzled enticingly in a pan, ready to become a match made in heaven with the slices of buttered, morning-fresh white bread already laid out on a thick wooden chopping board in front of me.

'I'm surprised any of the women who stay here ever leave,' I said a few minutes later as I tucked blissfully into the sandwich.

Luca threw me a brief questioning look as he finished preparing his own sandwich. I waggled mine at him.

'Oh. I thought you were referring to my irresistible company and charm for a moment.'

'Sorry. I've known you for too long to think it was that.'

He gave a tight smile. 'Funny. And my penchant for a weekend bacon sarnie hasn't exactly gone down well with a few dates.'

'Really?' I asked, savouring the perfection of the bacon cooked just to the right point of crispy and the soft white bread with just the right amount of chew about it. 'I'd marry you just for these.'

Luca's sandwich paused halfway to his mouth.

I rolled my eyes. 'It's all right. I wasn't proposing. You can relax. I was just saying. You don't need to look quite so panicked.'

'I'm not panicked. I already told you I was looking for something more serious. Isn't that what this damn challenge is all about?'

I swallowed my mouthful. 'OK.' I frowned. 'What's up? If you don't want to do this challenge, please say because it's not exactly filled me with glee so far and I'd happily stop. I thought you wanted to do it – to find The One.' I did my best to keep any hint of sarcasm out of my voice as I took another bite. From the expression that crossed Luca's face, I didn't quite nail it.

'I do,' he said.

I waited for more, but it turned out that was it. We sat in silence for a few minutes, enjoying the food. Luca's brow still had a hint of wrinkle about it.

'You're still frowning.'

'I'm not.'

'You are. I can see your face.'

'Then you're mistaken. Sandwich all right?'

'Perfect, as always. Thanks.'

'You're welcome.'

'Is something wrong?'

'Nope.' He glanced back at me as he loaded the dishwasher and the frown had gone. Mostly. Maybe he was just tired after a long day yesterday. Whatever it was, I knew from experience that you couldn't force anything from Luca. If there was something he wanted to tell me, he would. But only when he was ready.

'So, what did you mean that the food puts some women off?' He looked like a movie star, was kind and funny and an amazing cook. I wasn't exactly sure what else they wanted. Perhaps to have him dipped in gold plate?

'Oh, a few that have been on what seemed pretty extreme diets who weren't exactly fans of the amount of parmesan I like on top of my pasta.'

'Surely what you eat isn't really any of their business. You weren't asking them to eat it.'

He gave a one-shouldered shrug. 'There was a vegetarian who demanded I not order any meat when I took her to dinner.'

'Oh. How did that work out?'

'Well, I didn't order any, but I don't appreciate being told what I can and can't do, especially when it comes to food, which I love, so that obviously wasn't going to go anywhere. And, of course, there was the awkward moment with the vegan. To be fair, when

I offered her a bacon sarnie, I didn't actually know she was vegan. It hadn't come up.'

'Oops.'

'We met at a bar one night. And...' he did a thing with his hands '... one thing led to another.'

'Which led to you offering her a bacon sandwich.'

'Which led to her letting off a rocket at me about my lack of consideration and selfishness before storming out of the apartment.'

'Ah.'

'Funny, as earlier she'd been pretty complimentary about my generosity.' He grinned at me and waggled the dark brows.

I gave him a momentary look with just the right amount of long-suffering patience mixed in. 'I guess people can be passionate about their beliefs.'

'As they've every right to be. What annoyed me was having those forced on me or her acting like I was being purposely malicious when I hadn't been given all the facts.'

'Yep, I get that. Well, if you ever have any unappreciated food, you know where to send it. And for the record, if they'd taken the time to get to know you, they'd realise that you would never dismiss anyone's feelings or beliefs like that.'

A dimmer version of his killer smile showed. 'Thanks, Bee.'

I shrugged. 'It's true.'

'What you up to today?' he asked as I pushed both our bar stools back under the kitchen island.

'Oh, I don't know. Probably ought to clean the flat a bit and then maybe do something worthwhile and mind-expanding like binge-watching a series on Netflix.'

He smiled. 'Want to come to dinner at home? Mum and Dad would love to see you.'

'Oh, Luca, that'd be lovely. But I couldn't really just descend at the last minute without your mum knowing.'

'I'll tell her now.'

'You know what I mean. She'll already be preparing a dinner for a set number of people.'

He pulled a face at me. 'Bee. You've been coming to my parents' since you were five. Since when has there not been way too much food?'

There was that.

'Are you sure they won't mind?'

Luca was looking at his phone. Just as I finished speaking, another voice began. 'Hello, my darling. Are you still coming to dinner?' Luca's mum was born in England but her voice still had that sing-song quality of Italian cadence.

'Yep. Is it OK if Bee comes?'

'Of course! Oh, that would be lovely! You know you never have to ask.'

'I know. But Bee was worried.'

'Is she there with you now?'

'Yep. She had a crappy date last night and ended up staying here.'

'Oh... Well, I hope she's OK now. It'll be lovely to see her. Have you both had breakfast?'

'Yes, Mamma.' Luca laughed. 'We'll see you in a bit, then.'

'OK, darling. Drive carefully. Love to Bee. We can't wait to see her again. It's been too long.'

They said goodbye and hung up.

'Satisfied?'

'Yes. Thank you.'

'You know you're always welcome, Bee. Here or there.'

'I know,' I said, leaning against the window I'd now wandered over to, looking down on London as it went about its Saturday morning.

'You don't sound like you know.' He came to stand next to me. I looked up. When we were seven, I'd had a growth spurt and there was a momentary period – probably about a week and a half – when I was taller than Luca. It hadn't lasted and now, at six four, he had almost a foot on me.

I looked up at him. 'No, honestly. I do.'

'Why am I having trouble believing it, then?'

I returned my gaze to the street.

'Bee, I know your parents always told you not to get in the way at our place, but you never were. You never will be. Not there.' He inclined his head, making me meet his eyes. 'And not here.'

I gave him a brief smile. 'Thanks. Although your next date might have something to say about that.'

'Then there won't be a second one. You're part of my life. You always will be.'

'Yep.'

He let out a sigh. 'Why do I feel you're not convinced?'

'Things change, Luca. We don't know what the future holds or what demands on our time there will be. Or what will become important.'

He stood away from the window. 'You'll always be important to me, even if you don't feel the same.' He began walking away.

'Luca, that wasn't what I meant.'

'It's fine, Bee.'

'It's not fine. I don't want you thinking that. It's not what I meant.'

'What did you mean, then?'

'That... people get busy. Get other interests. No matter what they say, things can change.'

'I'm not your mother, Bee.' His eyes fixed on me. 'I will never be too busy for you.'

I swallowed and looked away from him, back out of the window.

'I take it you've heard from her.'

'Yesterday.'

'She's not coming back for Christmas, is she?'

'No.'

'Was there a reason given?'

'Something about a trip with her husband to see his family.' I'd never been able to think of my mother's second husband as my stepfather. I'd only met him twice and he'd shown zero interest in becoming any sort of father figure. He had a family from a previous marriage and that was clearly all he needed, and it was all my mother needed too, it seemed. Even at Christmas.

Luca had returned to where I was standing at the window. 'I'm sorry, sweetheart. She doesn't deserve you.' He reached around from behind me and gave me a hug.

'No. You're probably right.' I forced some conviction into my voice. He was right. She didn't deserve me. But the hurt still burned, even all these years on.

'Obviously you'll come to us.'

'No, Luca. It's OK. It's just a day anyway.' I rested my head briefly back against his broad chest. 'But thank you, anyway.'

'It wasn't really open to discussion, but we can talk about it nearer the time for appearances' sake if you prefer.'

I laughed and bumped my head back gently against his solid chest. 'You're such an Alpha.'

I heard and felt his laugh in his chest as he gave a quick squeeze in response before I turned and Luca's arms dropped away from me. 'Anyway, if this dating thing all works out, you might be taking Ms Right to your parents'. Tia did declare that Christmas was the deadline, after all.'

Luca remained silent. I gave a brief raise of my eyebrows.

'And who knows? Maybe I'll have met Mr Right by then.'

He looked down at me for a moment before moving away. 'Yep, maybe you will. So, do you want to go via your place to change or have you got something here?'

'I'd rather wear something a bit nicer than the stuff I have here. Is that a pain?'

'Not at all. Want a shower before you leave or at your place?'

I was still wearing the T-shirt he'd lent me to sleep in, which had become a sort of habit, and, unlike my place, Luca's modern eco-forward apartment was always lovely and warm. Our height and size difference meant that there was no chance of the T-shirt being in any way revealing so I was more than happy to loaf about in it. At home, I'd be bundled up in my enormous fluffy dressing gown. I weighed up the options. Lots of hot water with divine-smelling shower gel under a rainfall head shower here or possibly warm, more likely tepid, on a standard, partially lime-scaled shower head at home.

'Can I do it here?'

He smiled. 'Still not got that boiler fixed?'

'It's on the list.'

'It's been on the list since you moved in.'

'I know. I was going to do it with the bonus that year.'

'The year they stopped giving bonuses.'

I pulled a face. He shook his head. 'Why did you stay? You can do so much better than that place. You're hugely under-valued – not to mention underpaid – there.'

'Money isn't everything.'

'That is true. And you know I don't think that.'

I knew he didn't. Even though he had plenty to be 'comfortable' – as people always describe it when comfortable is rather an understatement, like saying it's a little breezy in the middle of category five hurricane. And, of course, people with money always say money isn't everything. But try taking some away from them…

'If you were following your calling, or in a position you loved, I could see why you stay there but you're not, and you don't.'

'I like computers and I believe we've had this conversation,' I said, straightening from where I'd been leaning on the back of the bar stool and heading towards the shower.

'We have. And you've still never given a decent reason as to why you stay there being underappreciated and underpaid.'

'I'm off to have a shower.'

'Bee…'

'What?' I said, turning but still walking away.

Luca said nothing but his look spoke volumes.

11

Under the blissful soak of the shower, I turned the question over in my head. Luca was right. He knew it and I knew it. I was all the things he said and more. So why did I stay? *Because it's easier...* a voice inside my head whispered.

'It's not that,' I snapped out loud, getting a mouthful of water for my trouble, causing me to burble and cough at the same time.

'You all right in there?' Luca's voice drifted through the door from a distance.

'Yep!' I called back once I'd recovered.

'Who are you talking to?'

I could hear the amusement and almost see the smile in his voice.

'Myself. It's the only way I can get decent conversation in this place.'

'It's really easy for me to go and flush a toilet, you know...'

'You wouldn't dare.'

He'd totally dare but I also knew he had swanky plumbing that meant if you flushed a toilet or ran a tap in one place it didn't scar for life the person using the shower – unlike my own plumbing. My stomach gave a squeeze at the thought that all this would change, possibly soon, no matter what Luca said about always having time for me. Things changed. It was the way of the world. It was just that sometimes I felt as if the world was leaving me behind. Pointing my face towards the shower head, I let the water flow over me to wash the thoughts and those secret fears away.

Luca was waiting when I returned from the shower wearing a pair of old jeans and a T-shirt I had stashed at his apartment. We headed towards the lifts and then descended to the ground floor in expensive, muffled silence.

'Good job I had these here.' I tugged at the clean clothes as we headed to the car, Luca having stopped at Reception to check his mail first. 'Although I don't suppose your concierge would be too surprised at another woman leaving your apartment in the same clothes she arrived in the day before.'

Luca shifted his gaze and gave me a patient look. 'Funny.'

'What?'

He beeped the key fob and the lights flashed twice on his BMW as we walked towards it.

'You.'

'Me what?' I waited but Luca just leant around me to open the door. I stayed where I was.

'Are you getting in?'

'Are you answering my question?'

He let out a sigh. 'Just that I'm pretty sure you think I'm way more of a Lothario than I actually am.'

'I don't think so. I'm pretty astute.'

Luca didn't reply but the way he avoided my eyes suggested he didn't agree. Instead, he stood back, one hand on the car door, waiting for me to enter the vehicle. I hesitated for a moment, then got in.

The traffic was light, and the journey out to my flat was surprisingly quiet for London. Even Luca was quiet.

'Is everything all right?' I asked as he squeezed into a visitor space that was built for a car made many decades earlier and therefore far smaller. Luckily, one of my neighbours was out, which made things easier.

'Yep. I'll wait here in case your neighbour comes back and I have to move the car.'

'OK,' I said, unconvinced. 'I won't be long.'

He nodded without looking up and slid his phone from his jacket, already concentrating on another task.

Under ten minutes later I was back out in a casual but feminine dress and the still niggling feeling Luca was pissed at me. I slid back into the leather seat and reached back to grab the seat belt.

'Can we stop somewhere for me to get some flowers for your mum?'

'You don't have to do that.'

'I know I don't, but I'd like to. If it's possible.'

Luca pressed the dash button to start the car and a throaty burble emitted from the exhaust.

'Fine. I know a layby on the way that has a good choice.'

'You take me to the nicest places.'

His face was partly turned towards the oncoming traffic as he waited to pull out, but I saw the smile.

'Just you remember that.'

* * *

He'd been right about the flower seller and as we pulled up to his parents' house, and parked behind a car belonging to one of his sisters. I gave the bouquet I'd chosen another sniff. The scent from the freesias within it, one of Mamma Donato's favourites, wound itself around my senses. The rest of the journey had been just as quiet and as Luca turned the engine off I looked across at him.

'Are you sure something isn't wrong?'

He paused, his hand on the door handle.

'Nope.'

'So why didn't you say much on the drive here?'

'Not much to say.' He gave a shrug and made to move again. I laid a hand on his arm.

'I've known you far too long to buy that excuse, Luca Donato. You always have something to say.'

He turned his dark head slowly; eyes the colour of melted chocolate met mine. Humour danced in them but there was something else. Something I couldn't quite make out. And apparently something he didn't want to share with me. I felt the twist in my stomach again. It seemed the change I'd worried about had already begun.

We walked up to the front door and Luca glanced at me as he separated the correct key from the bunch.

'Stop churning things about in your mind. You'll set fire to something in there. Everything's fine.'

'I'm not churning things about.'

'You are. You have that "my mind is currently on spin cycle" look on your face.'

I stopped. 'OK, fine. It's just that... you're sure we're OK? You just seem a bit... distant this morning since we left your place.'

He looked down at me for a moment before wrapping one muscular arm around me, pulling me close and dropping a kiss on my temple.

'I'm not distant. It was just a long day yesterday. I expect it's catching up a bit, that's all.'

'You sure?'

'Yes!' he said, taking my face within two large hands, dark eyes fixed on mine. 'I promise. How could I ever be distant from you? Who would I have to annoy me and keep me grounded?'

'Well. Quite.' I tried to smile.

'Want to try a bit harder with that smile?'

'Sorry. Just a feel a bit... out of sorts. I'm sure it's just the whole dating-disaster thing. It's not exactly doing much for my confidence.'

'The right person will change that. They're the one that will always be there for you. The one who will make you feel like you can do anything.'

'Kind of like your family has always done for you.'

He smiled, nodding, but I saw the sadness in it.

'Don't look at me like that. I don't need pity. I'm fine.'

'I know you are. And you know you'll always be a part of this family, whether you want to or not.'

'Why would I not want to?' I asked him, genuinely confused.

He shrugged. 'I don't know. You're the one saying things change.'

'But what if we don't want them to change?'

He looked at me for a long moment, before taking a step closer to me, our bodies practically touching. 'Look, Bee, I need to—'

'There you are!' The beaming face of Luca's mum appeared as the heavy front door suddenly swung inwards. 'I thought I saw your car. What are you doing standing out here? Come in, come in!' She bustled us both in and there was a flurry of exchanged hugs and kisses as more members of the family gathering came out to the hallway to greet us. Relieved of our coats, we were swept along and whatever it was that Luca had been about to say was swept away with it. The unusual seriousness of his expression had me wondering if that wasn't a bad thing.

* * *

The serious look that had clouded Luca's face just before we'd entered his parents' house had, for the moment at least, dissipated and been replaced by that fabulous smile he'd been blessed with, along with plenty of laughter. This was standard for dinner time in this house and I loved it. I'd always loved it. People reached across others, talked over each other as they playfully argued and enjoyed the great food and the company in such a relaxed, natural manner. I'd thought Luca's family were perfect from the first time I'd been invited, despite at that time sitting quietly in awe at the way things were done here, so different from the meals I occasionally shared with my parents. There everything was ordered and quiet and rigid. Here it was noise, and chaos and entirely wonderful.

Full of delicious food, I'd wandered outside after dinner with Luca's dad, who was telling me about the veggies he'd grown over the summer and those he was still growing on in the greenhouse. The weather had taken a turn and the late summer warmth we'd been enjoying had now certainly bid arrivederci, leaving behind it a cold breeze and a crisp bite to the air.

'You go back in and get yourself warmed up,' Luca's dad said, bustling me out of the greenhouse. 'I'm just going to have a talk with some of the plants in here. Make sure they know what's expected of them.' He winked. 'Then I'll be in. Go, go. Get yourself a warm drink. Maria will probably have brewed the coffee by now. Tell her to save me a cup.'

I promised I would and walked quickly back up the garden path, my arms wrapped around myself for warmth, and in through the side door of the utility room, which led through to the kitchen. As I bent to undo the zips of my boots I heard raised voices in the kitchen. When I was a child this had worried me, but I'd soon come to learn that raised voices here didn't necessarily mean an argument as it generally did at home. I pulled my second boot off and paused as I stood back up, listening. Something was off. This was too lively. And even though I only spoke about ten words of Italian, I'd known Luca long enough to recognise his tone. This wasn't his usual laid-back, laughing one. I hesitated a moment, not knowing quite what to do. But I couldn't stand here all afternoon, so I stepped forward from the utility room into the large, warm kitchen still swathed in the delicious smells and fug of cooking.

Luca and his mum were both waving their hands as they spoke rapidly in Italian to each other, talking over the ends of each other's sentences as each apparently made their point. There were no smiles and as they noticed me the speech halted mid-sentence, their faces both flushed, upset showing on each of them. For a moment, we all just stood there in silence.

'Is everything OK?' I asked, mentally kicking myself as I did so for such a lame question. Even in another language, it was pretty obvious things were far from OK.

Maria pushed her hair from her face with the back of her hand, summoning up a wide smile for me as she did so. 'Perfectly fine,' she said, reaching for my hand. 'Goodness, you're frozen. Whatever was Frank thinking, taking you out there in this weather?' She rubbed my hands together within her own warm ones. Luca remained silent and avoided my eyes.

If I was of a suspicious nature, I might have thought that Frank was thinking he'd get me out of the way while you two had this conversation... The thought popped into my brain before I dismissed it. The awkwardness that his mum was now doing her best to dispel wasn't anything to do with me personally. I'd just walked in on an argument and, despite the fact they'd always treated me like family, the true fact was I wasn't and had interrupted what was clearly a family argument.

'Frank said could you save him some coffee, please, and that he'll be in when he's finished giving the plants a talking-to.' I'd begun to babble with nerves now. It might have helped if Luca would look at me but he didn't. Instead, he turned away and began pulling crockery from the cupboards, ready for coffee, cake and biscotti.

'Of course. Now, why don't you go through and find the others? I think Anthony wanted to ask your advice on a new laptop he was thinking of buying. Would you mind?'

I fetched up a smile and nodded, getting that strange feeling once again that I was being manoeuvred out of the room. As if on cue, Anthony appeared and began questioning me on storage capacity, video capabilities and screen resolution. I listened as we walked from the room. Luca had often told me I read too much into situations. Maybe he was right. But as I glanced back, still listening to Luca's brother, I saw Luca and his mum, heads close together, speaking fast, hands gesturing, faces serious. If he tried to tell me that this time, I'd know he was lying.

'Everything all right?' I asked as we drove home. We'd been sitting in silence for a while now, which in itself was unusual. To be fair, days with the Donato family could be pretty exhausting in a good way, so there was that. But still, my Spidey senses weren't happy.

'Uh huh.'

I tried again.

'Everything OK with you and your mum?'

'Yep.' His eyes remained focused on the road.

Obviously he didn't want to talk about it... but I did, so I kept going.

'It's just that things seemed a bit heated when I came in from the garden.' He flicked his gaze to me momentarily before returning it to the road. I rushed on. 'That's pretty unusual for you two. And now you're doing the moody silent thing, which isn't like you either, so it just seems like something happened and ordinarily you would already be talking to me about it so...'

Luca slowed to a halt at a set of traffic lights and looked over at me.

'There's nothing to talk about.'

'People always say that when there's something massive to talk about but they just don't want to.'

'Well, maybe I don't want to, then.' His tone was a mixture of tiredness with a hint of unusual sharpness.

'Oh.' I swallowed, trying not to be stung.

He put a hand out and touched my leg briefly. 'Sorry, Bee. I didn't mean to snap. I'm just tired, OK? And there's really nothing to talk about. Ma just gets the wrong end of the stick about things occasionally and it can be a bit frustrating.'

'OK.' I nodded. I felt his eyes linger on me a little longer, as if waiting for something before the lights changed and he had to return his attention to the road. I didn't believe him. Luca's mum was as sharp as the huge knife she used to slice through tomatoes as if they were made of air. She didn't miss a thing and she certainly wasn't the type to get the wrong end of the stick about anything. But Luca clearly didn't want to share so I turned my face to the window and stared out at the darkness, riding the rest of the way in silence.

12

'Hi!' Tia waved at me as I answered the video call while finishing my Frosties the following Monday. She had one eye closed as she applied a strip of false lashes, making her green eyes look even more striking than they already were. I'd never got the hang of false lashes. The one time I tried them was on a date with a guy I'd really wanted to impress. I'd gone all out and, even I had to admit, I looked pretty damn good. He'd been complimentary and I loved the way his eyes had kept drifting over me as we sat at the swanky restaurant he'd taken me to.

Things had started to unravel when the soup arrived. I'd taken a couple of spoonfuls of the delicious watercress creation when I spotted something swimming in it. A caterpillar! At least that was what I thought it was before it dived below the surface again. Horrified, I'd called the waiter over and explained, quietly, that there was a creepy-crawly doing the backstroke in my soup. My date, previously showering me with compliments, had now gone suspiciously quiet and appeared to be looking everywhere but at me. The waiter had apologised profusely and swept the bowl away, offering something else. At this point, my date had found his voice and requested the bill. I'd thought that was a bit harsh but there was also something slightly sexy about the take-charge manner in which he did it. Clearly, he hadn't thought this restaurant was good enough, if that was their level of service, and he wasn't standing for it.

There was, however, nothing sexy about the way he'd then dumped me on the pavement the moment we left the restaurant, claiming that it wasn't worth continuing the date as he didn't feel we were compatible, or some crappy excuse like that. I forgot his exact words, not that it mattered. The outcome was the same whatever he said. And then he walked off, not even pretending to care if I could get home safely. It was only when I'd got home and dropped my keys in the small bowl I kept by the front door and glanced up at the mirror above it that I noticed that only one of my eyes was now adorned by false lashes. The evening flashed before my half-naked eyes. My date's sudden lack of interest in me, which I then realised was embarrassment, the waiter's over-politeness, the caterpillar... which clearly hadn't been a cater-pillar at all. It had been my bloody expensive false lash! If I'd realised that I'd have damn well fished it out, if only to have the satisfaction of chucking them dramatically in the bin.

Of course, Luca thought it was hilarious. At least the lash bit. He was less impressed about the guy dumping me in the middle of London without ensuring I had a safe way home.

Hence I was now staring at Tia through narrowed eyes.

'Do you have to do those in front of me? You know it brings back traumatic memories.'

Tia finished applying the lashes and grinned. 'Don't be such a drama queen. He didn't deserve you anyway. Would you really want to be with a man who couldn't see the funny side of your fake lash dropping off to have a swim in your soup?'

She was right, of course. 'That's not the point.'

'Of course it's the point. How was your weekend?'

'OK, I guess. I went to Luca's parents' for dinner on Saturday.'

'Oh, cool. No need to eat for the rest of the week, then.'

I smiled, fiddling with the handle of my spoon. 'Have you spoken to him?'

'Today? Nope. Why?'

I shrugged. 'He just seemed a bit off.'

'Did you ask him about it?'

'Yep. He didn't want to talk about it.'

Tia paused in her task. 'Really?'

'Yeah. I know. Weird, right?'

She rested her chin in her hand. 'Maybe he just had stuff on his mind.'

'But still. Ordinarily he'd tell me what those things are.' I gave a shrug, feeling strange inside. 'Just feels odd.'

Tia tilted her head slightly. 'I guess things can change.'

There it was again. Everything was changing.

'What if we don't want them to?' I asked, trying to sound neither petulant nor terrified.

'I'm not sure we always get a choice. But honestly, it's you and Luca. I'm pretty sure you two are set in stone. Don't worry about it. I'm sure he'll be back to normal today.'

I forced a smile that felt awkward on my face, uncomfortable suddenly that I sounded like a whining child.

'Yeah, I'm sure you're right. So, what does the day hold in store for you?'

'Well, I've got a meeting at ten, hence the need to look absolutely fabulous.' She waved her hand across her face.

'Which you always do, obviously.'

She winked at me. 'Thanks, love. What sort of day have you got?'

I gave a non-committal 'same as usual' kind of shrug. 'Average, I guess,' I said as I picked up my phone and reached for my jacket and bag.

'Thought any more about leaving?'

'Not really.'

'Why not?'

I'd heard this same refrain from the entire group, with extra doses from Luca, for years.

'I will when I see something I feel is worth the move. It's not as bad as you all make it out to be.'

'Yes, it is.'

Tia was right, but that wasn't the point.

'We've had this conversation.'

'Yep. And we're going to keep having it until you see the light and take Luca's offer and finally work with people who appreciate you.'

'Got to go!' I trilled, giving her a big smile and waving at the screen.

'This isn't over!' she said, pointing one elegant and perfectly manicured finger at me.

Unfortunately, I had a feeling she was right about that too.

* * *

'So, in conclusion, I am sure you can understand why, unfortunately, and much to our regret, this year we are unable to offer you the bonus we would have very much liked to have been able to.'

'And the raise you'd promised I'd be getting, as I didn't get one last year?'

My boss began wringing his hands again, looking at me with a mixture of pity and condescension. 'As I explained, the firm...' I switched off. This was the third year in a row I'd been denied either a raise or a bonus despite some of my colleagues getting them. Colleagues who I knew for a fact did a hell of a lot less work than I did. 'I hope you understand?' I tuned back in as my boss finished.

Actually, no. I didn't understand. I worked my bloody arse off every day for this company and always had done, just to watch others less qualified and less dedicated get promotions, bonuses and pay rises while I stayed resolutely where I was. It wasn't fair.

When I didn't answer, I saw my boss give a sideways glance at the clock and shift in his chair. 'If you could send Colleen in on your way out, that—'

I looked up, meeting his small, piggy eyes. His expression was a combination of bored and smug. Something inside began to boil and before I knew what was happening, I was standing up, words were falling out of my mouth and my boss was staring at me, his mouth opening and closing in surprise like a startled trout.

'Is Colleen getting a pay rise?' I asked. Colleen had joined the company a little over six months ago, been given a pay rise just over a month later and, by the way my boss had now gone as red as the cockerels strutting about on his tie, I guessed she was about to get another. Colleen was beautiful, tall with long legs that she didn't mind showing and frankly, if I'd had them, I'd have been proud of them too. But she was also terrible at her job. Which was why I spent a proportion of my time doing tasks she should have done, or fixing the ones she'd attempted. And yet I was the one being continually passed over. Until now I'd sat there and accepted it. Never said a word. I'd made excuses for the company when, inevitably, Luca or one of the others had started on why they continually undervalued me. Apparently, I had now decided to make up for it. In spades.

* * *

Luca wasn't answering his phone. Ordinarily I wouldn't have worried. He'd be in a meeting or something. But since Saturday something had been niggling at me and this morning had been the first time in forever he'd not said good morning either in person, by video or text. Today there had been nothing. And then my boss had picked today to, once again, show me what a dick he was.

Although apparently that wasn't something I needed to worry about any more as I had just resigned. And not subtly. I'd done it in a dramatic, you-can-stick-your-job, completely unlike-me manner. What the hell had I been thinking? And now I couldn't even talk to the one person I wanted to about it. Not to mention the tiny matter of no longer having an income. Oh, God! I felt sick. Maybe I could get my job back? Tell them I'd had an allergic reaction to my prawn sandwich at lunch and it had affected all my sensibilities. That could happen, right? I plopped down on one side of a battered leather sofa in the coffee shop I frequented and dropped my head into my hands. They would never take me back and, deep down, if you waded through all the fear and panic and nausea, there was a minuscule part of me jumping up and down in elation that I'd finally walked out on a job I'd hated for years. But the other 97 per cent of me just wanted to throw up.

'You all right?' The deep voice, full of concern, made me jump. I snapped my head up to see Luca dropping his laptop bag beside the sofa and sitting down next to me, scanning my face. 'I had a meeting early. Whoever invented breakfast meetings needs a lobotomy. I tried calling you when I came out but your phone's been off for hours.' He flopped into the seat beside me. 'That's not like you.'

Once I'd tried Luca with no reply, I'd switched the phone off as soon as I'd left the building. I didn't have my thoughts together enough to speak to anyone else coherently about what I'd just done and I knew, if anyone did ring, they'd be asking me the question I'd been asking myself since the moment I stepped outside the building. What will you do now? And frankly, I didn't have the foggiest idea! While my mouth had been racing off ahead of me, my brain and common sense had been charging after it, trying to rugby-tackle it into submission before it said anything stupid. Unfortunately, they were too slow and my mouth had well and truly scored a try. A try that might just about have resulted in me walking out with my dignity but was unlikely to result in a reference.

I gave Luca a vague reply that I was fine and turned back to the barely there coffee now placed in front of me. Luca's gaze flicked to it then back to me. Usually he smirked at my 'hot milk' – I liked the idea of having a coffee but couldn't bear the taste so they put the merest hint of coffee in and frothed milk around it. But today he said nothing about it and left me in peace to take a sip. The warm soothing liquid trickled down, comforting me from the inside. It didn't fix anything but it was a start.

'So, what's going on? Your mobile is off. Your work phone rolls immediately to voicemail and you're sat in a coffee shop in the middle of a workday.' He tilted his head at me before briefly acknowledging the waitress who put down his usual order in front of him. I watched her. It was obvious she'd have liked a little – or a lot – more acknowledgement than that from Luca and her eyes drifted over me briefly before she smoothed her perfectly smooth skirt over her perfectly shaped thighs and moved on. I'd found situations like this amusing in the past – when I'd sit with Luca and be silently but obviously dismissed by women who had an interest in him. Luca would wave it off and the others in the group would be supportive and kind, saying that sort of woman would dismiss anyone who wasn't them and to take no notice of it. And I didn't. Until now. Not really. But now, on top of my meltdown, it dug into me, burrowed into my insecurities and twisted its knife.

'I think you have an admirer. You should go and talk to her.' I lifted my drink again, still not having met Luca's eyes.

'Huh?'

I gave a brief tilt with my chin towards the counter, where the woman was laughing with another customer but darting her eyes back towards Luca with a frequency that was designed as if willing him to notice her. When he followed my indication, her eyes locked onto his and a wide, very white smile lit her features. Luca looked back at me. From the corner of my eye, I saw her smile fade and her eyes focus on me. From the look, I decided it would be safer not to order any more coffees while she was still on shift.

'Not interested,' Luca said.

'Why not?'

'Too young, too flirty and too obvious. And I don't suppose any of those are PC things to say but you asked and I answered.'

I turned my face to him. 'Talking of asking and answering, how come you won't tell me what you and your mum were arguing about at the weekend?'

His face tightened, the dark brow clouding. 'Because it's nothing.'

'Doesn't normally stop you telling me.' His continuous ducking of the question on top of the events of the day was making me feel more belligerent and argumentative. I should have just left it. Accept the adjustment in our friendship. Move on. My parents had always pretty much left me to it, and when my father died, things had only got worse. I'd managed then, and

I would deal with Luca beginning to distance himself too, if that was what he wanted. Feeling like seeing me was becoming an obligation would be far worse. Maybe the events of today were actually an opportunity. A chance to do something different. Move out of London. It was so bloody expensive and I was only just on the fringes now. I could get more for my money elsewhere and pretty much everyone had computers. Jobs in my field certainly weren't limited to London – so long as they weren't too fussy about my references. I took a deep breath. I could do this. I had to do this. And maybe the pond of potential suitors would be a little more varied somewhere else too and I'd get that perfect date for Christmas after all.

If my mind had eyebrows, it would have raised them at this moment. None of this sounded like me. But then being 'me' hadn't exactly been working out so well. So perhaps it was time for a new me. I could temp until I found something, and somewhere, I wanted to move to and in the meantime I was going to take this dating thing more seriously. Just because my parents, my now ex-boss and a variety of short-lived dates and relationships hadn't appreciated me didn't mean that I was unworthy of that appreciation. The little voice that had been jumping for joy at me finally walking out of my dead-end job got that tiny bit louder and a tingle of excitement, although still mixed with a good deal of nausea, swirled around me.

'So? You going to tell me what's going on?' Luca asked again.

'Nope. It's nothing.' I turned his own words around and sent them back. I knew I couldn't – shouldn't – rely on Luca always being there for me. I couldn't expect, or ask, him to be there every time I had a crisis or even something I wanted to share and there were obviously things he didn't feel he could share with me now. I had to get on board with that rather than stressing about it. I couldn't help but wonder if things had gone differently at the weekend and I hadn't wound myself into such a knot about it all that I might have acted differently today. I hadn't been feeling myself and I certainly hadn't acted like myself. Oh, bloody hell. I had no job and it was all Luca Donato's fault!

I gathered my things and made to stand. Luca placed a hand gently on my arm. 'Bee. What's going on? I know there's something. Why won't you tell me?' The dark, thick brows were now practically meeting with the severity of his frown, the deep brown eyes locked onto mine, searching for my answer.

Because I know you're not always going to be here to tell...

'Bee, come on. Just—'

'Can I get you anything else?' The waitress from earlier appeared, all plump lips and soft curves. We probably had about the same waist size but hers was bookended in a more obvious way than my more 'athletic' figure, as my mother would describe it. Other people had been less kind over the years – including a recent date who'd bluntly told me I hadn't looked quite so flat-chested in my profile picture. The evening had never really recovered. But I'd done a fair bit of thinking today on my aimless walk once I'd left the office. Thoughts had tumbled and raced through my head – thoughts about everything. And everyone. And the main conclusion I'd come to was that, when it came down to it, I was on my own. So, I'd better make the most of it.

'No,' Luca snapped distractedly before immediately turning to the girl momentarily, softening his reply. 'Thank you.'

She gave a nod, clearly still offended, before sweeping my empty cup up and stalking off.

'I think you just lost your fan,' I said, slinging my bag up onto my shoulder.

He gave a shake of his head. 'Seriously not what I'm concerned about right now.'

'No. Well, I guess there's always more where she came from

when it comes to you.' It was supposed to be amusing but, even to my ears, came out wrong. Luca's eyes darkened.

'What the hell is up with you today? You shut your phone off. You won't talk to me and now you're making catty comments.'

'It wasn't meant to be catty,' I snapped back, hurt and embarrassed. 'It can hardly be said that you're ever short of offers. That's all I meant.'

'And it's never bothered you before.'

'It doesn't bother me now!' I said, flinging my arms out, palms upward. 'It was just an observation that came out wrong. That's all. Forget I said anything.'

'That's not hard. You've barely said two words.'

'Perhaps I'm taking lessons from you.'

'What does that mean?'

'You barely spoke to me on the way home Saturday and I can't remember a time you "didn't want to talk about it".'

'That's what this is all about? You're pissed off I didn't talk to you on Saturday?'

'No. That's not all. But yes, if you want to know the truth, I am upset about it. For the first time I felt like I was in the way at your parents' house. Like an interloper.'

'Don't be ridiculous.'

'I'm not! And don't call me ridiculous!'

'I didn't. I said what you're saying is ridiculous. That's different.'

'No, it's not, Luca. I don't even care about what you were talking about. I could just see that it had upset you and I wanted to help and you shut me out.'

'I wasn't shutting you out! It's... complicated.'

'Since when has that ever stopped us?'

He said nothing.

'God knows I had enough complications with my parents and

we always talked about it. Man trouble. Women trouble. Family trouble. World trouble. We always talked. Whatever it was, we always talked about it. Until now.'

'It was a family thing.'

I swallowed hard, trying to push the tears pricking my eyes back from their treacherous precipice.

'Then I guess all that stuff about me being as much a part of your family as any of your siblings was just talk.' I tilted my chin up a little more. 'Thanks for the clarification.' With that, I turned on my heel and made to stride out of the coffee shop, suddenly aware that everyone was either overtly, or covertly, staring at us. Obviously, I could never come back to this café again.

A bitter wind was forcing itself down the tunnel created by the high-rise glass and steel blocks that dominated this part of town; a sharp, biting blast took my breath away as I stepped out into the street from the warm fug of the interior. I hesitated for a moment, catching my breath, before turning towards the nearest Underground station to catch a train home. Once in the relative quiet of my flat, perhaps I could start unravelling just how, in the matter of a few short hours, it felt as if my life had imploded. I had no job, and a friendship I had thought would last for eternity suddenly no longer seemed to be the rock I had always leant on.

13

I battled against the wind for a couple of minutes, head down, eyes squinting almost closed until abruptly it stopped and I bumped into something. I looked up, ready to apologise, but then I saw the object was Luca so I didn't. His comment about 'family' was still churning in my brain.

'I wasn't finished.'

'I was.' I made to step around him. He sidestepped to match me.

'We clearly need to talk.'

'Oh, so now you want to talk?' I snapped.

'About this?' Luca flapped one large hand between us. 'Yes.'

'I think you said all that needs to be said.'

He frowned, his mind running back over his words. I didn't have the patience to wait.

'Look. Things were never going to stay the same between us. That's just a given. Especially once you find Ms Right and take her home to the family.' He opened his mouth to say something, but I ran on. 'And that's how it should be. You want someone to build a life with, Luca. You deserve to have that. And I think I do too.'

'Of course, you do!' he burst in, unable to wait, reaching for my hand. I pulled it gently away.

'Then perhaps we need to concentrate on doing that. We already know that you having a female best friend has caused problems in the past in relationships. I don't want to be that obstacle any more, Luca. Not now. Not when it's so important to you.'

'You're important to me!' he said, running a hand back through his short, midnight-black hair.

'I know. And you are to me. But something's changed.'

'No, it hasn't!' He tried again. 'Saturday was... complicated. It's a one-off.'

I shook my head gently, seeing it all clearer now. 'No, Luca. It was just the start of something that's been coming a long time.' I thought about telling him about the fact I'd just finally stormed out of the job he'd wanted me to leave since about a week after I'd started it. And any other day I would have, but it didn't feel right now.

He took a step back and looked down at me and I saw recognition in his expression. Luca had known me forever and he knew the look on my face now. I wouldn't change my mind.

'So where does that leave us?' he asked. His face had taken on a blank expression but I knew it was masking hurt. That made two of us.

'In the same place.'

'Well, obviously not,' he snapped. 'Yesterday you were the closest friend I've ever had and today you're walking away.'

'I'm not. I'm just giving you the space you need.'

'I don't want any bloody space! I want you!'

Two passers-by turned their heads, eyes widening at our

exchange. Luca caught my hand and guided us both to a doorway, affording us a little more privacy from gawpers. In truth, I was now the one gawping. I snapped my jaw shut quickly.

'Judging by the horrified look on your face, I'm guessing that's come out wrong but do remind me never to propose to you.'

'Sorry. I didn't mean... I'm not horrified. I was just...'

'It doesn't matter.'

Going by the look on his face, it really did matter, but his expression brooked no further discussion. Something in my stomach twisted.

'Luca—'

'Bee, it's fine. All I meant was that I wasn't asking for space, but maybe it's not a bad idea.'

I swallowed and saw his features soften. 'I'm sorry I couldn't talk to you before. The whole thing with Ma... It's just something I need to get straight in my own head before I can talk about it. To anyone. I'm sorry I didn't realise until now how that made you feel.'

'It's OK.' I tried to wave it off. 'Maybe I was just overreacting, like you said. I think my mum blagging off Christmas again has bothered me more than I thought and made me more sensitive right now.'

'I think you have a right to be sensitive about that.'

I gave a shrug before wrapping my coat tighter around me. 'It's time for me to make some new rules, I think. The first of which is to stop letting my parents' lack of interest in me keep affecting me now.'

'Sounds like a good place to start.'

'Thanks.' A shiver rippled through me. 'I'd better get home before I freeze to death. I've got a few things to do.' *Like find a new job...*

'Yep. Sure.' He remained there, looking down at me.

'What?'

'I don't know. It just feels weird suddenly.'

'What does?'

'Everything.'

I knew what he meant.

'It's fine.' I tried to make light of it. 'Besides, you're going to be busy enough trying to win this damn bet anyway to even notice.'

'Believe me, I'll notice.'

I shook my head. 'I have to go.' Quickly, I reached up and hugged him. For a moment I wanted to stay there. Safe in the arms of my friend as I poured out everything I was feeling. But I couldn't. I had to do this on my own. I placed a quick kiss on his cheek, gave him a final squeeze and then turned back into the wind and the direction of the Tube.

* * *

'Why are you in your pyjamas?' Tia was squinting at me through the screen. 'Are you ill?'

'No.'

'Then what? Why didn't you tell me you had some holiday? We could have met up for coffee.'

'I'm not on holiday. I'm...'

'What?' Tia prompted when I didn't follow through with the sentence.

'Unemployed.'

Her eyes widened and her full, fuchsia-painted lips began to form an 'O' that was getting bigger by the second.

'It's not a big deal.'

'It is *such* a big deal!'

'No. It's not. And don't tell Luca, for God's sake.'

The 'O', and her eyes, got even larger. 'You haven't told Luca?'

'No.'

She snapped her lips together. 'OK. What's going on with you two? He's being all weird and distant and now apparently you haven't told him about a major life event. It's like the whole universe is out of whack.'

'Don't be dramatic.'

'It is dramatic. You two are like... the earth and moon. You're just there. Together. And now it's all going to implode like a dying star.' She paused. 'Dying stars implode, right?'

'Yes.'

'OK, so yeah, it's like that.'

'No, it's not.'

'If you two implode then the rest of us are like all the other planets around you, and we'll all be shot off into the farthest reaches of space, never to see each other again. Or sucked into some black hole. Whatever happens in that situation anyway. I know it's bad though.'

'I think you're taking this metaphor a little too far.'

Tia reeled herself back in. 'Maybe. But my point is still the same.'

'We can't be glued at the hip forever.'

'Why not?'

I gave her a look, which she shrugged off.

'Most of us thought you'd have got together by now anyway. You already cost me twenty quid by not doing so last New Year's Eve.'

'You've been betting on us?'

She was unapologetic. 'You have so much in common.'

'We argue literally all the time.'

'No. You disagree. That's different.'

'No, it's not.'

'It is. But even if you did, think of the make-up sex...'

'Tia!'

'What? Oh, come on. Even being best friends with him you can't ignore he's hot as...' She glanced over her shoulder to where a passing colleague had now entered the office break room. 'As something I can't say right now.'

'I'm not going to even dignify that with an answer.'

'So, yes. That's what I thought.'

'I am not thinking about it. It's Luca. It's... weird.'

'Weird is not what I think it would be, but have it your way.'

'Anyway, it's never been like that. You've seen the kind of women he goes out with.'

'Yeah, and they never last. You, however, have lasted decades.'

'It's different. And besides, things change.'

'Not with you two. You and Luca are... you and Luca.'

'I know.'

'Do you want them to change?' she asked, her voice soft and quiet. She'd brushed her long, straight extensions forward like a curtain between her and the rest of the room.

'As you said, I'm not sure we always get to decide. Sometimes we just have to ride the roller coaster and see where we end up.'

'That's a total cop-out answer.'

'But an honest one.'

Tia let out a sigh. 'So, what are you going to do about a job? And also, how the hell am I just finding out about this? Did you get fired?'

I bristled. 'No, I didn't get fired!'

'OK!' She held up her free hand, palm out. 'I was only asking. It's just that... well, we've all been on at you to leave that job for so long and you never did so I just wondered if you were, kind of, made to.'

'Nope. It was all me, I'm afraid.'

'What brought that on, then?'

Good question!

'I guess everyone has their breaking point. Even pushovers like me.'

'You're not a pushover.'

'Well, I don't suppose it matters in the end. The end result is still that I'm out of a job.'

'So what made this week different from any other?'

'I don't know. I was feeling a bit out of sorts anyway and then I was called into the boss's office to discuss my bonus and pay rise. Which turned out, yet again, to be no bonus or pay rise due to a multitude of factors that apparently don't apply if you're a mouthy bloke or a leggy blonde and I just sort of... exploded a little bit.'

Tia's concerned expression slid into a grin. 'I'm not exactly sure how you explode "a little bit". Explosions are generally fairly sizeable things.'

I chewed the inside of my lip.

Tia's grin widened. 'I just have to say this, and I know you're probably stressing about no job and the rest of it, but, girl, I am so proud of you!'

14

I couldn't help the laugh that accompanied the feeling of warmth that swirled around me.

'You are?'

'Of course, I bloody am! We all know that place has been taking you for granted for years and that you could be earning twice what they were paying you.'

Having now looked more seriously into what jobs were out there, I'd discovered everyone was right and although it was something I'd sort of known, I just hadn't had the gumption to follow through on it. Which apparently was something my boss must also have known, otherwise I guessed he'd have been less inclined to keep passing me over when it came to bonus and promotion. I wasn't the type to toot my own horn – but in this case the odd peep might not have been a bad thing, just to show him that I was aware of my own value.

'Bee?'

'Yes?'

'You know Luca has been trying to hire you as his head of IT for years.'

'I know.'

'The package he gives his employees is really good.'

'I know that too.'

'So?'

'I told you before. It'd just be weird.'

'Seems like a lot is weird between you two at the moment.'

'It's not. It's just different. We're... maturing.'

'Um hmm.' Tia gave me that look that said she didn't believe a word of it. 'I don't know what it is. But I do know I don't like it.'

'You're not even going to notice. You have a wedding to plan, for a start.'

'Of course, I'll notice. So does all this...' she waved her hands around '... oddness mean the dating challenge is off?'

'Absolutely not!'

'Still think you're going to win?'

I worried a thread on my pyjama bottoms. And yes, as Tia had pointed out, I was still in my pjs and knew that there were those who would judge me for that, but I had bigger worries.

'Bee?'

'Yes?' I avoided looking at the screen.

'What's up?'

'Nothing really.'

'I've known you far too long for you to tell porkers to me, Bee. Come on, spill.'

'Is it strange that I want to win this thing?'

'No. Not at all. I can't remember a time where you didn't want to win when it came to a challenge against Luca.'

'True. But... the only way for me to win this is to end up alone. There's something wrong about that, isn't there?'

Tia's face softened. 'Oh, honey.'

'I mean, when we started, I didn't really think about it in that way. I guess I've just had more time to analyse it now and...' I shrugged, unsure how to finish off the sentence. I didn't quite have it straight in my own head yet, so trying to explain it to someone else wasn't exactly easy.

'Then maybe you need to forget about the whole challenge side of it. Forget about beating Luca for once. Focus on you for a change. You've clearly taken one huge step this week with the job situation. Maybe it's time to rethink this too. I know you're not a fan of online dating, and, granted, there's always a lot not to love about it.'

'You can say that again.'

'But good things do come out of it sometimes. It's not beyond the realms of possibility that good things could happen for you too.'

'Maybe.'

She grinned. '"Maybe" is an improvement on your view several weeks ago so I'm going to take that.'

'I think Luca's probably still got the edge on me though, even if I do throw myself into it.'

'What makes you say that?'

'Oh, come on, Tia. The server is probably crashing regularly with the amount of messages zooming towards his inbox.'

'So what if it is? You've only got to find one.'

'Yes. The One. Something that's easier said than done.'

'But it's still just one.'

'The odds of which are far better if you have a large choice.'

'Or maybe it's harder. Too much choice isn't always a good thing.'

'I suppose.' I rubbed my hands over my face. 'I don't know, Tia. Sorry. I just feel a bit out of sorts. I've never been out of work in my life.'

'Have you seen anything you fancy?'

'I've had five interviews over the last two days.'

Tia burst out laughing.

'What?'

'You! There you are, stressing yourself out and making me worry about you when you're being trampled with job offers already.'

'They're not offers. They were just interviews.'

Tia tapped one long clashing-coloured nail against her brightly painted lips. 'You know Luca is going to be pissed if you take a job elsewhere when he's been offering you a position for ages.'

'He'll be fine. That was all just Luca being Luca. None of you liked me working at that place but he has the ability to take charge and fix it.'

'You know that's not what it's about.'

It was my turn to give her the look.

'OK, so maybe that's a tiny bit of what it's about, but for the most part it's because Luca always wants the best person for the job and, when it comes to IT, that's you. That's why he keeps offering you the job.' She pulled a face. 'This could feel like a bit of a slap in the face.'

'And that's exactly why I could never take a job with him. Because I'd just be swapping one place that I felt I could never leave because I didn't have the confidence to for another place I could never leave because I would be worried about hurting Luca's feelings! Business and pleasure never mix well.'

Tia gave a wicked grin. 'I know a stationery cupboard three jobs back that would disagree with you.'

I shook my head, laughing. 'Thank goodness you've finally found Jono, then, and stationery cupboards countrywide are now safe.'

'Oh, come on, don't tell me you've never stolen a moment or two in one.'

'I haven't! But then I'm not as exciting as you.'

'Well, that's a shame and you're not less exciting than me, or anyone. You're clearly just more picky.' She gave me a wide grin and winked.

'Don't let Jono hear you say that.'

She threw her head back, her laugh loud, clear and happy. 'He's fine. I've got more discerning as I've got older. Got all that quick-fling stuff out of my system. And to be honest, cupboards are not the most comfortable of places for a romantic tryst.'

Tia flashed her eyes at me wickedly before tapping her phone. 'Oh, crap, is that the time? I've got a meeting. You sure you're OK?'

'Yeah. I'm fine.'

'And, Bee?'

'Yep?'

'You need to tell Luca. Whatever's going on with you two, he'll want to know, and finding out from someone else? I'm not sure he deserves that.'

She was right. 'Yeah. I know. I'll tell him, I promise.' Now I just had to work out exactly when and how to tell him.

'OK. Good. Gotta dash. Love ya! Talk to you later.' She blew me a big kiss through the screen and then she was gone.

I sat staring at it for a few moments, turning her words over in my head. What Tia had said was true. This was a pretty big thing I'd done. Some people changed jobs like their underpants, but that most definitely wasn't me. To continue the metaphor, this was the equivalent of me going from Victorian bloomers to a thong. (And seriously, who invented those? Given the choice, I think I'd go with the bloomers.) I needed to tell Luca before someone else did. Tia was a wonderful friend, but she couldn't keep a secret to save her life. If I didn't tell him soon, one way or another Tia would. Now I just had to decide on the best way to do that.

I picked up my phone, toying with it, scrolling up and down the contacts aimlessly. As I took a deep breath, about to press Luca's name, the phone began to ring, making me jump and drop it on the floor. Thankfully, it hit the rug and continued ringing. A smashed phone was not what I needed right now. I leant down and picked it back up, took another deep breath and swiped up on the video call.

'I was just about to call you.'

'Great minds.' He smiled out at me from the phone, looking more like his old self. But there was a hint of hesitation. 'Bee, I need to apologise.'

'For what?'

'The other day. At my parents' place, and after.'

'No, it's fine. You really—'

'I do. I can see how it might have made you feel excluded. Although, believe me, that definitely wasn't the intention. You might have a different last name but you're most certainly a part of this family and I never want you to think that you're not. OK?'

'OK.'

'And it's not that I don't want to talk about things. This is just something no one but me can deal with. Despite what my mother thinks.' He pulled a face, knitting the dark brows together.

'I'm sure she only wants what's best for you.'

Luca blew out a sigh. 'She does. But sometimes she wants what she thinks is best and life isn't always that black and white, or that simple.'

I gave him a sympathetic smile, unsure of what else to say.

'How are you, anyway? Been on any more dates?'

'No, but I have got one lined up for tomorrow evening.'

His expression gave little away. 'You don't sound particularly enthusiastic.'

'He seems nice but it's hard not to let my experience so far in all of this colour my expectations somewhat.'

'That's understandable.'

'Are you still thinking this is a good idea?'

'What?'

'This whole challenge thing.'

'Yes.' His answer was quick and definitive.

'Oh.'

'You seem disappointed.'

I shrugged.

'At least it's giving you a chance to meet people. See what you might be missing out on.'

'Very little if my dates so far are anything to go by.'

'Someone might surprise you. You have to push yourself out of your comfort zone sometimes, Bee.'

'I like my comfort zone. That's the whole point. The clue is in the name.'

He smiled, shaking his head at me affectionately. I was glad he'd rung. I'd hated that feeling of tension between us, which was so unfamiliar. Of course, I still had to tell him that, right now when it came to work, I was so far out of my comfort zone, I'd need a NASA-strength telescope to even see it.

'Actually, there's something I need to—' I was interrupted by my phone ringing with a regular call. The name of the job agency I'd signed up with dropped onto the screen.

'Call you back?' I said, making a phone shape with my finger and thumb and holding it to my ear. Luca nodded and I ended the video call and slid into professional mode to take the call.

'Oh, Beatrice. Good. I've caught you. It's Camilla from Top People.' I tried not to cringe at her using my full name, despite me asking her not to. I'd never been a fan of it, but apparently I'd been rather drunkenly conceived after my parents had been to see a particularly good adaptation of my mother's favourite Shakespeare play and I'd been named for one of the heroines. I think, to give them some credit, they had been initially excited about my arrival into their world, until it had become apparent that I took up far more of their time and energy than they'd anticipated or were prepared to give over. Either way, I was stuck with the name.

'Please, do call me Bee,' I reminded her.

'Oh, yes. Of course.' Had I been in front of her, I was pretty sure I'd have been able to see the request go in one ear and fly straight out of the other. She dealt with a tonne of people a day, I imagined, and it was fair enough if she didn't remember requested nicknames.

'Absolutely perfect position for you. It's temporary to start but if you're the right person, which I am convinced you are, it will lead to a permanent position. I've told them you're a perfect fit already. Hope you don't mind. I knew you wouldn't turn this down. Sensible girl like you. Good head on your shoulders. Great package, excellent pay and lovely offices. Hardly ever get any positions come up within it as everyone loves it too much to leave. Got someone retiring for this one though, so going to shoo you in while there's the chance. Start Monday. You don't mind working over your gardening leave, do you? I didn't think you would.'

'No, not at all. Sounds great, Camilla.' Had I actually had a garden, a week or two off might have been nice but, as it was, extra money coming in would alleviate some worries.

'I've just sent the details through. You should have them now. OK?'

I switched screens on my phone to email and saw the one

from the agency. 'Got it,' I replied as I clicked on the link to open the details. 'Oh!'

'Something the matter?' She sounded distracted, as if she was already moving on to the next task.

'The company is Donato Solutions?'

'Yes. I've always got a raft of people begging me to get them in there, but I knew the moment it came in that you were the best person for the position. They'll love you! Got to go. Speak soon.' And she was gone.

'I can't take it...' I said, half-heartedly into the silence.

15

'You have to take it!' Tia said, when I rang her. 'What's the big deal?'

'You know exactly what the big deal is. It's Luca's company.'

'And? I know one of your worries, if I remember correctly, was that you were concerned others would think you'd only got the job because you're friends with the boss.'

'Exactly.'

'Well, bearing in mind he still doesn't know you flounced out of your last job and are on an agency's list at all, you can scrub that reason, can't you?'

'I didn't flounce out.' Actually, I'd totally flounced. The one and only time I've ever flounced anywhere but that wasn't the point.

'Of course you did. And if you didn't, you should have. Anyway. At least try it, Bee. You deserve something good after slogging away at that dead-end place for so many years.'

'Thanks for that.'

'You're welcome.'

I pulled a face at the screen but Tia waved it away.

'You going to tell Luca now?'

'I guess I have to.' I shrugged again. 'I was talking to him when the agency rang so I've got to call him back anyway.'

The call rang for a while before Luca picked up. There was a brief flash of his face before he darted off again, the phone resting on his bedside lamp, giving me a view of him dashing about his bedroom throwing various items into a holdall.

'Am I interrupting?' I asked. 'I didn't realise you were heading off somewhere.'

'Last-minute thing,' he called back across the room. 'Couple of the guys have organised a climb in the Peak District.'

'When are you leaving?'

I saw him give his expensive but remarkably simple watch face a quick glance. I knew he'd be changing it before he left for a far more complicated one that seemed to do everything but make the tea. (That omission by the manufacturers was a big mistake if you asked me.)

'In about five minutes. Everything OK?'

Five minutes wasn't enough to explain this past week. I could in theory say, 'Yeah. Just letting you know I finally walked out on my crappy job last week and start at your place as a temp on Monday' within that time but I knew Luca would stop and want the details and I wasn't about to mess up his trip.

'Yep. Nothing that can't wait. I'll leave you to your packing. Have a good time and try not to fall off, or into, anything.'

'I'll do my best.'

Luca came closer to the phone, gave me his trademark grin and blew an only slightly sarcastic kiss. I gave him a wave and hung up. Quickly I messaged Tia.

Rang to tell Luca. He's heading out on another daft adventure trip so didn't get a chance. Will tell him when I can. Please don't blab if you speak to him!

Almost immediately I could see that she was typing a reply.

I am not a blabber!

Three shocked emoji faces followed this declaration.

OK. Just advising haven't told him yet in case you thought I had xx

She sent a thumbs up followed by a couple of kisses. Twenty minutes later she sent a shot of a delicious-looking lunch accompanied by a tall glass of ice-cold champagne, if the condensation on the glass was anything to go by. A 'yummy' gif was returned and I got on with the far more menial and boring tasks queuing up for my own attention.

* * *

I shifted in my seat and tried to relax while Adrian paused in pouring the excellent wine he'd chosen. I'd let him choose as, with them just listed on the wine list, my usual method of going by the prettiest label was a little harder to employ.

He placed the bottle of white carefully back in the chiller, before turning pale blue eyes on me.

'You're not having a good time, are you?'

'No! I mean, yes! I am.' I felt the colour rush to my face, feeling a second rush as I got embarrassed about being embarrassed.

He pulled a kind of adorably puzzled face.

'OK. This might sound weird.'

He folded his hands together on the table.

'OK.'

'It's just that I am enjoying myself and it seems to be going well. At least I think it is...' If my cheeks got any brighter, I was in danger of distracting planes landing at Heathrow.

'I think it is too.' He smiled at me.

'Oh. Right. Good. That's good,' I gabbled, giving myself a mental slap. 'It's just that I've been on a few dates through the app now and it's never gone this well.'

He raised a questioning brow.

'That's kind of an understatement actually.'

Adrian nudged the now full glass towards me. 'This sounds like it could be interesting...'

Two hours later I was rattling along on the DLR, staring out at the little squares of lights in the office and apartment blocks and gazing at the bright lights of London City Airport before gathering my coat around me as the train pulled into the terminus, ready to battle the chill that had drifted in during the evening and set firm for the night. All the while I was thinking of Adrian and did my best to adjust what I was sure was the slightly dopey look plastered on my face.

We'd talked, laughed and eaten well. The wine had flowed just as easily but thankfully the food at the Italian restaurant he'd chosen had done a good job of absorbing most of the alcohol. Or at least enough of it to make me relaxed but not plastered. Adrian was interesting and funny and he'd appeared to feel the same about me, listening when I spoke and asking questions. It was... nice. And, I had to admit, a surprise. I had got used to feeling as if I was either an extra, or, more often, invisible. That was, until someone wanted something. Then, of course, there I was – when I could prove useful.

Tonight, for the first time in a long time, I felt as if maybe I did have something to offer the world after all. Adrian had been keen to see me again and had said goodbye with a gentle, and very chaste, kiss on my cheek. Secretly, I'd hoped for more and certainly wouldn't have objected. Something told me he felt the same way but he'd been a perfect gentleman – which kind of made it all that much hotter.

* * *

'You're seeing him again, then?' Tia squealed excitedly down the phone as I strode towards the Tube in order to start my first day of temping at Donato Solutions.

'I am.'

She squealed again and I held the phone out a little from my ear until she'd finished.

'Are you done?' I laughed.

'Probably not.' She laughed back. 'I'm so happy for you, Bee.'

'It was just a first date, Tia,' I reminded her, trying not to let the excitement bubbling inside me leak its way into my tone.

'Yes, but I can hear it in your voice.' So much for that tactic, then. 'You're excited. And, no offence, but that's pretty unusual for you.'

'I'm not entirely sure whether to be offended at that or not as it makes me sound terribly dull but, because I'm in a good mood, I'll give you the benefit of the doubt.'

She laughed that great laugh of hers. 'Thanks. How you feeling about today?'

A little knot of anxiety popped up in my stomach. 'Bit nervous, if I'm honest. But I need a job and this is what came up. At least it will give me a chance to see how it is working there without any need to actually commit.'

'Wow.'

'What?'

'Nothing.'

'Well, it's obviously something. You said wow.'

'It's just that you sound... don't take this the wrong way.'

'That doesn't sound good.'

'It's coming from a good place.'

'Spit it out, then.'

'It's just that you sound a bit less terrified of everything. Like you're finally sticking a toe out from that comfort blanket you normally cling to so avidly.'

I didn't say anything, but the fact that Luca had made a very similar comment about me and comfort zones was flitting around in my brain.

'Bee? You still there?'

'Yes.'

'Are you cross?'

'No. I'm just... I didn't realise that was how everyone saw me.'

'It's not a bad thing. They're called comfort zones for a reason. We like them. It's just that we all know you have so much more to offer than you were allowing yourself. And now you seem to be realising that too. We love you and it's hard to watch you not fulfil your potential. This is a big step and I'm so proud of you.'

'Are you crying?'

'No! Of course not,' she said, sniffing loudly. 'It's hay fever.'

'I'm pretty sure it's several months too late to use that particular excuse.'

'Allergies, then.'

I grinned. 'Love you, Tia.'

'Love you too, babe. Knock 'em for six today.'

'I'll do my best.'

'Let me know how it goes with Luca.'

'Hmm. Yep. You'll be the first to know.'

We hung up and I headed through the entrance to the station, beeped my Oyster card and stepped onto one of the driverless trains heading into the City.

* * *

'This is your desk,' Jo, the lady from HR, settled me in, smiling and checking if I needed anything else. This was a new experience for me as, although I was sure there were plenty of nice HR people around, most of the ones I and my friends had encountered had been people who seemed to be a little short on both sympathy and empathy and, on occasion, even humanity. All of which seemed as if they should be necessary for such positions. But Luca seemed to have found someone for his own HR department who had all those qualities and more. Of course, he had.

'Normally Mr Donato would be here to say hello but he's out today.'

I actually knew this, which was why I was a tiny bit more relaxed. Well, as relaxed as you could be when you were the new kid. As I'd exited the station and my phone had reconnected to a mobile signal a message from Luca had come in, saying they were taking an extra day to do some more climbing and that, yes, he would still do his best not to fall off. I'd sent a quick reply telling him to have a good time, before pushing open a heavy glass door and entering the lobby of his building.

'Oh, that's OK.'

'He'll be sure to come and see you when he's back in. He makes a point of meeting all the new staff. He's a great boss. Always has time for everyone.'

I smiled, feeling a little awkward. Should I say I knew him? If I didn't say it now, would she wonder why I hadn't when she found out? But I also wanted to prove that I'd got the position, albeit temporary, off my own bat and not just because I was pals with Luca. However nice people were, it was human nature to think that it wasn't what you knew but who. Argh! What should I do?

'Would you like a tea or a coffee?'

'Oh! Umm, no. I'm fine, thanks. I have some water in my bag.'

'OK. Well, don't forget there's a variety of drinks and snacks in the kitchen, Just help yourself.'

'Thanks, I will.'

'Ah, here's Colin. He'll get you all set up with the work. Colin, this is Bee, our IT saviour.' She laughed and touched my shoulder. 'I've told her you'll get her all settled in.' Colin smiled and shook my hand as Jo turned to me. 'In the meantime, I'm on extension 232. Any questions, just give me a bell.'

'Thanks, Jo. I will.'

'Right,' Colin said as Jo walked away, her neat little hair-bun bouncing happily. 'I've seen your CV so I'm pretty sure you could probably already run rings around me, but I'll get you set up so you can get going.'

'I'm sure that's not the case.' I smiled, feeling a little awkward.

Colin laughed, good-naturedly. 'It really is, but that's all right. I like what I do and I do it well so everyone's happy.'

'That sounds fair enough.'

He smiled, pulled up a chair and set about showing me the ropes of the system.

* * *

Five o'clock came a lot faster than it usually did and, for once, I wasn't ready to rush out of the door, breathing a sigh of relief that another work day was over. I'd actually enjoyed it, which was a novel feeling. I'd concentrated and got to work but I didn't feel exhausted as I usually did as I walked back towards the station to catch the train home. A twist of emotions fizzed around my body at the thought that I'd wasted all those years at a dead-end job I hated purely because I was, as Tia had put it, too unsure to put a foot outside my comfort zone. I was already loving what I was doing at Donato's but I was still aware that I hadn't told Luca I'd walked out of my old job yet, let alone started temping at his place. Plus, all the people there had been so nice – would that change once they knew I was close with Luca? He was clearly popular but he was still the boss – I didn't want them thinking I was a spy in the camp.

'You're totally overthinking it,' Tia said when I laid this out to her as I cooked some pasta for dinner. For once, I wasn't just binging a ready meal in the microwave. All right, it was just pasta and sauce but it was still a step up.

'Am I?'

'Yep. As usual.'

'Thanks.'

'You're welcome. Have you spoken to Luca yet?'

'No. I got a message saying he'll catch up with me tomorrow as they won't be back until late tonight.'

'Ah.'

'Yes. Ah. I don't think he'll be expecting to catch up with me in his own office.'

'He'll be fine.'

'I just don't want him to feel I've done something behind his back.'

'You're doing it again. Stop worrying. Now, when are you seeing this Adrian guy next?'

16

Luca did an almost comedic double take when he saw me sitting at the desk in his offices early the next morning. I gave a small, slightly sheepish wave and pasted on a smile as he changed direction and began walking towards me. Someone waylaid him and I could see him trying to concentrate but still glancing over towards me, as if pinning me in place with his gaze until he got an explanation as to what I was doing there. He clapped the chap that he'd been speaking to on the arm and resumed taking long strides towards me.

'Hi,' I said, as normally as I could manage.

'Hi,' he said, his expression a mix of smile and utter confusion.

'How was your weekend?'

'Good,' he replied distractedly. 'Really good.'

'Excellent.'

There was a long pause and Luca leant over my desk a little, his voice low. 'Don't take this the wrong way, but what the hell are you doing here?'

'Working.'

He blinked, then frowned, then blinked again.

'But... you don't work here.'

'I do now. Well, for the next two weeks at least.'

'Since when?'

'Since yesterday.'

He stood up straight. 'OK. I'm confused. Do you want to come into my office and explain things a little more clearly to me?'

I glanced around surreptitiously. 'Isn't it going to look a bit odd if you take the temp into your office within two minutes of meeting her?'

'Bee. I've known you since you were five, not two minutes ago.' He made a gesture indicating his office, a large glass cube at the end of the room. 'Besides, I always try to meet all our staff. It won't look odd.'

'So why is everyone trying not to stare?'

'They're not. You're just paranoid, as usual. Come on. Don't make me fire you on your second day.'

'Oh, ha ha.'

It was clearly meant in jest but I couldn't stop my stomach doing a small rhumba as my previous reservations about working for Luca resurfaced.

'I was joking.' Luca sighed, pinching the bridge of his nose.

'I know.'

'Try telling your face that, then.' Luca's grin was hovering.

I needed to work on the nonchalance.

Luca closed the heavy glass door behind me and indicated the seat opposite his desk as he took his own in a large, buttery soft leather one and glanced briefly at the memos and paperwork placed neatly on the pale ash wood desk.

'So, what did I miss? I was only gone four days!'

'Umm... I kind of left my job.'

'You kind of left your job or you actually left your job?'

'Actually left it.'

'When?'

'A little over a week ago,' I said, bluntly. There was no point skirting round it now.

His eyebrows shot up into his hairline. 'A week ago? And I'm just finding out now.'

'You seemed distracted with whatever else is going on with you at the moment.'

'I would have had time for this.'

'I was about to tell you on Friday but when I called back – after I'd had the call that they wanted a temp here – you were rushing out the door and I didn't want to delay you.'

'You should have.'

'Why?'

'Because this is important.'

I shrugged. 'It's no big deal.' I glanced at his face. 'Unless you think it's a big deal I'm here.'

'I do.'

'Oh.'

'But not for the reason you're thinking, judging by the look on your face. You know I've been trying to get you here for years and you've always refused. I'm just curious as to what momentous thing happened in order for you to leave that dead-end place and come here.'

I let out a big sigh. 'I got called into the boss's office to be told that, yet again, I wasn't getting a pay rise or a bonus. Several others did, despite the fact it was always me that's sorted out their messes and made them look good.'

'You should have left the messes for them to clean up themselves.'

'I know. But I'm not made that way. Plus, somehow, it would still come back on me.'

'But, correct me if I'm wrong, that situation has been going on for some time. I can't remember the last time you got a pay rise or bonus. So why now?'

'I guess I was just having a bad day.'

Luca tilted his head and raised a brow. Sometimes others knowing you so well can be incredibly annoying.

'OK. I was upset that we'd had a falling-out—'

'We hadn't,' Luca stated emphatically.

'Well, it felt like it to me.'

He gave a small head shake.

'It did! Anyway, I was already not in a great place and then that happened and I guess it was just one time too many.'

'Good.'

'Good?' I repeated. 'Not exactly! I hardly think they're going to be writing me a decent reference any time soon after I flounced out.'

His white teeth were highlighted against the soft olive of his skin as the wide smile broke through.

'You flounced?'

I tried not to smile but, with Luca looking at me like that, it was hard not to. 'I may have done.'

'You did. You totally flounced!' His laughter filled the room and beyond the glass walls I saw a few people turn their heads in what was clearly meant to be a casual manner.

'Shoosh! You're drawing attention.'

'Did you just shoosh your new boss?'

'No. I shooshed my old friend. It's completely different.'

Luca laughed again.

'But how did you end up here? I mean, obviously there was always a door open but—'

'The agency don't know I know you! I didn't get it that way. I went for a bunch of interviews for permanent positions last week and then, when I was talking to you on Friday, the agency rang and said they had a temping position here for a couple of weeks.'

'If I'm not directly headhunting, I've found it can be a good way to try people out and see if they're a good fit.'

'Makes sense.'

I hesitated.

'I nearly didn't take it.'

'Why?'

'For all the reasons I've listed to you over the years.'

'So what makes this time different?'

'I have bills to pay and no job. Beggars can't be choosers.'

He said nothing.

'That came out wrong.'

'I'm not sure it did but I can let it go. The main thing is you're here. I just wish you'd told me you'd left your other job when it happened. As you said the other day, I thought we talked about everything.'

'We do. Mostly.' I gave him a look and a hint of colour tinted his cheeks.

'Point taken. But those are special circumstances.'

I shrugged.

'These were too. I knew you'd want to fix things and give me a position here and I'd never feel like I'd been wanted for who I am and my skills.'

'That's exactly why I want you!' Luca exclaimed, throwing his arms up just as a tall, slim woman with flaming red hair and a figure to die for knocked and entered, without waiting to be invited. She kept her face immobile but I'd seen her eyes dart between me and Luca as she caught his declaration. Oh. Excellent.

'Sorry to interrupt, Luca. I just wanted to remind you that you have a meeting with Mr Takahashi about the Tokyo project at eleven.'

'Yep. Thanks, Carrie.' She nodded, gave me a brief smile and then turned and left the room, the underside of her four-inch stilettos showing a flash of red as she did so.

'Wow.'

'What?'

'She's a knockout.'

'She's a good personal assistant. That's my main concern.'

'Who just happens to look amazing. How come you've never got together?'

'It would be too complicated. Plus I never mix business and pleasure.'

I gave him a wave.

'You're different.'

'How?'

'Because...'

'I hope you're going to be more erudite than that at your eleven o'clock meeting.'

'Smart arse.'

'So why's it different?'

'Because it just is. You're excellent at what you do and I've known you forever. It's not the same as...' He searched for the words.

'Friends with benefits?'

'Something like that.'

'But what if she's The One?'

'She's not.'

'How do you know?'

'She's engaged to a Viking type called Olaf.'

'Olaf?'

'Olaf. Can we move on now?'

'Yep. I guess. I need to go and get on with my work before I get fired.'

'You're not getting fired.'

'I've only been here two days. There's plenty of time.'

'For you to flounce out?'

'It's been known.'

'Well. I am extremely glad you finally found your flounce and told them where to stick their job. It made me so mad to see you taken advantage of for so long. But I would hope you don't find anything here that would cause you to leave now we've finally managed to get you in the door. Are you enjoying what you're doing?'

'It's obviously all new but, from what I've been shown and the tasks I have right now, yes,' I answered honestly. 'I really am. It feels good to be able to actually engage my brain in work again.'

He smiled and pushed his seat back. I rose too, turning towards the door. Quickly I spun back, unaware that Luca had followed me, and I bounced off his broad chest. Warm, large hands at my waist steadied me momentarily.

'I'm sorry I didn't tell you about everything before. It felt really weird not to. It was just an odd week.'

'I know. And I know a lot of that was on me. I'm sorry.'

I went to pull on the glass door but Luca was there before me, opening it.

'Thanks.'

'Catch up later.'

'Yep. Good luck with the meeting.'

'Thanks.' He held up crossed fingers and I smiled, before heading back to my desk. Automatically I dropped my head, trying to make myself less of a point of interest. But something prodded at my mind. I hadn't done anything wrong. So, I knew the boss. So what? That wasn't how I'd got the position. With a rush of effort, I lifted my head, focused on my desk and headed towards it. I'd spent years being invisible at work. It was time for that to change.

* * *

'Want to come round for dinner?' Luca asked as I was packing my things at the end of the day. The neighbouring desks were empty, as I had stayed on a little longer to finish a particular task.

'I'd love to.' I smiled and Luca returned it, the twinkle in his eyes highlighted by the eco, people-friendly lighting in the office. The harsh fluorescent strip lighting of the previous place, along with the headaches they frequently caused, was something else I wasn't missing. 'But I have a date.'

'Oh!' The smile dimmed momentarily. 'Right. Another time, then.'

'Definitely.'

'I'm surprised you don't, to be honest.'

'No one's caught my attention.'

I gave him a disbelieving look as I dropped my phone into the side pocket of my bag.

He gave a shrug. 'It's true.'

'I'm sure there will be another bevy of potential dates when you look at your inbox again in about five minutes.' I grinned.

'Ha ha. So who are you meeting?'

'He's called Adrian.'

Luca screwed up his nose.

'What?'

'I just can't see you with an Adrian.'

'Is that so? So who do you see me with?'

He shrugged.

'Excellent argument.'

'What does he do?'

'Financial sector.'

'That covers a lot of sins.'

17

'Fine. He's a stockbroker.' Luca had had a thing about stockbrokers ever since a crooked one had skimmed a load of money from a bunch of accounts, including his own and some of his friends', and made off to Rio de Janeiro with the proceeds. Extradition attempts were still proving difficult and he'd pretty much kissed the money goodbye. Thankfully, he hadn't lost a lot in the grand scheme of things, but another friend had lost almost everything, followed shortly by his fiancée, who clearly didn't fancy the life she was likely to have as opposed to the one she'd planned for. Luca and others had tried to console him that it was better for him to find out her motivations now, but it had still left a nasty taste in his mouth.

'That's exactly why I didn't tell you.'

'What? I didn't say anything.'

'You didn't have to. It's written all over your face.'

'First date?'

'No. Third.' The second had been a few days ago, when we'd met up for a meal after he'd finished work and just spent the evening chatting and laughing. When he'd suggested the third date, I'd been surprised at how excited – and thrilled – I was.

'Wow. Right.'

'What does that mean?'

'Nothing.'

'It so means something but I'm going to be late, and I probably don't want to hear what you think it means anyway, so I'd better get on.'

'Where are you meeting him?'

'At Bar Rodin.'

He nodded. 'Not a bad choice.'

'I'm so glad you approve.'

He condescended to give a small smile.

'Thanks for the invite though.'

'No problem. You know you're welcome any time.'

I glanced at the wall clock, gave Luca a quick hug, as the office was now empty, and headed towards the door.

'Just let me know when you're home, OK?'

I gave him a wave in acknowledgement and left.

* * *

'So, how's the new job?' Adrian asked as I took a seat on the stool next to him, this time in a manner that didn't flash my knickers to the entire bar.

'It's good. I mean, I've only been there two days but so far.'

'An improvement on the last place, then?'

'Definitely. Although it's probably hard to find somewhere that wouldn't be an improvement.'

'That Donato guy seems to have his head screwed on. Got the Midas touch, it seems.'

'He's worked hard to get where he is.'

'I guess.' He shrugged. 'Just seems a bit too good to be true.'

'He's really not.'

Adrian looked at me. 'You seem quite the fan.'

'He's actually a friend.'

'Oh, really?'

'That's not how I got the job though. He didn't even know I had the position until he came in to work today.'

Adrian smiled. It was a good smile. Not knockout, movie-star type like Luca's, but not many people got to swim in that privileged end of the gene pool. But I liked Adrian's smile. I liked Adrian full stop.

'Let's talk about you instead,' I said, resting my chin on my hand. He met my eyes and held the gaze before leaning closer.

'I've been thinking about you all day.' His voice was low and intimate, close to my ear.

I felt myself flush and warmth flooded and fizzed throughout my body.

'Have you?'

'Oh, yeah,' he replied, his lips still close to my ear before one hand gently pushed my hair back and he brushed them against my jawline. The fizzing increased and without thinking I leant closer. I felt him smile against my neck.

'Shall we go somewhere else?'

Speech seemed to be temporarily out of the question, so I nodded and heard him laugh softly. Taking my hand, he put some notes down on the bar and waited as I dismounted from the bar stool. By the flicker on his face, I'm guessing I didn't quite manage the same degree of decorum that I had earlier.

'Had I known there'd be high stools involved, I'd have worn a longer dress.'

Adrian grinned. 'Believe me, I'm not complaining.'

I bumped against him and his other hand slid to my waist. 'Where do you want to go?'

'I really don't mind.' And for once, I didn't. For once, I didn't feel the need to plan. To cater for all eventualities. I was caught up in the moment and I loved it.

* * *

What I did not love was the raging hangover currently bouncing about in my brain. Champagne had seemed like a good idea as I'd relaxed in the high-end restaurant with Adrian. He had nodded towards a group of people at a table near the window.

'Reality stars,' he noted, the tone of his voice not hiding that he didn't exactly approve.

'Oh, are they? I don't really watch anything like that.'

'I knew I liked you for a reason.' He smiled.

'I hope that's not the only reason,' I replied, emboldened by the cocktail of earlier, which I was currently chasing with a glass of ice-cold Cristal.

Heat flashed into his eyes and, under the table, a warm hand touched my thigh tentatively. Should I move it? The thing was, I didn't want to. I wanted this. I'd never been one for being the centre of attention and still wasn't. But being the centre of one person's attention, someone I was beginning to have real feelings for, felt heady and wonderful. He made me feel sexy. I wasn't sure I'd even known I could feel that way. I never felt I quite made it. But tonight, here, now, I did. I laid my own hand over his and interlaced my fingers with his. The hand moved a little higher.

'Definitely not.'

* * *

'Wow. You look like crap.' Luca's voice broke into the cocoon of quiet I was endeavouring to build around myself within the office. 'I thought you were going to let me know when you got home, so I knew you were safe?'

I looked up from my desk and met his dark eyes, irritation and concern mixing within them. His full lips were set in a stern line and the ice-grey shirt was open at the neck, revealing a triangle of smooth, tanned flesh.

'Oh. Yes. Right. Sorry. Forgot. It was a bit later than I'd planned.' Was I shouting? It felt like it. It felt as if everybody was shouting.

'I see.'

I didn't answer.

'I'm not sure it's a great move showing up on your third day at a new job with a raging hangover, Bee.'

My head shot up, a movement I immediately regretted as my brain had apparently broken loose from its moorings somewhere during the second bottle of champagne and was now rolling unsecured within my cranium.

'This is exactly why I didn't want to work here,' I whispered. 'But don't worry. I am more than capable of doing my job. I'm sorry I have a headache but don't appreciate you assuming it's a hangover.'

Obviously, it was a massive hangover but I wasn't about to admit that.

'I see,' Luca said, clearly seeing exactly what he wanted to, which in reality was probably the truth. I hadn't meant to get drunk. I'd never once turned up to work with a hangover before. It just kind of happened. But, of course, it would happen today. Here. 'Perhaps it would be better if you took the day off to recover.'

'No. I'm fine. Thank you. I've taken some headache pills and

I'm sure they'll start working shortly.' I risked a look up and found Luca's eyes on me. He leant over the desk briefly. 'If this is the state this guy gets you into, I'm not sure he's good for you. Anywhere else and he could have got you fired.'

'He didn't make me drink!' I snapped back, forgetting momentarily that I was supposed to be denying the whole hang-over thing.

'That's not the point. He knows you're in a new job and impressions count.' He placed a large glass of water on my desk. 'Drink that and take some more paracetamol as soon as you can. And eat something. There's plenty in the kitchen. It will help.'

With that he turned on his expensive heel and strode between the desks back to his office. He closed the door without looking back and sat down. His jaw was set and tension radiated from him. I'd let him down. The belief he'd had that I'd be a valuable member of his team was clearly less definite now and, as I caught a glance of myself in a mirrored wall panel nearby, I could hardly blame him.

Luca was on the phone when I left that evening and, having exchanged a few messages with Adrian, a couple of which had me blushing the colour of the little red train I was now riding in, I switched the phone off, headed into my flat, and went straight to bed.

* * *

When I switched the phone on the next morning, feeling far more human, I saw several missed messages from Luca come in. I pulled the front door closed behind me and dialled his number.

'Hi.'

'Hi.'

'I got your messages. Sorry. I had the phone off.'

'That's OK. I hadn't planned to interrupt your evening. I just wanted to see how you were.'

'You didn't interrupt. I went home and straight to bed.'

'Oh.' He paused. 'You feeling any better?'

'Yes, thanks. I'm on my way to work. Assuming I still have a position there.'

'Of course you do.'

'That's good.'

'I just think it's a bit irresponsible of Adrian—' he put on a tone when he said his name '—to risk your job.'

'We just got a bit carried away.'

There was silence for a moment. 'Right.'

'Luca, would you be like this if I was working somewhere else?'

'Yes.'

'Are you sure?'

'Absolutely.'

'OK. But can you stop now? It was a mistake, I know that, but you're not perfect either.'

'I never claimed to be.'

'I know, but I already felt bad and you're making it worse.' I headed towards a seat just as a woman with a massive bag, and her phone on speaker, cut across me and plonked herself down in it.

'Oh, for...'

'What?'

'I seem to have my invisibility cloak on again this morning.'

'So take it off.' This was always Luca's reply when I said anything like this. He never took it seriously and it frustrated me that he thought it was so easy to change. He'd never been invisible to people. His family had made sure of that and his confidence had had a strong foundation. My foundations, however, were built on sand. Shifting beneath me whenever I attempted to steady them. But maybe one day that would change. I'd had a taste of it with Adrian. Maybe that was what it took. For someone to believe you were worth noticing. I mean, Luca had always said that, but I'd known him so long, it was different. Of course, he'd say that. But Adrian was independent and he'd noticed me. Really noticed me, and when I was with him, for the first time, I felt as if I was seen. Even if Luca didn't approve of him, he would when he met him. I was sure.

* * *

'I don't like him,' Luca said, when Adrian disappeared off to take a call. A bunch of us were having a quick meet-up in the pub before we all separated off to do our own thing. It hadn't been a planned meeting and I'd apologised to Adrian before too many people turned up, telling him we could go if he wanted.

'I don't want you to think I'm pushing you into meeting people.' I'd flapped, hesitating outside.

He'd waved the comment away, stroked my hair back from my face and kissed me instead, pulling me close to him as he did so. What would my mother think of me, standing in broad daylight (OK, under a streetlamp in the chill of late Autumn), snogging a man. I thought she'd probably be horrified and I smiled against his mouth.

'What are you smiling about?' he asked.

'Nothing,' I said, leaning into him, ready to smile all over again.

'Evening.' Luca's deep tones broke the moment and I pulled back, a little startled.

'Luca, hi!' His eyes were fixed on me and he smiled but there was something off about it. He leant and kissed me on the cheek. 'Umm, this is Adrian.'

'I kind of guessed that,' he said, holding out his hand, which Adrian took. 'Luca Donato. A friend of Bee's.'

'Hi.' Adrian nodded. 'Nice to meet you. We were just about to go in. Can I get you a drink?'

'Sure.' Luca stepped forward, held the door for us both and followed us in.

* * *

'Why not?' I asked, dropping my tone to as much of a whisper as I could in the noisy pub.

'I don't know. There's something about him.'

'Right.'

'I mean it. Be careful.'

'I know what I'm doing, Luca.'

He sat back, nodded and held his hands palm up.

'You just don't know him well enough.'

He repeated the nod and I gave up, pulling a face at Tia just as Adrian came back to join us, glancing at his watch.

'We'd better leave if we're going to make those reservations at Nobu.' From the corner of my eye, I saw Luca roll his eyes.

'Great!' I said, standing and grabbing my bag. I hugged Tia and waved at the others. Tia nudged Luca, who had turned in his seat and was chatting to some long-legged blonde at the next table.

'Bye, Luca.' He gave a brief wave and returned to his conversation. I glanced at Tia, who looked as uncomfortable as I felt. Luca never let his friends go without a hug or a kiss on the cheek.

When we got outside, I checked the message on my phone.

Ignore him. He's just distracted. Her legs go up to her armpits and carry on up.

Bless Tia for trying to smooth the situation but we both knew Luca was acting out of character, and neither of us knew why. But I wasn't about to let it ruin my evening. Instead, I turned to someone who had the time and inclination to be with me and snuggled against Adrian as he flagged down a taxi and we climbed inside.

18

———

'You seem nervous,' Adrian said softly, pausing as his hands moved deftly, slowly pulling down the zip of my dress. 'We don't have to do this, you know.'

I turned, pulled him towards me and kissed him, giving him all the indication needed to continue.

As his hands pushed the filmy fabric from my shoulders, a loud, obnoxious tune began to fill his apartment.

'It's my work phone. I'm going to ignore it,' he said, dropping his head to kiss my shoulder, but his jaw had tightened and I could tell his mind wasn't really on the job. The sound stopped and peace once again reigned. But the moment was short-lived as the noise began again.

'You should get that,' I said, taking a step back.

'I really don't want to,' he countered. His eyes, not to mention other parts of his anatomy, told me he meant it.

'I know. But they seem rather insistent. It could be important.'

Adrian held my gaze for a beat then strode across and snatched up the phone from a glass side table in the open-plan living room.

'Yes?' he snapped.

I remained where I was while he talked, barking questions and a few expletives. Feeling a little awkward and exposed, I subtly pulled the straps of my dress back up over my shoulders.

'I'll be there as soon as I can. Don't do anything else!' He stabbed at the phone's screen to hang up then turned to me.

'It's fine,' I said before he could say anything.

'Bee, I'm so sorry. Someone's cocked up on the foreign markets and may have just lost one of my clients several million.'

'Then you really do need to go.' I smiled. 'Really, it's fine. I hope you manage to sort out the mess.'

'Shit. So do I!' He buttoned up the few buttons I'd undone, made a few adjustments and grabbed his jacket from where he had thrown it over the back of a chair earlier, peering out of one of the large windows that I imagined flooded the apartment with light on brighter days. 'It's bloody pouring out there. Let me at least call you a car.' Adrian had use of an exclusive limousine service as a perk.

'Thanks, that'd be great. Although perhaps a walk might help me cool off.' I laughed, feeling my cheeks tint pink.

He stopped momentarily, snaked an arm around my waist and pulled me to him. 'I prefer it when you're hot,' he whispered into my ear and the tint matured to full-on postbox red. Pulling back, he met my eyes. 'We'll pick this up another time, OK?'

I nodded, feeling a little shy and wishing I could be far more confident and sure about it, parrying back some witty retort. Adrian let go and grabbed both our coats from the floor where we'd dropped them earlier, helping me into mine as we hurriedly left the apartment.

'Your car should be along any minute,' he said, seeing the one he'd requested via the exclusive app approaching down the street.

'Thank you. Good luck with the millions.'

He kissed my cheek, held up crossed fingers and then dashed from the cover of the doorway canopy to the waiting car.

I wrapped my arms around myself as I watched the tail lights disappear into the sheet of rain and out of sight around a corner. I was glad of Adrian's offer to arrange the car. The wind was building now and the rain was almost sideways as I hurried towards the sleek black car that pulled in, the driver advising who his pick-up was. Memories of my parents sighing if I needed taking anywhere still hovered in the back of my mind – I'd never quite been able to shake them off. I had always felt as if I was an inconvenience to their lives and they had made no effort to dispel that thought. I'd joined an after-school club or two but it'd always been up to me to get the bus back.

If it had been one with Luca in, his parents would pick me up and drop me home, repeatedly telling me it was no problem. When I'd done my ballet recital at the end of term, my parents hadn't attended. I'd looked at their calendar and seen they already had an engagement that night. It was just a casual dinner with friends that could easily have been rearranged, had that been their wish, but I'd learned by then if there was anything on the calendar, that was that. On the rare occasion the day was free, my mother would often be resting. Having a busy social life was clearly exhausting. The Donatos, however, had all come. Every single one of them, cheering and whooping when I'd entered the stage. They had been shooshed, which had made them and me laugh, relaxing me and resulting, according to my teacher, in one of my best performances.

It had encouraged me to continue the classes when I'd begun university, which I had, and loved. Of course, that had come to an abrupt halt along with the rest of my studies when I'd returned home after Dad's accident. Sometimes it felt as if someone had pressed pause on my life that day and I was still trying to find the play button. Maybe tonight, all of this with Adrian, was a start. But there was something niggling at the back of my mind that I couldn't put my finger on. I pushed it away, dismissing it as nerves, and continued towards home.

* * *

'Oh my God! Talk about timing!' Tia exclaimed when I rang her from the car.

'I know. I guess it could have been worse though.' I left her imagination to fill in those particular blanks.

'Doesn't bear thinking about!'

I giggled.

'So, how was it before the Phonus Interrruptus?'

'It was... nice.'

'Oh, no.'

'What?'

'Nice? You've got to admit it's been a while since you got this far with anyone and all you can say is that it was nice? It doesn't exactly ring of hot sexual tension and screaming the walls down.'

'We didn't get as far as the screaming.'

Tia laughed again. 'Fair enough. But what about the rest of it?'

'I really do like him.'

'I sense a but coming.'

'But—'

'Thought so.'

'Shoosh. But... is it weird that I sort of felt a sense of relief that he was called away?'

'A little. I mean, not necessarily weird but, Bee, you don't have to go that far if you're seriously not comfortable with someone.'

There was concern in her tone now. 'This challenge wasn't about sex. Please don't tell me you're feeling pressured to—'

'No. It's not that. I don't know. I guess I'm just nervous. It's been a while.'

'Honey, don't worry about that. It will be fine. But only when and if you want to. You know what men and their egos are like. Any bloke who thinks he's the first one you've wanted to go to bed with for some time will be strutting around like a peacock showing his colours off. Seriously, don't worry about it. And if he's as good a guy as he needs to be for you, then he'll take that into consideration and make sure you're comfortable with everything.'

'Yeah, I guess. I just don't want to make a fool of myself.'

'Hon, you won't. Jeez, girl, you really do need to stop worrying so much what other people think.'

'It's not always as easy as it sounds, is it?'

'Yeah, I know. Your parents really did a number on you, but you've got to remember you're worth more than that. Other people can see your value and appreciate you. You just need to believe that and the only person who can help you with that part is you.'

Tears sprang unexpectedly to my eyes.

'Bee?'

'Yeah?'

'Can I ask you something?'

'OK?' I drew out the word uncertainly and my skin prickled.

'What's up with Luca? I thought you two made up after your spat or whatever it was.'

'I don't think it was a spat really and we've talked about it and he was fine. Until I turned up to work with a hangover, that is. I know that wasn't professional and could put him in an awkward position, but I can't imagine he's ever not done that either.'

'We both know he's definitely done it.'

'Exactly.'

'So, what's his problem? I tried to ask him after you'd gone but he just clammed up.'

'Too busy chatting up the blonde, I imagine. He was certainly too busy to say goodbye properly.'

'Yeah, I saw that. It's not like him. I don't know what's going on with him lately. As soon as you left, he turned back to the rest of us and she left a short time after. Not that he said much even when he was back with us.'

'Me neither. He definitely doesn't like Adrian – he thinks he's a bad influence on me, apparently. But I think it's more his prejudice against stockbrokers rather than anything else.'

'Yep. Out of all the occupations you had to choose.' Tia laughed.

'I know,' I said, fishing in my bag for my keys as we pulled up to my flat. 'Although to be honest, I'm not sure it would have mattered what he did for a living. Luca would still find something to criticise about him. I know I haven't exactly had a bevy of boyfriends but every time I have met someone, there's something wrong with him, according to the Law of Luca.'

'That's true,' Tia replied in a thoughtful tone. 'But then again, you've never been overkeen on any of his girlfriends either.'

'It's not that. I don't mind them. It's more that whenever I'm next to one, I immediately look like an old bag lady. I'm sure they're nice women in their own right.'

'You do not look like an old bag lady!'

I closed the front door behind me, looked in the mirror and gave a private smile at my slightly dishevelled look. With a bit of luck the driver had put it down to the weather. 'Thanks. I'm going to jump in the shower now and head to bed.'

'OK. Sorry your evening got interrupted, but then again,

maybe from what you said, it might have been for the best after all.'

* * *

'Hi.' The deep voice behind me made me jump and spill the hot water I was pouring onto a sweet rhubarb herbal teabag in the staff kitchen.

'Shit!' I half turned at the same time as grabbing a wodge of kitchen towel and mopping up the mess. Luca was standing in the doorway. 'Oh. Hi. Sorry, miles away.'

'You looked it. You OK? Did you burn yourself?' He crossed the room and was standing beside me, trying to take my hand. I could smell the expensive shower gel he used and noticed a tiny nick on his face where he'd cut himself shaving this morning.

'I'm fine,' I said, brushing him away and grabbing more towels. It went over the counter, not me.' I looked up again briefly and met a concerned gaze. 'Seriously. I'm fine.'

'I'm sorry about last night.'

'What?' I flushed and made a mental note not to tell Tia anything else about me and Adrian.

'I know I was rude when you said goodbye.'

'Oh. That.'

He tilted his head. 'What did you think I meant?'

'Nothing,' I replied, far too quickly.

'Bee. What happened?' His expression had darkened, the planes hardened on his face and a muscle flickered on the right side of his jaw.

'Nothing happened, Luca.'

'Why don't I believe you? What aren't you telling me?'

'Luca. Stop being so over Alpha. I'm fine. And yes, you were kind of rude last night. What's up with you?' I swung the spotlight back on him and hoped he'd drop the other line of questioning.

'Nothing.'

'Why don't I believe you? What aren't you telling me?' I raised a brow, throwing his own questions back at him.

'Smart arse.'

I pulled a face, indicating he might be right, but said nothing more, leaving him to fill the silence. Luca glanced round, checking that we didn't have extra company. 'I just don't like him.'

'Who?'

'Adrian.'

'You started acting weird before that, but let's deal with one problem at a time. Why don't you like him?'

'I don't know. There's something about him.'

'The fact that he's a stockbroker, perhaps?'

Luca at least had the decency to shrug. 'I admit that doesn't exactly endear him to me.'

'And the rest?'

'Like I said, I don't know. I don't think he's good enough for you.'

'You don't even know him, Luca. And you made no attempt to get to know him last night. You seemed more intent on getting to know the woman on the next table.'

'She was interesting.'

'Yes, I could see that,' I said, dryly. 'It just would have been nice if you'd made an effort. I like him and he likes me. Shouldn't that be enough for you?'

'Not if he's not good enough for you.' He said it matter-of-factly, as if there were already irrefutable evidence.

'How would you even know that?'

'He got you drunk on a workday for one, just after you started a new job. That doesn't exactly scream respect to me, or indicate he has your best interests at heart.'

I threw the damp paper towels in the bin with more force than was needed. 'We've been over this. I've apologised. Drinking that night was my choice. He didn't force them down me. Just as he didn't force me to go home with him last night.' Luca's face lost some of its colour. I had no idea why I'd even told him that, but I'd had enough of his disapproval when it came to boyfriends, and specifically Adrian. Dropping that in probably hadn't helped my case but, God, he was infuriating sometimes. The silence stretched on.

'Morning!' Jerry's cheerful tones broke the silence as he bounced happily into the kitchen. Jerry always reminded me of a golden retriever with his sandy hair and almost permanent smile. He invariably seemed pleased to see people and had an enthusiasm for anything and everything. But even he stopped dead upon entering the room. The tension between Luca and me had melded itself into an almost physical forcefield.

'Hi, Jerry,' I replied, forcing as normal a smile as possible onto my face, but, from the look on his, it had more of a rictus quality to it than I was aiming for.

'Jerry.' Luca nodded. He gave a final glance at me and then headed out, striding towards his own office.

'Everything OK?' Jerry asked.

I shrugged. 'Think he got out the wrong side of the bed this morning.' *Or the wrong bed...*

Jerry smiled and nodded but I could see he didn't buy it in the slightest.

'Well, better get on,' I said, picking up my tea and making my way to my own desk. Burying myself in work, I kept my head down and ploughed through my current project for the rest of the day. Luca had gone out at ten-thirty and hadn't returned by the end of the day and I couldn't say I wasn't relieved. I glanced around the office as I left. I really liked it here. The work was interesting and the people were lovely. But if Luca and I couldn't sort out whatever the hell it was that was going on between us, I knew I'd have to say goodbye to it all.

_____

19

As I rounded the corner to the train station, Luca's car sat idling on a double yellow line. He stepped out and I met his gaze.

'The traffic news just said your line was shut. Reports of a person on the line or something. I can give you a lift home.' He paused for a moment. 'Assuming you don't have other plans.'

Like most things in life, the Tube was excellent when it was functioning but when a spanner went in the works, it was a huge pain in the bum and I definitely wasn't having much luck with my journeys lately. This was another disadvantage of living further away from the city than the others – there was always extra potential for travel chaos.

'No, no other plans.' Adrian was away for a few days and the only plans I'd made were to get home, eat and curl up with a new book. 'It's rather out of your way.'

'I don't mind.' He glanced up at the sky as large plops of rain began to fall around us. 'Come on, Bee. Please. Plus, I'm going to get nicked if I hang around here much longer.' At that, a white van beeped at him, accompanied by a hand gesture. Luca wisely, and thankfully, ignored both of them.

'I'm sure there are replacement buses.'

He gave me an even look. Nobody in their right mind ever wanted to take a replacement bus if there was a better alternative. And Luca's car, warm, comfortable and offering door-to-door service, was definitely a better alternative.

'OK. If you're sure.'

'I am,' he said, moving to the passenger side to open the door for me. I slid into the soft leather, out of the rain, and tucked my bag down in the footwell.

Luca got back in, closed the door on the noise of London and pulled out into the traffic, joining the slow snaking crawl of vehicles heading out of the city. Classic FM played quietly in the background and we both just sat there, for once, short of words for each other.

'At least it's not weird or anything,' he said at last, and a bubble of laughter burst from me, breaking the tension.

'No. That would be awful.'

He looked across at me briefly, as the traffic stopped yet again, and laid a hand over mine. His large tanned one making my small pale one look like a child's.

'Sorry, Bee.'

'For what?'

'I know things have been a bit awkward and I shouldn't have said anything about you having a hangover at work the other day.'

'It was a headache, not a hangover.'

He threw me a quick glance, a smile tipping the corners of his mouth up. Even in the low light of the car's interior, I could see his dark eyes twinkling with amusement. 'It was totally a hangover.'

'OK, fine. It was. But it's not like I make a habit of it. And if I'd done it at my old company you wouldn't have said anything.'

'I know you don't make a habit of it. It just seemed... a little out of character for you, and I guess that bothered me. I know you like this guy, but...'

He leant back against the headrest, his eyes focused on the row of tail lights in front of him.

'But what?' I asked.

'I guess I don't want you to change. I like you the way you are.'

'What? Sad and alone?'

The traffic remained stationary and Luca turned to me. 'Is that really how you feel?'

'Of course not!' I said, doing my best to laugh it off. From the look on his face, Luca wasn't entirely convinced. And if the truth be known, neither was I. The words had just tumbled out. Flippant and without thought. *Was that how I really felt?* 'Stop looking at me like that. It was just a joke.'

He held the gaze a moment longer before turning back to the road, inching another few feet forward.

'I'm not changing, Luca. I just got a bit carried away. It won't happen on a school night again. I promise.'

He shook his head but I saw the smile.

'So where is he tonight?'

'Away. Some friend's stag do. But you know how it is. It's never just an evening these days, is it?'

'Rarely. How long's he gone for?'

'Five days, I think.'

'Anywhere nice?'

'Las Vegas.'

Luca didn't say anything but, then again, he didn't need to.

'I know what you're thinking.'

'I doubt it.'

'Blokes on a stag do and that whole "what happens in Vegas stays in Vegas" thing.'

'OK. So you do know what I'm thinking. Which probably means you're thinking the same thing.'

'Not at all.' I shrugged. 'It's not like we're serious or anything. We've only been out a few times.'

Luca suddenly pulled the car off towards a side road. 'Sod this. Just come back to my place. We can eat there and I'll run you home later when the traffic's died down. Is that OK? We're both getting older just sitting here.'

'Yep. Why not? My train line should hopefully be back up running by then. I can always jump on that, save you going out again.'

'I'd rather drive you.' Luca could be a pain in the arse at times, but he had a chivalrous heart.

'Thanks, Luca. That would be great.'

He turned the car and headed towards the sleek modern apartment block where he lived.

* * *

'So, the Vegas thing really doesn't bother you? You know what it's like.' He was adding ingredients to a pan, stirring as he did so. 'Here, taste that. Careful, it's hot.'

'Mmm. Yum! When will it be ready?' I peered forward into the pan from my vantage point on one of the kitchen island's bar stools.

'About half an hour. But I have these to keep you going.' He pulled a small tray of anti pasti from the counter and placed it in front of me before turning the heat down and covering the pan with a lid. That done, he came round and took the seat beside me, joining me in picking at the nibbles.

'It really does amaze me you're not married already.' I laughed, forking up a piece of salami.

'I know, right? I'm quite the catch.' His mouth was serious but his eyes shone with merriment.

'Shame about the ego.'

He pulled a face at me and stabbed at some wild rocket. 'What is it about blokes and Vegas?'

'I don't know. You tell me. You're a bloke. I was the one practically shoved out of the way so the touts could hand you sex workers' business cards when we went.'

'Yeah, that was kind of weird. I mean, you could have been my girlfriend or wife and they all just leaned across you to try and shove those cards into my hands. Who does that?' He shook his head, stabbing a roasted tomato stuffed with cheese. 'Weird place.'

'Obviously they didn't think my league was high enough to have been attached to you.'

'Oh, ha ha! It wasn't that. And all that league crap is just rubbish anyway. You know that.'

'Says the man who only dates women who could feature in a high-end glossy magazine.'

'That's not true.'

I gave him a sidelong look.

'It is not.'

'It is too!'

'You're imagining things due to your own insecurities.'

'I'm bloody not. Right. Hang on.' I leant down and fished about in my handbag, retrieving my phone. Balancing it in front of us both, I video-called Tia.

'Hi, hon! You all right? Hi, Luc.' Tia was reclining against Jono on their sofa. Her hair was shoved up, her face was bare and she still looked bloody amazing. Luca waved and let me speak.

'Yep. Quick question. I've just told Luca he only dates women who look like they fell out of *Vogue* magazine, a fact he vehemently denies. Would you agree with the statement?'

Jono looked at the screen briefly, grinned and turned back to whatever they were watching on TV.

Tia pulled a face. 'Sorry, Luc, babe. You kinda do. You definitely have a type – and that type is super-glam, long-legged model-looking types.'

'I do not have a type.'

'Mate. You have a type,' Jono interjected.

Luca puffed for a moment or two. 'Thanks for the solidarity, pal.'

Jono shrugged and grinned. 'You did ask.'

'Actually, Bee asked,' Luca replied pedantically and Jono just laughed, returning again to his viewing.

'Did you seriously not realise?' Tia asked.

Luca frowned, dark brows knitting together. We both waited for him to say something but he seemed lost in his own thoughts.

'Thanks, both of you. Sorry for the interruption.' They waved and I hung up.

'Wow. You really didn't realise, did you?'

He shook his head.

'No one is criticising you, you know. It doesn't matter. Lots of people have a type.'

He didn't reply. Instead, he got up and went round the other side of the island to the hob and gave the pan a stir.

'How's it looking?' I asked, sensing he needed a change of subject.

'Good. So you like this guy, yeah?'

I looked up at Luca. 'I think so.'

'You think so? Bee, you slept with him. Unless you've changed personalities in the past few weeks, I'm guessing you really like him. It's not like you to just jump into bed.' I blushed furiously, the colour deepening as I got annoyed with myself for blushing in the first place.

'Don't make me sound like such a prude.'

'I'm not! I'm saying you're discerning, not frigid!'

'Oh. And yes. I do like him. But, if you must know, I haven't slept with him.'

Luca's brow wrinkled as he looked back up from stirring. 'I thought you said you went back to his place. I assumed that meant that things had...' he made a rolling motion with the hand not occupied stirring our dinner '... moved to the next level. Which, like I say, seems pretty fast for you.'

'Just because I don't sleep with my dates on day one like some people...' I glared at him, but it was pointless trying to make Luca Donato look apologetic for that particular scenario.

'Not always. I just don't want you thinking you have to do something you're not ready for just to get this guy to like you.'

I sat up straighter. 'You think the only reason a guy would like me was if I was easy? Thanks for that.' I could feel my cheeks flaming from a mixture of anger, hurt and embarrassment.

'No! That's not what I meant.' Luca dropped the wooden spoon back in the pan and strode round to where I was now pushing myself off the stool. Suddenly, I'd lost my appetite.

'It bloody well sounded like it.'

Luca held my upper arms, gently but firm enough that I had to look at him. 'Bee. Seriously. That isn't what I meant. You know I think you're amazing and beautiful and funny and smart and loads of other things. I'm just not sure you always realise that, and I don't want you feeling pressured to do anything you don't want to.'

'I wanted to,' I said, defiantly, tilting my head up to meet the intense dark gaze. For a moment a shadow flickered across Luca's features. But then it was gone. Maybe it was a trick of the light.

Maybe I just imagined it, but he dropped his hands and shoved them into the pockets of his suit trousers, stepping back as he did so.

'OK.'

'But as it turned out, there was a work emergency and he had to leave before anything much happened.'

'Right.'

Should I tell him I was relieved about that? But that I didn't know why?

'How did you feel about that?'

'About what?' I asked, stalling for time and ruing the fact that Luca Donato knew me far too well.

The patient, half-amused, half-frustrated expression dropped back onto his face. He gave a small head tilt, telling me that he knew exactly what I was doing.

I shrugged in reply.

'That's it?' he said, repeating my gesture.

'I guess.'

'Interesting.' He moved to walk back to the hob, but I caught his arm.

'No. No,' I corrected, 'it's not interesting. It's not interesting at all, at least not in the way your tone suggests.'

'I beg to differ.' He was almost smiling now.

'It's not! It's exactly the opposite of interesting.'

'That would be uninteresting.'

'Exactly! It's entirely uninteresting.'

'If you say so.'

'Argh! I hate it when you do this!' He smiled even wider. 'I know I'm going to regret this, but why is it so interesting?'

'You really want to know?' He flicked the long-lash gaze up at me as his lips tasted the sauce. 'Almost done.'

'Good. I'm starving. And yes. I really want to know.' I wasn't sure that I did but I had to now.

Luca laid the spoon down and came back round to where I was now leaning against the kitchen island.

'Because your reaction tells me something.'

'Oh, does it really?'

'Yep. It tells me you're not as ready to commit to this guy as you thought you were.'

'I'm not committing to anyone! It was just going to be sex.'

Luca's gaze fixed on mine and I wanted to look away, but something kept me held there, like the tractor beams in *Star Trek*.

'It's never just sex with you, Bee. You're not made that way. If you're with someone like that, they mean something to you. And it should be reciprocal, otherwise he's not worth it.'

'Maybe I'm changing. Maybe I've had enough of being dull, quiet old Bee, destined to be the maiden aunt and godmother to everyone else's kids!'

Luca's face darkened. 'Sweetheart, you're none of those things. The only person who thinks that is you. And, while I said before I didn't want you to change, I maybe need to correct that. Because that perspective you have of yourself is so wrong. You're strong and smart and beautiful and the man you're with should make you feel all of those things. And I know that perhaps I'm biased against The Stockbroker, but if he's not making you feel all that then there's something wrong there.'

'He does make me feel... things.'

'I just know that no phone call in the world would have made me give up a chance like that.'

'It was important. These things happen. You know that.' Luca was close to me now and I could smell the fading musk of his aftershave. He never wore a lot. Just enough to tempt the senses.

'Some things are more important.'

'Someone was about to lose millions of pounds.' I heard the

falter in my voice and put a hand behind me, resting it on the back of the bar chairs at the kitchen island, suddenly feeling light-headed. My pulse kicked up and a warmth flooded my body. Luca was looking down at me, close now, not saying a word. My own brain, however, was talking nineteen to the dozen. *It's just because you haven't eaten and has absolutely nothing to do with Luca Donato.*

Of course it was right. It had to be right. I'd been this close and more with Luca plenty of times. We'd shared a bed on the odd occasion when we'd been away. Nothing ever happened – it just saved money and it was company. Someone to chat to once the lights went out. But right now... *Were we having a moment?*

'If it had been your money, I'm sure you'd have rather he answered it.' My voice came out more raw than usual and Luca's head tilted ever so slightly.

'Oh, I'd definitely want him to answer it.' He held my gaze a beat longer, then dropped a gentle kiss on my forehead before stepping back to return to the shining induction hob where goodness simmered. 'This is done. You ready to eat?'

I blinked and found the edge of the stool with my hands behind me, hoisting myself onto it. Nope. No moment. Just a lack of food. Luca was just Luca. Which was a good thing. Obviously.

'Absolutely,' I forced out, finding my voice again. 'I don't think I ate enough at lunchtime. I feel a bit light-headed.'

Luca's gaze lifted and locked with mine for a moment but he said nothing.

20

The next few weeks passed in a blur. The two-week placement at Donato Solutions had been extended to a four-weeks, but yesterday Jo from HR had handed me a letter formally offering me the position on a permanent basis. The salary was a vast improvement on my previous job, plus it had perks. I'd never had perks before! Private medical insurance, a pension contribution, an extra five days' holiday plus the option to earn more the longer you stayed, not to mention the stocked kitchen, which had already enabled me to begin having a more healthy lunch each day. It had also helped me to actually *have* lunch, which sometimes still felt like a novelty. It was company policy that everyone took their lunch hour away from their desk. As well as the kitchen, there was a lounge area to sit in with lots of natural daylight, plus a selection of books that rotated as people read and swapped them. A polite notice on the wall requested that anyone watching films, etc, must use headphones so as not to disturb others. I wasn't sure when the whole 'I'm just going to be obnoxious and play my video/music to everyone whether they want to hear it or not' culture became a thing, but it was a real bugbear of mine, and it was good to see that everyone abided by this simple rule. Now we just needed the world at large to do the same.

Luca and I seemed to have fallen back into our old pattern, and the weirdness that had begun at his parents' house that day, thankfully, seemed to have dropped away. Although both of us were definitely busier these days. Luca was working on a big project for a prestigious Japanese client, and, by the sounds of it, now once again dating most of the women on the site we'd signed up with.

'Still not found The One?' I asked teasingly as I caught him scrolling a profile in the kitchen while waiting for the kettle to boil. It was just me and him in there and my voice was low. The rest of the staff by now knew we were friends and I was pretty sure there were rumours and suspicions we were more than that, but neither of us entertained that idea or were bothered by it. It wouldn't have been the first time people had misunderstood our friendship. At one hotel we'd gone to for a walking weekend, the lady had checked us in and then smilingly advised that she'd given us the honeymoon suite, proudly announcing that she could always spot a couple in love. I'd been about to correct her when she'd continued her spiel, telling us that strawberries and a chilled bottle of champagne were being sent up on the house. I'd leant my head against Luca's arm and he had squeezed my waist as we'd both smiled and thanked her. OK, so maybe we should have corrected her, but we hadn't wanted to make her feel awkward and the champagne was delicious.

Luca flicked his eyes up to me then back to the screen. 'I'm choosy.'

I snorted in my head. Well, keeping it in my head had been the plan.

'What's that supposed to mean?'

'Sorry. You weren't supposed to hear that.'

'But I did. So explain.'

I nudged him out of the way and made us both a cup of tea. 'It doesn't mean anything.'

'Clearly it does."

'All right,' I said, putting his mug in front of him. 'I suppose when someone says they are choosy, people—'

'You mean you.'

'People,' I reiterated, 'tend to associate "choosy" with those who have a specific list of requirements before they go out with anyone. That just doesn't really sound like you at the moment.'

'It's hard to tell what someone's really like from a few lines on a bio. How else am I supposed to find out what they're really like?'

'That is true. And I'm not criticising you. Just saying.'

'Well, I could say that you aren't choosy enough.'

'What's that supposed to mean?'

'You've only been out with a few blokes off the site and then settled with Stockbroker Guy. How do you know if he's the right one for you? The fact you felt relief when he got called away just as you were about to have sex indicates you're not sure.'

I flapped my hands, shooshing him! 'I knew I shouldn't have told you about that,' I said, pushing his mug towards him before picking up my own. 'And I'm not "settling", as you put it. I just like him.'

'You might like someone else better.' Luca gave a shrug, then watched me over the rim of his mug.

'What do you suggest I do? Treat the site like a sweet shop and try one of everything like you are?' I put the mug down. 'I'm not like you, Luca. You know that. I don't enjoy the whole dating process at the best of times, and now we're embroiled in this bloody competition thing, I'm already way out of my comfort zone.'

'You pushed yourself out of your comfort zone with work – finally – and look what's happened. You already seem happier and more fulfilled, and you're certainly valued here a lot more than you ever were at your old place. Comfort zones are nice, but stepping outside them can bring things you never dreamed of.'

'What is it that bothers you so much about me and Adrian?'

'Nothing. Except he's not good enough for you.'

'You always think that. I'd need to be a bloody nun for you to be happy and then even wedded to God wouldn't be good enough for you.'

Luca grinned. 'You are extremely keen on *The Sound of Music*. Perhaps there's a hankering for the convent life in you after all.'

'Maria left the convent, if you remember, and got married. So, there's that argument down the drain.'

'Do you want to get married?'

'Oh! Oh! I'm so sorry! I didn't mean to interrupt!' Gloria from Accounts was standing in the doorway blushing bright red, shuffling her feet awkwardly and doing a poor job of hiding the grin that had spread across her face.

Luca glanced at me, bemused at her reaction, before it dawned on him.

'Oh, Gloria. No! You didn't interrupt anything. We were just chatting about life in general.'

'So... I didn't interrupt a proposal?' Disappointment cloaked her features.

'Umm, no.'

'Oh.'

Luca looked back at me again, his eyes begging for help. I shrugged.

'Sorry,' he added, with his own slight shrug.

Gloria smiled, but it was obvious her heart wasn't in it. 'Oh, don't be daft. I just love a good wedding and seeing two people in love making that commitment. Probably a bit old-fashioned now, I suppose.' She bustled in and retrieved a mug with a photo of a dog on it from the cupboard.

'No, not at all.' Luca smiled. 'I'm with you on that.'

She turned and smiled up at him, then patted his hand. 'It's about time you found someone to look after you, duck.'

'Put up with him, you mean,' I mumbled quietly. Luca shot me a look, pulling a 'very funny' face over Gloria's head.

She glanced around, including me in the conversation. 'That's probably a bit old-fashioned too these days, but you know what I mean.'

'I think the ideal is that you both look after each other, really.'

'Quite right,' she said, smiling at me. 'And do you have someone?' she asked with an innocent tone to her voice, but it was pretty obvious to both of us she was fishing madly.

'She's seeing a stockbroker.' Luca answered for me.

'Oh!' Gloria stirred her low-fat, low-sugar and likely zero-taste hot chocolate, clearly doing her best not to appear disappointed. 'That's nice.' I saw her sneak a glance up at Luca, but his face remained impassive.

'Well, I'd better get back to work before I get fired.' I smiled at Gloria, who smiled back, more naturally this time.

'Somehow I don't think that's going to happen.'

'Oh, I don't know. I heard the boss here can be a real tyrant when he wants to be.'

'You're hilarious.' Luca quirked an eyebrow at me.

'I know. I put that on my CV. I'm pretty sure it clinched me the position.'

'I'll clinch you in a minute. Get back to work and stop causing trouble.' He grinned at me and I wandered back to my desk, tea in hand. As I glanced back, Gloria had backed Luca into one of the walls and their discussion seemed quite intense. Back at my desk, I rang his mobile.

I leant back a little in my chair so I could see into the kitchen.

'Luca Donato.'

'I thought you might need extricating,' I whispered into the phone.

'Right. Yes. OK. That's a great idea actually. Let me find the paperwork. If you can give me a minute, I'm just away from my desk but I'll ring you straight back. Thanks for the call. Speak soon.'

I hung up and, moments later, Luca walked past my desk and headed towards his own. After a minute a message popped up on my phone.

Life saver. Xxx

* * *

I'd been seeing Adrian for several weeks now and the situation of a few weeks ago hadn't yet been repeated. He'd mentioned that perhaps it had been just as well, and that things had moved quite fast, and he got the sense that I might not really have been ready. I'd felt awkward and embarrassed but he'd brushed it aside and told me that he actually found it quite a turn-on and that the waiting just made it hotter. But tonight, things seemed different. Whatever Luca said, I didn't want to try dating a tonne of different men when I felt happy enough with the one I was with. I could relax with him, and the more I saw him, the more I relaxed with him. Which was why tonight I'd put on my sexiest undies and packed a toothbrush in my handbag...

'Wow.' Adrian ran his eyes up and down me when I met him in the bar. 'You look amazing.'

'Thanks,' I said, accepting the kiss and loving the feel of his hands around my waist as he pressed me closer.

A lecherous cheer went up nearby and I pulled away. Adrian kept his arm around me and, with the other hand, gestured impolitely that the group could go away.

'Do you know them?' I asked.

'Yeah.' He laughed, looking back at the group of men and shaking his head. 'Lads from work. We often come in here to wind down a bit. Thought it would be easier if we met here. You don't mind, do you?'

'Umm, no. Of course not.' Adrian was still in his work suit and had clearly been here since the close of day. 'Did you want to go on to the restaurant now?' I asked, thinking that perhaps some food might help soak up some of the alcohol he'd already started on.

'Yeah. Sure. If you want.'

I looked at the big station clock on the wall. 'It's just I thought we had reservations for seven.'

His eyes followed mine. 'Oh. Shit. Is that the time? Yeah, right. We'd better go. Ha, time flies when you're having fun, eh?'

'Yes,' I said to his retreating back as he dropped his arm and left me standing in the middle of the bar while he went off to say goodbye to his mates. I guessed he wasn't ready to introduce me to them just yet. That was fine. I got that. Men were different that way. I saw a couple of them look over and then back to Adrian, saying something that was followed by a loud, drunken guffaw. I pulled my coat tighter and waited. A group of people coming in from the street bumped into me, knocking me forwards. I stumbled and regained my balance. No one else appeared to have noticed. I moved further towards the door, out of the way of the main Friday night crowd, and waited.

Ten minutes later Adrian finally appeared through the crowd. 'Ready to go?'

I'd been ready for over a quarter of an hour but I bit my tongue, gave a smile that felt a little too tight for my face and pulled open the door, my breath taken by the northerly bite to the cold night air. Adrian hailed a cab and rattled on about something one of his mates had said, which was apparently hilarious. I didn't quite get it but smiled along with him and surreptitiously glanced at the time on my phone. We were now nearly half an hour late for our dinner reservation. My stomach growled loudly, thankfully drowned out by the chugging of the black cab, and I hoped the restaurant hadn't yet given away our table.

No longer with his raucous friends, Adrian became more attentive and glanced at his Rolex.

'We're a little late, I think.'

He threw an arm around my shoulders and planted a kiss on my neck. As his lips remained there, I shifted subtly, pulling away, smiling almost apologetically, but the last thing I needed as I was settling into my new job was a giant love bite on my neck. I'd never been a fan of them and rather thought they'd gone out of fashion, but the fleeting expression on Adrian's face showed that he felt differently.

'Sorry,' I said, suddenly feeling I had to explain. 'New job and all that.'

He shrugged. 'Fair enough.'

The cab pulled up and he paid before exiting, waiting for me to follow. Catching me as I did so, a possessive arm clutched my waist, pulling me closer. I could smell the beer he'd been drinking before I'd arrived. It wasn't exactly the evening I'd imagined so far but there was time for it to improve. 'I'll just have to find somewhere that's less visible...' His words were soft in my ear and suddenly things felt as if they might be looking up. I definitely still wasn't a fan of love bites but, pressed up against Adrian in the chill night, with his breath warm and full of promise, there was every chance of me being persuaded otherwise.

The restaurant was busy and looked full to capacity as Adrian held the door and I stepped through before he followed me in. We were greeted by the maître d'.

'May I help you?'

'Hi. Yes. Got a table booked, name of DeVere.' Adrian made a show of checking the expensive watch again. 'I know we're a bit late.' He held out a hand to shake the other man's and I noticed the subtle exchange of a high-value bank note between the two. 'Hope that's not a problem.'

'Not at all, sir. May I take your coats and then I'll have you shown to your table?' I studied my shoes, and shifted my weight, slightly uncomfortable with the whole transaction and wishing we had instead just been able to be on time, therefore bypassing the whole need for the charade.

I slipped my coat off and handed it to another obliging member of staff, who had magically appeared from nowhere, thanking him as I did so. Adrian handed his over but barely glanced at the man, his eyes scanning the room and then landing on me.

'Wow. Sexy dress.' He tilted his head behind me and checked out the low back, exposed as it was, my having pinned my hair up. I'd ummed and aahed about both the dress and the hair for over an hour before finally ringing Tia and being told to 'Yes, definitely wear it' and 'Hair up. That way it shows off the dress, plus you can shake it out sexily later on'. I wasn't convinced I could pull off the sexy-shake-your-hair thing. It usually looked as if I were trying to escape a wasp when I attempted such things. Tia, however, was a natural and, at the look on my face, had given me brief instructions and a demon-

stration. I was still unconvinced of my capabilities as a seduc-
tress and decided I'd just take my hair down like a normal
person if it came to it and that would have to do. Better that
than completely humiliating myself. The last time I'd tried it a
concerned look had come across the face of the man in question
and all I'd done was put my back out. Not really the effect I was
going for and the episode had put rather a damper on the
evening's subsequent activities.

But, so far, now that Adrian's focus seemed to be back on us,
the dress, at least, was having somewhat of the desired effect. I
followed the waiter showing us to our table, doing my best to
push away visions of other diners who weren't in the position of
being able to buy off their tardiness (like me!) being turfed off
'our' table and being stuck with one by the toilets.

'You all right?' Adrian asked when the waiter had melted
away into the background, leaving us to make our choices.

'Yes. Of course.'

'You don't seem quite yourself.'

I glanced at the woman on the next table. A huge diamond
perched upon a platinum band on her left hand and several
other assorted rings caught the candlelight and sparkled and
flashed as she moved. I suspected that just her rings alone would
buy my flat, with change left over. I tucked my bare hands onto
my lap and tried not to feel quite so out of place. And out of my
depth.

'I'm OK.' I smiled and began to scan the menu.

'Is this because we were late or because I handed the guy
money?' Adrian had leant across the table, his voice low and
brow darker than it had been a moment ago.

I looked back up from the menu. 'Huh?'

'You seem pissed off for some reason.'

I shifted in my chair, aware that the woman at the next table had now stopped talking and was fiddling with her glass stem and trying not to be seen earwigging our conversation.

'I'm fine, really. I'm just... used to more casual dining and I don't want to mess up.' There. I'd said it. He could either laugh at me or pity me. But I wasn't going to lie. I did feel uncomfortable. I'd been to posher places. Luca had money and liked good food but I'd never felt so conspicuous before, worried about saying or doing the wrong thing and showing Adrian up. One time, my parents had gone out for a meal and, unusually, I'd been allowed to accompany them. It was my parents' favourite – a swanky French restaurant tucked away in a corner of London. The hush I heard the moment I entered tonight had reminded me of that night, taken me back there and brought up all my insecurities. But really, what did they expect, serving a twelve-year-old snails with neither consultation nor instruction? It wasn't exactly my fault when one escaped from my tongs and hit another diner. The sudden snap of his head caused his toupee to dislodge and fall onto the romantic candlelit set-up he'd been sharing with his much younger companion. I watched in a sort of fascinated horror as he snatched it back, hurriedly smothered the flames with a linen napkin and then returned it to his shiny pate as tiny wisps of smoulder twisted into the air above him. I never went out to dinner with my parents again.

Of course, when I told Luca he'd roared with laughter, dragged me in and begged me to retell the story to the rest of his family, who had reacted in the same manner, finally enabling me to see just how ridiculous the entire scenario had been. While I'd been with the Donatos, the tenterhooks I'd been on during the meal, which had obviously increased tenfold following the snail flinging, had dissipated. They'd made me see it wasn't my fault. But the feeling had returned the moment I went home. And right now, those same feelings had reared their heads. Suddenly, I felt twelve years old again and scared I was about to show myself, and others, up.

'You'll be fine.' Adrian smiled and squeezed my arm before leaning in again. 'Besides, looking at you in that dress is making me doubt we'll be here long.'

I felt colour rising to my cheeks and tried to hide behind the menu. 'It's cute that you blush. I have an idea you're going to be doing a lot of that...'

'Shall we order?' I asked, my voice a little higher pitched than usual.

Adrian watched me for a moment, then smiled and nodded. 'Snails to start?' he suggested, studying his menu. 'You do like them, don't you?' I felt my stomach drop.

21

'Bee?'

I turned to see Luca about to sit at another table with two smart-looking gentlemen. One had a pleasant, smiling face while the other looked as though he'd begun the morning by treading barefoot on a slug and the day had gone downhill from there. Luca excused himself and approached us. He bent and kissed me on the cheek and then held out his hand to shake Adrian's.

'Nice to see you again, Aidan.'

'Adrian.'

Smiling, Luca made an apologetic gesture and I kicked him from the side of the table, knowing full well he knew my date's name and was doing it for no other reason than to wind me up.

'Snails?' he asked, looking down at the now empty dishes. 'Didn't think you'd ever eat those again after SnailGate.' He grinned.

'SnailGate?' Adrian asked, his head tilted enquiringly.

I waved my hand around. 'Something silly from when I was a child. Don't worry about it. I love snails now. Obviously.'

Actually, I'd hated every mouthful, praying that the next one would taste better. It didn't.

Luca studied me a moment. 'Obviously.'

'What are you doing here?' I asked brightly, while shooting him a private look that belied my tone.

'Business. Nothing exciting.'

'Trying to impress your clients,' Adrian noted and nodded, approvingly.

'Actually, they're trying to impress me,' Luca replied.

I fiddled with my hair and looked away.

'Nice dress, Bee. You look gorgeous.'

'Umm, thanks.' My hand returned to its nervous fiddling.

'Glad to see you're treating her well.' Luca smiled at Adrian but I could see the steel beneath it. Oh, perfect. Luca was always protective of me – always had been – but right now I didn't need any knights in Savile Row armour.

'What makes you think I wouldn't?'

'He didn't mean it like that,' I said quickly. 'Hadn't you better return to your guests, Luca?'

'Like Bee says, didn't mean any offence.' Luca held up his hands. 'It's just she's met some right ones since we started this challenge thing.'

Adrian frowned and glanced at me. 'Challenge thing?'

'Yeah. I'm sure Bee must have told you. She's never believed in all this online dating. Doesn't reckon you can find anything meaningful.'

'Luca! I think your companions are waiting.' I laid my hand on his arm and gave him a subtle shove. Unfortunately, between Luca's bulk, and my far smaller size and current position, it did absolutely nothing.

'Anyway, I think you can, so our friend challenged us to find out. Bee's had such bad luck so far I thought she was going to prove me wrong and win but—' he glanced between us '—seems like she's found someone that might change her mind about the whole online dating stuff.'

'I see,' Adrian said, smiling tightly at Luca. 'I guess that would mean you'd lose after all.'

'Maybe.' Luca returned a trademark winning smile and the woman on the next table knocked over her glass. I rolled my eyes and gave him another kick. 'Well, I'd better get back. Catch up tomorrow, Bee. Nice to see you again, Adrian.' With that, he turned and walked back to his table. Within moments, even the sour-faced chap had the hint of a smile about him. Luca could charm the birds from the sky. I, however, wasn't so charmed by him right this moment.

'Sorry about that.'

'No problem. He doesn't really like me, does he?'

'Of course he does. Well, he would if he got to know you, I mean. But that doesn't matter, does it? I mean...' I gripped my hands together on my lap and met Adrian's eyes '... I like you. That's the main thing, isn't it?'

Adrian grinned and, underneath the table, his hand slid to my thigh. 'That's definitely the main thing.'

Although I was cross with Luca for interrupting us and then purposely saying the wrong name, his appearance had, oddly, seemed to focus Adrian's attention on me even more. Unintentionally, he'd actually done me a favour.

The main course was delicious and, despite Adrian's earlier insinuation, we did order dessert. I was completely full but he insisted on the waiter bringing two spoons and, as a good person, I agreed to help him out with the disposal of a wickedly delicious warm chocolate pudding that melted in the middle, pouring forth yet more scrumptiousness into the dish, mixing with the single cream moat that surrounded the creation.

'So, you weren't a fan of online dating, then?'

I dabbed at my face and tried to subtly check in the back of an unused teaspoon as to whether I was now sporting chocolate smiles around my mouth.

'Not really, no. I mean, I know it can work out for some people, but I'd also heard a lot of horror stories too.'

'Oh God, yeah,' Adrian agreed as he paid the bill, refusing my offer of any contribution, and made a gesture to a waiter to retrieve our coats. 'I mean, I've had women who won't leave me alone. They seem to think that just because you go out for a while, it's suddenly something all meaningful and deep. But I'm with you.'

Despite having just belted my warm winter coat, I suddenly felt a chill trickle through me.

'You're with me?' I repeated, not quite understanding. At least, hoping I hadn't understood.

'Yeah,' he said, gesturing me to go through the door the doorman was now holding open for us. I thanked him and Adrian followed me through. 'About online dating not being about finding anything serious. It's more about just meeting different people and having fun. Like we are.' He smiled, but with a hint of something else to it as he hooked one arm around me and hailed a black cab with the other. 'People like Luca who think you can find something meaningful through all this are a bit delusional, I think. No offence.'

I shook my head but inside it was spinning.

'I mean, some people seem to, of course. But it's like you said. It's not about meaningful. It's about having fun, right?' He moved closer and began to nuzzle against my neck, one hand moving up my thigh.

'That's not exactly what I meant,' I said, pulling away a little.

Adrian sat up straighter, studying me for a moment in the low light of the cab.

'You don't want fun?'

'Of course I want fun. Doesn't everyone? But... with something more. I mean, eventually.' I put a hand across my brow for a moment then fiddled with my hair again. 'That's how this stupid challenge thing with Luca started in the first place. He thinks you can find both of those things – together – using dating apps.'

'And you don't.'

I lifted my gaze, which had dropped to where I was worrying the beginnings of a hangnail on my thumb with my ring finger. 'I didn't, no...' I left the sentence there, unsure of both how to finish it and how it would be taken by Adrian.

'Until...' he prompted me, gently catching my hand and removing it from where I was now gradually ruining my updo and folding it within his own.

I still didn't reply. I felt hot and cold all at the same time and wished I'd never got dragged into this stupid dating thing. It was too hard and too complicated and too—

'If it helps, I thought the same as you.'

I met his eyes.

'I was just looking for fun, like I said. I admit that. And some women wanted more but I wasn't interested. But then you walked in and, incredibly, you wanted to see me again. If I'm honest, the smart and beautiful ones don't usually want to do that when it comes to me. I know I can be a little rough around the edges at times. Making us late this evening, for example. But...' He took my other hand and held them both within his own now. His voice was low and close to me. 'Meeting you makes me think there could be more to this.' He gave a low chuckle. 'As much as I hate to admit Luca Donato might be right, for no other reason than he clearly dislikes me, I fear I may have to. There's a lot of horror stories out there, as you said, surrounding online dating. I expect a few involve me, if I'm brutally honest, but that's because I never took it seriously. Nobody ever made me want to take it seriously before.' He paused and lifted one hand, placing it gently under my chin, tilting my face to his. 'But I'd like to now. With you – if you'll let me.'

My mind was spinning. A whole stream of emotions rushing through me – excitement, fear, wonder, distrust. Did he mean it? Why was I the special one? It sounded as if he'd had his pick.

'You don't believe me, do you?' He sounded amused.

'It's not that...' It was exactly that and we both knew it.

'Is it because you don't trust me or because you don't think you're worth it?'

My head snapped up. No one had ever been that blunt before. Well, other than Luca but that didn't count.

Adrian moved, trailing the softest of kisses just under my ear. 'I don't know what happened to make you think that, but I would like to. What I do know right now is that you are absolutely worth it. You should have confidence in the fact you're a smart, gorgeous woman with a hell of a lot to offer.' His fingers moved to my hair and found the hair clip, deftly undoing it so that my careful updo tumbled down. He wrapped his fingers in it and gently pulled me closer. Any closer and I'd have been on his lap, although right now I probably wouldn't have objected, except that we were still in the cab. But maybe it was time for me to loosen up a little. Live a little bigger. Start actually believing those who believed in me and stop second-guessing both them and myself. I'd made the change in my work life and, despite all my fear and reservations, it was turning out pretty damn good. Maybe it was time to try that in my personal life...

'I'm sorry I made us late earlier, leaving you standing there waiting for me. I promise it won't happen again.'

'It's fine.'

'No, it's not,' he said as his hand slid down behind my back and shifted me against his thigh. 'It's really not. It was rude and I apologise. I wouldn't have blamed you if you'd turned round and left me in that damn bar.'

'Well, I didn't,' I said, my voice not sounding like my own, low and with a hint of unsteadiness as Adrian kissed down the front of my throat.

'Thank God for that,' he replied, gruffly, moving back up to my lips and brushing them gently with his own. 'And frankly, had I known what was under that coat then, believe me, there's no way I'd have been wasting my time on that lot!' His mouth pressed against mine, softly at first then gained pressure, his arm tightening around me as our lips parted and he began to explore with his tongue. One hand slid further up my thigh, finding the suspender belt, and a deep growl rumbled in his throat as he began to move further.

'Here you go, mate.' The cab pulled to a halt and Adrian sat back, subtly adjusting things as he reached for his wallet. He glanced at me as I made my own adjustments and grinned wickedly which, without control, I returned.

'Keep the change,' he said as another large note got passed through.

'Cheers, mate. Have a good evening.'

In the rear-view mirror, I caught a glance of smiling eyes and felt myself blush. But there was no time to fixate on what the cabby thought of me as Adrian was helping me from the taxi and out into the crisp night air. The car pulled back out and its lights disappeared around the corner, leaving me alone on the pavement with Adrian. It was only then I realised I didn't have the faintest idea where I was.

'Where are we?' I asked, looking around at the buildings surrounding me.

'My place.' Adrian moved closer again. 'Is that OK?' I closed the tiny gap left between us.

'Perfectly OK,' I whispered, my voice sounding hoarse and low. He grinned a slow grin in reply and took my hand.

* * *

Late the next afternoon, I was sitting in my favourite café, sipping a hot chocolate with all the toppings, watching the rain outside streak down the large pane glass windows. A book sat open on my lap but I'd only half read one page so far, mesmerised instead by the raindrops – not to mention a little sleep-deprived from the previous night. My phone, resting on the sofa cushion next to me, began to buzz. I declined the video call from Luca and messaged him instead.

Can't video. In café.

Immediately the phone began to ring. I picked it up.

'Hi.'

'Hi.' I'd been irritated with Luca initially for being childish about Adrian, getting his name wrong in the restaurant on purpose, but the rest of the evening had rather made all that slide into insignificance. Luca's pettiness had actually backfired and had the opposite effect of bringing the subject of online dating, and what Adrian and I both wanted out of it, to a head. It had forced the conversation... which had led to last night. I tried not to smile too widely as I thought about it.

'Where have you been? I've been trying for ages.'

'I had my phone off for a bit.'

'All morning,' Luca corrected me. 'I was worried.'

'You didn't need to be. I'm a big girl, Luca. I am allowed to turn my phone off if I want.'

'But you never want.'

'Well, I did last night.'

'This was this morning.'

'Last night led to this morning.'

'I see.' Wasn't it amazing how much weight could be loaded into two tiny words? There was a long pause. 'You all right though?'

'Yes. Just sat here reading.'

'Where are you?'

'The usual.'

'OK.' Another long pause.

'What are you up to?'

'Not much.'

'No hot dates?' I asked, trying to inject a teasing note into what had turned into an unexpectedly awkward conversation for reasons I was a little unsure of.

'No.' There was no undercurrent of laughter to his words as there usually was when we discussed this subject. If anyone was going to hold a grudge about things, it would be me until he made me laugh, which never took long, but it seemed that Luca was the one with the stick up his backside today. I thought back to the previous evening. Adrian and I had left before Luca and his prospective clients. I'd raised a brief hand in goodbye as he'd looked around, seeing us leave, but Adrian had then moved behind me so I wasn't sure if Luca had responded or not.

'How did the meeting go yesterday evening?' Maybe that was the reason for his mood.

'Yep, really well, actually.' There was suddenly a little more animation to his voice. 'They're coming into the office on Monday to sign the final paperwork.'

'Oh, Luca, that's great. I'm really pleased.'

'Yeah. I tried to call you last night to let you know but... well. Anyway.' Another awkward silence drifted in.

'Luca?'

'Yep?'

'What's the matter?'

'Nothing.'

'You're not you. We're not us.'

Luca let out a long sigh. 'Well, I guess, like you said. Things change. Whether we want them to or not.' In the background I heard his security buzzer ring. 'Jez's here to watch the rugby. You free later or you out?'

'No, I'm free.'

'OK. Maybe catch up then.'

'OK.' And then he was gone. The conversation left an odd taste in my mouth and strange feeling in my stomach, neither of which I liked. I let out a sigh and went to the contacts on my phone. Finding Adrian's number, I dialled, just to say hi. It rang a few times and then the call was cut off. I stared at the phone for a moment then put it down beside me again. Maybe I'd try later. As I turned back to my book, the phone began to ring and Adrian's number showed on the screen. I smiled and answered.

'Hi.'

'Hi.' There was noise in the background and it was a struggle to hear him clearly.

'Sorry. I thought you were at home working this afternoon. Just thought I'd say hi.' I felt a little awkward suddenly. I didn't want him thinking I was clingy. My mind went back to the women he'd mentioned who wouldn't leave him alone after they'd dated. But then again, he'd also said I was different. So that meant something... didn't it? Shit. I literally had no idea what you were and weren't supposed to do in these situations. The rules of etiquette when it came to dating seemed to change every five minutes and, as I'd rather been out of the circuit for a while, I had no idea whether ringing him now was in the acceptable column when it came to the rules. My calm from earlier had by now evaporated entirely and I felt my shirt get sticky. Nice. I should have just left it. Let him call me. If he was going to. At least I—

'Yeah,' Adrian's voice, raised to cover the clamour of what sounded like a very noisy pub, came through the line. 'That went quicker than I thought in the end so came out with the guys.'

'Oh. Right. That's good. I'm glad you got it done.'

'Yeah.' The phone muffled and I could hear talking followed by some laughter before Adrian came back on the line. 'You OK?'

'Yep. Absolutely. I'll let you get on.'

'Great. I'll call you.'

'Sure,' I replied, ensuring I injected as much casualness as possible into this one word to make up for any possible faux pas I'd already made in actually dialling him at all. 'Bye.'

22

'Don't worry about it,' Tia said airily when I called her later to catch up and request her sage advice.

'But what if I've blown it by calling too early? Did I call too early?'

'There are no rules, Bee.'

'Of course there are rules. Everyone always goes on about the rules! There have to be rules.'

'Love doesn't go by rules.'

'I don't think we're at that stage yet!'

'No, but you must really like him to go to bed with him. That's just you.'

'Why does everyone keep saying that? It makes me sound like a prude.'

'Rubbish. You just have taste and class and are a little shy. None of those things are bad. It's fine. Stop worrying so much and tell me all about last night.' On the video screen, she plumped a cushion behind her, poured herself a glass of white from the bottle sitting on the coffee table and settled in.

'It was... nice.'

Tia pulled a face. 'Honey. I have a whole bottle here and hours until my fiancé gets home. This is the first man you've slept with in a-a-a-a-a-ages. I am going to need a whole lot more than "nice".'

I shook my head, half laughing, half blushing and Tia pointed at the screen. 'There! That's what I'm after. Now spill!'

* * *

I didn't see Adrian for a few days and tried not to think about it too much. He'd been honest and sweet, and even apologised for what he felt were faults. He had a very full-on job and although Tia and Jono had spoken and texted all the time when they got together, that didn't mean everyone proceeded like that. Right?

'Out with Aidan again tonight?' Luca's deep tones made me jump as I peered in the fridge for something to eat. I pulled out a fruit energy bar thing and closed the door to find his large bulk behind it, encased in a deep charcoal suit that made him look as if he should be advertising for the company who'd designed it. I drew myself up. I was in heels today so I got a four-inch advantage on my usual height.

'It's very childish insisting on getting his name wrong every time you refer to him, you know.'

Luca shrugged and gave a half-smile. 'I know. But it winds you up and that's always fun.'

'How are you the CEO of such a successful company when in reality you're a total child?'

'I'm good at fooling people.'

'Apparently so.'

'Maybe I'm not the only one.'

Here we go. Don't rise to it. Don't bite...

'And what's that supposed to mean?' So much for that plan.

He held his hands up. 'Calm down. I just meant that I'm glad we've finally managed to secure you for the company after you'd spent years pretending you were happy at the previous place, that's all. Jo just told me you've signed your contract. She may even have squeaked with excitement. I think you have a fan there.'

'She just likes me because I managed to get her a new computer.'

'She needed it. I don't know why she didn't ask me.' He shrugged with that blissful ignorance that was at once both sweetly endearing and highly annoying, depending on what mood you were in.

'Because people don't. Especially quiet, sweet people like Jo. People like you can intimidate people like her.'

'You're quiet and sweet. I don't intimidate you.'

'No, but I know what a dork and a pain in the arse you really are. People here have only seen your shiny outside. They don't know any better. And I'm not sweet.'

'I see. And yes, you are.'

'Am not.'

'I bet Adrian's said you're sweet.'

I turned away and began faffing about, making a cup of tea I didn't really want.

'What's that teabag ever done to you?'

'Do you want one?'

'I'm not sure I want to be involved in the abuse of a second teabag.' I gave him a look as I threw another teabag, admittedly with greater force than was needed or it deserved, into a mug.

'Too bad. You're in it up to your neck now.'

'Then it's a good job I have an excellent solicitor.' He laid one large hand on my arm, stilling my furious drowning of the teabags. 'What's going on?'

'Nothing.'

He gave me the look he'd been giving me since we were little. The one that called 'bullshit'. Although, admittedly, that probably wasn't what I categorised it as back then. Then it was more something along the lines of a 'you're telling porky pies' look.

'OK. Fine. He has called me sweet.'

'Oka-a-a-a-a-a-ay. And that's a problem because...'

I splashed milk into the mugs, and over the worksurface. Grabbing a paper towel, I mopped up the mess and dried Luca's mug before handing it to him. He made no attempt to fill the silence. This was a technique I guessed he'd learned at one of the many business conferences he'd attended over the years, one with a title like 'How to be a shit-hot CEO' or something similar because, coming from the household he did, there was rarely any silence left to fill and if there was, momentarily, a lull in the conversation, it was immediately swallowed by the hubbub of laughter and noise. Silence was not a concept Luca Donato had grown up with, but clearly one he had no problem with it now. I caved. Sort of.

'It doesn't matter.'

'Yes,' he stated, softly. 'It does. If it's getting you worked up like this, it matters a lot. To me, anyway.'

Luca took a step closer, and I looked up. Concern creased his features and his normally smiling mouth was set in a line that gave nothing away. More techniques. Growing up, I'd been able to read Luca like a book, just as he could still read me.

'It really doesn't, Luca.' But even to me, my words didn't seem to have the oomph behind them I'd intended.

'Tell me.' His voice was soft, low and determined. One arm rested casually on the wall beside my head, his taut, toned body only inches from mine. Had circumstances been different, I could easily have imagined that such a set-up could have a person's deepest secrets gushing out like Mentos dropped into a bottle of Coke. I met his gaze. And began to smile.

'What?'

'These tactics don't work on me, remember?' I said, ducking under his arm.

'What tactics?' He turned, looking genuinely confused. *Did he really not know he was doing it?*

I wasn't quite sure how to describe it, so I waved my hands over him and just went, 'That.' This obviously made things much clearer but Luca continued to stare at me.

'I'm not doing anything.'

Oh, wow. He really didn't know.

'OK,' I said, agreeing now that I truly realised he wasn't doing it intentionally.

'Now can we get back to you? What did Adrian say that upset you?'

'Ugh!' I dropped my head back and looked at the ceiling for a moment. 'Nothing. It's me, not him.'

'It's totally him.'

'You don't even know what it is.'

'And yet I still know it's him.'

'You're just prejudiced.'

'Probably. But tell me anyway.'

I let out a sigh. 'You're not going to let this go, are you?'

'Nope.' He sat down at the table opposite me, filling the chair and the space.

'It's just that...' I paused and glanced around. 'It feels weird talking to you about it.'

Another frown creased Luca's brow. 'Since when?'

Good point.

'I don't know. Things have just been a bit... off.'

'I know.'

'Is it this stupid challenge?'

There was a beat before he answered. 'No. And I will tell you everything. I promise. It's just not the right time. I hope you understand that.'

'Yes.'

Sort of.

'So? Adrian called you sweet? That's good, right?'

I shrugged.

'You're going to have to elaborate.'

'It's just that... sweet wasn't really what I was going for.'

Luca did his thing with the silence and, like a lemming, I walked straight off the cliff into it. 'People always call me sweet, or serious or studious or... well, one guy even said I reminded him of a librarian. Obviously, I like librarians. They like books and they like quiet and I'm a huge fan of both of those things.'

'In which case I'm not seeing the problem. And believe me, bearing in mind this is The Stockbroker, I'd love to see the problem. Maybe the guy who said about the librarian meant it in a sexy way? You know...' He waggled his eyebrows. 'Looking disapprovingly over the top of your glasses. That sort of thing.'

'I don't wear glasses.'

'Maybe you should.' Luca grinned and then stopped when he realised I wasn't smiling. 'Sorry.'

'He didn't mean it in that way. He texted me later that night and said I was "sweet" but too quiet.'

'Then he's an idiot.'

I took a sip of my tea, unconvinced.

'But what about Adrian? Because...' he cleared his throat and fiddled with the handle on his mug for a moment '... I saw you both leave the other night. That dress is a knockout and he was looking at you like you were dessert.'

'We'd had dessert.'

'Then he was after second helpings.'

I kept my features focused closely on my mug. 'I kind of thought so too. And for once...' I looked up at Luca, whispering, 'For once in my life, I felt like someone noticed me. Someone thought I was sexy. Not just quiet or sweet or bright but sexy with it. And I realise that I'm probably breaking about a million feminist rules, but it felt good. Actually, it felt quite empowering that someone thought that about me. Especially someone I really like.'

'Bee, I can guarantee people think that about you.'

'No, you can't.'

'I really can.'

'Who?'

Luca gave a tight smile and a slight twist of his head. 'I'm afraid I can't reveal my sources.'

I rolled my eyes and took a big mouthful of tea. 'Yeah, that's what I thought.'

'So, Adrian didn't think you were sexy in that dress? He needs his bloody eyes testing.'

'No, he did. It's just that... after...' I swallowed and Luca disappeared behind his mug of tea. 'He said I was really sweet, which is nice of course. But I suppose I really wanted him to say something... different.'

'Like what?'

I gave him a look and a half-smile tilted up one corner of his mouth. 'Maybe he's just not good with words. Numbers are more his thing, I guess.' He rubbed a hand over his face. 'I can't believe I'm defending a stockbroker.'

I knew how hard this was for Luca and smiled. 'Thank you.'

He shrugged but it was a little stiff. Considering he liked neither Adrian nor stockbrokers in general, I really did appreciate him making the effort. 'Do you think that's really it? I'm just thinking that maybe I'm not as—'

'However you were going to finish that sentence, don't. You need to stop comparing yourself to other people, Bee. You're you and you're brilliant and funny and kind and sweet—' he made a pointed face when he said that '—and there's no question you're sexy. I've already had to avoid a couple of tongues this morning when you walked by in those shoes.' Luca took another look at them.

'I can't remember the last time I saw you in heels, apart from the other night with Aidan.' I let the name dig go and shrugged.

'I always used to wear the same old things at the last place. I don't think anyone noticed what I wore anyway and I had sort of got past caring.' I looked back up. 'That's terrible, isn't it? That I so didn't want to go to a place I returned to day after day that I didn't even care about what I put on.'

'It's easy to get into a habit. A rut. Ploughing a new furrow can often be scary but you did it.'

'I did. And I guess the clothes thing is just a part of that. Trying to get out of the rut.'

'I'm glad to hear it.'

'So how do I get out of the rut of being sweet?'

Luca shook his head, smiling. 'You don't, Bee. You are what you are. But just because you're sweet doesn't mean you aren't all those other things too. People are complex. We're not just one thing or another, we're a whole blend. That's what makes us interesting.'

'Says someone who's never once been told he's boring.' I winked at him.

Standing, Luca let out a sigh before taking the now empty mugs and stacking them in the dishwasher. I followed him and headed towards the door. As we got there, he caught my arm and pulled me gently back. In the privacy of the corner behind the door, Luca gently took my face between his hands and the deep chocolate gaze lasered into me.

'Believe me, I have been called plenty of other things, but you are not and never have been boring. Don't let anyone tell you different. And I would say if they try then send them to me, but I know you're completely capable of kicking their arse all by yourself. You just need to have a little more belief in yourself because good things can happen when you do.' With that, he dropped the briefest of kisses on my forehead and pulled back. 'OK?'

I smiled. 'OK.'

'Good. Now get back to work. I don't pay you to sit around here gossiping.'

'I was keeping the boss company. I thought it would be rude to just leave.'

'Good one. See? You can think on your—' he glanced down and grinned with a wicked waggle of dark brow '—feet.'

'You know I can complain to HR about you leering at my shoes.'

'I wasn't leering. I was admiring them from an aesthetic point of view. I'm just happy you've begun your kick-arse programme here. Going after what you want. Those—' he gave another quick, appreciative look '—are a symbol of that. You're bound to have blips but just keep believing in yourself like I believe in you. Like Tia does. And anyone that doesn't certainly isn't worth your time.'

'Right.' I nodded, with more conviction this time.

'Right.'

I started to walk out, stopped and turned, finding myself closer to Luca than expected. 'Whoops. Just wanted to say thanks.'

He tilted his chin down further, now I was closer, to meet my eyes. 'You're very welcome.'

23

'Is there anything wrong?' I asked Adrian as we walked along the Embankment after a dinner that had been pleasant but not exactly full of... sparkiness.

'Huh?' He put away the phone he'd been furiously texting on. 'Oh, no. Sorry. Work thing.'

'You seem a bit distracted tonight.'

'Me? No. Not at all.' He stopped and caught my hand, resting my back against the balustrade. 'Only by you.'

I smiled. OK, yes, it was the cheesiest of lines and, if I thought too hard about it, I wasn't utterly convinced it was true. For most of the night, he'd seemed more interested in his phone than me. But people had busy lives and demanding jobs. I got that and accepted it. I wasn't about to turn into one of those women he mentioned, demanding all his time. But a little of it when I was with him would be nice. Was nice. He seemed to take my silence as something other than my brain having an inane conversation with itself.

'OK, that was cheesy.'

I laughed. 'It was a little.'

'But I am sorry. And cheesy though it may be, you are quite the distraction.' A loud beep beep emanated from his pocket. Neither of us moved. 'Although I could quite understand why you would believe my mind is elsewhere tonight.'

'Do you need to go? Is it a fire you need to put out?'

Was it me or did he look a tiny bit relieved? OK, it was me. Definitely me. Remember what Luca said. I am fierce. I am woman. Hear me roar!

Squeak squeak.

'Was that you?'

'It was my phone.'

'Your phone squeaks?'

Normally I turned my phone to silent on dates but tonight I'd been behind schedule and, once I'd messaged Adrian to say I'd be a little late, I'd been so caught up with trying to get ready and arriving as close to on time as possible, I'd obviously forgotten.

'I thought it was cute. At the time.'

'It's sweet. Like you.'

I was absolutely changing my notification sound at the next available opportunity.

There was a pause.

'Do you need to get it?' he asked.

'Nope. I'm here with you. If it was urgent, they'd ring.'

'Does anyone actually ring any more?'

'My friends and I ring.'

'Really? You don't just message?'

'Well, we do that as well. But yeah, we talk on the phone and on video.'

'Interesting.'

I wasn't sure quite what he meant by that so remained silent.

'Would you really mind if I went? I mean, I feel like a dick leaving early but, as you said, bit of a fire.'

'Oh! Right.' When I'd said it, I didn't think I'd really expected him to say yes. 'No. Of course not. Emergencies are emergencies.'

'Exactly. You're so great. I'll call you.' He pecked me on the cheek and started to walk away. I might not be all that great at this dating lark but even I knew when something didn't feel right. At least it didn't feel right to me. I looked up as I heard footsteps approaching me quickly. I readied myself for my loudest scream. But it was Adrian.

'Oh! Was your emergency cancel—?' I didn't get the rest of the word out as his mouth caught mine and his hands dived under my coat, pressing me to him, his tongue exploring my mouth hurriedly. As he drew back, I blinked up at him.

'Sorry. Knew I'd forgotten something. I'll call you later, OK?'

'OK.'

* * *

When he said later, I didn't realise he actually meant *later* later. About quarter to twelve, my mobile rang and Adrian's name flashed up. I'd showered, got into my jammies and was about to climb into freshly laundered sheets. Did I want to answer it? Should I even have that question in my mind if he was The One? I was rubbish at ignoring calls. I even took cold calls and once spent about ten minutes trying to politely tell the person on the other end that I wasn't interested in a maintenance plan for my Sky box – the chief reason being that I didn't and never had owned a Sky box.

I'd got a little better since then. I'd managed to ignore my mother on the one time she rang for my birthday. I say for it rather than on it as it was two days late, which she did admit to in the message she left, telling me she had just been so busy. Too busy to wish your only daughter a happy birthday. Well, it was good to see some things didn't change. But then, ignoring her call had been easier as I realised I didn't really like my mother. That concept still made my stomach knot a little, but I thought most of that was sadness rather than regret. Adrian, on the other hand, I did like.

'Hey!' He sounded brighter than he had earlier.

'Hi. Did you fix the emergency?'

'Oh, yeah.'

'That's good.'

'You still up?'

'Well, unless I'm a very erudite sleep talker, I guess so.'

Silence.

It had been meant to come out as funny but I wasn't sure now if it just sounded sarcastic.

'Yes. I am.' I started again. 'Although I was just about to go to bed.'

'Want some company?' His voice had dropped an octave. Randomly, I suddenly wondered if Luca ever did that sort of thing. I'd never heard him change his voice, but then again, Luca kind of already spoke from his boots so it'd have been pretty tricky for him to drop it any more.

I really did want to see him, but...

'I'm guessing by the pause, that's a no.' I couldn't tell if he was pissed off or not, but, to be fair, he was the one who'd disappeared part way through the date.

'It's not that I don't want to. It's just that I've got a presentation to prepare for and it's the first one I've done at this place so I really want to make sure I'm firing on all cylinders.'

'And you think I'll distract you.'

I laughed. 'I know you'll distract me.'

'Good. Then I won't give up hope just yet. I'd better leave you to get some beauty sleep. Although I don't think you need to worry on that score.'

Again, a little cheesy but again, kind of sweet.

'Thanks.'

'Besides, Donato's hardly going to fire you, is he? Don't worry about it.'

'I got this job on my own.' I reiterated what I'd already told him once before.

'No. I know. I'm just kidding.'

He clearly wasn't but I tried not to let it bother me. People were bound to think that strings had been pulled with Luca and me being so close, and Donato Solutions being such a hot ticket. Although it would be nice if it felt as if the man I was seeing had a bit more faith in me... Maybe I was just tired and overthinking things. The night hadn't exactly gone to plan with him ducking out part way through the date so that probably wasn't helping. I'd told Adrian I understood, and I did. But that didn't mean I was overly thrilled about it.

'I know. I'm just tired.'

'OK. Hope the presentation goes well.'

'Thanks. Night.'

'Night.' And then he was gone.

* * *

'Oh my God! You got a booty call.' Tia laughed as I sat at the pub with her the following night.

My new HD brows shot up as I put down my drink. 'I did not get a booty call!' Next to her, Jono gave the merest incline of his head. 'Oh, don't you start joining in.' I pointed a freshly painted nail at him and he grinned.

'What did I miss?' Luca's deep tones joined the conversation from behind me as he leant down and put the pint he was holding on the table next to my drink, before shrugging off his coat and laying it to the side, dropping the scarf he'd had wrapped around his neck on top. He'd been away on business for the last couple of days and up to his ears in negotiations; he'd been quiet online too so this was the first time in a few days we'd all been able to catch up.

'Nothing,' I replied quickly at the same time as Tia gleefully announced her misguided assumptions.

'It was not,' I repeated.

Luca blew air from his nose. 'It totally was.'

'It was not!'

'The guy rings you out of the blue late at night and asks to come round...' He let the rest of the sentence hang there as he took a seat next to me.

'It wasn't out of the blue. We'd been out earlier in the evening.'

Luca frowned, not understanding.

'He had to leave early. Some work emergency.'

A dark brow flickered.

'What?' I asked, turning.

'Just seems to have a lot of work emergencies for a stockbroker.'

'You know nothing about them or him, other than they lost you and your friends money, which means you automatically hate them. Which,' I added, 'is completely understandable. But I do think you could perhaps judge people in their own right rather than as a whole group, just because of their job.'

'Believe me, I am judging him in his own right. He disappears halfway through dates and then rings you up later, clearly expecting sex.'

'It wasn't like that!' I reiterated but a quick glance at the faces of my friends showed me this was not a battle I was going to win. And I suppose, laid out in black and white like that, it didn't sound great. But there were always greys when it came to life, whatever the others thought.

'So how come you're here on a Friday night slumming with us instead of out schmoozing Ms Possibly Right?' Tia asked.

'I'm meeting her here.'

'Oh!' Tia flicked a look at me. I returned the look and went back to studying the menu. Now that my salary had increased, my dining out choices had also increased. No longer did I have to just order a side and pretend I wasn't hungry. None of the others ever said anything but I knew they hadn't believed me when I'd told them I only wanted something light. Luca would often ask me to share some of his, saying he'd eaten at lunchtime and his eyes were bigger than his stomach. I knew it was a lie. Luca could finish off whatever you put in front of him if he wanted. The fact he wasn't the size of a house often surprised me; then again, he was pretty active, what with all the off-roading bike rides, Three Peak runs and dangling off rock faces, so I guessed he burned most of the calories he snaffled.

But tonight I could choose what I wanted. I'd had my first couple of payments from the employment agency clear and signed the contract with Donato Solutions. The thought I'd stayed in the old place so long, forcing myself into situations like that, annoyed the hell out of me now. All that time wasted. But thinking like that got me nowhere, and I'd been going nowhere for long enough. Finally, I'd begun to move and now I just needed to stay on that path.

'Hey, Luca.' A soft, low voice behind us interrupted my perusal of the menu. Luca turned. Actually, we all turned because we were nosy like that.

'Aneeka. Hi!'

The woman smiled a full-wattage smile as he stood and only just about gained height on her. For someone six four, this was quite some going. I glanced down subtly. Her heels were six inches and her legs made up most of the rest of it. They were probably, quite literally, twice as long as mine and encased in matt black, skintight leggings that showed off a perfect bum to, aptly, perfection, and the spikes of her heels should have been classed as deadly weapons. Outside the weather was threatening to fall below freezing and I'd thought my knee-length, low-heeled boots were a good choice. But perhaps wearing shoes that could also double as ice axes was a good approach too. She spoke quietly to Luca for a moment as he took her coat and I thought I caught a Scandinavian accent, which could explain the shimmering curtain of white-blonde hair that swung as she moved. Unlike most women, that was the only thing that moved. Everything else remained firmly, and pertly, in place.

'Sorry I am a bit late,' she was explaining to Luca. 'The shoot was supposed to finish earlier but the photographer couldn't get the shot he wanted for ages.'

I felt my eyebrows ping. If a photographer couldn't get a decent shot of this image of perfection, then perhaps he needed a new camera. Or a new career. God forbid if he ever had to take pictures of regular people.

'Would you like a drink?'

'Sure. I'll come with you.' And off they went, her hair and backside swaying perfectly.

I spun to face Tia. 'Isn't this deal supposed to be that we find someone online? There's no way he's met her on a dating app! Just look at them. There's a trail of tongues lolling after her just going up to the bar!'

Tia shrugged.

'That's the rules though, right? The whole thing about this stupid challenge is to prove love can be found online.'

Tia frowned. 'If it's so stupid, why did you agree to it?'

'Because I didn't have much choice.'

'And you're fed up of being on your own?'

'No. I'm more than happy on my own.'

Tia began sniffing the air.

'Yes. Fine. Someone would be nice but there's got to be rules. Surely?'

'Nothing to stop you picking up a model,' Jono added, I assume with the intention of being helpful.

'Yeah, hang on. I've got David Gandy on speed dial. He's taken but maybe he's got a friend.'

'Bee!' Tia snapped.

I let out a sigh. 'Sorry. Sorry, Jono.' I stood and leant across the table and stupidly, tears sprang to my eyes. 'I didn't mean to be such a bitch. I didn't mean it like that.'

Jono reached out and accepted the hug. 'It's fine. I know you didn't.'

I sat back down and Tia pulled a face at me.

'Everything all right?' Luca asked, returning to the table.

'Yep.' Tia smiled and held out her hand to the woman standing at his side. 'I'm Tia. This is my fiancé, Jono, and this is Bee.'

'Hi, it's nice to meet you all.' She folded her Bambi legs up elegantly and took the seat next to me. I shifted to make a little more room for her. Although, to be fair, she really didn't take up much. Tia, sensing my usual move-away-from-the-stunner play about to go into action, kicked me under the table. Except she didn't.

'Ow!' Aneeka cried, leaning down to rub her shin.

'Oh, God, I'm so sorry. I've been having this problem with my knee and the nerve just jumps,' Tia improvised quickly while Jono buried his nose in his drink and I buried mine in the menu. 'Usually Bee is on the receiving end!' she added pointedly.

I briefly looked up, nodded and returned to the menu, doing my best not to explode with laughter. I really didn't want Aneeka to think we were laughing at her.

'That's OK. I know a wonderful physiotherapist. I will give Luca the number for you. I'm sure he will be able to help your knee.'

'Oh, that's so kind of you. Thanks!'

'What's that?' Luca asked, coming in halfway through, having been distracted by someone he knew.

Aneeka explained.

'Dodgy knee?' he asked, screwing his face up. 'You haven't got a dodgy knee.' I leant back a little on my stool, ostensibly stretching and, behind Aneeka's head, pulled a face at Luca. He looked at me blankly for a moment.

'Oh! Right, yeah, the knee. Sorry. Forgot for a moment.'

'So how did you two meet?' Tia asked, going for the jugular.

Aneeka smiled and laughed. 'On an app, would you believe?'

I would believe. Just not necessarily the app we were both supposed to be using. But had we stipulated it was only to be through that app? Could I have been swiping around on Tinder and all the rest of them to increase my chances? I gave an involuntary shudder. Dealing with one app was bad enough.

'A dating app?'

Luca saw where this was going. 'Yes. The one Bee and I signed up to,' he said, meaningfully.

'Wow.'

'What?' Aneeka turned; perfect teeth showed in partially parted perfect lips. If her top had been loose fitting, which it definitely wasn't, I'd have comforted myself with the reasoning that she was probably hiding a hump in there or something, but I was clearly out of luck.

'Umm... I just. Well...' Everyone was looking at me now. Luca had a quizzical brow raised and a half-amused smile on his lips. I tried to ignore him. 'It's just that I didn't think someone like you would use dating apps.'

The flawless brow creased a little. 'Someone like me?'

'Yes,' I added hurriedly, worried that she was preparing to be offended. 'I mean, fourteen blokes would have asked you out if it hadn't been for that lump—' I nodded towards Luca '—just on the way to the bar. I guess I'm surprised you have trouble meeting people.' My face felt warm and I really hoped it was because the pub had heated up and not because I was now glowing like a harbour wall signal light, but I knew which one I'd put money on.

Aneeka studied me a moment then smiled. 'That's very sweet of you. I guess you are right. I do meet people in my work but they are not always the right sort of people. I am looking for...' She paused for a moment. 'More, I guess you would say. The people I meet tend to want to just party, party, but I am not really like that. Family is important to me. I miss my own and go home to see them when I can. Many of the people I meet don't get this.' She turned to Luca and gave him a smile that could launch a toothpaste. 'Luca gets it.'

I smiled. 'Yes. I could see that. His family is very important to him.'

'So I hear.'

'Bee knows all the family secrets.'

I thought back to that Saturday when I'd come across him and his mum arguing heatedly in Italian. *Not all of them...*

24

Luca and Aneeka finished their drinks and left.

'She seems nice,' I said.

'Mm hmm,' Tia replied, her mind clearly elsewhere.

'What?'

'What? Oh, nothing. I just...' She waved her hand. 'Doesn't matter. Have you decided what you want to eat yet?'

Intrigued by the look on Tia's face as she watched the retreating figures of Luca and his date, I'd been about to question her further but a loud rumble from my stomach interrupted us both. Gathering our food order, I headed up to the bar.

A typically busy night meant the place was now heaving. I squeezed my way through a couple of gaps – being petite did sometimes have advantages – and found myself at the shiny, granite-topped bar. Placing my foot on the silver rail that ran all around it a few inches from the floor, I hefted myself up to gain a little more height. A tender appeared to notice me and began sauntering over. They always sauntered here, whether it was empty or heaving. Although to be fair, it was rarely empty. I wasn't sure if this was their instructions – saunter to be cool – or if it was the fact that the staff were nearly all laid-back Australians and sauntering was just their natural setting. I smiled at him and opened my mouth to place my order.

'Can I have sex on the beach?' a loud, Estuary accent beat me to it. This was followed by a high, piercing laugh as the woman turned back to her five friends huddling at the edge of the crowd, giving them a thumbs up. To be fair, the guy was good-looking and I didn't imagine it was the first time he'd had that request. He smiled good-naturedly and pointed to me.

'I'm afraid this lady was first, love.' He turned his attention back to me, the smile widening. 'What can I get you?' From the corner of my eye, I saw the woman's jaw drop.

I placed our food order with the smiley Australian and paid with my card. The woman he'd bypassed was still waiting to be served and was now tapping her own in an irritated manner on the bar, her annoyance radiating out. Handing the receipt to me, the barman half slid his gaze to her then back to me and grinned.

'You're in trouble there,' I said in a tone that was quiet enough not to travel but still loud enough for him to hear.

'Ha! No worries. I've been here long enough to know how to avoid trouble.'

'Probably a wise tactic,' I said, folding the receipt into the back pocket of my jeans.

'Not noticed you in here before though.'

I looked back up, surprised at the fact he was both still in front of me and at his comment. We'd all been coming here for years and I'd certainly noticed him before. He had one of those great Australian smiles – relaxed, easy and sexy – although the last bit could just be my own addition.

'Oh! I've, umm, been in here loads.'

'Really? Maybe I've just never had the pleasure of serving you before.'

I knew he had, in fact, served me plenty of times.

'That must be it.' I smiled.

'Well, I'd better get on. Maybe I'll get to serve you again later.' He gave me a grin, this time accompanied by a wink, and turned away towards the woman who was still waiting and was practically now steaming with fury at having to do so.

Buoyed up by a number of things, not least getting served at the first attempt, I turned to find my way through the crowd back to Tia and Jono, forgot I'd been resting my foot on the pole and fell flat on my face. That was, I would have had I not instead face-planted against a very broad and, from the feel as I peeled myself off it, remarkably muscled chest. Two matching arms helped me regain my balance.

'You OK?'

'Yes, yes. Absolutely!' I said, feeling myself glowing with embarrassment. 'I'm so sorry. I'm not drunk. I just tripped over my own feet.'

Because that makes it so much better.

I looked up and met a smiling face that was as good as the muscles. 'Not a problem. I'm glad I was here.'

'I'm not!' I laughed and the smile wavered. 'I mean! I am too, obviously,' I said, raising my voice above the noise. 'I'm just thinking it would have been less embarrassing if you hadn't been.'

'Falling on your face on the floor is preferable to falling into my arms?' The man folded said arms and my stomach did a little happy dance. The smile was now back on his face in full force.

'No! Of course not. I just meant, umm...'

He leaned closer. 'I know what you meant. It's just fun teasing you.'

'Is it now?' I replied, a smile on my own face. Oh my God, was I flirting? I never flirted. I was notoriously bad at flirting.

But tonight seemed different. Was it a full moon or something? People were acting weird. I was being noticed! OK, fair enough. The current guy couldn't help but notice me because I had literally fallen into his arms. Oh, God. I hope he didn't think I'd done it on purpose.

'It is...' he replied, leaving the sentence to tail off as he waited for my name. I was about to give it to him when we were interrupted by a tall, willowy woman with great hair and large dark eyes. Eyes that were now laser focused on me.

'Who's this?'

'Oh. Nobody.' There was an edge of panic to the man's voice and it had gone up two octaves.

Ouch.

Despite his size, he seemed to shrink in the company of what was obviously quite a forceful presence. And, to be fair, now I noticed the flashing diamond on her third finger, she clearly needed to be forceful if her fiancé had a tendency to start chatting up random women in bars.

She turned the lasers towards him. 'It had better be nobody. I warned you what would happen if it was a somebody.'

Wow. But also, good for her.

'Excuse me.' I headed through both the almost non-existent gap and the extremely existent atmosphere back to where Tia and Jono were getting cosy.

'None of that now, thank you!' I said, plopping down back on my seat.

Laughing, they turned back to me. 'That was quick.'

I pulled a face. 'I know. I ducked through some tiny gaps and that cute Australian barman served me almost straight away.'

'Oh, well done!'

'And then a bloke started chatting me up when I turned to leave.' I left out the bit about me tripping arse over tit. Sometimes not all the details were needed.

'Oh, rea-a-a-ally?' Tia leant forward for more information. I took a swig of my drink and shook my head.

'Engaged.'

'Huh?'

I inclined my head towards where the man and his fiancée were now leaving. Her face still looked like thunder while his was very contrite. I couldn't help thinking she could do better.

'Very engaged.'

Tia tried to follow their progress unobtrusively. 'Oh!'

'Quite.'

'Good for you though. Getting out there. You do seem like you've got a bit more confidence these days.'

'Do I?'

'Definitely.' She turned to Jono. 'Right?' Jono nodded. I thought back to what Luca said about me wearing heels to work. Was the fact I'd felt ignored because I'd let people ignore me? Growing up with my parents, it had been pretty hard to get their attention, to make them notice and realise they had a daughter, and not just an inconvenience. Kids only have so much control and I'd had two choices. Accept them for who they were and retreat into my own world or go the opposite way and head off the rails spectacularly. The second option seemed such a lot of work and, frankly, just hadn't appealed to me.

Plus I had Luca and his family. Getting into trouble would have felt more like a betrayal of their attention and kindness than an act of rebellion against my own parents. And there was always the possibility that my parents either wouldn't have noticed or alternatively, seen it as an opportunity to completely wash their hands of me and claim to their friends that they had tried everything, but they just didn't know what they'd done wrong. Given a notepad, a pen and half an hour, I could have given them a list. But that was then. I'd taken the first step with Mum now. Her new life and new family were clearly her priorities – just as Dad had been, even when he'd gone. Even when I'd given up my degree to be there for her. To be there for each other. She'd had the chance and she'd blown it. And for once, at last, I wasn't going to let it get to me. Sometimes life didn't go the way you wanted it to, and you just had to accept it and not let it ruin any more of the time you'd been given on this earth.

Home life had transitioned into work habits and I'd let it happen all over again. Don't rock the boat. Don't make a fuss. Don't draw attention to yourself. But sometimes you needed to do all of those things – even if it was only to get a drink at a bar.

'What are you grinning about?' Tia asked.

'Nothing,' I replied.

'Liar.' Tia grinned back.

A few minutes later our meals arrived and we tucked in, chatting about everything and nothing, enjoying the food and company and the atmosphere of a Friday night in a great pub in one of the best cities in the world.

* * *

Sitting on the DLR back to my flat, I turned things over in my mind as I stared out past my reflection into the dark of London, its lights blinking, shining out and lighting up the sky. Somewhere up there in the clear, cold sky, stars lurked, hidden by the all-encompassing light pollution, but I imagined them in my mind with help from the stories Luca's granddad had told me about the village his family were from back in Italy. Midnight-blue skies stretching out across the Bay of Naples, millions of points of starlight twinkling way, way up and as far as the eye could see across the vast darkness of the sea. Millions of chances for a wish, he would say.

Luca had been devastated when his grandfather had passed and, although I couldn't begin to imagine the loss he and his family had gone through, when Luca rang me I dropped every-thing and rushed round to be with him. I was already crying when he opened the door and we'd sobbed in each other's arms for what felt like hours. As Luca had finally fallen asleep that night, his head resting in my lap, I'd laid my head back against the sofa and wondered what it meant that I'd felt more pain, and more loss, at the passing of Luca's granddad than I had with my own father. I'd always harboured some guilt about that, but I realised now I didn't have to. Sometimes you got back what you gave. Clearly not always. I'd tried to give and give to my parents but had got little back, but perhaps, when it came to his daugh-ter, my father had reaped only what he'd sown. And it was time I let that go.

I smiled, seeing the reflection of my smile in the now rain-streaked window of the train. It was time to let go of what no longer served me, to live my best life and go after what I wanted. I wasn't invisible after all. I just had to make sure people realised that.

Pulling out my phone, I found the chat thread between Adrian and me.

Hi. How's your evening? x

It was a while before I received a reply.

Hi. It's OK. Pretty quiet. Sorry, nodded off for a bit. Did you have a good time with your friends?

Yep. Just caught up with Tia and Jono in the end. Everyone else had things on but kids can do that.

I added a laughing face here.

Just on the train home now.

Oh? No Donato tonight?

I gave a little eye roll. Luca liked to get Adrian's name wrong and I'd noticed Adrian had taken to referring to Luca purely by his surname. Maybe it was a private-school thing or maybe it was just because he knew Luca wasn't sold on him. But hopefully, if things moved on, that would change.

No. Out on a hot date.

I followed this with a winky face.

Surprise surprise…

I let it go and waited while I saw he was still typing.

Would you be free for a hot date next week?

I might be…

Meet you at 7 at Bar Rodin on Friday? I've got some team building course most of the week unfortunately.

That wouldn't give me enough time to get home and go back again but I could loiter a bit at work, then change and go from there. As this seemed to be Adrian's favourite bar he'd likely be going straight from work too, although his place was far closer to the centre than mine. Perhaps it was time I made a suggestion of a place that was more middle ground for us both.

Sure x

Looking forward to it x

The online notifier disappeared and it seemed he was gone. Adrian didn't really seem one for chats or just to pick up the phone for a natter, whether real or online. That took a little getting used to as I was used to friends that did, but everyone was different, right? So long as he was present when he was actually with me, then that was good. I slapped away the little voice in my head that reminded me about the times he hadn't been present, having to dash off or put this or that fire out. As Luca had pointed out, he did seem to have more than his share of work emergencies but then, I had to admit, I'd never dated a stockbroker before – and as far as I knew, neither had Luca – so this could be the norm. He always seemed apologetic if plans changed and I was sure he'd rather be out than working at ten o'clock at night – I knew I would, despite loving my new job.

There was enough stress involved in Adrian's job already. A few months ago there'd been a story in the *Metro* about a stockbroker who'd stepped off the ledge of his office building twenty floors up after he thought he'd made a mistake on a deal. Heart-breakingly, it turned out he hadn't made a mistake and the deal had gone through, making the investors billions. He'd died for nothing. But the poor man had obviously been suffering from an enormous amount of pressure in the first place to have got to that point. I wasn't about to judge Adrian. He was responsible for a hell of a lot of other people's money and it wasn't a responsibility I'd have liked, no matter what the possible financial rewards, so if the odd shortened date was the way to him keeping sane and happy, then I was more than OK with that.

* * *

Weather looking pretty chilly and windy on Sunday for the walk. How does everyone feel about a picnic in our conservatory? Kids can still run around in the garden while we stay warm inside?

The group WhatsApp pinged up Bella's message. Several of the others replied, agreeing with the change, as did I. I'd clearly been watching the same weather forecast as Bella and Jesse and had no desire to spend the afternoon freezing my sandwiches off, so I added my vote of approval too.

Is it OK if I bring Aneeka?

Luca asked.

Of course!

Jesse answered.

The more the merrier.

Tia sent me a private message.

Bringing Aneeka, eh? Seems like he's getting pretty serious.

For Luca, going out with anyone more than twice was serious. Bearing in mind he'd been seeing this woman for a few weeks and was now including her in group activities, something else he didn't tend to do, this was, as Tia suggested, quite monumental.

I guess so.

I didn't really know what else to say. Luca hadn't talked to me much about her and I hadn't asked. I wasn't exactly sure why.

Are you bringing Adrian?

Haven't asked him.

Why not?

I sent the shrug emoji. Why hadn't I?

I'll do it now.

I clicked off the chat with Tia and sent one to Adrian, asking him.

Sounds great. Bit chilly for a picnic though?

It's going to be an indoor one. Friends have a huge conservatory and a big garden so kids can run around.

Oh. Thought you meant just you and me.

Maybe this was why I hadn't asked him. Luca hadn't exactly been all warm and fuzzy the last time he'd met Adrian and perhaps part of me was trying to avoid that, but, if he was going to be busy with Aneeka, it might not be so bad. The others had better manners when it came to my boyfriends.

It will be fun. They're really nice, I promise. I know Luca was off last time but he has a new girlfriend so will be plenty occupied.

I sent a funny-face emoji after this, hoping it would be enough to convince Adrian. I could kick Luca for being so rude and making Adrian, and me, feel uncomfortable at the pub.

I'm not worried about Donato. What time is it?

Half 12. About half an hour from my place.

I've got a rugby thing in the morning but I could come along a bit later?

No problem.

I sent a big cheesy smile.

Looking forward to seeing you xx

Me too. Catch up later x

He clicked off the chat and I went back to Tia.

He's coming but going to meet me there. Some rugby thing in the morning.

Great! Do you want a lift there?

That'd be fab, thanks.

25

I'd sent Adrian the address and he'd said he'd be with us by two o'clock. It was now nearly three and I still hadn't heard from him and was beginning to worry. Picking up my phone, I wandered out into the garden to find a quiet place and dialled his contact. He picked up on the third ring.

'Hi, Bee. I was just about to call you.'

'Is everything OK?'

'Yeah. I just don't think I'm going to make it today.'

I looked over to where Aneeka and Luca were playing with the children. She'd fitted right in from the moment they'd arrived together as though she'd been part of the group from the start, and, despite looking like a goddess and clearly used to attention, seemed genuine and down to earth. I think sometimes our humour went over her head, but she'd smile graciously when that happened and occasionally Luca would explain but, more often than not, he'd just leave it and touch her hand or give her a squeeze instead, which she appeared to be happy with. It was always hard penetrating a pre-formed group, but Jono and Lucy had both integrated so well that we didn't even remember they hadn't been a part of the original school gang. The way it was going, it wouldn't be long before Aneeka made that leap too. I watched as Luca caught her and wrapped his arms around her. She snuggled back against him, laughing. They looked like an advert for a luxury brand as the low sun caught their faces and bathed them both in a golden glow. Luca turned his head, catching me staring. We locked eyes for a moment before I turned away, tuning back into what Adrian was saying.

'Took a bit of a bump on the field. Not sure I'll be that much company.'

'You don't have to say much if you don't want. It'd just be nice to see you, if you feel up to it.'

'Yeah, sorry. Not sure I do really. Probably best if I leave it today. Did mean to ring you earlier. Was just seeing how I felt but things are still a bit sore.'

'Oh, right. OK. Yes, that's probably best, then. I'm sorry you're hurt. I hope you feel better soon.'

'I'll be fine. Just need a bit of rest.'

'Yes.'

'I'll call you tomorrow and we can arrange something for the week?'

'Sure. I'll look forward to it.' I put a smile into my voice, trying to hide the disappointment of Adrian baling at the last minute. Obviously, it wasn't really his fault that he'd got hurt but I couldn't help thinking he sounded a little relieved. It had been clear that he hadn't exactly been sold on the idea from the start – unlike Aneeka. Luca had invited her in the pub when we were all gathered for a quick after-work drink and she'd been thrilled at the prospect and, from the look exchanged between the two of them, perhaps realised this was another step in their relationship.

'OK. Have a good time, then.'

'Bye,' I said, but I wasn't sure he caught it. I stood for a moment trying not to read too much into it. Accidents happened. This was just bad timing and so long as Adrian was OK, that was the most important thing.

'He's not coming, is he?' I was lost in my thoughts and Luca made me jump, a hand going to my chest.

'No.'

'There's a surprise.'

'What's that supposed to mean?'

'It means I doubt he had any intention in the first place.'

'That's unfair. You have no idea. You don't know him and you haven't made any attempt to. If he wasn't keen, then I can't imagine your frigid welcome at the pub before did much to entice him to spend several hours in your company!'

'If he's any sort of man, it wouldn't matter what I think of him. It's what he thinks of you that matters.'

I bristled at the insinuation behind the words.

'He got hurt in rugby, if you must know.'

'Right,' he said, his tone disbelieving. 'That was convenient.'

'I'm sure it wasn't planned!'

'No, but he wasn't exactly enthusiastic about being part of today, was he?'

'And how would you know?'

Luca shrugged. 'You told Tia. Tia told me.'

I'd forgotten it was almost impossible to have any sort of secret within the group unless specifically requested.

'He was still planning to come, despite your previous rudeness.'

'Not here though, is he?' Luca did an exaggerated look around, like something out of a cartoon.

I shook my head. 'Why do you care, anyway? Shouldn't you

be with Aneeka rather than abandoning her just to come and give me grief?'

'I'm not the one giving you grief.'

'Huh! Could have fooled me.'

Luca ignored the jibe. 'Anyway, she's fine. Getting on like a house on fire with everyone.'

'Yes. I noticed.' I took the higher ground. 'She seems lovely.'

He glanced back to where a roar of laughter echoed from the conservatory. 'Yeah, she's nice. Everyone seems to like her.'

'You certainly seem to. This is a bit of a record for you, isn't it?'

He gave another shrug. 'Like I said, I'm looking for more now and she's a good person and we have some common goals.'

'Plus she's hot as...'

He conceded to give a head tilt. 'That too.'

I gave a small smile, sensing the truce.

'I am sorry Adrian didn't come through for you today.'

'Accidents happen.'

Luca didn't say anything.

I looked up at the pale sky. 'You still won't admit it, will you? And how about apologising for perhaps being part of the reason that he didn't want to come, if that's even part of the issue?'

'I'm not sorry. That's his problem, not mine.'

'Except it's actually mine, isn't it, Luca? You being an arsehole to him means it's bounced back on me.'

'Then he should have more balls. If I really liked someone, I wouldn't give a shit what others thought. I'd be wherever it was for her, and her alone.'

'God, it must be nice to be so perfect!'

'I've never claimed to be perfect. I'm just not an idiot like him and, frankly, I can't believe you're wasting your time on him.'

'You know what, Luca? It would be nice if, just for once, you could show me some support when it comes to dating. All you ever do is pick holes in my choices. You were the one who wanted to pursue this challenge and now I've found someone I might really like, all you've done is be an arrogant arse about it.'

'That's rich. You think I'm the arse, and yet you're the one who's been stood up.'

Tears sprang to my eyes at his cold, unkind response. 'Bee, that didn't come out—'

'Just forget it, Luca.'

He reached out for my arm and I snatched it away. 'Don't!' I began to walk away but after a couple of quick strides, I turned back. 'You're not always right, you know that? Just because you find it easy to do all this doesn't mean everyone does, and for once it would be nice if you thought about that instead of just immediately putting down every choice I make.'

'That's not how I meant it!'

'I don't care, Luca! It's how it comes across and how everyone else sees it too. You were unforgivably rude to Adrian in the pub, and you made me look foolish, the way you ignored us when we tried to say goodbye. If you are the reason he didn't want to come today, I don't blame him. Perhaps he's just not as cocky as you, expecting everyone to like him and not being bothered when they don't. Some of us actually have fears and feelings.' I turned away from him.

'And you think I don't?' he called after me.

'No, Luca. Right now, I'm not sure you have any idea.' I turned back towards the house and continued walking, smiling at Aneeka as she came the other way, clearly looking to see where her boyfriend had disappeared off to.

'Is everything all right?' she asked, slowing.

'Yep.' I smiled, hoping she would blame my watering eyes on the cold. 'Luca's round there, if you're looking for him. Are you having a good time?'

'Yes, I am. Thank you. Everyone is so kind, making me feel a part of things.'

'It can be a bit daunting sometimes, things like this, can't it?'

'Definitely.' She looked around. 'Your boyfriend is coming still?'

'Oh. No. He's not going to be able to make it after all.'

She pulled a sympathetic face, unlike her own boyfriend had done. 'I'm so sorry.'

'That's OK.' I made light of it. 'These things happen, don't they?'

'Yes. I wasn't sure if I would be able to come but I managed to rearrange some things and I'm so glad I did. Although I seem to have lost Luca now!' She laughed but I recognised a little insecurity in the sound. For all her beauty and poise, underneath Aneeka was like a lot of us. It had taken a certain amount of courage for her to come today but she'd made the effort. I wondered if Luca appreciated, or even realised, that.

'He's over there by the pond.' I pointed her in the right direction.

'You two... are OK? I... no, I shouldn't say anything.'

'It's fine.' I smiled in what I hoped was an encouraging way.

'It's just that you two are close, yes?'

Oh, God, I hoped this wasn't going to be a problem. Luca really seemed to like this woman and I didn't want to be seen as a bone of contention again. Although, with his attitude lately, right now I had no desire to be anywhere near him.

'Yep. Most of the time.'

She gave a half-smile, not quite getting it. I waved my comment away, indicating it didn't matter.

'That is good. You seem like a good friend to Luca.' OK, this was new – and refreshing. 'It's just that, you seemed upset when I first saw you and I thought I heard loud voices?'

'Oh, no. It's fine. Luca and I just... we get on each other's nerves sometimes.' *And right now, Luca was getting on my very last one.*

'Ah, I see. I hope you are not upset?'

'No, no. Not at all. Just the cold. My eyes always run in the cold. Don't yours?' I asked, almost hopefully looking up at her perfect face. Today she was pretty much bare of make-up and still looked stunning. She was the epitome of a 'woke up like this' hashtag, except, unlike the many staged ones, Aneeka probably did.

'Sometimes, yes.' She smiled at me but it seemed she was as good at telling fibs as I was and it was clear she'd never once had the problem, but it was kind of her to pretend for my benefit. I really liked her and, as mad as I was at Luca right now, I was glad he'd found her. I just hoped he'd wind his neck in enough to keep her.

'We're fine anyway, don't worry. I didn't push him in the pond. Yet.'

She laughed, a twinkly, gentle sound unlike my far more raucous one.

'There is still time, yes?'

'Oh, definitely. That's why I thought it best to come in and get some intelligent conversation.'

She grinned.

'I'll see you in a bit.' She nodded and I took a step to pass her. 'Thanks, Aneeka.'

'You're welcome.'

Perhaps spending time with this gentle woman might soften some of Luca's rough edges. He could be as charming as he wanted when needed but he could also be a bull-headed arse.

I made my way back in, getting mobbed by the children as I did so, and made apologies on Adrian's behalf for his absence, hoisting Lucy and Jack's youngest onto my hip as she tried to clamber up my leg.

'Oh, that's a shame,' Bella said, a chorus of agreement following her. 'We were hoping to get to meet him properly.'

'I know. Came a cropper in rugby or something.'

'Oh, really?' Jesse said, scooting one of his children back across the floor from where she kept crawling off, like a continual resetting of a clockwork toy. 'Looks a bit skinny for a rugger bloke. Which position does he play? Winger?'

When we were at school we'd all chosen what our *Mastermind* subject would be. Jesse's, predictably, had been sport and little had changed from those days. Mine had been the Mr Men.

'I've no idea.' I shrugged and Jesse looked disappointed as I took a seat on the rug next to Tia.

'Should I know that?' I asked her quietly.

'What position he plays?'

'Yeah. Is that the sort of thing I should know?'

'Do you like rugby?'

'Not especially.'

'Do you care about it?'

'No.'

'Then no. He plays and that's enough to know. Jono does all that weird Dungeons and Dragons stuff and I haven't got a clue about it.'

'It's not weird. And it's not DnD. That's a completely different character set.'

Tia held her hand out as if Jono's comment proved her point, which it kind of did.

'Do you think Luca would know what position Aneeka played?' I whispered to Tia.

'I'm pretty sure she doesn't play rugby, hon. She'd be snapped like a twig, bless her.' Tia was tall and willowy too but she had a kick-arse line of steel running through her.

'No. I know. But if she did?'

'What does it matter? I know this thing started off as a competition, but it's not a contest to find out who knows the most about their choice of partner.'

'I know.'

'You don't have to share each other's hobbies to take an interest in that person. I know Jono likes these character things and that it makes him happy, and that's enough for me. You know Adrian plays rugby, but you don't have to know all the ins and outs of it. What's brought all this on?'

I shrugged.

'Has Luca been winding you up out there again?'

'It seems he expected Adrian not to show and was being unbearably smug about it.'

'I hope you pushed him in the pond.'

'Believe me.' I leant closer as Luca and Aneeka came back, hand in hand, into the conservatory. 'I was this close.'

Tia grinned.

'There's always next time.'

I comforted myself with that thought and turned to where Lucy had just pulled out an enormous chocolate cake and was asking who was up for a slice. Aneeka was the only one who abstained, tasting the tiniest bite from Luca's fork at one point but refusing to be drawn into having more.

26

I need to talk to you. You free for lunch? Xx

Luca's message popped up on my phone screen. There was an internal chat function within the office but Luca still used WhatsApp when he needed to ask anything. Habit, I guessed. I picked up my phone from the smooth oak surface and typed.

Sorry. Going shopping with Helen. She has a wedding next weekend and wants some advice. Xx

I glanced over at his office. He was pacing about in it. I waited. Having read my reply, he turned and looked across at me. The momentary expression of confusion was hurriedly replaced with a blank one and he turned back to his phone.

OK. That's nice. I'm glad you're making friends here. Xx

And???

And what?

I looked up again. To be fair, I had no clue either why Helen felt I was the one to turn to for sartorial advice, but I would do my best. Across the room, Luca was facing me and shrugged. I shook my head subtly and tried not to smile. Two desks across, a man glanced up from his screen and locked eyes with me. I froze for a moment. For a second, he froze too, and then he smiled back, adding a little wave to it. Oh, God, he'd clearly thought I was mooning over him as his desk was in line of sight of Luca's glass walls. Behind those walls I could now see Luca laughing. I stabbed at my phone.

Stop laughing. That was your fault.

You really are making friends…

Oh shoosh. What did you want me for? Can you tell me on here?

The man across from me was now engaged in what looked like an in-depth telephone conversation and was furiously scribbling on a pad beside him. I glanced back up to Luca. The smile had gone from his face.

Not really.

AM I FIRED??

Nooooo!

He added a line of rolly-eye emoticons to this, then began typing again.

Free for dinner?

No. Sorry. Meeting Adrian.

Across the room, Luca's door opened and he strode across the office. I noticed a couple of my fellow workers watch and then turn to each other when he'd passed, pulling a lustful face. I suppose, objectively, he did look pretty good today. Luca never really had off days like us mortals. Today, he wore a deep blue suit, the jacket of which was hanging in his office, paired with a pale blue shirt with the neck open, the sleeves of which were rolled back to just below his elbows, displaying permanently tan, muscular forearms. It worked well for him. And apparently also for the two employees now fanning themselves theatrically behind his back. I pretended not to notice and turned to my screen.

'Hi.'

'Hello.'

'Have you got a minute?' he asked, casually.

'Hi, Bee! You ready?' Helen smiled at both of us as she came up to my desk.

'Hiya. Yep. All ready.' I nudged my computer into sleep mode and pushed my chair back. 'I'm just off out. Do you want me to come and see you when I get back?' I asked Luca, bending to pick up my handbag.

'No. I've got a meeting this afternoon, but I do need to talk to you today.'

'OK. Give me a shout when you're free, then.'

He nodded, gave Helen a quick smile, then turned on his heel and headed purposefully back to his office.

'He really does have the most gorgeous bum,' Helen said, watching it all the way across the floor. Suddenly her head snapped round to look at me. 'Oh, God. Please don't tell him I said that.'

I grinned. 'Of course I won't.'

'It's just I know you two are... friends.'

I rolled my eyes at her and gave her arm a tug. 'Come on. And yes, we are friends,' I said, leaving out the rather pregnant pause she'd added. 'But believe me, if I passed on every compliment directed his way, he'd need a far bigger office door.'

Helen grinned.

'Are you really just friends?'

'Yep.'

'How? He's lovely.'

Helen was of a similar age to Luca's mum, and happily married to a lovely chap called Bill, but that didn't mean she couldn't appreciate the finer things in life. And Luca Donato was undoubtedly fine.

'We just are. It's a bit different when you've known each other as long as we have. There's definitely no mystery when you know all the other one's secrets.'

'Ohh, but it would be so romantic. Literally childhood sweethearts.'

'Helen?'

'Hmm?' She had a dreamy look on her face.

'The lift door is open. Are you coming?' I was standing in the foyer. She'd been so caught up in her dreaming she hadn't even noticed we'd arrived at the lobby, let alone that I was no longer beside her.

'Oh! Yes. Right.' She did one of those hurry-walk-not-quite-a-run things you did when a motorist waved you across the road in front of them.

'Where do you want to start?'

'I'm not really sure. I wondered about John Lewis?'

'OK.' We turned towards the Tube station. 'Or we could try somewhere a bit off the beaten track. My friend, Tia, could represent Great Britain at the Olympics when it comes to shopping and absolutely trounce the competition. She's taken me to a couple of places that have some great stuff, if you want to try there.'

'For my age?' Helen asked, hesitantly.

I gave her arm a hug. 'For any age.'

'I suppose somewhere more boutique would lessen the chances of me running into someone wearing the same thing at the wedding.' We exchanged a quick grimace at that prospect.

'That is true.'

'Let's do it!' Helen announced.

Half an hour later we had a gorgeous new outfit for Helen and the assistant was talking her into trying some adorable (and undoubtedly sexy) shoes that she hadn't planned on buying.

'I have shoes,' she told the assistant.

'Honey, I have shoes too but a girl always needs more shoes.' A valid point, well made.

'Well, I think I'll probably... oh! Ohhh. Those are rather lovely,' she cooed as the assistant pulled a pair of strappy numbers off the shelf.

'You could just try them on and see what you think?' I suggested. The assistant nodded along with me. Of course, once they were on, Helen was sold. They looked amazing.

'I'm not sure what Bill will think.' Helen giggled as the assistant took the items off to wrap up. We both glanced down at her feet, now back in her own shoes. She always looked nice but clearly had a tendency to veer to the 'sensible' side of the scale when it came to footwear. The ones currently being lovingly placed in a shiny gold box definitely didn't fall into that category.

'Believe me. I think Bill will like them.' I looked back at the box then Helen. 'I mean, rea-a-a-ally like them.' Helen giggled, gave me a nudge, blushed, then giggled again.

Luca's office was empty when, with a minute to spare, we returned to the floor where Donato Solutions resided, but the boardroom, also glass, had a group of seven or eight people sitting around it with tablets, laptops and a projection screen pulled down. Luca was standing beside this, talking animatedly and pointing occasionally with a stick to the various slides. I liked that he was still a bit old school when it came to doing things like that.

Luca glanced up as he finished his presentation and gave me the briefest of smiles before turning back to the others. One woman sat to his right, her dark hair slicked into a chignon with professional-level make-up and a slash of red lips, and she followed Luca's eyeline and studied me for a moment. I had the feeling of being a specimen of some rare but extinct creature in a museum, but something made me hold my position. Ordinarily I'd have been intimidated by such a person. OK, let's face it. I still was. But I gritted my teeth against my natural impulse to look away and instead effected a friendly smile instead. Her cool gaze drifted over me before flicking briefly back to Luca. After one more brief study of me, she returned her attention to the meeting.

My internal office phone rang and I went off to sort out a computer that had just shown its user the dreaded Blue Screen of Death before switching off completely. When I returned to my desk half an hour after clocking-off time, Luca's meeting was still going on. I looked up as I grabbed my bag and saw he was looking out. I raised my hand in a brief wave. I couldn't wait any longer. I had to go and sort myself out in the bathroom and then head off to meet Adrian. A Tube strike they'd been hoping to avert had now gone ahead at the last minute, beginning from four this afternoon, throwing the city into chaos, and now I had to figure out buses to get to the bar, which would take longer, especially at this time of day. I had no idea what time Luca's meeting would actually finish, and it had obviously gone on longer than he'd expected. Whatever it was he wanted to talk to me about would have to wait. A small furrow appeared on his brow. I shrugged and turned away.

* * *

'Hi!' I said a little breathlessly as I finished pushing my way through the crowd to where Adrian was standing with his mates. He peeled away from them and came towards me.

'I was beginning to think you'd stood me up.' He grinned, bending to kiss me.

'I'm only...' I had been about to say two minutes late but got momentarily distracted as his warm lips met mine and his hands moved slowly down from my waist.

'I've missed you,' he whispered, his voice low.

My fingers slid around his neck and pulled him closer. Ooh! Apparently, he had missed me.

'Told you,' he said, reading my features. 'Let's get out of here.'

'Sounds good. I'm starving.'

'Let me just say 'bye to the guys.'

'OK. Do you... umm... want me to come with you?'

'Won't be a sec.' He dashed off.

'OK... I guess that's a no,' I said to myself as he disappeared back to his mates. One craned his neck around, glanced at me then spoke quickly to Adrian, his face serious. Another of his friends gave him a shove and pushed Adrian back towards me with a laugh. Momentarily, I met the eyes of the serious man. He dropped his gaze and turned away.

'Who's that?' I asked when Adrian returned to me.

'Who?' he asked, elbowing his way through the after-work crowd.

'The chap you were talking to. Dark hair. Serious face.'

'Oh. That's Damon.' He stopped and turned. 'You eyeing up my mates?' He laughed.

'No! It's just... he didn't seem that happy about you going off with me.'

We popped out from the throng onto the pavement like peas from an overripe pod and Adrian pulled me towards him. 'Do you mind if we stop talking about my mate? It's kind of a mood killer.'

'Oh, I didn't mean... I just wondered.'

'What?' he asked half distractedly as he waved for a cab.

'Why he doesn't seem to like me.' Adrian turned back to look at me as a taxi pulled into the kerb. I shrugged. 'I'm nice really. I mean, I think I am.'

Adrian pulled me close. 'You are nice. I'd think you were even nicer if you were thinking about me rather than him.'

'Where are we going?'

'There's a new restaurant opening tonight. Invite only but I've managed to wangle one. You up for that?'

'Sounds great.'

'And then... maybe back to your place?'

I thought about the state of my floor, which was due its weekly tidy up, but not until tomorrow. It was also way out on the end of the DLR, which tonight meant a bus ride from hell, whereas Adrian lived near the centre.

'Or yours,' I suggested with a smile.

'I've got a friend staying with me at the moment so...' He left the sentence unfinished. I shrugged OK, still a little confused. Adrian's apartment was not what you'd call 'bijou' and he had a guest room that was actually used for guests, and not a dumping ground as I knew I'd be tempted to use it as – if I'd had a guest room. As it was, my bedroom was the size of Adrian's en suite so second bedrooms were something I could only dream of.

We made our way to the restaurant and as we were about to go inside my phone began to vibrate inside my bag. I pulled it out. Luca. I declined and quickly typed out a message to let him know I was about to go into the restaurant and would call him later. It went blue, showing he'd read it. Then the phone rang again.

'Sorry.' I turned to Adrian. 'I have to get this. Do you want to go in and I'll meet you in there?' He nodded and headed in. Once he'd gone, I stabbed at the phone's screen to accept the call.

'Hi,' he said, almost casually.

'Luca. I'm on a date. We were just about to go into the restaurant.'

'I know. But I told you, I need to talk to you.'

'Luca, this is going to have to wait. I don't know what's going on but you're acting weird.'

'Adrian's cheating on you.'

For a moment everything was silent, followed immediately by a loud ringing in my ears, drowning out the traffic.

'What?' The word snapped out like a short, sharp burst of machine-gun fire.

'I'm sorry. I didn't want to tell you like this. That's why I wanted to see you today. To tell you in person.'

'Why would you say that?' I asked, quieter this time.

'Because he is! I'm sorry, Bee. I know you like him but he's playing you. I saw him last night.'

'Well, you couldn't have. I spoke to him last night and he was at home and had been all evening.'

'Is that what he told you?'

'I spoke to him.'

'What time?'

'God, Luca. I don't know! Let me dig out my minute-by-minute account of yesterday's events, shall I?'

'Bee, I know you're upset but I think you're getting mad with the wrong person. I'm just trying to help.'

'Are you?'

'What's that supposed to mean?' he snapped.

'You haven't liked Adrian from the start.'

'And you think I'd make something like this up and risk hurting you, just because of that!'

'I don't know!'

'Yes, you do, Bee. You know me a hell of a lot better than that! I'm just trying to protect you.'

'I don't need your protection, Luca. I need your support. I need you to be happy for me!'

'I would be if he deserved you, but he's lying to you and you don't deserve that.'

'Luca. I don't know what's got into you and I'm not sure this bloody challenge has done anything good for our friendship. But right now I can't deal with that. I'm out, on a date, and I'm sorry if your pride is hurt that I might not need to rely on you as much as I have for the last thirty years, but things change and I can't believe you'd say something like this just because you don't like the guy I'm seeing.'

'He's using you!' Luca snapped. 'Can't you see that?'

'No! I can't. But clearly you can. I mean, why would a success-ful, good-looking man be interested in a little nobody like me? I can see that would be hard for you to wrap your head around as you only date women who either are, or could easily pass for, models. I may not be Aneeka but that doesn't mean I don't have things to offer. Just because you can't see that doesn't mean others don't.'

'You're taking this all wrong. That's not what I meant. Of course I know you have a lot to offer. I just think – no, I know – you're offering it to the wrong guy!'

I glanced inside. Adrian was sitting at a table near the window and was perusing the wine list. As if sensing he was being watched, he lifted his head and met my eyes before tilting his head in question.

'Everything OK?' he mouthed, frowning.

I pushed a wide smile onto my face, beating back the tears that were threatening to overtake me. I couldn't believe Luca was being like this. He was my best friend. We were supposed to have each other's backs, support each other through thick and thin and all the other clichés that went along with that. And yet since this whole challenge had begun, there had been a shift, small at first, but whatever it was had grown. There was something different about him. I'd get moments of the old Luca, but there were secrets now, pettiness with Adrian that I hadn't seen before. He'd never been overkeen on my boyfriends and I probably hadn't made as much effort as I should have with his dates either, but I'd never, ever try and break them up, no matter how much I disliked them. They were Luca's choice, just as Adrian was mine, and Luca was supposed to support me on that. Had Adrian actually been cheating, I would still be mad at Luca, but purely because I'd be shooting the messenger. Believe me, I'd have plenty enough bullets left for the man in question. But Adrian had been at home yesterday. I'd spoken to him on video so Luca's story had one big hole in it. And I was afraid the best part of our friendship was seeping away down that same hole right now.

'I have to go, Luca. I'm sorry you can't support me on this.' I took the phone from my ear, hearing him still talking, and hung up. Then I switched it off and headed into the restaurant, trying to swallow the huge, painful lump in my throat as I did so.

27

'Everything all right?' Adrian asked as a waiter pulled out a chair for me.

'Yep, yep. Fine.' I waved my hand casually, nominating myself for an Oscar as Adrian seemed to buy this. Inside I was angry, sad, hurt and a whole other raft of emotions I couldn't name right now but they would stay inside. I'd learned from an early age how to hide my emotions when required and had naively hoped I wouldn't need those skills as I grew up, that 'everything would be better'. But something else I'd learned back then was that the ones you should be able to rely on were the ones that let you down the hardest. There was a certain sense of déja vu about the whole situation.

'You sure you're OK?'

I withdrew my award nomination.

'Definitely.' I added in a big wide smile for bonus points this time. 'Sorry to keep you waiting. Did you find a wine you'd like?'

'I did. Shall I order or do you want to take a look at the list first?' This was kind. We both knew my knowledge of wine extended to which end of the bottle it poured out of and that was about it, but it was good of Adrian to play along.

'No, you just order. I'm sure it will be great.'

The waiter brought the wine, Adrian tested it, deemed it acceptable and the waiter then proceeded to pour us each half a glass. Finishing, he made a tiny bow and backed away, disappearing into the lowly lit interior of the restaurant. I tried to relax and put the phone call with Luca out of my head. Reaching out, I picked up my wine and necked it.

'Would you like another?' Adrian gave me a slightly quizzical look.

'Oh. Um. Yes. Thanks.'

'You might want to, er, savour it a little more this time. It has notes of honey and blueberry underlaid with a woody base,' he explained as he poured the golden liquid expertly. I nodded and tried to concentrate. Right now, all I wanted was for it to have notes of alcohol underlaid with yet more alcohol.

'Yes.' I sipped at it, resisting the urge to repeat my previous action. 'Hmm, yes, I can taste those.' I couldn't but it seemed the right thing to say and would hopefully make him forget I'd just necked a glass of wine from a bottle that probably cost more than my monthly flat payment.

'We discovered it on a trip to the Napa Valley vineyards.'

'We?'

'Oh... just a group of us. Such a beautiful place. Have you been?'

I shook my head. Croydon was more my budget than California.

'I think I'll probably go and live there for a while before too long.'

I swallowed the wine I'd been holding in my mouth, searching for its elusive blueberry notes. 'Umm, sorry?'

'America. I've often thought about living there. I think I'll probably try it before too long.'

'Oh. Right. But... umm...'

'Hmm?'

I smiled. 'Never mind.'

'Shall we order?'

I opened my menu and stared at the contents. What with Luca's call and Adrian's announcement that he was likely to bugger off to live in America any time soon, my appetite seemed to have waned. The rumblings of earlier had drifted away like an ebbing summer storm.

'So, would this be a temporary move, or a permanent one, do you think?' I was aiming for a casual conversational tone. Apparently, I nailed it.

'Temporary to start but, if I liked it, I'd probably stay. I don't think I'd have any visa problems.'

'Anywhere in particular?'

'Probably California. I like that whole vibe and, of course, there's all the tech stuff there I could invest in so there's opportunities on the ground.'

'Right. That's, um, quite a long way from your friends and family, isn't it? Wouldn't that bother you?'

'Pop is always dashing about and could easily drop in, and, so long as they serve champagne on the flight, Mum would come as often as I'd like her to.' He laughed and I tried to join in.

I wanted to ask him what those plans meant for his love life. More specifically, us. He'd told me he was looking for something more. Something special. He'd told me he might well have found that with me – and it seemed to be going OK, so far as I knew. I ignored Luca's claim. There was no way he could have seen him out yesterday. He'd had a nap after a long day and then I'd seen him at home on a video call. It was clearly a case of mistaken identity, which Luca was more than happy to cling onto for whatever reason. But... if Adrian really was looking for something deeper and more meaningful, shouldn't the tiny subject of moving continents be something that was discussed? I didn't want to live in America. I liked it here. It had a lot of faults but I was less likely to get shot here, for a start. And I got more than two weeks' holiday.

'You'd love it.'

'Pardon?'

'California. You should go sometime.'

Sometime?

'Well, maybe I will...'

I grabbed his gaze with mine. His was blank for a moment and then seemed to get the message. A smile slid onto his face. 'Great.'

We enjoyed the rest of the meal. Well, Adrian did. To me, everything tasted oddly of cardboard thanks to Luca's interference and Adrian clearly making huge plans that might or might not include me. Due to the eye-watering prices, obviously I exclaimed everything to be absolutely delicious.

'Ready to go?' Adrian asked.

Outside the darkened skies had made good on their threat to drizzle and had actually pushed the boat out and hit the switch for full-on rain.

'We'll just get a cab back to your place.'

'That'll cost a fortune!' I once had to deal with an emergency at my last job and had been there until the early hours. The Tubes had stopped running and I had to get a cab all the way home. When I handed my expenses in, all I got was grief about it. I explained that next time I would fix the emergency in work hours only, thereby avoiding such a circumstance arising again. That was quite brave for me and had more to do with having got in at five in the morning and being back at work for nine than any sudden inclination to make a stand for myself. It wasn't mentioned again.

'My treat.' Adrian winked at me, hailing a cab as he did so. Something inside me sat uneasy. Tonight just felt off. I knew it was me and not him and I felt bad about that but right now I just wanted to go home – alone – crawl under the covers and not think about any of it.

'Adrian?' I began as a cab rolled towards us, its windscreen wipers slapping in time with the rain. He turned to me.

'Do you mind if we, um, leave it tonight?'

'Oh.'

I placed a hand on my tummy. 'I'm not feeling too great.'

'Oh. Right.'

I wasn't exactly lying. I didn't feel great, but it was nothing to do with the food.

'Perhaps I can take your mind off things?' He ran the back of his hand down the side of my neck, fingers teasing the top of my dress.

I laid my hand gently over his and wrapped my fingers around them. He paused in his nuzzling as the message got through, then stepped back.

'Sure. Of course. You take this cab. I'll grab another.'

'I can get the bus.' I waggled the Oyster card tucked into the back of my phone case.

'I told you, I don't mind.'

My brain suddenly skittered back to his unexpected announcement that, despite what he had said about getting serious, he might be taking himself off to America, possibly indefinitely, at some point soon.

'Actually, that would be good, if you don't mind.'

A cab pulled up and Adrian handed the cabby enough cash to cover the journey and left me to give him the exact address.

'I hope you feel better soon,' he said, pecking me on the cheek.

'Thanks. And sorry to ruin the evening.'

He shook his head. 'You didn't. Don't worry.' He closed the door and the cabby pulled out into the road, the wipers making a hypnotic sound as they sloosh-slooshed back and forth across the windscreen. I sat back and all the thoughts I'd held back this evening rushed in.

I felt bad about curtailing the evening with Adrian, but I really wasn't in the mood and pretending I was wasn't fair to him or me. All because of bloody Luca. I could kill him. I didn't believe his accusations for a moment, of course. But the doubt was there now, and, even if I didn't believe it, it had cast a pall on the night for me, wriggling around in my head.

I leant forward. 'Actually, could you take me somewhere else instead?' I asked the driver.

'Wherever you like, love. What's the address?'

*   *   *

The rain was coming down in torrents and, not being dressed for deep-sea fishing, after even a short dash from cab to building I now found myself drenched to my underwear and dripping unceremoniously in the swish foyer of Luca's apartment block.

'Miss Bee! You're soaked!' Igor was an upright, striking-looking Russian who suited the livery of the complex to a tee. He took absolute pride in a job many of our own country would sniff at and refused to not add a prefix to my name, even though I'd asked a tonne of times. In the end, it seemed to make him happy so I let him.

'It's drizzling a little out there.'

Igor gave me a grin and began to lift the handset. 'I shall tell Mr Luca you are here.'

'That's fine. I'll just head on up, if that's OK?'

Igor replaced the receiver. I'd been there so many times, there was nothing to let on to the concierge that there was every chance I might actually strangle one of the inhabitants of this swanky address this evening. I pondered this in the lift. I'd have to find a way to excuse Igor for not following strict protocol, should that happen. Being so mad at Luca that I could happily bump him off was one thing, but I definitely didn't want to lose Igor his job – I liked him. Luca, I wasn't so sure about right now.

Reaching the correct floor, I strode out of the lift and headed towards Luca's apartment door and began hammering on it. Moments later, it swung open mid hammer and I overbalanced. Luca's hands wrapped around me and steadied me back into a more upright position.

'Bee? What are you doing here? Bloody hell. You're absolutely soaked! Come in.'

'No, thank you.' I stood my ground, with said ground getting wetter every second. 'I just have something to say and then I'll be going.'

'You'll be going straight into hypothermia at this rate.'

'Don't be so dramatic,' I said, punctuating the sentence with a loud, unladylike sneeze.

'Oh, for God's sake.' Luca reached out, grabbed my hand and tugged me into the apartment. Disappearing for a moment, he returned with a large, fluffy bath towel. 'Take off your coat.'

'No.'

'Bee. This is ridiculous! You're soaked to the bone. What the hell are you doing out in weather like this? I thought you had dinner plans anyway.'

'I did!' I snapped back at him, feeling the shivers start to ripple throughout my body. 'Very nice dinner plans, actually, but you ruined them.'

'Please take that coat off. You're going to make yourself ill out of pure stubbornness!' I took the coat off but only because it was beginning to feel as if a large wet sheep had settled around my shoulders and the combined weight and chill made me feel as if I were sinking.

Luca took the coat and replaced it with the bath towel, which was deliciously warm. An overwhelming feeling of wanting to snuggle down into it began to creep over me.

'Better?'

I snapped my head up. 'Drier. Yes. Thank you.' Manners still won out even when I was mad. Some people were pithy and sharp when pushed to a limit. I, on the other hand, was over-polite. It didn't have quite the same impact. And certainly not the one I was aiming for.

'You're welcome.' The towel began to slip a little and Luca's hand reached out to adjust it.

'Don't,' I snapped.

He paused, gave the merest hint of a head tilt, then slowly dropped his hand and placed it casually in his trouser pocket. He was still in his suit from earlier, which meant he hadn't been home that long himself. Probably had his own hot date following the meeting. One that hadn't been ruined by interfering friends. A thought suddenly struck me.

'Am I interrupting anything?' Tearing Luca off a strip because he'd been an arsehole was one thing but – and perhaps this came back to the whole manners thing – I wasn't about to do that in front of company.

'Nope.' He shrugged, hands still in pockets.

'I just—' I waved at his attire '—assume you may have been out.'

'The meeting finished far later than we planned. I haven't had a chance to change yet.'

'Right. But you did have a chance to call me and try to sabotage my date.'

'I wasn't trying to do that.'

'No.' I waited a beat. 'Just trying to sabotage the whole damn relationship.'

'You're overreacting.'

'I'm overreacting?' I took a step back and my fake Louboutin squelched.

'Yes. I'm not trying to sabotage anything. I'm trying to help you.'

'Help me what? Be alone forever? Always be there for you to call on for when you're bored and have nothing better to do or no one else to talk to?'

Luca's dark eyes flashed with anger. 'I have never, ever thought of you like that and you know it. If you do think that, then it's your own insecurities generating it, not the truth.'

'Oh, you're a fine one to talk about truth!' I shot back. 'How about your claim that my boyfriend is cheating on me? A man you immediately decided you didn't like purely because another stockbroker stung you years ago. Now whose insecurities are on show?'

'You think that's why I said something?' Luca took a step back from me.

'Why else would you? It's clear you don't like him. But then you don't seem to like anyone I meet. There's always something, isn't there, Luca? I can never quite get it right. You know, sometimes you're just like my parents! I'm just never quite good enough.'

'I am nothing like your parents!' He turned and strode away from me, muttering something in Italian. This was always a good indicator of Luca's temper. Rattling away in Italian meant he'd hit the red zone. He swivelled back suddenly. 'I can't believe you'd say something like that.'

'Well, what, then? It's true, isn't it? Poor little Bee. She tries so hard and never quite gets it right. But I note you never bothered to make the effort to set me up with anyone. Would it have been that hard? You meet people all the time, know lots of interesting people and if you like to spend time with them, they must be decent. But I guess perhaps I'm not quite the right type to mingle with them.'

'What's that supposed to mean?'

'God, it's obvious, isn't it, Luca? Some of them had to be single but it didn't once occur to you to think, oh, maybe this guy and Bee would hit it off. But that wouldn't sit well with your impressive CEO status, would it? Introducing someone in your business life to a simple data input clerk!'

'You're the bloody head of IT, not a data input clerk. You weren't an input clerk at the other place either. You ran the damn department there too but you were too scared to stand up for yourself and tell them so you let them pay you those rates, let them believe that's all you were worth. Don't blame me for you not wanting to go for things when the offers were there.'

I swallowed, trying not to accept that he had a point, but knowing that he did. On that aspect at least.

'So?'

'So what?' he snapped.

'Why wasn't I good enough for anyone?'

'I never said that.'

'But you never did anything about it either. There must be a reason? Surely with all your sport and business and all the other bloody things you do you must have met one person who wouldn't think I was a complete—'

'Stop it!'

'What?'

'You! This! Putting yourself down! You know I hate it.'

'Well, how do you think that all makes me feel?'

'Did it ever occur to you that it was the other way around?' he yelled at me. I stared at him blankly. 'That I didn't think they were good enough for you?'

I considered that for a moment. 'No.'

'No. Well, it wouldn't, would it?'

'Isn't that for me to decide though?'

'While I stand back and watch someone I introduced you to hurt you?'

'I'm not as easily hurt as you think I am.'

Luca gave a laugh that contained zero humour. 'Since when?'

'Since always!'

'You are. You just think that because your parents couldn't or chose not to see your hurt that no one else can. Newsflash, Bee. You show a hell of a lot more than you think you do. And so no, I wasn't prepared to watch that hurt if someone I hooked you up with upset you.'

'And what if they'd made me happy?'

Luca remained silent.

'That's what I thought. You think I'm so hopeless at relationships that that scenario was pretty unlikely.'

'I never said that,' he snapped. 'And why the hell are you here shouting at me anyway? It's obviously Adrian you're angry with!'

'Oh! It's "obvious", is it?'

Luca's jaw was set so tight I could probably file a nail on the sharp plane of his jawline, now dark with the day's stubble.

'Once again, you don't know me as well as you think you do because it's not him I'm angry at. It is most definitely you.'

'Why? I'm not the one cheating on you!'

'And neither is he!'

'Bee. I saw him!'

'When?'

'Yesterday evening.'

'Where?'

'At a cosy, pricey little restaurant in Bermondsey.'

'People are allowed to eat out.'

'With a woman.'

'A friend, a colleague. It could have been anyone!'

He gave me a look. 'They were kissing, Bee.' He held up a hand, pre-empting my interruption. 'And no, I don't mean peck-on-the-cheek type. Proper kissing.'

'Then you obviously have the wrong person.'

'I was two tables away. It's pretty hard to get it wrong from that distance.'

'Did he see you?'

'No. He was... occupied. I asked the waiter to move us and we ended up behind a large pot plant.'

I took a deep breath and let it out slowly. 'Well, you must be mistaken because we video-chatted. He was at home.'

'What time?'

'I don't know. About ten, I guess. I'd rung earlier but he was asleep.'

'Asleep?'

'Yes. He told me he'd had a long day and had nodded off.'

The look on Luca's face made me boil. 'Stop it! You're not ruining this. I don't know who you saw but it wasn't Adrian. He wouldn't do that. And if it wasn't for you and your insidious little remark, your determination to hate him and stir trouble, I'd be with him right now. We were on the way to my place and your stupid, vicious accusation had been spinning round and round in my brain all evening so I ended up crying off and sending him home alone.'

'Good.'

I stared at Luca. The air in the apartment was thick enough to spread on toast and yet it felt as if there were no air at all. As if someone with an overpriced vacuum had put it on boost and sucked it all up. We stood there, neither of us saying a word.

'I need to go.'

'I'll drive you.'

'No.'

'Come on. I know there's a Tube strike, the buses will be a nightmare and it'll be twice as hard finding a cab in this weather.'

'I think you've done enough for one night, don't you?' I looked up at him. I could feel my mascara running but I wasn't sure if that was due to the rain or the tears spilling over onto my cheeks. I took the towel from around my shoulders and put the cold, heavy, rain-soaked coat back on.

'I've never lied to you, Bee, and I wouldn't start with something like this. I know you like him. I'm not sure why.' He gave a shrug that ordinarily I'd have smiled at but I was beyond smiling now. Everything was wrong. As if the world had rocked off its axis just a tiny bit. Luca and I had argued before, of course we had. But something about this felt different and as I glanced at Luca's face I knew he felt it too. 'But I care about you. I don't want you hurt again, ever. You've had more than enough pain.'

Tilting my head up, I met his serious eyes. There was a deep crease in his forehead and the tie that had been merely loosened when I got in had been yanked off and discarded. Luca didn't really do dishevelled, except in that morning way that good-looking men always managed to pull off so well. But right now, he definitely fell into that category. This was different. In nearly thirty years, it had never felt like this.

'Please let me drive you.'

'I think it's better for us both if you don't.'

'Then let me get Igor to call you a car.'

The thought of protesting at this too skated across my mind but the sound of my teeth chattering was drowning out my brain.

I nodded and Luca lifted the phone and briefly made the necessary arrangements. I opened the door as he returned the entry-phone receiver to its cradle. Luca gently pushed it shut.

'Don't go like this, Bee. It feels wrong. I hate it.'

'I hate it too. And it is wrong. But it's done and I'm tired and just want to go home.'

He waited and then opened the door again. I stepped out into the hallway and walked towards the lift at a slower pace than I'd taken on the inward journey. Sadness and confusion clouded my thoughts and all I wanted to do was sleep. I entered the lift, which was thankfully open and waiting. Without turning, I knew Luca was still there, so I let the doors close behind me before I turned back to face them.

28

'The car is outside, Miss Bee.'

'Thanks, Igor,' I said, mustering up the best smile I could manage. Even without the slight flicker of his expression, I knew it had been a pretty poor imitation of one. He picked up a large umbrella and walked to the door with it.

'Oh, that's fine. I can just run to it. I don't think I can get any wetter but there's no need for you to come out in it too.' The wind had picked up now and was blowing the rain round and sideways so I wasn't convinced the umbrella was going to be a lot of good anyway.

'Is fine.' Igor smiled and held out his elbow for me to take.

'Thank you,' I said, stupidly feeling as if I was going to burst into tears again at this gentle act of kindness.

We walked to the car and Igor kept the brolly over me as much as possible until the last minute.

'May I say something, Miss Bee? It may be out of place. Is that the right word?'

'What is it?' I asked, softly.

'I worry about you. You and Mr Luca. Always smiling. Laughing.' He linked his fingers together. 'Like this. But tonight is first time I've seen you leave so sad. I worry.'

'We're fine, Igor. Just a difference of opinion.'

Igor nodded under the umbrella. It was so much more than that though and he clearly knew it too. Shutting the door, he gave a couple of taps on the roof and the driver pulled smoothly away into the dark and motored towards the edge of London and home.

* * *

The following couple of weeks were odd. Luca and I were talking – but not really talking. This was another first in our relationship and not something I'd ever seen coming. We kept it professional at work and did our best to keep it natural too. The last thing I wanted, and the last thing I wanted for him, was for people to be gossiping about 'us'. For the most part, I think we did a pretty good job, although I did catch Helen throwing a few sideways glances between the two of us when she thought no one was looking. I'd already figured out that Helen's character was much underestimated. Her voice tended towards the squeaky side and her mannerisms could imply that she was a little bit ditsy but I – and clearly Luca, having hired her in the first place – had soon realised she was sharp as a hungry shark's tooth. We had gone for coffee together a few times, but I was always careful to steer the conversation towards her life rather than mine – or Luca's. Having just welcomed a new grandchild, she was easily, and luckily for me, distracted and happy to chat about him.

There was another reason I was keen to keep the conversation focused away from me. Since the evening I'd cut short our date, and, if I thought about it, longer than that, Adrian had seemed a little more busy, and a little less keen to meet up. When we had, I'd asked him if something was wrong but he'd just dismissed it as a 'crazy work schedule', so I'd accepted that. I was still confident that Luca's accusations had been wrong and so I'd pushed them from my mind. But I couldn't help wonder whether Adrian's enthusiasm for seeing me had gone off the boil somewhat. He hadn't called for a few days and if I messaged him, he did reply but there were often large gaps before he did. But perhaps work was just tiring him out.

Tia nodded when I was telling her this as we made our way through a bottle of wine, having already demolished a large takeaway pizza and cheesy garlic bread.

'What?'

'What? she asked. 'I'm agreeing.'

'No. Your gesture says you're agreeing but your face is saying something entirely different.'

'It is not.'

'It is too!'

'Jono!' Silence. 'Jono!' Tia yelled louder. Jono poked his head around the door from the spare room, tiny paintbrush in hand from where he was putting the finishing touches to a *Lord of the Rings* model. One earcup of a pair of wireless headphones was pushed back so he could hear his beloved's yells. Tia conceded to having a couple of these models on display in their living room, but I noticed they were getting more and more obscured by the stripy fronds of a spider plant draping itself over them. This, I suspected, was no accident.

'Yeah?'

'Bee's questioning my "I agree" face.'

'Oh.' Jono looked at her, then at me, then down at the model as though that might tell him what his next move was supposed to be.

'Look.' She turned to me. 'Tell me again.'

'What?'

'About it being perfectly normal for Adrian to not be so responsive. You know, the whole being tired thing.'

'No.'

'Yes. Come on.'

'It's fine. I believe you believe me.'

'No, you don't. Come on.'

I knew from long experience this matter would not be dropped so I let out a long sigh, exchanged an eye roll with Jono and repeated my earlier statement as per Tia's request. She did the same nod.

'See?'

'Yeah. You still look like you're merely humouring me.'

'I do not! Jono?'

He shrugged. 'Bee's right. You're nodding but this—' he circled his face with the paintbrush '—tells a whole different story.' Tia's mouth dropped open but before she could say anything Jono pushed the headphones back on straight and closed the door for added emphasis.

'Obviously he's wrong.'

'He's not. It does. But it doesn't matter. I don't want to be living in someone's pocket anyway. I like doing my own thing.' Glancing up, I noticed the exact same expression on Tia's face as before.

'I do!'

'You don't. You just got used to it because you were always left on your own. That's a different thing altogether.' This was the most annoying thing about people knowing you for most of your life. It was hard to get shit by them.

'Anyway...' I said in an attempt to change the subject.

'Anyway, yes. You'd know if something was up.'

'Exactly!' My stomach knotted as it had been doing for several days. 'And it's not. So that's fine.'

'Absolutely.'

There was a lull in the conversation and we both knew the other one was stretching the truth but, in the interest of friendship, and unlike Luca, each kept silent.

'Have you spoken to Luca?'

'Yep. Saw him at work today.'

'I rather meant about something other than ordering printer paper and ink.'

'I don't have to talk to him about that. There's a lovely chap called Amir who does a stationery inventory once a week. It's marvellous.'

'You know what I mean.'

'Yes. And no.'

'Why not?'

'There's nothing else to say.'

'There's always been something else to say when it comes to you two.'

'Then perhaps we've said it all.' I fiddled with the twisted stem of the wine glass, catching the light with it, sending sparkles and shapes across the room. 'Or maybe we've both said a little bit too much.'

'I hate this.'

I looked back at her. I did too but what was said couldn't be unsaid. I knew he'd been trying to protect me, but I didn't need protecting. I needed supporting. That was what Luca didn't seem to get. Or be able to offer.

'I'd better get going.'

Tia rose from the sofa, untucking her long legs, still shown off in cut-offs despite it edging steadily to Christmas. I dreaded to think what their heating bill was.

'Bye, Jono!' I yelled. The door opened, a hand popped out and waved happily as we heard a snippet of discussion about what exact shade of green an Ork's underpants should be. I wasn't sure that was exactly what he said but it was definitely something along those lines.

'Love you.'

'Love you, too.'

'You've got this, you know.' This time Tia's expression coincided with her words.

* * *

I leant back in my trendy, expensive but surprisingly supportive office chair and stretched. We were in the process of researching for an upgrade of the whole IT system and time had got away from me. While I'd been immersed in brochures and websites, the sky outside had turned from cool winter blue to burnt orange to a deep midnight without me much noticing and when I looked up, nearly everyone in the office had gone. In the corner, Luca's task lamp still shone, casting a pool of soft yellow light onto his desk, and I could see him leaning back in his chair, talking hands-free on the phone, gesticulating animatedly as he did so.

Gathering up my things, I pondered on what I had in my fridge for when I got home. An image of a rather sad and mostly empty interior filled my mind. I really needed to get into a routine of shopping properly now that I was cooking from scratch a bit more rather than just bunging in the cheapest ready meal I could find. The thought that I'd done that and what they might have contained was one I didn't want to spend too much time on, so I made a note to go shopping first thing tomorrow instead of having a lazy Saturday lie in. In the meantime, I decided to head for Adrian's favourite bar. That way I could get a double whammy both of seeing him and getting food at the bar. We'd never stayed long enough to sample it – at least I hadn't, but Adrian had told me it was good and, from what I'd seen float past me on occasions balanced atop adept waiting staff's trays, it all looked pretty appetising. Adrian had said he was probably going to be there tonight when we'd talked yesterday but, with us both having busy work schedules right now, we hadn't made any definite plans. But sometimes surprise dates were the best.

I knew me baling part way through the last one hadn't been ideal and I had the idea that it had thrown things off kilter. I wanted them back on kilter and I thought Adrian did too but that whole male pride thing was getting in the way of him actually spelling it out. If he didn't, I told myself, then he'd be ghosting me, not calling me. It was certainly easily enough done and wouldn't have been my first experience of such treatment, but it wasn't like that this time. Sometimes things just took a bit more effort and, having felt as if I'd been sitting back almost my entire life letting things happen to me, it was time to be more proactive.

'Hi.'

Packing away my stuff, I hadn't noticed Luca had left his office and was now standing a few feet from my desk, resting on the one in front of mine. His long legs were crossed casually at the ankles and his shirt sleeves were rolled back. It was a 'no tie' day and the crisp white shirt contrasted with the skin it exposed.

'Hi,' I said, dropping my phone into the outer pocket of my bag.

'You're here late.'

I glanced up and threw him a quick smile. 'Got caught up researching.'

'You look like you're enjoying it.'

'I am.' I gave a quick shrug before hoisting my bag onto my shoulder. 'I'm kind of nerdy that way but you already knew that.'

He gave a flick of his eyebrows that both questioned and acknowledged the statement, but accompanied it with a soft smile.

'You look tired. Are you not sleeping?' There were dark shadows under his eyes that I hadn't noticed before and there was just a little less... vitality about his manner.

'I'm OK.'

'Too many hot dates with Aneeka wearing you out?' I teased.

He pulled a face. 'No.'

I paused. 'Is your family OK?'

He nodded.

'Is it something about the business? Is everything all right?' I'd stepped a little closer now, my hand on his forearm, naturally falling back into our old ways without thinking amid my concern. 'You can tell me, you know that. I won't say anything.'

Luca touched the fingertips of my free hand, a soft laugh in his voice as he responded. 'Everyone at home is fine and everything here is fine. You're not about to lose your job.'

I stepped back, stung. 'That wasn't why I was saying it.'

'I know. I was just trying to reassure you.' The smile was gone now, replaced with a frown, which he followed with a head shake. The moment of familiarity had gone, dissolved as quickly as it had manifested. 'Why is everything so difficult between us now? I feel like I have to walk on eggshells around you.' There was a sad resignation to his tone and it made my stomach twist and felt so much worse than if he'd said it angrily.

I looked up and met his eyes, the gaze holding between us. 'I don't know,' I replied softly. Sadly.

'I hate it.'

'I know. But you did accuse my boyfriend of cheating on me. That's kind of a problem.'

Luca broke the gaze but didn't answer.

'Apologising would be a start.'

Luca took a step back. 'I'm not going to apologise when I haven't done anything wrong.'

I took my own step back. 'Of course you did something wrong!'

'No. I didn't. I told you something in good faith. Just because you refuse to acknowledge that and are happy for him to continue making a fool out of you, then that's your decision.'

I snapped off my desk light with a vigour it didn't deserve.

'And you wonder why things are difficult between us? Unbelievable.'

'What? Because I'm honest with you? Because I'm not pandering to you and pretending everything is fine, like Tia is because she doesn't want to upset you?'

'Whereas you're apparently just fine with upsetting me!'

'Of course I'm not. Don't be ridiculous.'

'You know what? I'm hardly surprised that you're not out on a date tonight if this is how you treat Aneeka. If you want to beat me on this damn challenge, then I'd suggest readjusting your attitude.'

'I treat women with the respect they deserve and you bloody well know that. My relationships didn't last because I was looking for that one person who lights me up, who has the right chemistry, who I feel I can be myself with. That's why. Not because I treat anyone badly and I don't appreciate you suggesting that I do.'

I'd said the words in anger and hurt and I could see both of those reflected in his face. We each knew he was right on that front. Luca was charming and chivalrous and respectful and, knowing it was an unfair accusation, I felt my cheeks heat at his words. But I remained silent, childishly refusing to apologise purely because he hadn't either.

'And I don't give a shit about winning, Bee. I just didn't want you getting hurt, much less by an idiot like Adrian who doesn't deserve you.'

'You made a snap judgement on him and you've stuck to it and when you saw someone who looked vaguely like him, you automatically decided it was definitely him seeing another woman.'

'It was him.'

'Did you go up to him? Say hi?'

'No.'

'Why not?'

'I didn't think you'd want me to. Plus I didn't particularly trust myself. I've not hit anyone since I was seven years old and Ben Copperthwaite pushed you down the stairs at school. But this guy has kind of a punchable face and I didn't want to tempt fate.'

'Aren't you the hero?'

He let out a long breath.

'His dating profile is still live. Did you know that?'

'What?'

'On the site. It's still live. I take it you've paused yours.'

I cleared my throat. 'Yes. I have.'

'Well, he hasn't. So he's still accepting matches while he's supposed to be building something with you as you're "special".'

'I knew I should never have told you that – that you'd just make fun of me.'

'I'm not making fun. I just think he's full of shit.'

'Right. Well. Thanks for that insightful psychological opinion and, as much as I'm enjoying this conversation, I need to get going.'

'Where are you off to?'

'Why do you care?' I snapped back, petulantly.

Luca stared at me for a moment before throwing his hands

up. 'I've absolutely no idea.' With that, he turned on his custom-made Italian shoe's heel and stalked back to his glass box. The door swung heavily as he shoved it closed.

Tears pricked at my eyes as I rode down in the lift. I hated this. I hated all of it. I had no idea why Luca was being so different, and so difficult. After decades of being so in tune with one another it felt as if we were now completely out of sync, like a badly dubbed foreign film. The words were still flowing but the mouths had long stopped moving. But I didn't know what to do. It seemed that every time we tried to take a step towards where we'd been, the ground opened back up. And now I'd begun to wonder if it was fixable. Or if this was really it...

29

I swiped a thumb under each eye in the lift mirror and gave a sniff. Attractive. I dug in my bag, reapplied my lipstick and gave my hair a brush. Not perfect but better. The lift slowed to a stop, and I stepped out into the echoing foyer, the lights of the huge Christmas tree now dominating it twinkling brightly, and out onto the cold street of the city. There was an icy chill to the air that made my eyes water. At least I could use that as an excuse should anyone question the slight red rim to my eyes. Head down, scarf up, I marched along the pedestrianised area next to the office building towards the nearest Tube station. A message pinged on my phone. Tia.

Hey hon. You ok? What you up to?

Hi. Fine.

I didn't have the energy to get into explaining yet another fight with Luca to her. Plus it would only upset her.

Just on my way to surprise Adrian at the bar.

Oh. Right. He doesn't know you're coming?

No. Hadn't really arranged anything but thought it might be nice to see him. Long day.

Yep. Sounds great. OK. Speak later then.

OK. Love you

Love you too. Be safe xx

I clicked off the chat, dropped the phone back in my bag and made my way to Adrian's favourite bar.

Just as I was about to enter the bar, my phone rang. Luca. I was still angry with him and I didn't want to say anything else I might regret so I stared at it, waiting until it finally rang off. No message popped up so he'd obviously chosen not to leave a voicemail. I tucked it back in my bag and headed into the crowded bar.

Pushing my way through the people, I edged my way towards where Adrian and his friends tended to gather. I rocked up onto my tiptoes and peered through a gap between two suit-jacketed shoulders and saw the side profile of the guy who'd looked at me before falling into a short but deep conversation with Adrian on a previous occasion. Damon, was it? I excused myself through and popped out between them, coming to a halt beside him. He turned and glanced at me, then looked again.

'Hello.'

'Hello,' he said, a hint of insecurity in the soft Irish lilt of his voice. He had short, chestnut-brown hair cut into a neat style, and deep blue eyes set in a kind-looking face.

'It's Damon, isn't it?' I offered my hand. 'I'm Bee.'

He shook it, nodding. 'Nice to meet you,' he said, but his manner didn't seem to back up the words. 'Does, um, Adrian know you're here?'

'Not yet. I was late out of work so thought I'd surprise him and get some food at the same time. I've heard it's good.'

He nodded again.

'Is Adrian here?' I asked, peering around.

Damon gave me a look that in any other circumstance, I would have interpreted as pity. I'd seen it enough times after Dad's accident to know what it looked like. Damon took a small step to the side. A short distance behind him, Adrian was leaning against the very end of the bar, chatting to an exceptionally short man wearing a loud striped shirt and clashing braces who'd clearly watched *Wall Street* one too many times.

'OK, thanks.' I smiled up at Damon. He looked back at me and smiled but there was something off about it. An awkwardness. Maybe he just wasn't very good with women. Or maybe Adrian had told him about my poky little flat and clearly I wasn't dressed from head to toe in Designer. Perhaps all that signalled to him that I was after Adrian's money. Perhaps Damon himself had been hurt in such a way and didn't want that for his friend.

'I'm not after his money, or anything,' I blurted.

Damon's deep blue eyes widened slightly. 'I never thought you were.'

'Oh. Right. It's just that before I saw you and Adrian talking a bit animatedly and I seemed to be the topic and now you don't really seem keen...' I stopped, not sure exactly where I was going with the conversation and also halted by the incredulous look forming on his face.

'No.' He shook his head. 'I don't have a problem with you at all.'

'Oh. Right. Good. OK.' If this was a play the stage directions would have *insert awkward pause here*. As I couldn't rewrite this particular script, I smiled, nodded and headed off towards Adrian. The short guy noticed me first and nudged Adrian, who turned, the laughter on his face shrinking away. Not exactly the reaction I was hoping for. I tried not to misstep and continued towards him, the smile on my face now feeling a little forced.

'Hi!' I said.

'Hi,' he replied. He waited a beat then kissed me on the cheek. It was hardly the stuff of romantic novels, but I got that some people weren't always that demonstrative in front of their friends. 'What are you doing here?'

I opened my mouth to reply just as a stunning brunette of the calibre Luca tended to go for approached. Long, shapely legs strutted on impossibly high heels, their stilettos so thin I was waiting for them to bend at every step. A very short red bodycon dress with long sleeves topped off the endless tanned legs. Shiny hair artfully waved tumbled across one shoulder and framed the perfectly made-up face. She strutted with hips swaying leaving a wake of admiring looks behind her. Adrian was watching her intently and when she noticed, a Hollywood smile broke onto her previously pouting face. A smile he returned. She came up to him, slipped her arms around his waist and placed a long, lingering kiss on his lips, which he also returned. I guessed he wasn't so shy after all.

'I missed you,' she breathed.

'She's only been to the toilet.' A soft whisper came from beside me and I turned to find Damon standing there. He pulled a sympathetic face. I swallowed and did the tiniest of nods in acknowledgement.

'Who's this?' she asked, seeing me standing there, still rooted to the spot while my brain took its own sweet time in processing all the information before me. There was an accent to the words. American. A light bulb went on... *California.*

'This is Bee. I told you about her.'

He told her about me?

'Oh. Right. Yes.' She smiled but there was no warmth behind it. 'Did you two have arrangements tonight?'

Umm, right here!

'I don't think so.' He looked at me questioningly.

'Err. No,' I managed to get out, trying to process the fact that this woman clearly knew he was seeing someone else and was just as clearly not bothered about it. But then, I supposed if you looked like that, you probably knew you had the edge on any competition. It was a shame Adrian hadn't had the decency to share that same information with me.

'I, umm...' I cleared my throat. 'I just wondered if I might be able to catch you here. See if I could grab a quick word.' I summoned up what I hoped was a casual tone and tried to adjust my face to suit, unsure as to whether it was working. Damon glanced at me and gave the merest hint of a nod and smile. I realised the discussion before probably hadn't been about Damon not liking or trusting me, but his own friend's behaviour. I didn't really know him but I liked him already. What he was doing being friends with someone who was clearly a huge eejit was a question for another time.

'Sure,' Adrian answered, his arm still around the brunette's tiny waist. He didn't move.

'Perhaps in private?' I elaborated.

'Oh. Right. That OK with you, babe?' He turned to the woman and I was quite proud of myself for not actually screaming.

She shrugged one elegant shoulder and picked up a cocktail that matched her dress and took a seductive suck on the straw. Adrian faltered. Bored now, I interrupted.

'It will only take a minute and I'm on a schedule, so if you don't mind.' I just hoped Damon wouldn't dob me in, having already blabbed to him my original reason for coming to the bar. He didn't say a word. In fact, there was the hint of a smile on his lips, which disappeared behind a pint glass.

'Right. Yeah, sure.'

I walked across to a slightly less crowded area in the most confident manner I could muster and then turned to face Adrian.

'Are you going to make a scene?'

'A scene?'

'Yeah. About Brandy.'

I shrugged, although it felt a bit as if someone had stuck a coathanger in my shirt. 'Why should I?'

'Some women are funny. They expect all this monogamous stuff.'

'Well, I suppose when you tell someone that you're looking for something special and think you may have found it with that particular someone, it's easy to see a justification for them getting "funny".'

'Yeah, but everyone says that, don't they? It's all part of the game, right?'

It was a game to him. It had all been a game. And I'd just been a pawn in it. Not to mention a total idiot.

'No, Adrian. Not everyone says that. That's the sort of thing that should only be said if it's actually meant.'

'See. I knew you'd be funny. This is why I didn't tell you about the others.'

Others? Plural? I decided I didn't want to know.

'You know what, it's fine anyway. I came here tonight to tell you that I don't think this is working for me.'

'Oh, right. Yeah. I did wonder.'

'What does that mean?'

'Just a few things really. Like, you don't always seem comfortable in higher-end places I tend to like so that's a bit of an issue.'

'I'm fine with them!' I snapped.

'It's OK.' He laid a condescending hand on my arm. 'Some people who aren't used to them can feel a bit out of their depth.'

'I said I was fine.'

'And you're kind of... No, it doesn't matter now. Anyway, it was fun. Good luck and all that.'

'I'm kind of what?' I reached out and stopped him.

'It's fine. Doesn't matter.'

'Tell me,' I said, tightening the grip on his arm, something I didn't notice until he winced. Luca had always said I was stronger than I looked.

'OK,' he said, rubbing his arm. 'Tense in bed. Not exactly the most fun.'

My face burned with humiliation and only increased in heat when a small group nearby turned and began exchanging looks, clearly having overheard Adrian's declaration.

'Funny. I've never found her to be that way at all,' a deep voice stated as strong arms snaked around me from behind and pulled me close, leaving the suggestion in the air that perhaps the problem wasn't with me at all. My skin prickled as the colour rose in it, but now I wasn't sure if it was due to Adrian's accusation or the rough rasp of lust in the voice contradicting him.

I knew the voice and I knew the arms. I also knew he had absolutely no idea what I was like in bed. Luca dropped a kiss on an exposed piece of my neck. 'Sorry I'm late. Something came up last minute.' I turned and caught a breath as Luca's eyes locked onto mine with a look that could start a forest fire. Stunned, I stared a moment longer and Luca's resulting smile fanned the flames. Swallowing hard, I snapped back to face Adrian. I wasn't exactly sure what Luca's plan was but, in this moment, I supported it wholeheartedly purely to witness the look on Adrian's face right now.

'You're seeing him? I thought you said you were just friends.'

I gave a shrug, knowing I was absolutely crap at lying and wanting to get out of here with at least some shred of dignity left intact. The group to our right were now surreptitiously watching and I saw a couple of the women mentally comparing Luca and Adrian. From their exchange of glances, I guessed Luca was winning.

Luca filled in for me. 'You know how these things happen sometimes. Suddenly you realise the right one has been there in front of you all the time. And everything just fits.'

'Huh.' Adrian's lip sneered and I realised I hadn't really known him at all. I'd known what he wanted me to know. And perhaps only seen what I wanted to see. 'I didn't think you were the type to sleep around,' he snapped, as Brandy drifted over towards us. Luca tensed behind me but I rested my hands on his, signalling I was fine. I remained silent but regarded Adrian levelly with an expression that told him in no uncertain terms what I thought of his comment. He looked away.

'And who's this?' Brandy breathed dreamily, staring at Luca. 'Aren't you going to introduce us?'

'Luca Donato,' Luca answered after a moment when it was clear that Adrian had absolutely no intention of doing so. He shook her offered hand very briefly before dropping it and returning it to my waist. Disappointment and a little shock flitted across her face. Clearly she was used to having far more impact on men than that. To be fair, she wasn't the only one in a slight state of bewilderment.

'You ready for dinner? I thought we could try *Bianco Nero*,' Luca said, turning me to face him.

Adrian gave a snort. 'You'll never get in there. It's booked up months in advance. You have to be Hollywood A-list or major royalty to get a table.'

Luca tucked a loose strand of my hair back behind one ear and smiled, his whole being for that moment focused on me as if I were the sun and he were the earth, orbiting happily and dependently. I swallowed, remembering not to get caught up in this. That, for whatever reason, Luca was playing a part and if it meant not looking like quite such an idiot in front of Adrian and the rest of them, then I could go along with it. But it did seem that Luca had completely missed his calling. If tonight's performance was anything to go by, there was a Golden Globe with his name written all over it. He turned his head to glance down at Adrian and gave a shrug.

'I guess that depends on who you know.'

Brandy was practically drooling, and suddenly looking a lot less enamoured with her own date. Adrian, meanwhile, had turned puce.

'Ready?' Luca asked me, before Adrian could form any sort of reply.

I nodded.

'Oh, just one more thing, Adrian. I was once told you didn't deserve me, but I thought that person was wrong. I realise now that they were correct all along. I deserve so much better than someone like you.'

We turned our backs, Luca taking my hand, squeezing it

gently in support as we made our way back through the throng and out onto the street. We took a few steps like this, until we were out of sight of the bar. Luca hadn't spoken but I had *all* the words whizzing round my head and now they began to tumble out.

30

'What the hell was that?' I asked, stepping away from him and wrapping my coat around me, only partly against the cold. Part of me felt as if the action might help protect me from at least some of the confusion and disappointment I was feeling right now.

'What?'

My eyes widened to a point where I thought they might actually pop out. 'What do you mean what? You know exactly what!'

'That?' He gave a small tilt of his head back in the direction we'd come from.

'Yes! That!' I retorted, sarcastically echoing his gesture.

'Tia rang me and told me you were heading off to surprise the idiot.' He gave another directional jab with his head, hands rammed into the pockets of his petrol-blue, beautifully cut and very expensive merino wool coat. I'd been with him when he bought it; he'd handed over the equivalent of one month's rent in my world as I'd stood rigid, making sure I didn't touch anything in the shop just in case I had to pay for it.

'Why would she do that?'

'Because she's worried about you. We all are. No one wants to see you get hurt again and, from everything we've seen and heard about him, things were definitely heading that way.'

'So, what? She sent you to spy on me?' I had begun pacing up and down now in a short section of the street. Luca remained firmly rooted to the spot.

'Of course not!' His hands were out of his pockets now, gesturing as he spoke.

'Oh, you came just so you could witness my humiliation first-hand, then? Make sure you got it right so you could tell everyone the story accurately.'

The streetlight we'd stopped under gave enough illumination for me to see Luca's face darken. 'That's not the reason and you bloody well know it. That's unworthy of you and disrespectful to people who care about you.'

I knew he was right but I couldn't stop. 'You, you mean? Sorry, am I supposed to throw my arms around you and thank you for galloping in on your white charger to rescue me from my hope-less predicament and be thankful for ever more?'

'No. I was referring to Tia and Jono. They've been worried about you.'

'They're only concerned because you told them Adrian was cheating and made them concerned!'

'He was cheating! Bloody hell, Bee. How much more evidence do you need? He told you what you wanted to hear to get you into bed, just as he probably told the blonde he was with when I saw him and that woman tonight. He's not on that site to meet people for anything more than sex. Even you must realise that now!'

I did realise that. But realising and accepting were two different things. The second promised a whole new wave of humiliation and I wasn't sure if I was ready for that just yet.

'Bee?' We both turned at the voice to see a man walking

swiftly towards us. 'Hi.' He smiled but I could see the concern and pity in Damon's face. 'I was hoping to catch you but lost sight of you.'

'Oh. Well, here I am.' I smiled back awkwardly. 'Thanks for not dropping me in it as to why I'd actually gone there, by the way.'

He shook his head quickly. 'No problem. I'd never do that. I just wanted to check you were all right. Adrian can be a real dick at times. Oh, sorry.' He stuck his hand out to Luca. 'Damon Reilly. You're Luca Donato, aren't you?'

Luca shook his hand and nodded. 'I am.'

'Design's one of my pet hobbies so I read all the magazines and saw the feature on you and that amazing place you designed in Barcelona last year. It's stunning. So innovative too.'

'Thanks.'

I chewed my lip, waiting. Damon turned his focus back to me.

'Yeah. So anyway, I just wanted to make sure you were OK. I mean, Adrian does this all the time. I can never keep up with which woman he's seeing on which night. I'm amazed he can. Sometimes it's two on one night.'

I cast my mind back to the time he'd said he had a work emergency then called me late, saying he was free. Had he been with another woman on a flying visit in between and been planning to come back to my bed straight after? I felt my stomach lurch.

'I keep telling him he can't treat people like this. Not if they don't know. Some don't mind. They're not exclusive either, like Brandy in there. They've had some sort of deal in the past and she's over from the States staying with him at the moment.'

We discovered it on a trip to the Napa Valley... I've got a friend staying with me at the moment... It all made sense now.

Damon continued. 'But I knew he hadn't told you and when

he told us you weren't quite so easy to get into bed, he made it like a challenge to himself. We argued about it more than once.'

My head spun and by the sudden look of concern on both men's faces, my face looked as green as the rest of me felt. Luca put a steadying hand at my back.

'You OK?'

I nodded, keeping the action gentle.

'Sorry. I didn't mean to be so blunt. I'm not always very good at tact. Cara, that's my fiancée, she's a doctor and keeps telling me my bedside manner needs practice.' His expression was grave.

I smiled to tell him it was OK.

'You seem like a decent bloke. Why are you even friends with someone like him?' Luca asked.

'We've worked together for a long time at different places. I guess part of it is habit but, also, he never used to be like this. There's a pretty decent guy under there. I think the money's gone to his head a bit, which is a shame.'

Luca looked disbelieving but I got it. There had been something good in Adrian. It just hadn't been enough. Maybe I'd known that and hadn't wanted to believe it, or maybe I'd known it and believed it but enjoyed the feeling of being a part of something. A part of someone else's life. Someone who wanted me. Someone to whom I made a difference by being there. But in the end, none of it had been true. He'd wanted me but briefly and only as a challenge. A way of proving something to himself, all the while shopping around for someone else. It had all been lies. My parents made little effort to cover up the fact I was excess to requirements, while Adrian had merely pretended I wasn't. I wasn't sure which was worse.

Damon's phone began to ring. He pulled it out and glanced at the screen. 'It's Cara. I'd better take this. I just wanted to check you were all right.'

'Thanks.'

'I'm glad you've found someone who's good for you now.'

'Oh, we're no—'

'Thanks, mate. You'd better get that. Nice to meet you.' Luca offered his hand and Damon shook it as he answered the phone with his left, nodding as he did so to Luca and then touching my shoulder gently before lifting the hand in a waved goodbye, all the while chatting warmly to his fiancée.

'Why did you stop me telling him this isn't real?' I flapped a hand between us.

'Because he doesn't need to know. He seems a nice guy, but people can say things accidentally when they're with their friends, especially after a few pints. At least this way, he's not going to feel bad if he blurts something accidentally.'

It made sense. Damon had been sweet and I'd hate to think of him feeling bad if it came out that Luca's stunt had been exactly that. Just a stunt.

'You didn't need to come tonight. I can take care of myself.'

'Just because someone can take care of themselves, doesn't mean they always have to, that it's against the rules to let others help you. You do it for others. I've lost count of the times you've been an emergency babysitter or helped out in an IT crisis and, with the amount of screens we've all got now, that's only got more frequent. You do all that without complaint.'

'I don't mind it.'

'So why is this different?'

'Because...'

He tilted his head to one side, waiting, and I flicked him on the arm. 'I'm trying to get the wording right.'

Luca took a deep breath and blew on his hands to warm them before shoving them back in his pockets.

Why was this different?

I formed the words. 'Because it feels like none of you think I can take care of myself. That you're behind my back, talking about my disastrous job and my disastrous love life and you're all so together that it can make me feel worse. It sometimes feels like I'm some sort of pet project or charity case, just like I was for your family growing up.' My throat was hoarse and raw and I was doing my best not to cry, but the warm trickle against the cold skin of my face told me I'd failed on that front too.

Luca remained silent as I hunted in my bag for the mini pack of tissues I always kept in there. Blowing my nose in a most unladylike manner, I reflected that it was a good job Luca's romantic gestures tonight were an act because I'd have probably just dampened the ardour somewhat. I never understood how women could cry and end up with delicately red-rimmed eyes and dab gently at their noses when any tears on my part resulted in blotchy skin, a red nose accompanied by determinedly indelicate nose blowing and eyes like I'd had an argument with two very pissed-off bees.

'That's what you think you were, what you are, to me and my family? A charity case?' His face was taut with emotion and his hands were out of his pockets now. One dragged across his tense jaw. I looked up at him and saw the hurt in his eyes.

'I didn't mean that in a bad way...' Even to my own ears that didn't sound great and Luca's expression showed he agreed with me.

'What other way is there exactly, Bee? From the moment they met you, you've been part of the family. End of. That's it. Nothing more, nothing less. There was never a thought of it being to do anyone a favour or because they felt they had to show some care when your own parents didn't have the time. It's how they are. I thought you knew that and frankly I'm not that happy about you thinking they did it for any other reason.'

'I'm not saying they aren't kind! You're taking it wrong. I don't mean that!' I tried to explain.

'No. But you're saying they had an agenda. Their only agenda was to welcome a friend of mine and, because they immediately loved you, any chance for you to be part of the family was a joy to them. It still is. They'd be heartbroken that this is what you thought.'

'But I don't even speak Italian!'

'So? Neither does Marco's wife. It doesn't matter. That's not a prerequisite for them loving you or you being part of our family. I can't believe we're having this conversation all these years on!'

Shame brewed inside me and more tears dripped down towards my chin, where I suspected most of my eye make-up had by now also accumulated.

He gave me a look. 'Is this about you walking in on me and Ma that time?'

I shrugged and he dropped his head back a moment, staring at the sky before returning his gaze. The frustration in it, clearly aimed at me, made me sort of wish he'd remained focused upwards.

'If it makes you feel any better, no one else in my family knows what that's about either. Well, I suspect Dad does because that's how it is. But it's between us. You're no less a part of things because of that. Families don't always share everything between everyone.'

'But you always seem to...' I felt a little idiotic now. Said out loud, this thing that had been bugging me for so long didn't seem such a big deal. It probably hadn't been about me at all anyway. It was just something private. They really did consider me as part of the family. 'I'm sorry. I just assumed that's what happened in families, especially yours. I guess I overreacted.'

Luca raised one agreeing eyebrow.

'To be fair, you were kind of off for a bit afterwards.'

He accepted this. 'I was. And I know knowledge of family interactions isn't exactly your strong suit, with being an only child and your parents' interesting take on childcare.' He took a step closer and I lifted my chin to meet his eyes, somehow unable to look away now. 'But every family is different, Bee. They all work in different ways. Your own will probably work differently again.'

I dropped my gaze. 'I can't see that happening any time soon.'

Luca tucked his little finger under my chin, gently encouraging me to resume the gaze. 'Don't be so sure. You're an amazing woman when you let yourself, and other people, believe it.'

'You were at the bar, right? I've ended up allowing myself to be made a fool of, just like you said. That, my friend, is not amazing.'

'I should never have said that. I was angry and frustrated and said something I now regret. There's only one fool here and it's him, not you. He had the chance to be with you and he gave that up. He actually deserves a prize for being that big an imbecile.'

I tried not to smile.

'And don't think I don't see that.'

I tried harder.

'As for the rest of your rant. Disastrous job?'

'Not the current one, obviously. I meant before. You all told me to leave so many times, and I should have. Just like you all told me to go back to uni, but I was scared. Scared to leave the comfort zone I'd built around me, but I think now it was more of a hindrance than a help. I relied on its walls so much that I never wanted to leave them.' I wiped away a tear with the back of my hand, my make-up well and truly given up for dead. 'And clearly Tia thought I was being blind about Adrian too. I can't believe she didn't say something.'

'She wants you to be happy. She was hoping for the best, I think.'

'But put a rescuing knight on standby just in case.'

'I was passing.'

'Why?'

'Why what?'

'Why were you passing? Your place is in the other direction.'

He paused for a second too long.

'Oh my God, you have a date! You said you didn't.'

'I had a date. Past tense.'

I stepped back and yanked up his sleeve a bit. His hands were like ice. 'What time is it? Can you still make it? And where are your gloves?'

He laughed, catching my foraging hands. 'My gloves are in the car.'

'Well, they're not doing you much good there.'

'That is true. And no, I can't still make it.'

'Because you stopped to faff about here?' My voice tilted up a pitch.

'No. Aneeka cancelled last night.'

I frowned. 'So you were going in this direction because?'

'I'm not about to waste a great restaurant reservation just because I don't have a date.'

I chewed my lip again.

'Go on. Ask it. I know you're dying to.'

'Why did she cancel?'

'Turns out I'm not as irresistible as rumours would have it.' He winked.

I didn't smile back. 'Is that it?'

'With Aneeka?'

'Yes.'

'Yep. She made that pretty clear.'

'I'm so sorry, Luca. You should have said. I know you really liked her.'

'I did. But, to be honest, I also know she wasn't The One.'

'You seemed happy together.'

'I think I wanted to be. But in the end...' He gave a very Italian shrug that summed up the rest. 'You want to go and get some dinner?'

'Why not? We can't have you looking sad and lonely at a table for one.'

He gave me a side eye and hailed a taxi in favour of walking as the clouds had now formed a union and voted to release bone-chilling rain over the city.

'Tia and Jono have made this finding love on the Internet look such a doddle. Personally, I think we should have them for false advertising.'

'Yep. It's harder than it looks. Or perhaps easier.'

I pulled a face. 'That's very cryptic. Do explain.'

'Another time. I'm starving.'

'Where are we going?'

'Told you. *Bianco Nero*.'

My eyes lit up. 'Really? I thought you just said that because I'd mentioned Adrian has been trying to get in there for ages without success and you wanted to annoy him.'

The taxi pulled up and we bundled ourselves in, Luca giving the address before continuing the conversation.

'That was just a happy accident and an added bonus to see the expression on his smug face.'

I looked out of the window for a bit, taking in the colours of the Christmas lights reflected in puddles and wet, shining pavements. The streets were still busy with people heading out for the night and the usual drifting mass of tourists that London played host to, whatever the time of year.

31

'How do I manage to pick them?'

'What do you mean?'

'I mean, is it me? Do I just have an inbuilt chip I don't know about sending out signals to oddballs and arseholes?' I said, doing the best repair job on my make-up I could with the little I had on me.

'Possibly. Who knows?'

I gave him a Paddington stare and he laughed, wrapping an arm around me. 'No. I'm pretty sure you don't. Loads of people have the same experience.'

'Which is exactly why I didn't want to do this flippin' challenge in the first place.'

'But sometimes you have to take chances, Bee.'

The taxi slowed outside a subtle and tasteful restaurant frontage in Mayfair. Luca paid, waving away my offer before leaning over and opening the cab door. Thanking the driver, I got out and hurried through the rain to shelter under the fixed canopy of the building and wait for Luca. Following quickly, he pushed open the door, signalling me to go through first.

'Aah, Mr Donato. We're so glad to see you again!' A maître d' came across in a sort of fast walk that gave the impression of a glide. It was both elegant and efficient and I spent a moment or two wondering how much practice that took.

'Peter.' Luca extended his hand. 'And you. Thanks for fitting me in. This is my friend, Bee.'

Peter did a little bow and I had an almost overwhelming inclination to curtsey but just about managed to restrain myself. 'Very pleased to meet you, Ms Bee.'

'Oh, it's just Bee.' I smiled.

Peter nodded graciously, then extended an arm to indicate which way we should go. I leant close to Luca.

'He's still going to call me Ms Bee, isn't he?'

'Without a doubt.'

Luca turned his head just slightly and dropped the lightest of kisses on top of my hair. 'Don't worry about it.' With that, he gently laid a hand at the small of my back, and we made our way through the tables, with Luca nodding to the odd person here and there. I didn't miss the admiring glances he drew as we did so, but he did. It was one of the things I liked most about him.

'Holy poop!' I whispered. 'Have you seen these prices?'

Luca looked across the table and raised an eyebrow.

'OK. I want to go halves with you. But I'm going to need a raise, like immediately.'

'Done.'

'Really?'

'Yep. It was on the agenda of the meeting last week anyway. HR is just drafting the paperwork.'

'What for?'

'Your raise.' Luca gave a brief, confused look before turning back to the wine list.

'No, I mean what is the raise for?'

'You completed your trial period with flying colours, and although your predecessor was a good guy and efficient at his job, he wasn't as up to date on all the new technologies coming through and the world of IT in general as you keep yourself. That you do so has meant that you've suggested and integrated new ideas and tech within the firm that has already made things easier for staff and created a more efficient working process for all. That skill and dedication was noted and it was agreed that a raise should be given in acknowledgement of that.'

'Blimey.' I sat for a moment, taking it in.

'Everything all right?'

'Yes! I mean, definitely yes. Thank you!'

'No need to thank me. It's all on your merit.'

A niggling thought began to gnaw away at me. 'Is it though?'

He looked up again. 'Huh?'

'Is it just on merit or did you... sort of have something to do with it?'

Luca blew out a sigh. 'I really hope we're not going to have this conversation every time bonus or pay-rise time comes around and you get one. Which isn't guaranteed, as you'll have noted from your contract.'

'No, I know.'

'But no. I did not "sort of have something to do with it". In fact, I was against it.'

'What? Why?' I asked, just a little too loudly, causing a couple of diners to very consciously *not* turn to stare at me, which was almost the same as if they'd been gawping at me like guppies waiting for fish flakes. I flushed and Luca grinned. But unlike when I'd dined with Adrian, I didn't feel out of place sitting here with Luca. I could be myself and not worry I wasn't good enough for the establishment – or the company. I readjusted my volume.

'I mean, what? And why?' I repeated quietly.

'Because I felt your package was already good enough.'

'Oh.'

'The others were worried we might lose you to another firm. I told them that was pretty unlikely.'

'Oh?' I repeated, this time as a question.

'Bee, it took all the planets in every universe to align before you walked out on the other job, which paid badly and you hated. I know you like working at DS and have made yourself another little comfort zone there. You're not exactly one for taking chances if you have the option to play it safe and stick to something familiar. I didn't think there was much danger of you taking another chance elsewhere any time soon.'

'That's pretty cold, isn't it?'

'What? Do you want white or red?'

'I don't care so long as it's wet. I mean about using your knowledge of me like that. And I do not always play it safe!'

'Bee, I'm a businessman. In this world you have to use whatever knowledge you have. And I know you don't want people thinking I'm favouring you because of our history.'

'Well, no. Obviously...'

Luca stared at me for a moment and then laughed, his whole face animated and joyful. 'You can't have it both ways, sweetheart.'

I pulled a face. 'It's good to know that others recognise my contribution and are happy to reward me for it, then, as I clearly can't rely on you.'

'I didn't say I didn't recognise it. I just said you were already well renumerated for it.'

I didn't have an answer for that, so I blew a quiet raspberry instead and made him laugh again.

'What about this wine?' he asked, tilting the list towards me.

I choked on the sip of water I'd just taken as I clocked the price. 'Does it have gold leaf in it or something?'

'No, but they have that if you want it?'

I looked up. Luca's face was dead serious.

'Of course I don't want it!' I replied, my face incredulous. 'What on earth is the point?'

Luca remained silent for a moment before shrugging. 'Some people just like the idea, I guess.'

'Do you?' I asked him, serious now.

'God, no. I think it's as ridiculous as you do.'

I tilted my head slightly. 'But you've bought a bottle to impress a woman in the past, haven't you?'

He made a gesture that could have been yes or no, but was, in this case, most definitely a yes.

'And did it?'

'What?'

'Impress her?'

'It impressed her so much I ended up taking her home in a taxi and handing her over to her flatmate.'

'Blimey, how much of it did she drink?'

'The best part of two bottles.'

'Oh, Luca, and you didn't even get a bonk out of it.'

'Nope.' He laughed. 'I did, however, get a ruined pair of favourite shoes out of it though.'

'How come?'

'She went to kiss me and threw up all over me instead.'

'Oh, wow.'

'Yeah. There was no chance of getting a cab home in that state so I got a good walk out of it at least.'

'I'm so sorry.'

'What are you sorry for? It wasn't you that threw up on me. This time.'

'Hey. That was one time and I had food poisoning. And you had a T-shirt and knackered old jeans on. That's hardly the same thing.'

'True.'

'Did you see her again?'

'I did, actually.'

'Lots of people wouldn't have.'

'I know. I guess I thought maybe it was just a one-off thing?'

'Ordering alcohol with precious metal in it?'

'The after party.'

'Oh. And was it?'

'Let's just say there wasn't a third date.'

'Ah.' I pulled a sympathetic face.

He laughed. 'C'est la vie.'

'It's funny. I guess I imagined all your dates had gone really well. I can't really imagine you having a bad one. They're always these gorgeous glamour-puss types and you're...' I waved a hand vaguely encompassing his being '... well, you. I suppose it hadn't really occurred to me that any date hadn't gone smoothly.'

'Why not? You think you have the monopoly on bad dates? Believe me, you don't.'

'I can't tell you how much better that makes me feel.'

He laughed. 'You're a mean one.'

'No.' I laughed along, 'You know what I'm getting at.'

'That it's not just you.'

'Yes! It's hard not to have doubts when none of mine seem to work out. That it must be me.'

'Bee, listen to me. I've said it a million times and I'll say it again, but this time, listen. There is nothing wrong with you. You didn't do anything wrong. It's just that you weren't compatible with those particular people for whatever reason, not because there's anything wrong with them or you, but because we're all different in what we look for. What makes us click with that one, special person.'

'What if my click is broken?'

'Your click is just fine.'

The waiter, who had chosen that particular moment to approach the table, hovered for a second. I looked at Luca. Luca looked at me.

'Click!' he said, suddenly, looking up at the waiter. 'Click!'

The waiter nodded, gave a small, slightly uncertain smile and asked if we were ready to order.

'Would you mind giving us a minute?'

'Of course, sir,' he said and headed off towards another table. Luca began studying the menu.

'You know he thought you said—'

'Yes. I do. That's why I was clarifying.'

'And you know you just made it worse?'

'Yes. I'm aware of that too.'

'OK. Good. Just checking.'

Luca lifted his gaze from the menu and looked over at me. Laughter danced in his eyes and his smile was wide and relaxed. That was the moment it hit me. Tia's words drifted back to me.

According to this, Luca's looking for someone exactly like you...

'Everything OK?' he asked, the smile fading. 'You've suddenly got a really strange look on your face.'

'Umm, no, yeah! I'm fine.' I pushed Tia's words out of my head. 'Fine!'

* * *

'Did you see anything that takes your fancy?'

Having hoovered up our mains, we moved onto pudding. The choice was overwhelming and in the end we chose three to share between us. I couldn't imagine doing this with anyone else... I didn't want to do this with anyone else... I pushed the thought away.

Don't be ridiculous. It's Luca. You're just fed up about Adrian and—

I cut my racing thoughts off and tried to get back to a more normal line of conversation – and thought.

'So, bearing in mind we're getting pretty close to Tia's deadline, do you think you're going to be able to win this challenge? Not a lot of time left now.' I waggled my eyebrows and squished down the building waves in my stomach.

'Quite possibly.'

'Huh?'

This wasn't the answer I'd been expecting. *Or hoping for,* my subconscious added unhelpfully.

'I think I may well be able to prove that love can be found even when online dating is involved.'

'Oh. Right. So you... umm... think you've found The One, then?' My stomach was roiling like a sea swell that would be a danger to shipping and I felt a sticky heat wash over me followed immediately by a cold sweat.

'I do. Are you OK?' He leaned forward. 'Do you need a glass of water?' he asked, already pouring me one.

I swigged the water and made a rolling motion with my hand for him to continue, willing myself not to repeat the gold-flake date on him.

'It wasn't entirely unexpected, to be honest.'

'So this is someone you've been out with before?'

'Yes.'

'Was that in the rules? Bit of a head start there,' I teased him, forcing a casual tone into my voice that I most certainly didn't feel.

'She's on the app. That means it counts.'

I couldn't argue with that.

'She's still single too, then. That was lucky.'

'Very.'

'So? Come on, then,' I prompted, not wanting to hear any of it but unable to not know, wanting to masochistically know everything about this woman who had finally stolen Luca Donato's heart. Realising far, far too late that I had wanted it to be me and knowing now that it never would, never could be.

Luca glanced up at the waiter, nodding his thanks as he talked when the man brought coffee and a small plate of tiny handmade chocolates. One part of me wanted to take the plate and tip the entire contents down my throat as I wallowed while the other half was trying to control a churning stomach that didn't want to touch, see or smell any of it. Currently the latter was winning but it was close.

'She's amazing,' Luca began and I felt the bile rise. 'She's beautiful and funny and really clever. Runs rings around me, although she'd never admit it. She makes me laugh pretty much every day I speak to her or see her and when I do, I feel like someone's turned the brightness up on the world a little bit. Everything, even the crap days, are better just for being near her.'

'She... umm... sounds brill.' I'd suddenly turned into a teenager from the eighties. Luca didn't appear to have noticed. His face had taken on an almost luminescent quality as he spoke about his new love. It wasn't one I'd ever seen on him before. That was when I knew. I knew I'd lost him and hadn't realised quite how much I loved him until that moment. The pain was so raw, so excruciating it felt physical, sucking all the breath from my lungs and squeezing my heart until there was nothing left.

32

Shoving my chair back hastily, I caught it as it threatened to topple with the sudden movement.

'Bee? What's wrong?'

'I... just... sorry. I just remembered I have to do something.'

'What?'

Kick myself about a thousand times for falling in love with my best friend who's fallen in love with someone else.

'Nothing. I mean, something. Of course. It's just that it's not that important.'

'If it's not that important, why do you have to leave in the middle of dinner?'

'I thought we'd finished.'

'Is everything all right?' A waiter glided over.

'Yes. Would it be possible to have my coat, please?'

'Of course, madam. Would sir like his?'

Luca was watching me, confusion written all over his face and his mouth set in a line.

'Yeah. I guess so.' The waiter drifted off again before I could tell him which coat it was. Oh, well, with a bit of luck I might get an upgrade.

'No. You don't need to leave.'

'Right. So I'll just sit here on my own instead while you have your crazy moment.'

'It's not a crazy moment!' I said, in a hushed snap. I was aware that to anyone watching, including Luca, it looked very much like one and I could hardly blame him for the description. But I needed to get out of there. Put some space between us, and fast. Luca paid as we waited for the return of our coats.

'I'll split that with you, obviously.'

'Whatever,' Luca replied, waving the comment away.

'Thank you,' I said as I took my coat from the waiter and Luca did the same, shrugging his on easily while I fought with a sleeve in my flustered state, only making myself even more flustered.

'Here.' Luca reached to help me, but I stepped away.

'I'm fine.' I glanced up as I finally shoved my arm down the sleeve. He looked as if I'd slapped him.

'I mean, thanks though.'

'Right.' His brows were drawn down and the tension in his jaw was so tight I had concerns about his teeth exploding. But right now I couldn't focus on the confusion and anger resonating off him in waves. I just had to get away. Get home. And now, I realised, get a new job. The door closed behind us and I turned briefly to face him.

'Well, um, thanks for dinner. I'd better get on with my... thing.'

Luca remained silent, staring at me intently with those dark, long-lashed eyes.

I'd never been very good at the whole not-filling-the-silence thing. Luca, however, was an expert. But I wouldn't crack. Not this time. I couldn't afford to. I turned to begin walking towards the nearest Tube station.

'So that's it? You don't even say goodbye now?'

I stopped, turning back to look at him. His face was half in shadow from the light spilling out onto the pavement through the etched privacy-glass plate window of the restaurant.

'Oh, right, yes. Sorry. Mind is on my... thing. Bye!' I took the few steps back and reached up to place the lightest of kisses on his cheek. He didn't move.

'And this thing is?'

'Does it matter?' I snapped, finally. I was a crap liar at the best of times and under Luca's scrutiny I knew I wouldn't be able to keep it up.

'Yeah. It kind of does, bearing in mind your hellishly weird exit in there and the fact now it feels like you don't want to be within fifty feet of me!'

How wrong he was. The real problem was that I didn't want an inch of space between us. I wanted his skin on mine, his hands on me, his lips on mine...

'You know that's not the case.'

'Certainly feels like it.'

'Well, it's not. I just have something I need to do.'

'OK. I'll call a car. It can take you.'

'No. It's no problem. I can get the Tube. I like the Tube.'

'You hate the Tube.'

'Only when it's crowded.'

'Let me get you a car. It's safer. I'd feel better knowing you were at least dropped at the door of your mystery location.'

'It's not a mystery.'

Luca's face disagreed.

'Anyway, the train is fine. But thanks.' I turned back to go and

Luca let out an expletive, just as a well-dressed older couple exited the restaurant. His outburst made all of us jump.

'I'm so sorry.' He held his hands up to them. 'I apologise. I didn't see you coming out.'

The man tutted as the woman pressed herself closer to her husband and they scuttled up the road a short distance to hail a cab. Luca shoved his hands roughly back through his hair before closing the distance to where I was still rooted to the spot.

'You know, you are one of the most infuriatingly stubborn people I've ever met!' He was so close now, I could smell the woody, smoky scent of his aftershave and if I lifted my hand, I'd feel the tantalising roughness of a day's growth on the strong, sharp lines of his jaw. I shoved my hands deeper into my pockets.

'If I'm so bloody infuriating, why don't you go and spend the rest of the evening with your Perfect Woman if she's so bloody faultless?'

'You know what? Maybe I will,' he retorted.

I spun on my heel so he wouldn't see the tears I'd been trying so hard to hold in now fall without pause as I began to stride away from him. I swiped them away with one hand and then felt someone catch mine within theirs. Startled, I turned as Luca pulled me back towards him. His eyes were dark and focused entirely on mine. Gently, he let go of my hand and transferred his own to my face, his thumbs softly sweeping the tears away, our gazes locked until he dipped his head and brushed his lips to mine. Electricity fired through me and I knew he had felt it too. A small sound issued from my lips as all the tension released, replaced by a far more basic feeling as Luca pulled me close to his body and kissed me properly and thoroughly, exploring my mouth with his own as his hands dropped lower to hold me as close to him as possible. I lost all thought and sank into it, feeling warm and wonderful and as if I was finally home. This was Luca. My Luca... *This was Luca!*

'I can't!' I pushed back hurriedly, struggling for breath and almost stumbling over an uneven paving slab as I did so. Luca's arms caught me and, once steady, I stepped back again, this time more carefully.

'What?'

'This. You. Us.'

'Yes, you can. You know it's right, Bee. I know you felt what I did.'

I looked up at him, unable to hide. I had felt it, and he knew it.

'Not everyone gets a chance like this, Bee. We both know that. We've both tried other people and it hasn't worked. And you know why?'

I shook my head, mute as myriad emotions spun around inside it.

'Because we're meant to be here. Together. You and me. I've known it for years, but I had to wait until you realised it too.'

'I don't understand. Why didn't you say something before?'

'Because I didn't think you were interested and I wasn't about to mess up what we had. But I couldn't make it work with anyone else because they're not you. I want more and I know you do too.'

'No! No, I don't!' I cried, shaking my head. 'And you don't either. It's all just this stupid bet. We've both had plenty of terrible dates and so when we end up in a date-like setting with good food and wine, and a romantic atmosphere, it just seems right because we're already comfortable with each other. There's no need for all the pretence and nonsense that we do when we think we need to impress someone. It's just screwed up our heads and made us lose focus.'

'For God's sake, Bee!' Luca exploded. 'My focus is finally

crystal clear and if you, for once in your life, got out of your own way, you'd see that yours is too.'

'What's that supposed to mean?'

'It means that you've been sabotaging yourself for years! Always afraid to just let go and see what happens.'

'That's not true!'

'It is true, Bee, and you know it!'

'I changed jobs, didn't I?'

'Yes. After over ten years at the same place, being ground down a little more every day despite the fact your skills and talent meant you could have walked out and got another position easily. It took being pushed to the absolute limit, being passed over for promotion and bonuses countless times, for you to actually do something about it.'

'There was no guarantee I'd have got a job.'

'You would have and you know it. People were falling over to offer you a position when you finally left that bloody place and you knew you always had an opportunity at DS as soon as it was up and running. I asked you to come in at the start.'

'I didn't want to mix business with our friendship and risk messing it up.'

'Argh!' He linked his hands at the back of his neck and looked up to the sky, turning away before spinning back to face me. 'You always do this! You always expect the worst.'

'I don't!'

'You do! This online-dating thing is the perfect example. You didn't look at it as an opportunity, just as something that had to be endured. You expected disappointment so that's all you saw, all you got.'

'I got a bunch of crappy dates and a cheater!'

'Perhaps if you'd just let go, let yourself really shine, life might be different.'

'So the terrible dates were my fault? Is that what you mean?'

'Of course not. Stop twisting things. I'm just saying this is what you do. It's what you're doing now. With us. You know it's right, I know you do. We have a connection. We always have had and that kiss just now, that proved it goes deeper than friendship. We're meant to be and you know it. I think you realised that earlier tonight and it's panicked you because you're afraid. Like you're always afraid.'

'That's not fair!' I was crying now, and my chest hitched and broke on the last word.

'No, it's not fair because I've watched you doing this to yourself for so long, it breaks my heart. You're capable of so much more than you think, Bee, if you just let yourself try. Look at the job thing. You took that leap and now you're so much happier.' He took a step towards me. 'I know you can make me happy and I would spend every day doing my best to make you happy too. But the truth is, I don't think we have to try. We fit, Bee. We've always fitted. I knew it a long time ago and I know you know it now. But it can only happen if you're willing to step off that ledge and try.'

My mind was spinning and I put a hand to my head as if by doing so I could still it. Luca moved to touch me but I stepped back and I saw frustration and hurt shadow his strong features. My heart cracked a little more.

'Remember that argument Ma and I were having when you came in from the garden that day?'

How could I forget? Luca's unusual secrecy had played on my mind ever since.

'It was about you.'

'Me?' I felt the food we'd eaten earlier churn violently in my stomach.

'Yep.'

'Why?'

'Because of this online thing. This challenge we had to find The One.'

'But why would your mum be upset about that and what did that have to do with me?'

'Because, like all good mothers, she knew I'd already found The One and by taking part in the challenge I was at risk of losing you. She thought I should just tell you as it's not only me she can read like a book. Even if you didn't know this was the real thing back then, she did.'

'But you disagreed?'

'Nope. I knew. I knew I wanted you and I knew we'd be amazing together, but I couldn't just tell you like I might someone else.'

'Why not?'

He let out a sigh and scratched the stubble on his cheek, his long, strong fingers making a raspy noise as he did so.

'Because I needed you to come to me because you wanted me. Because you wanted me above all others, and not just because I was the safe choice. The comfortable choice. I wanted you to come to me because I was the only choice.'

'I wouldn't have done that,' I said, trying not to colour.

'Yeah, Bee. You might.'

There was nothing to say. I knew he was right, and so did he. I also knew I loved him. More than anything or anyone. More than I knew was possible. I wanted him so badly it was tearing me in two...

Luca broke the silence. 'I think your lack of reply speaks volumes. Once again you're putting barriers up and limits on yourself, even when you know it could be amazing.'

'It could also go horribly wrong!'

Luca watched me for a moment, tipped his head to the sky

and then down at the ground. 'I'll call you a car,' he said, pulling his phone out of his coat pocket.

'And what's supposed to happen now? Now that you've kissed me and changed everything.'

'I'm pretty damn sure you were kissing me right back, if you remember.'

I did remember. I would always remember that kiss, of that I was certain.

Luca continued. 'But don't worry about the rest. Nothing's changed, Bee. Nothing will ever change because you won't let it. You're far too content to stay in that comfort zone, and maybe that's for the best.' The planes of his face had hardened, his jaw was set and his dark eyes, normally so warm and inviting, had shuttered against me. 'As for the kiss, just forget about it. Pretend it never happened. I'm away next week on an ice-climbing trip – it will give us both some space, which I think is probably a good thing.'

'Forget it?' I asked. 'Exactly how am I supposed to do that?'

'I'm sure you'll find a way, Bee.' His voice was as cold as steel. 'That's what you want after all, isn't it?'

I tilted my face towards his. *Did I?*

Luca let out a half-laugh that held no humour. 'This is exactly your problem, Bee. You don't even know what you want half the time and when you do? When you're sure of what you want, you're still too scared to reach out and grab the opportunity just in case it isn't perfect. Well, life isn't perfect, Bee. You know that. And there's no point pretending it is. But it's there to be lived and the only way you can do that is to try. Sometimes you have to risk everything, even if it could mean losing everything.' His gaze locked onto mine. 'I don't think you can do that.'

He turned to watch a car advancing down the street slowly and raised a hand. It pulled to the kerb beside us. Walking towards it, he greeted the driver, waving him back as he got out to open the door, which Luca did instead before turning back to me. I made my way slowly towards it, unsteadily, but not because of the alcohol. All that had happened since we'd stepped outside had more than sobered me up. Now it just felt as if the world was crumbling beneath me. Everything had changed but I didn't want to change it back. Not really. Not in my heart.

Luca was right. I was too scared to take that change forward in case it didn't work out. In case I lost him forever. But was that already done? In all the time we'd known each other he'd never told me he needed space from me. It was always him that had kept me close, which, of course, made sense now. I'd never suspected. I'd never allowed myself to suspect because I didn't think someone like Luca would have noticed me in that way. I hadn't thought I was worthy of his notice. I'd taken my parents' attitude and saddled myself with it for life, assuming everyone else would always feel the same way towards me. But they could only treat me that way if I let them. Luca had always seen me as more. I realised that now.

'It's getting late. You should get home.' Luca's expression was closed and his tone signalled the discussion was over. There was nothing else to say. I put a hand on the roof, steadying myself to enter the car. Luca's fingers gripped the top of the open door tightly as he turned to talk to the driver, avoiding any chance of eye contact with me. I slid in, the cool leather seat soft under my fingers. I saw Luca move to shift his weight to close the door.

He wasn't even going to say goodbye.

'Luca?'

He leant a little over the top of the door and tilted his head in question.

'What are we now? Are we...?' I swallowed hard to try and

shift the lump that had wedged in the rawness of my throat. 'Are we still friends?'

'Yeah, Bee.' There was nothing but tiredness and resignation in his voice now. 'Friends. Like always.' Before I could reply, he closed the door and gave two taps on the roof, signalling the driver to pull away. I turned but Luca already had his back to the car and his phone out, presumably calling another car for himself. We could easily have dropped him off en route but it was clear that, contrary to earlier, now Luca just wanted distance from me. And the only person I had to blame for that was myself.

Tia passed me another box of tissues, pulling the top one out for me in order, I suspected, to avoid another tantrum of frustration when the last one had got stuck with the result that my bedroom floor now looked like someone had plucked a large chicken, the carpet festooned with white shreds of tissue. She'd been on my doorstep that morning with all the supplies we'd need. I hadn't wanted to call her, but I'd finally realised I couldn't always deal with things by myself – and that I didn't have to. And right now, I needed her. When the doorbell had rung, I'd opened it to find her standing there with two large boxes of man-size tissues and an enormous hug. The fragile lock that had been keeping the floodgates closed had disintegrated and she'd guided me back in until I'd curled up in a foetal like position on the bed, and sobbed for everything I'd lost because I'd been too scared to just try – including now, it seemed, the one man I couldn't imagine life without.

'Was I the only one who didn't know?'

Tia pulled a face. 'Pretty much.'

'Since when?'

'It was always pretty obvious, but it's got more so to the rest of us over the last couple of years. Did it never occur to you the reason he disliked all your boyfriends?'

'Not really. I thought that was just Luca disagreeing with me to amuse himself like he always did.'

'To be honest, I thought it was mutual. I mean, the way you always shifted away from any woman he brought to the pub.'

'No. I never really looked at him that way. I suppose because it never occurred to me that it would be reciprocated and I always felt so drab next to them.'

'Honey, you didn't look it. You've always had this skewed view of yourself, like you're less than, and I can understand how that could happen. I mean, with your parents and everything. You know Luca was always stealing looks at you when he thought no one was looking?'

I rolled over and she met my eyes. 'Did you never wonder why none of his relationships lasted past a couple of nights at the most?'

'I just thought he was playing the field.'

'Maybe he was to start. But then he was just trying to find someone who made him feel the way you do. And he never could. Not even Aneeka, who was lovely, but she wasn't you. You walk in, he lights up.'

I shuffled and looked up at her from where I lay, cuddling a pillow. Tia looked back at me and nodded. 'Uh huh,' she replied to my questioning face.

'Well, I'm pretty sure I cooled any ardour he might have felt now. He hates me.' I felt the tears welling again.

'He does not hate you.'

'He didn't even say goodbye, let alone give me a hug. And now he's buggered off to God knows where for a week. I asked if we were still friends and there was just this flat tone to his voice.

He said yes but we're not. I know it and he knows it. He just told me what I wanted to hear so he could leave.'

'Honey. He'd just had his heart broken. Give it some time.'

'I don't want to. I want...'

'What do you want?' Tia asked, her tone serious. 'You need to think about this, Bee. This is Luca we're talking about. He doesn't deserve to be messed around. He's too good for that, and so are you.'

'I don't need to think about it.'

Tia raised her beautiful, dark HD brows a little in question.

'I want Luca.' I pushed myself up into a sitting position. 'I want Luca,' I said again, this time with a conviction in my voice and heart that felt so right I knew there was no mistaking. 'I've always wanted him. I just didn't know it until last night and then, when I had the chance, I ran away, just like I always do, just like Luca said. But I shouldn't. I should have reached out for it with both hands.'

'Then that's what you need to do.'

'But if I call, he might not answer.' Part of me realised that I was once again doing what Luca had accused me of – expecting the worst.

'He won't.'

I snapped my head up from where I'd pulled Luca's contact up on my phone.

'What?'

'The place they're ice climbing. He told me it's pretty remote and no signal. But he'll be back in a week. You can tell him then.'

A week felt like forever. 'Do you think he'll listen?'

'It's Luca. He's stubborn and he's mad at you but, yes, I think he'll listen.'

'Have I missed my chance?'

Tia shrugged and gave me a hug to try and soften the blow. 'I really don't know, Bee. I've never seen him as upset as he was before he left. I can't say whether he'll open himself to that again. All we can do is hope.'

I nodded and Tia hugged me again. 'I'm sorry. I know that's not the answer you wanted to hear but I've decided pretending to know or not know things, like the fact that Luca had seen Adrian cheating, doesn't do anyone any favours.'

Tia gave me another hug before she left and I headed straight to the shower and made an effort to dig myself out of the pity hole I'd dropped myself in. I washed my hair, put on a dress and slick of lipstick. Grabbing a warm, cream woollen coat that I hardly wore but loved, I pulled on boots and a woolly hat with a bobble that bounced gently with every step. Locking the door behind me, I headed out for a local park and fresh air. Or at least the nearest thing I could get to it on the outskirts of London.

Back at home two hours later, having walked for miles, thoughts turning over and over, I made a cup of tea and took a seat on the sofa, tucking my feet under me. Then I reached for my phone and pulled up Luca's contact. Thanks to Tia, I knew he wouldn't answer but I had to say what I needed to say and just hope that he listened to the message when he rejoined civilisation.

Taking a deep breath, I pressed the little green phone on my screen. A recorded voice told me the person I'd called was unavailable and to leave a message after the beep. It was now or never.

'Hi. It's me. I hope you're having a great time.' I paused and grimaced at the banality of the comment. 'I don't know when you'll get this message or if you'll even listen to it all, but I just wanted to say you were right. I'd say I've had time to do a lot of thinking, but I didn't need to. I knew you were right last night, just as you did, but I wasn't brave enough to take that leap. But like you said, the only thing holding me back is myself. I realise that now and I'm making changes and the only thing scaring me now is that I might have lost the only man I've ever loved. The best person I've ever known. The one who's made me laugh and cry and made me feel loved for so long. I'm scared that I'll never feel like I felt when you held me and kissed me. I knew I was exactly where I was supposed to be, and with the person I was supposed to be with, and that scared me, because it was you. But I'm not scared any more. I love you, Luca. I've always loved you. It's just that it's taken losing you to make me realise just how much and I'm so sorry for that.'

My voice had thickened and I ended the call, wiping away tears as I did so. I didn't know if it would be enough but, either way, I was glad I'd taken the chance. Glad I'd been brave enough, at last, to do that.

* * *

'I thought Luca was supposed to be back today?' Helen commented as I wandered into the office kitchen to get a smoothie from the fridge a week later.

'Umm. I'm not sure. Maybe his flight got delayed or something.'

'It's not like him not to let us know if his plans have changed though. He's really good like that.'

I nodded. Helen was right. Luca was supposed to be back today. From what Tia had told me, he was supposed to fly back on Saturday night as she'd rung me and asked if I'd heard anything. I hadn't. He would have received the message by now so either he hadn't wanted to listen, or he had but it had made no difference. My heart was now lying in tiny pieces in my chest and the only consolation I had was that I'd tried. In the end, it was always going to be up to Luca and his choice was something I had no influence over. Helen gave me a querying look, which I pretended not to interpret, dredging up a smile instead and making my way back to my desk.

The figures on my screen blurred and looked like the gobbledegook they were. Normally I could read code without thinking, just as though it were plain English, but today my brain was struggling to function. I stole a look at Luca's empty desk and felt my insides twist again as my phone began to vibrate. I snatched it up, my stomach dropping as I saw it wasn't Luca but some unknown number, most likely trying to sell me something or telling me they were aware I'd had an accident that had never actually happened. My finger hovered over the hang-up button but instead pressed the answer one. It would give me a minute's break from the screen at least.

'Hello.'

'Bee?'

'Umm... who's this?'

'Oh, Bee! It's Luca's mum.'

I felt the colour drain from my face and every bone in my body go soft. I couldn't speak.

'Are you still there?'

'Yes.'

'Bee, there was an avalanche where Luca and his friends were climbing.'

'Please, no,' I whispered.

'No, no, darling!' Her words rushed out. 'He's OK. He's safe. They were missing for a day or so but thankfully had managed to find each other and keep as warm and supported as they could until they were rescued and flown home. He's pretty bruised and managed to break his leg quite badly so has had surgery and they've pinned it, but he's still on some quite strong painkillers so a bit in and out of it.'

'OK,' I said, failing to find any other words as my mind tried to process everything and how near we'd all come to losing him entirely.

'The moment I saw him I asked if I should call you. I know what's happened, but in the circumstances...'

'Umm hmm.'

'He made me promise not to.'

'Right,' I replied, tears flowing now. I knew I was gaining surreptitious looks from over the tops of others' monitors but I didn't care.

'I told him you'd want to know but he always did have a stubborn streak. It's got him where he is today but, honestly, sometimes it drives me up the wall.'

A small, strangulated laugh escaped me, but it was wreathed in pain.

'He was finally awake long enough to look at his phone today for a few minutes. Somehow it survived all that.'

'He's got this super-robust case thing for it, like the military use, for when he goes out on adventures.' The reply was automatic. I knew all the little things about Luca, just as he did about me.

'Oh, right. Well, there we are, then. Just as well. Anyway, he listened to his messages. I understand there was one from you.'

'Yes.'

'I don't know what you said, but I've rarely seen my boy cry—'

'Oh! I didn't mean to—'

'No, no, *mia cara*. These were happy tears, I can promise you.'

'They were?' I said, my own happy tears now streaking my face and pooling on my chin before plopping onto the paperwork on my desk.

'Most definitely. He was already drifting off again as I took the phone back off him, but I had a feeling something had changed. Call it mother's intuition.' She gave a little laugh. 'I asked again if I should call you. He managed to nod and whisper the word please before the painkillers kicked in totally.'

'Can I see him?'

'Of course. I'm pretty sure the boss will be OK with that.' She laughed again and I could hear the relief in her voice as she told me which hospital to come to. Her son had been missing in an avalanche but had been found alive and mostly intact. It could have been such a different ending. For all of us.

I sat in the taxi and called Luca's right-hand man, unsure as to whether he knew or not.

'No! I've left a bunch of messages but I've not heard anything. God! Is he OK?'

I filled him in and explained about the painkillers and that I knew Luca would call as soon as possible.

'Absolutely. No rush. Are you seeing him now?'

'Yes.'

'OK. Tell him everything's under control and not to worry and just call me when he's ready.'

'Thanks, Andy. Will do.' I hung up just as the taxi pulled in front of the hospital. Willing the cabbie's pay machine to work faster, I rushed out and in through the doors, pouncing on the first desk I saw.

'I'm looking for Room 205. Luca Donato.'

'Down there, the lifts are on the right. Second floor.'

'Thank you,' I said, already in motion. When the lift hadn't arrived after two seconds I pushed through a door marked 'stairs' and ran up to the second floor, bursting through and looking for signage.

'About time you showed up,' Marco, one of Luca's brothers,

grinned as he turned from the coffee machine located near the door.

'I just found out,' I puffed. 'I didn't—' My protest was squashed as he enveloped me in a huge hug.

'I'm teasing you. About bloody time you two saw sense and got together though. We've all been waiting patiently for years.'

'Since when did a Donato ever wait patiently?' I giggled as my eyes filled once again.

'Good point. Here.' He handed me a clean tissue from a pack in his pocket. 'Come on, I'll take you in.'

* * *

The lights were low in deference to the sleeping form in the bed. A cage to keep the bed linen off his damaged leg covered the lower half and his beautiful face was a mass of rainbow-coloured bruises, visible even in this light. Butterfly bandages held together two cuts on his right cheek and another dressing covered a wound on his forehead. I felt the colour drain from me as I realised just how close we'd likely come to losing him.

His mum and dad both rose and hugged me close, his mum brushing my hair back from my face before placing a kiss on my cheek. There was no need for words. Their looks and gestures said it all.

I found an unbruised part of Luca's face and kissed him gently before taking a seat next to the bed and wrapping my hand around his. His eyelids fluttered briefly and sleepily before his eyes focused, heavy lidded, on me. That beautiful smile lit up his face as his hand turned to fold around mine before the medication claimed him once again. Laying my other hand over our clasped ones, I knew that I would risk everything for this man, now and always.

EPILOGUE

EIGHTEEN MONTHS LATER

The next time he woke up from the medication, Luca proposed, but I made him do it again when he was thoroughly lucid, just in case. He did so on Christmas Eve, thereby winning the challenge – according to him. I, obviously, disagreed. We're still discussing the technicalities of his so called win. Having waited so long to be together, neither of us wanted a long engagement and, six months later, I officially became part of the Donato family.

Donato Solutions continues to thrive and the Japanese deal Luca was working on when I joined the company brought us even more notice and prestige, allowing the company to expand. We moved premises and, as Head of IT and Digital Solutions, I got my own office (with a gorgeous view of the river), swanky business cards and an assistant.

My flat went on the market the day Luca was released from the hospital. I was spending all my time at his place anyway and neither of us wanted to be apart any longer. It sold within two days for above the asking price and Tia and Jono helped me move my stuff into Luca's permanently.

Today is their wedding and Tia looks stunning. Jono's totally going to cry when he sees her. Bella, Lucy and I are bridesmaids, giggling together like schoolgirls. Of course, my dress had to have some alterations and I'm not sure I'll be doing anything more than a slow dance with my gorgeous husband later this evening. Our son is due in a month's time and we've already started looking at places further out from London, still close enough to be with the family as often as possible, but also somewhere with a garden for him to play in. We'd both like more children but this one's keeping me busy enough right now.

My phone pings a notification and I pull it from my pocket. Tia made sure we all had pockets in our dresses. This is one of the many reasons I love her.

Got a minute?

I check with Tia and go to one of the other rooms in the suite and reply. Luca video-calls me. When I answer, he has his face pressed up to the phone, making me jump again. I tell him if I go into labour in the middle of the service, it will be his fault. He laughs that laugh and smiles that smile and I fall in love all over again with the man with whom I am finally living my best life.

ACKNOWLEDGMENTS

Well! Yet another book begun in yet another lockdown. Who'd have thought it? Between lockdowns, moving house and a bereavement, to say that writing this book was a challenge is putting it mildly. I'd like to take this opportunity to thank all the members of Team Boldwood for their support, understanding and humanity following Mum's move to the hospice and our subsequent loss. Their complete empathy took one large worry from my mind about my deadline in what was an incredibly difficult period. I cannot thank you all enough for that, and what that meant to me and my family.

Thank you also specifically to my editor, Sarah, copy editor, Sue, and proof reader, Rose, for helping make this book into the best it could be. You all put so much into it and I really appreciate your hard work. Thanks also to Debbie Clement, the highly talented designer responsible for the beautiful cover.

Writing can be a lonely occupation so knowing you have people you can call on to chat with, ask random questions of or just to say hi and know you're not alone is wonderful. Thanks to Rachel B, Rachel G, Sarah B, and Nat especially for the natters and also for helping spread the word about my previous book on its publication day when I was unable to. Your kindness and generosity is so appreciated and I owe you all mahoosive hugs as and when that's possible. Thank you, my darlings. Love you all!

Talking of friends, I couldn't forget the fabulous Jo P who has been such a massive support through a difficult time, despite having her own things to worry about. Also thanks to D who let me invite myself along for a couple of days walking in the beauty of the Welsh countryside shortly after the funeral – pure balm for my heart and soul.

I'd also like to send a big thank you to the bloggers who share lovely reviews and gorgeous pics of my books and help spread the word. It's a highly competitive world out there, and there are so many books vying for attention so your time, reviews and support are very much appreciated.

And, of course, you, my wonderful readers. Your support of my books means I get to keep doing this. Thank you so much. I love to hear from you all so do feel free to reach out anytime. I am so grateful for your lovely comments, and hearing that my books have brought a smile means such a lot.

And finally, thank you to James without whose love, belief and support none of this would have happened.

MORE FROM MAXINE MORREY

We hope you enjoyed reading *Living Your Best Life*. If you did, please leave a review.

If you'd like to gift a copy, this book is also available as an ebook, digital audio download and audiobook CD.

Sign up to Maxine Morrey's mailing list for news, competitions and updates on future books.

http://bit.ly/MaxineMorreyNewsletter

Explore more uplifting reads from Maxine Morrey.

ABOUT THE AUTHOR

Maxine has wanted to be a writer for as long as she can remember and wrote her first (very short) book for school when she was ten.

As time went by, she continued to write, but 'normal' work often got in the way. She has written articles on a variety of subjects, as well as a local history book on Brighton. However, novels are her first love.

In August 2015, she won Harper Collins/Carina UK's 'Write Christmas' competition with her first romantic comedy, 'Winter's Fairytale'.

Maxine lives on the south coast of England, and when not wrangling with words loves to read, sew and listen to podcasts and audio books. Being a fan of tea and cake, she can (should!) also be found out on a walk (although preferably one without too many hills).

Instagram: @scribbler_maxi (This is where she is to be found most)
Facebook: www.Facebook.com/MaxineMorreyAuthor
Pinterest: ScribblerMaxi
Website: www.scribblermaxi.co.uk
Email: scribblermaxi@outlook.com

ABOUT BOLDWOOD BOOKS

Boldwood Books is a fiction publishing company seeking out the best stories from around the world.

Find out more at www.boldwoodbooks.com

Sign up to the Book and Tonic newsletter for news, offers and competitions from Boldwood Books!

http://www.bit.ly/bookandtonic

We'd love to hear from you, follow us on social media:

facebook.com/BookandTonic

twitter.com/BoldwoodBooks

instagram.com/BookandTonic

Lightning Source UK Ltd.
Milton Keynes UK
UKHW041010080322
399742UK00001B/167